Then Came You

To Brenda —
follow your
heart!
xo
Jeannie Moon

Then Came You

A Compass Cove Novel

Jeannie Moon

TULE
PUBLISHING

Dedication

To my Long Island home…
You taught me, nurtured me, and gave me stories to tell.

Greetings and welcome to Compass Cove!

I'm so thrilled to welcome you to my new series that has been a long time in the making. Compass Cove, Long Island, New York, is a north shore college town that combines small town charm with New England sensibilities. It's a hearty mix of family, fun, laughs and tears, and of course, well-earned happily ever afters.

I've been waiting a long time to share these stories with you, and I can't send enough thanks to the publishing team at Tule for getting these books to readers. Meghan, Michelle, Sarah, Jane and of course my editor, Sinclair, your faith in these stories is humbling, and my friend and copy editor Jennifer Gracen made the book sparkle, as always.

But it's you, the readers, that these stories are for. Come have a sandwich at Rinaldi's Café and catch up on the town gossip, sit in one of the Adirondack chairs on the great lawn at Jennings College, go to a football game, or have a drink with friends at The Dock's End. Walk through town and find out about the town's history. Wander into a shop and hold an antique compass that might show you the way to your true north.

Ultimately, Compass Cove is about finding your way home. Once you do that, the love isn't far behind. It's a promise.

To experience the Long Island I know, follow me on social media. Stop by my website for links to all my online haunts, like Instagram, Facebook and Twitter, and so you can stay up to date on all news and shenanigans. (There are always shenanigans.)

Thank you so much for letting me share my stories with you. It's such a privilege. Please keep in touch! I love hearing from readers…it's the best part of what I do.

Much love,
Jeannie
jeanniemoon.com

In the year 1750, on the north shore of Long Island, a young woman named Lucy Velsor mourned her beloved husband, who had been lost at sea. Not long after his death, his shipmates, hoping to comfort the young widow, brought her his compass. It was a finely crafted instrument, made by the local compasssmith, whose family had settled the town of Compass Cove generations before. Lucy cherished the memento, taking care to kiss its face every day. One day, two years after her husband's death, the compass needle began to quiver and spin, never settling on a direction.

Desperate to have it fixed, Lucy brought it to the compasssmith's shop. The shop's proprietor, Caleb Jennings, had loved Lucy from afar, never knowing if he should pay a call on the beautiful widow. But when Lucy set the compass in Caleb's hand, it stopped spinning and the needle pointed at him, stunning them both. Taking the compass' strange behavior as a sign, Caleb put aside his fears and began to court Lucy. It didn't take long for the couple to fall in love, and marry. They spent many wonderful years together, making a home and family, living into their eighties, and dying just a few days apart. Before he left this world, Caleb credited the ghost of Lucy's first husband for setting the compass spinning and helping them find their way to each other.

To this day, Jennings Fine Compasses and Watches still resides on Main Street and is owned by one of Caleb's and Lucy's descendants. Many families in Compass Cove keep a compass in their home as a symbol of selfless love and as a reminder that hearts meant to love will always find each other.

Chapter One

I N ANOTHER LIFE, Mia DeAngelis would have been a star. In this life, she was doing damage control.

Again.

It was another day, another disaster.

"Aunt Mia, wait up."

Mia slowed and turned, doing all she could not to say anything until they got to the car. Ever since their move, Ben had been trying her patience. Three days in a new school, and she'd been called by the principal—twice. Today she'd had to leave work to come and pick him up.

"You're mad," he said.

Mia glanced down. It wasn't easy to be ten, and new in school. It wasn't easy to be ten, period. Mia had thought the rollercoaster tween years wouldn't be something she had to worry about, since she wasn't dealing with girl hormones. She couldn't have been more wrong. Boys had plenty of growing pains; they were just different.

His sandy brown head was bowed; she could see he was sorry. He was always sorry, and it was times like this that Ben still looked like a little boy. Other times, the sheer size of him gave her a glimpse of what he would look like when he was a man.

"Ben, I'm annoyed. This isn't a great way to start at a new school." They walked together into the bright afternoon sunlight, the smell of a nearby salt marsh tingeing the air. The whole ordeal made Mia's heart hurt. She wanted the move to be positive. So far, positive was a stretch. "Do you want to tell me what happened? I'd like to hear your take on it."

Ben shook his head. "No," he said. "The principal told you everything."

Thank goodness, he knew if nothing else, he shouldn't lie.

"Nothing to add? No excuses for your behavior?"

"Tyler was being a jerk, but I know I shouldn't have pushed him." Ben looked up at her, his blue eyes glassy. "The teachers think I'm a troublemaker now, don't they?"

Mia blew out a breath as she searched for the right words. "You're not a troublemaker, Benny. And the people at school know you're settling into a new routine, so I'm guessing you'll get a little slack." She reached over and wrapped her arm around his shoulder. "But you know what I always say about first impressions? People remember, and you *are* the new kid. You'll have to work at making things better." He nodded and wiped his eyes, fighting back the tears Mia knew he thought he was too old to cry. "We'll talk about it later. Do you have homework?" Mia was sure he did, there was just little chance he would actually do it. He was bright, but there was no denying he was a ten-year-old boy. A sometimes very unfocused ten-year-old boy.

"Uh huh. I'm going to work with you?"

"For a couple of hours," she said. "Nana has her yoga class this afternoon. You can hang in my office or find a table and start your homework while I finish up."

"Okay." Ben buckled his seat belt and stared out the window. Something was on his mind, again. "Do you think my mom knew I would be a bad kid and that's why she went away?"

Mia's hands gripped the steering wheel as she considered her response. *Went away.* It was the euphemism she had used when he was younger to avoid telling him what happened, and he still used it when he was upset. Thinking about her sister's death when Ben was a baby was something had Mia avoided for many years, but as Ben got older the questions came, and there was no way to soften a suicide. "Sweetie, there were many things that pushed your mother do what she did, but you were not one of them." Mia doubted Sara was thinking about him at all. "And let's get one thing straight. You aren't a bad kid. You don't always think before you act, but you aren't bad."

That seemed to satisfy him, at least for the moment. The day was so pretty, Mia almost wished the drive back to campus was longer. She could have used the time to clear her head. Whenever she visited Long Island as a girl, she'd always felt like she fit in, and that Compass Cove was her place. The gentle waves on the beach near her grandparents' house, the people, the smells... everything felt like home. And now it was.

When her good friend called about the job as an instructional librarian at Jennings College, Mia jumped on it, knowing she could provide Ben with a better environment, better schools, and more opportunities. That Compass Cove and the surrounding areas were beautiful was a bonus.

Ben was everything. When she became his sole guardian two years ago, her life took a left turn she never would have anticipated. The drunk driver who had mowed down her parents as they left a restaurant in Bethesda had killed her father, and injured her mother. After that, life went into a tailspin.

Finally, knowing things had to change, Mia took advantage of the chance to be close to family again—to give Ben what she knew he craved.

They pulled through the campus gates and Mia wondered if she'd ever stop noticing the elegant beauty of the college. Passing academic buildings and dormitories, remnants of the college's gilded Gold Coast past were everywhere. Formal and informal gardens, sculptures, and charming outbuildings dotted the grounds. The old stables, which were still in use, dominated a substantial portion of the property. Mia always slowed so she could catch a glimpse of the grazing horses, loving the feel of the place, and extremely grateful that it was their new home. Continuing the drive along the perimeter road, it was just a few minutes before she reached the North Quad, which included her library.

The Miller Library shared this part of campus with the administration building and the student union. Sitting on top of a hill, the views from the large windows, including the ones in Mia's office, were spectacular. Facing the Long Island Sound, she could see the gentle outline of the Connecticut shore. There was always a soft breeze, and on a warm day the smell of the salt water and the sound of the gulls were a perfect antidote for stress. It was the opposite of the congested city she'd left behind; exactly what she and Ben needed.

It was hard leaving Maryland, simply because it was familiar. But once her dad died, and Mom decided to move south to live near a pack of her friends who had also retired there, Mia didn't have any good reason to stay. Her mother had grown up in Compass Cove, and Mia cherished the summers she'd spent here visiting her grandparents. Memories of going to the beach every day, eating Italian ices, playing with other kids and experiencing that perfect freedom that only comes during the summers of your childhood helped Mia see that Ben deserved nothing less.

The family house where her mother grew up was in the area known as North Harbor. While moving in with her widowed seventy-nine-year-old grandmother wasn't the ideal situation for a single, twenty-nine-year-old woman, Mia did love that she had family. And Nana was hardly a typical little old lady. It had taken her a while to adjust to losing Mia's Grandpa several years earlier, and then her parents' accident had been another blow, but Nana fought to be happy and learned to love her life again. That included travelling to the most obscure places, working at a bustling indie bookstore, and doing yoga. She was busier in retirement than most people were in their working lives.

Mia adored her. It was Nana who'd really encouraged her to make a move, even before Mia had a job. She figured they had to stick together, especially since she'd been left alone to care for a ten-year-old.

The white Victorian where they lived had blue shutters, a colorful garden, and a big front porch. There was loads of room, inside and out, and it was right near a pretty beach. If Ben could settle himself down, he'd have a slew of playmates, because the neighborhood was crawling with kids.

Of course, if the kid Ben stood up to really was being a bully, Tyler probably deserved a lot more than a shove. Mia glanced at Ben and worry took over. He was tall for his age, with a strong athletic build; the problem with that was that other kids might see him as a challenge. Figuring he was built like his father, Mia also worried about his disposition. She'd never met Ben's father, but Sara had told her stories. And the stories weren't good.

As they walked up the main steps in front of the library, Mia knew she needed to find out more. More about the situation, more about what set Ben off.

"So, how did the whole argument start? All the principal could tell me was that you boys were on the playground and there was a lot of yelling and shoving."

Ben answered in a low voice. "It was dumb. Tyler threw a pass, I intercepted it and he told everyone I broke the rules."

"Excuse me?"

"No one's allowed to intercept anything when Tyler Jansen's the quarterback. We're supposed to let his team walk over the goal line." Ben was really angry; he was just going on and on and on, and that's when the pieces started to click into place. Mia stopped dead on the top step.

"You were playing *football?*"

The boy froze.

"Ben?"

"It's fun," he grumbled.

"It's against the school rules." It was, too. Contact sports, tag—even hide and seek had been banned in some places—it seemed everything was against school rules nowadays, except maybe hopscotch and pick-up sticks. Mia tended to be overprotective, she knew that. She'd learned it from her own mother. But she was starting to wonder if some of the rules were going too far.

She couldn't tell Ben that, though.

"We've discussed this. You can't just do whatever you want—"

"It's a stupid rule," he snapped. "Football's fun."

"Really?" Mia felt her face flush as her temper flared. "How much fun was it today when you nearly got into a fight?"

Ben spun at her, snapping, "I got into a fight because a stupid kid thinks he can pick on me 'cause I'm new." He threw her a look that was pure arrogance. "I showed him different."

Obviously, the principal didn't know what triggered the pushing and shoving, but at this point Mia didn't know if it mattered. She did wonder how the football detail had been missed.

"We'll discuss this later." Mia moved toward the doors and walked into the library lobby. She knew he didn't understand. He couldn't. It was her problem, her need to do everything right that sometimes made things hard for him. The problem was she sometimes didn't know what was right. "But from now on, you will follow the playground rules. Is that clear?"

"You don't get it."

"What is there to get? It's not allowed, you could get badly hurt and, obviously, in trouble. No football!"

"You don't let me do anything fun."

"Look, I'll ask around. I'm sure there are other things… art classes… or maybe you'd like to try tennis?"

The second she said it, Mia knew she'd made a mistake.

"Art classes?" The disdain in his tone said it all. Art classes

may have been fine for another kid, but not him.

As they walked into her office, Mia could feel his temper simmering.

"You don't care what I think," he growled.

Mia was doing her best to stay calm so the situation didn't get worse, but he was making it very tough to do so. "Benjamin," she began calmly. "I've had enough of your attitude. We'll talk about this later."

But Ben was the one who'd had enough. He threw his backpack across the room, causing Mia to jump as it crashed into a chair and the contents went flying in all directions.

"Hey! What was that all about?"

"I don't want to play tennis or take art!" he screamed, kicking a notebook that had landed on his foot. He was furious.

"Ben, calm down!"

"No! You don't listen! When are you going to listen?" And with a final shove at the door, he took off.

By the time Mia composed herself enough to go after him, Ben had disappeared.

ADAM MILLER CONFERRED with his assistants and could only shake his head as he looked at his roster. Their first game was three days away, and the offensive line had more holes than a cheap hooker's panties. The way things were going, he'd be down a quarterback by halftime on Saturday.

"I got almost 1500 pounds on that line, they should be able to block something," Adam mumbled.

"I don't know what to tell you," Drew Griffin, one of the assistants, said. "There's no way we could have anticipated those two injuries."

That was true. More than half of their starters from last year's team had either graduated or were no longer eligible to play. Then two of his veteran offensive lineman got hurt within days of each other. He had to get used to the fact that his team was green, and the best he could hope for was that they would get better with experience.

He flipped the playbook closed and stuffed the pen into his pocket.

"Adam? Looks like we've got company." Joe Rand, his defensive coordinator and best friend, pointed toward the end zone. There, sitting with his legs pulled up, was a kid. Alone.

"Damn." The last thing Adam wanted to deal with right now was a misplaced kid. He hoped one of the other coaches would make a move to check things out, because there was no reason a kid should be on this part of campus by himself. But no, eight of them stood there, and suddenly not one member of his staff was making eye contact with him. No one even looked up. Great.

"Here, take this for me." Handing off his binder to Joe, Adam walked down the field.

He guessed the boy was maybe eleven or twelve years old—hard to say, hunched over like that—but when the kid saw him coming, he scrambled to his feet and looked scared shitless. Adam had seen kids react to him in a lot of different ways, but this one was new. The boy shoved his hands in his pockets and when Adam got close enough, he could see the kid had been crying.

"Hey," Adam said. "You okay?"

"I guess."

"Lost?"

"Sorta."

"*Sorta*?" The kid sure wasn't giving much.

All Adam got this time was a shrug. He blew out a long breath and extended his hand. "I'm Coach Miller."

The boy met his eyes and shook his hand. Still nothing.

"You got a name?" More silence.

"Ben DeAngelis."

Finally something. Maybe he could figure out who owned this kid. "So, Ben, where are you supposed to be?"

Adam realized he'd asked the million-dollar question when Ben looked down and moved his feet uncomfortably.

"With my aunt at the library."

"Ah. She's a student?"

"No, sir. She works there."

"Does she know where you are?"

"No, sir," Ben whispered.

Adam widened his stance, folded his arms, and stared

down at the boy. Intimidation would go a long way with this kid. He was too respectful not to respond to an adult's request. "What do you think you should do?" He gave Ben some time to think through what he wanted to say. Sure enough, it came eventually.

"Go back to the library."

"Good answer." Adam was relieved he wasn't going to have to pressure the kid, but he had to regroup quickly as Ben turned to walk away. Yeah, that wasn't going to happen, not when Ben so much as admitted he was lost.

"Whoa." He reached out and took him by the arm. "Come back to my office and you can *call* your aunt."

Ben nodded and the two of them started toward the field house. Kids usually talked up a storm around him, but this kid wasn't saying much. Maybe a little activity would get him to open up. Adam pointed to two footballs on the sideline. "Go grab those two balls and toss them to me."

The kid's eyes lit up and he ran to the side of the field. He picked up the first ball, turned it in his hand a little and threw it to Adam. *Not bad.*

The second throw was better.

When Ben returned to his side, Adam stopped walking, dropped one football, and handed Ben the other. "Let me show you something. Put your fingers here and here." He moved the boy's fingers into position over the laces and Adam marveled at the size of the kid's hands. He was born to hold a football. "That's good, but not so tight. You want to have a little space between your hand and the football."

"Like this?" Ben had made an adjustment and the ball sat perfectly in his hand.

Adam nodded. "Good. Throw it."

It was poetry in motion. Ben dropped back a couple of steps, planted his feet and threw. The ball took off like a rocket. *Damn.*

They watched the ball's flight and Adam grinned at Ben's stunned expression. "Much better." Tossing him the other football, Adam said, "Now, do it again."

ONCE HE STARTED talking, Ben told Adam a lot about his recent move to Compass Cove. In the fifteen minutes he'd been with him, Adam had gotten an earful from Ben about why he'd run away, the ridiculous school rule about football that was at the root of his problem, and his aunt who wanted him to follow all the rules, no matter what.

That rule following thing sounded pretty boring to him, as did Ben's aunt. But she was a librarian; he could just picture her, all serious and uptight. It sounded like she needed to let the kid be a kid.

He thought about his own mother, who'd let Adam pursue every dream, even after his father died. He couldn't imagine being brought up in a bubble. Poor kid.

"So, what did your aunt say when you called?"

Ben took a drink from the water bottle Adam had given him. "That she was glad I found an adult and that I called. She said she'd be here soon."

Adam had been surprised to hear the kid was only ten. He looked older. "Do you go to school at Jennings Elementary?"

Ben nodded, but didn't look very happy.

"Don't like school?"

"School is okay. But like I said, we just moved here from Maryland."

Adam understood: it wasn't easy being the new kid. "Give it time." Adam took a long pull from a bottle of water that he had on his desk, processing the information. "Where did you live in Maryland?"

"Right near Washington."

"Yeah? I played close to there, in Baltimore. Now I live in Compass Cove, like you."

"Like you played pro football?"

Adam nodded. He didn't want to tell the kid it wasn't all it was cracked up to be.

"That's so cool."

A door opened and closed and decidedly female footsteps approached.

"That's my Aunt Mia."

Adam braced himself. He told himself she was probably a perfectly nice woman, and that he shouldn't judge, and that she—*she*—Adam swallowed hard when the librarian entered his office.

Oh. Damn.

This woman blew every librarian stereotype right out the freaking window. She was gorgeous. And she was young.

Her hair was a mane of loose brown curls, the same color as the toffee candy he used to find on his grandfather's desk. It was pulled loosely off her face, tumbling almost to her waist, and long, dark lashes surrounded her big brown eyes. Adam had to shake off his reaction before he could say something coherent. There had to be something wrong with this. Wasn't there some librarian rulebook that kept attractive off the grid?

She swept into the room and went right to Ben.

"Oh Benny, thank God." Her arms wrapped around the boy and Ben hugged his aunt's middle.

While the reunion took place, Adam adjusted to the real Aunt Mia. She was beautiful like an angel would be beautiful, soft and gentle. There seemed to be an aura that surrounded her.

Shit. What the... he had to get a hold of himself. It was enough that the sudden surge of blood to his groin was something he hadn't experienced since he was in his twenties, but *auras*? What the fuck?

Still, he couldn't deny that something about her made his heart pound, and the rush in his ears was freaking him out. Thank God her focus was on her nephew, and not him. Adam didn't need her to see how affected he was.

"I'm sorry," Ben said.

"Me too. But don't you ever run off like that again. I've been worried sick!"

Ben nodded and Mia finally glanced at Adam. She smiled and extended her hand. "I'm Mia DeAngelis. Thank you so much for taking charge of Ben, Mr...."

"Coach." *Shit.*

"Mr. *Coach?*"

"I mean Miller." *Damn,* he thought. She was standing there, grinning, probably thinking he was an idiot. *Jesus,* he thought. *When did he ever react this way around a woman?* "Adam Miller," he said as he took her outstretched hand. "Please call me Adam."

"He has the same name as your library," Ben said. "Is it named after you, Coach?"

"Ben, Miller is a fairly common name—" Mia began.

"My grandfather," Adam interrupted. "The Miller Library is named for my grandfather."

"Oh. Well," she said awkwardly. "I stand—um—corrected." Immediately her back stiffened and Mia looked away, keeping her hand firmly on Ben's shoulder.

An uncomfortable silence descended, the chill going right through him. Adam had blown this first impression big time. Mentioning his family was obviously a mistake. What a way to sound like a pretentious ass.

Then, as Adam began to gather his wits, Mia blinked those soft brown eyes, made a little noise in her throat and his vision clouded again. Just like that.

What the hell was going on?

Nodding deferentially in Adam's direction, Mia pointed Ben toward the door. "Thank you again. We'll get out of your way."

Damn. Where was she going? "You're leaving?" he said quickly.

"Is that a problem?" She stopped, confused, her twitching hands telling him she was nervous. *Think fast.*

"No, no… of course not. It's just…" *Recover, man. You have to recover.* "I'm done here. Let me walk you out."

She nodded, but Adam could see she was being polite. He watched her twist her hands and noticed her left ring finger was bare. With any other woman, he'd think the nerves were a sign she was interested. But given her earlier reaction, he figured the nerves were about his family name. Then again, maybe she just didn't like him. He looked at her again and what struck him was how innocent she looked, how young. Maybe she was thirty. Maybe.

The silence between them was once again uncomfortable, and before he could stop himself, Adam stepped on another landmine.

"Ben's got a great arm," Adam said as they walked toward the parking lot. Football wasn't the best choice of subject, but he really wanted to know what Mia had against football. "He could play quarterback right now with the way he throws."

"Football, again?" Her already icy manner cooled about another ten degrees. Wow.

Okay, maybe he was wrong about her not fitting the stereotype. The woman may not look like the blue-haired librarian of his nightmares, but she sure acted like her. "What's wrong with football?" He shouldn't have baited her, but he couldn't stop himself.

Mia slowed, straightened her back, and turned to him with narrowed eyes. Now she was on the defensive. "From where I'm standing, pretty much everything."

"He told me you don't want him to play," Adam said, recounting what Ben told him before she arrived.

He knew a lot of moms were nervous about contact sports. Sure, there were risks. Anything worth doing had some risk associated with it, but at Ben's level they were small. Now, though, as he watched her face tighten, he knew he'd pissed her off. Mia started to say something and then stopped, allowing him to continue. Like an idiot, he did.

"It's good exercise and a great way to channel a kid's energy."

"It's dangerous."

Adam looked away for a second, blew out a breath, and then looked back at her. "When a player is properly trained, and has the right equipment, at his age it's as safe as riding a bike."

"A bike? Are you kidding?" Yeah, she was mad. "I wonder if all the players with permanent brain damage, or their families, might disagree with you."

"That's not the same thing," he grumbled.

"No? Well, is playing tackle football on a playground with no equipment, no coaching, and no supervision safe? Is it? Is that as safe as 'riding a bike'?"

"I don't have a bike either," Ben shot out, but just as quickly, he snapped his mouth shut. The kid realized too late that after running away, and scaring her so bad, he shouldn't have said anything.

"Oh, don't start." Her temper flared, and Adam liked seeing her lose a little bit of that control. "I didn't want you riding around our old neighborhood. I don't have a problem with you riding a bike here."

"Then why don't I have one?"

"What? A bike?" She stopped at a very sensible small car. "Oh, gee… I don't know," she snipped. "Getting us settled in a whole new place has taken up a lot of my time, but once we get you one I'm thinking I'll need a degree in engineering to figure out how to put it together."

Adam grinned. He shouldn't do this. He shouldn't. It wasn't any of his business, but he couldn't just pass up an opportunity to look at her for an entire afternoon. "I could give you a hand."

"What? Oh, no. Truly, that's not necessary…"

"Really?" Ben's smile flashed like a thousand-watt bulb. Gorgeous aunt or not, that sealed it. Adam wanted to help the kid out and there was no way a bike was coming home in that compact.

"It's no trouble," Adam said. "We have a game Saturday, but Sunday I'm free. We could grab lunch and go bike shopping. There are a couple of good shops in town."

"I don't know…" Mia held her keys in a death grip while she examined him very carefully. Based on her expression, she didn't know what to make of what was going on between them any more than he did. God, she was something. Beautiful and smart.

Adam smiled. "It'll be fun. I'll show you around."

"Please, Aunt Mia?" When she looked at her nephew, Adam knew she was going to cave. Mia's shoulders relaxed, her eyes brightened—her whole demeanor softened. Ben's sad look was obviously her weakness. She might try to act tough, but the woman was mush where the kid was concerned, and Adam felt his opinion of her click up a couple of notches.

"Okay," she sighed. Adam almost felt bad as he watched a defeated Mia fish a piece of paper and a pen out of her purse and proceed to scribble some information before he could even offer to let her add the information to his phone. "Here's our address. And if you need to get in touch with me, calling the library would be your best bet. But here's my cell number, too. I don't get great reception on campus." She handed him the slip of paper and he smiled, hoping to crack the veneer.

"Twelve-thirty okay?"

"Fine." Mia swallowed hard and opened the rear passenger door.

As Ben got in, Adam reached out and gave him a fist bump. "Later, Ben."

"See ya, Coach."

The back door shut and Adam looked over. "Nice meeting you, Mia."

She barely said good-bye, mumbling something as she got into her car, and he walked toward his truck. Man, she was tough, but Adam smiled anyway. Saturday's game was probably going to be a bloodbath, but Sunday was definitely looking up.

Chapter Two

HOW DID IT happen? Mia ran the scene over and over in her mind as she made the left turn onto their street. How did he do that? How did he maneuver her into seeing him on Sunday? It was like they had a date. *A date*. It was absurd. Mia didn't date. She especially didn't date gorgeous six-foot-four-inch football jocks.

Oh, and he was gorgeous. Mia's breathing quickened just thinking about him. Dark hair, ocean blue eyes, a devastating smile. And he was big—tall, broad-shouldered, and muscular. And what was the deal with his voice? The deep, rich baritone played over and over in her head. Holy God.

Stop, Mia! Stop, stop, stop! He was being nice for Ben's sake. And he wasn't even that nice. It wasn't a date—like she would ever go out with a guy like him.

Oh, God.

Mia took a breath. What the hell was wrong with her?

Adam had been… well, he'd been very kind. He'd kept Ben safe, offered help with a bike, was gorgeous beyond words, and she'd acted like a bitch. *Great.* That was sure to go over well with the Millers.

"The Coach is cool, isn't he, Aunt Mia?"

"Oh, yeah."

"Why is the library named after his grandpa? You must be really important to get a building named for you."

"Mmm hmm." Important was one way to look at the family's influence. Since the Millers funded the faculty position that brought her to Compass Cove, she'd made a point of learning about them. Which meant that she knew Adam Miller came from serious money. Aviation money, shipping money, real estate money… the list went on.

"Coach says I can really throw. That I'm a natural. What does that mean?"

"That the ability is something that comes from inside you. No one had to teach you how."

She looked in her rearview mirror and saw Ben puff up a little at the thought. He was so happy, and since her father had died, he was rarely happy.

As soon as she parked in the driveway, Ben hopped out of the car, excitedly ran to the back porch, and went directly in the house. He'd gotten in trouble at school, run off for over an hour, and sassed her in front of a complete stranger. This had not been a great day, but Mia couldn't help but be relieved that her boy had a smile on his face.

He needed to get involved in something, she knew that. And she also knew an art class wasn't going to cut it.

When Adam questioned her about Ben playing football, she could see he didn't understand that it wasn't about the game. Okay, maybe it was, a little, but her problem today was more about Ben making a bad decision. Rules were in place for a reason. She didn't run the school, and regardless of what she thought, or Ben thought, he had to do what was expected of him.

Ben's runaway attempt and her encounter with Adam had left her completely wrecked, but all her nerves melted away when she went into the kitchen and saw her grandmother, still in her yoga clothes, clutching Ben. The savory smells drifting from the stove, the familiar glow from the overhead light, even the bubblegum pop music coming from the iPod on the counter relaxed her. *Home.*

"What were you thinking? Running off like that?" Nana was holding Ben in a grip so tight, Mia wondered how he was breathing.

"I'm sorry," he said. "But it was so cool!"

Tilting her head back, Nana pushed the hair away from his face. "How is throwing a tantrum, running away, and scaring us half to death 'cool'?"

Ben pulled back and dropped his backpack by the stove before launching into his story. The story Mia wanted to forget. "I saw part of football practice and I met the coach. He taught me how to throw a spiral."

Nana looked in her direction and raised an eyebrow. Ben was so excited he was ready to detonate. "Is that so?"

"And he thinks I should play football. And do you want to know the best part?"

"That wasn't the best part?" she asked.

"No! He's helping us get my bike on Sunday."

"A bike?" This time, Mia saw that Nana's gaze was squarely on her, not Ben, and a sly grin tilted her mouth. "The football coach is taking you out for a bike?"

Mia felt her insides twist as a vision of Adam and his sweet smile flashed through her mind.

"Yup." Ben opened his backpack, took out a notice from school, and tossed it into the basket on the counter. "I know just what kind of bike I want, too."

"Ben," Mia began, "Why don't you take your things to your room and get started on your homework. I'll be up in a few minutes, because you and I have a few things to talk about."

He tensed and nodded when he realized the talk was going to be serious. But for a change, he did just what he was asked to do. When she heard his feet on the stairs, Mia collapsed into the chair at the head of the kitchen table. For a few seconds, her grandmother simply regarded her before taking two wine glasses from the cabinet and filling them from the open bottle of Cabernet sitting on the counter.

"I don't think I've ever been so scared in my life." Mia dropped her head into her hands. "I had security looking for him. People on staff, even a few professors, were searching classrooms."

"And he was playing with one of the football coaches." Nana chuckled. "You should have called me when you needed him picked up."

"No," Mia said. "We made a deal when I moved here. Your life doesn't get interrupted for things like that."

"*Like that?* Mia, he ran away and was lost for almost over an hour! Interrupt me!"

Mia was about to say something, but stopped herself. Nana was right. She should have called. It was hard to remember that she wasn't doing this alone anymore.

"You want to tell me about the football coach and the bike?"

Mia groaned. There was no good way to spin this. She'd been nicely maneuvered by the coach who had more than likely figured out that she wasn't going to say no to a pleading ten-year-old, especially after the day he'd had. Mia took a long drink from her wine. "I'm not sure. One minute, we were discussing Ben's athletic ability, and the next he was offering to take us to lunch and the bike shops on Sunday."

Another splash of wine went into her glass. "Spill! There has to be more," Nana finally demanded. Her grandmother was a busy body, and the alcohol was clearly part of her plan to get information.

"Not much to tell." As soon as she said it, Mia felt her face flush and Nana laughed.

"You, my dear, are a lousy liar."

Mia met her eyes, and saw the familiar glimmer of awareness. Nana knew her too well. Much too well. "He's good looking. Gorgeous, in fact. I don't know. We don't seem to have any common ground. He didn't think what happened at school with Ben was a big deal."

"Pssht." Nana waved her hand as she rose to start dinner. "They have so many rules at school nowadays, it's impossible to keep track."

"That may be true, but it didn't mean Ben had to go off half-cocked and get into a shoving match with another kid."

"Don't be too tough on him," Nana said. "He's a good boy."

Mia turned and nodded. "I know, and I want him to stay that way."

The job and her grandmother aside, the biggest reason Mia moved was Ben. The city wasn't right for him, and his behavior and attitude were taking a not-so-nice-turn. Getting him to a better place before puberty hit was the only thing on her mind.

The walk through the old house generated so many memories. And as Mia climbed the stairs to Ben's room, she knew she wanted him to have good memories of his own, but she couldn't tolerate his outbursts, or his outright defiance. And what he did today? Forget it—that was downright dangerous. Yes, it all worked out in the end, but there would be consequences for his actions.

She hated to admit it, but Adam may have had a point about channeling Ben's energy. Football probably wasn't going to work out this year, but being a man gave Adam an understanding of Ben that Mia would never have.

As Ben got older, she was going to understand him less and less. Without a doubt, this single mom thing wasn't going to get any easier. Her mother, who was overbearing on a good day, was trying to run the show from Hilton Head, and her dad wasn't there anymore to run interference. Mia knew what was right, but she was on her own.

Turning her face toward the heavens, Mia spoke to her dad and her sister. "I hope I don't mess this up, guys."

When she looked in Ben's room, the scene was exactly what she expected. Ben should have started his homework, but instead he was lying on the bed, balancing a basketball on the balls of his feet. Yeah. That kind of said it all.

WHEN ADAM STEPPED onto his deck and looked out at the bay, he wondered if he hadn't made a mistake pushing himself on Mia DeAngelis. He'd have a good time on Sunday simply because the woman was eye candy, but it was pretty obvious she wasn't happy about being trapped into spending an afternoon with him. Ben was cool, though. He liked the kid. At least he could make sure he got a good bike.

Adam sank into the Adirondack chair and watched the golden light from the now invisible sun play with the clouds. He never got tired of his view. No matter where he'd traveled in his life, Long Island was home.

Leaning his head against the back of the chair, Adam

closed his eyes. He didn't know how he was going to win any games this year with the crew he was putting on the line. His only gift was Kelvin Grant. The kid was as dedicated as he was talented. Though he should have accepted an offer from a big football school, he didn't, because Kelvin's mother trusted Adam.

And he didn't take her trust lightly.

Kelvin's experience wasn't going to be like his own. Once he took the scholarship offer to the big ass football school, classes were the last thing Adam thought about. It was a miracle he graduated. Hell, considering how much he partied, it was a miracle he survived. School was only the beginning of Adam's problems; his arm was golden, so the pro contract came, and the money... and it was downhill from there.

It took him flipping his car and almost ending up in a wheelchair for Adam to change his ways.

No, Kelvin wouldn't go through any of that. The kid came from a shit neighborhood, but had managed to stay out of gangs and away from drugs, thanks to his mother. She wanted her son to get an education, and Adam was going to make sure he did just that.

Without warning, Mia's face flashed through his mind, and again he wondered if he'd done the right thing getting her to go out with him. He thought about canceling, but something wouldn't let him. He wanted to see her again.

But at the same time, he didn't.

There was no doubt Mia was gorgeous, but he wondered if there was a way to chip through the ice. The frost coming off her as they left campus told him she was majorly uptight, and he'd always liked his women more laidback. And easy. He liked easy women. The kind that wouldn't expect a relationship. The kind that worshipped pro-athletes.

Yeah, there was no way the librarian was going to worship him. She hadn't said as much, but she didn't really have to. Based on her response, it was fairly obvious Mia thought he was pond scum.

"I'm going out with a woman who hates me. Perfect," he mumbled to himself. Adam blew out a breath. He'd get through this like he'd gotten through that root canal he'd had last month. He'd just suck it up. They'd go out Sunday and get the kid a bike. Good deed done, and that would be it.

"Yeah, right." This time it was her scent that he remembered... something light, flowery. She'd gotten inside him. Ten minutes with her and now she was embedded in his brain.

Damn. He was thirty-seven years old and had always had control where the women in his life were concerned. He'd walked the red carpet with the most beautiful actresses, been photographed with the hottest models, but the thought of going out with the pretty little librarian had his stomach in knots. It could have something to do with living like a monk for months on end, but as he thought about her, Adam knew it was more. There was something in her eyes, in the way she looked at him—it was different, and his reaction left him feeling at odds with who he'd always been.

His sailboat bobbed against his dock. The flag at the top of the mast snapped away in the stiff breeze. It was the perfect time for a sail, the perfect thing to keep his mind off the book lady. Putting his tongue against his teeth, his ear-splitting whistle shattered the quiet.

"Bubba," he called. Down on the beach, the black lab mix looked up and his tail wagged like crazy. The dog was a mess: big, dumb, and always getting pinched by the crabs that wandered onto shore. The dope couldn't figure out the crabs didn't want to play.

"Come on, pal. We're going on the boat." Bubba bowed down and barked before running down the dock and hopping onto the boat. Adam laughed.

His dog, a sail… yep, the diversion was just what he needed.

THE DAY AFTER her close encounter with Adam, Mia sat staring at the computer screen in her office. She was supposed to be doing research for one of the professors, but her mind kept wandering. Somehow, gathering the latest criticisms referencing modern journalistic ethics wasn't keeping her attention.

She was too busy thinking about the gorgeous football coach, and for the briefest moment, Mia allowed herself to imagine his offer to help with the bike was as much about her as it was about Ben. Immediately, she knocked the thought out of her head. There was no way, no possible way, he was the least bit interested in her.

A light tapping at her door brought her out of her trance. Mia looked up.

"Hey," Fiona said. "Where were you?"

Fiona Gallagher, who also went by Finn, had become one of Mia's closest friends when they were in library school. Through the years, and several moves, they'd stayed in touch. When the opening at Jennings came up, Finn had called Mia immediately. Her friend knew this was exactly the kind of job Mia wanted, and where she wanted to raise Ben.

"Nowhere," Mia responded. "Just daydreaming, you know."

Fiona came into the room and sat in the chair facing Mia's desk. "Want to go to the mall Sunday? I noticed you aren't on the schedule."

"I have plans, actually. Ben and I are going to lunch and then going bike shopping."

"Bike shopping?"

"I've been promising him, so Sunday we hit the bike shop."

"Cool. I'll give you a hand."

Crap. When Finn offered to lend a hand, she meant to

do it. Now Mia would have to explain to her friend why she didn't need help. Maybe she could be vague.

"Oh, don't worry about it, we'll be fine. I have help."

Fiona's perfectly plucked eyebrow shot up beyond the rim of her glasses. "Really?"

Vague wasn't going to work.

"Yeah." Mia squirmed. She could see Fiona's sixth sense had kicked in. Should she explain? If she didn't tell her something, Fiona would be after her all day—she'd want details.

"Who's helping you?"

Mia stood and walked to the shelf that held some old print resources and ran her finger over the spine of one of the books. "Just a guy I met."

"Oooohhh." A smile spread across her friend's gorgeous face. "It didn't take you long. Tell me."

"There's nothing to tell."

"Sure there is. Give."

"We met. Started talking." Mia offered quietly. *Vague. Be vague.*

"Where did you meet him?"

"On campus. He helped when Ben ran off."

"So, yesterday. And?" Fiona was leaning forward, her eyes wide, waiting for more information.

Mia looked out the window, distracting herself with the view. She couldn't just blurt it out. It was personal. No one was supposed to know, were they? How was she going to get around this? It was so out of the blue and Fiona tended to blow everything out of proportion. If she held true to form, Fiona would have her married to Adam before they'd had a meal together. Just then, Kelvin Grant, one of the student clerks, popped his head into the room.

"Miss DeAngelis?"

Saved! Mia thought. Someone needed her assistance, and she could escape the interrogation. "Yes, Kelvin?"

"Phone call for you." He was grinning.

"Thank you." Looking at the console on her desk, she saw three lines were flashing. "What line?"

"One-five." He paused, looked at Mia and Fiona, and then spoke again, "It's Coach Miller."

Fiona's gasp was audible. "As in Adam Miller? He's the one…"

Could his timing have been worse? Mia doubted it. Kelvin, who was on the football team, was grinning ear to ear. Fiona was dumbstruck. Great. When she didn't pick up right away, Kelvin took the hint and vanished. Hand on the receiver, Mia shot Fiona a look before she drew a breath and pressed a button on her phone. "Mia DeAngelis."

"Hello, Miss DeAngelis." His voice rolled over her, deep and sexy. "I wonder if you could tell me the last fifteen winners of the Super Bowl?"

Mia bit her lip, but the smile escaped anyway. If she didn't know better, she might think he was flirting.

Realizing after she'd told her Nana all about what had

happened, that her anger toward Adam was rooted in the fear surrounding Ben's disappearance, she found herself more than a little receptive to his charms. "You could always look it up," she answered softly. "I would think even you know how to use Google."

"But then I wouldn't have an excuse to call you."

"Oh, I see," she replied, her face burning as Fiona watched. "What can I do for you, Adam?"

"I just need to push our date back until one o'clock. I have a couple of things to do in the morning."

Their date. She felt her heart speed up when he put it that way, but maybe he was just looking for a way out? "I really don't want to put you out. If you would prefer to cancel—"

"Are you kidding? I'm looking forward to it. Is one o'clock okay?"

"It's fine." Mia noticed she'd stopped breathing. She had to calm down. "Thanks again for offering. Ben's really excited."

Mia cringed. *Don't gush*, she told herself. She couldn't give him the upper hand for even one second. Why did this have to be so complicated? On one hand, she couldn't shake the stereotype that he was the typical over-confident and self-absorbed jock. But he was doing something for Ben that would have been hard for her to do without his help. When she looked at it from that angle, the gesture was genuinely sweet.

"Not a problem. Tell Ben I said 'hi'," Adam said.

"I will."

"Take care, Mia."

"Bye."

Hanging up, Mia slumped back into her chair and clutched her hands to her chest, hoping the pressure would settle her pounding heart. She'd forgotten that Fiona was watching her every move.

"Do you like red wine or white?" Fiona asked. Her arms were folded across her chest and she was tapping her foot steadily.

"Huh? Red, why?"

"Because tonight," Fiona said while rising from the chair, "I'm bringing the wine, and you're telling me all about how you met him. See you around nine."

SHE HAD THE sexiest voice—soft and feminine, just like everything else about her.

Calling Mia at work was a dirty trick and he knew it. But she *did* tell him it was the best place to get in touch with her, and just because he didn't like his notoriety on campus, didn't mean he wasn't going to use it to get her attention. Calling and identifying himself would start the gossip flying. If nothing else, it would keep her thinking about him.

Then again, it could backfire. She might feel pressured,

or embarrassed, and ultimately see it as a reason to put one more check in the "asshole" column, and he didn't want that.

He couldn't get her out of his head. The night before he'd taken a long sail, worked out, done some prep for Saturday's game, and still his brain had circled back to her. And the more he thought about her, the more he realized he'd made a snap judgment about her being an ice queen. No one who responded to a child the way she had could be unfeeling or cold. So, he called her to test his theory, and he was right. Not cold at all.

She was sweet, flustered, and adorable.

She had the face of angel and a body that could stop time—a little lusher, a little rounder than his usual type. Mia was built like a real woman, not some stick figure. She was shaped like she was meant to have a bunch of kids, and be worshipped by the man she married.

Mia was real, all right. And all Adam could think about was what it would be like to get his hands on every full, soft inch of her.

MIA DIDN'T HAVE much experience with heart-to-heart talks about guys. But after a few glasses of wine and some amazing chocolate strawberries, Mia told her friend the Adam Miller story.

Finn pulled her auburn hair back in an elastic and let out a long, low whistle when the story was finished. "He's the hottest man on campus, and *you* have a date with him."

Mia bit her lip, leaned forward and set her glass on the table. "It's not exactly a date. We're taking Ben for a bike."

"It's a *date*."

"He's being nice to Ben." Mia sank into the cushions as she leaned back.

"He's being nice to *you*."

"Finn, look, men just aren't interested in me like that. Especially men like Adam Miller."

"I doubt that. He's a lot of things, but he's not stupid."

"What he has are opinions. Too many."

"Seriously? I heard he left his jerky self back in the NFL."

Mia shrugged. Getting angry with Adam was all projection. She was upset about Ben and she'd turned it on him. It wasn't fair, but the man got her back up with all his questions.

"If you don't like him, then why are you going out with him? I told you I'd give you a hand with the bike."

Again, Mia shook her head, and sipped her wine. "I don't know."

"You're attracted to him, and I'm guessing he's attracted to you, and…"

"I don't think so. I'm not his type."

"Do you truly believe that? Truly? Because it's such crap."

"No, it's not! Men like him want gorgeous, sophisticated women. That's not me."

"You need to pay more attention, honey."

"What do you mean, *pay attention*?" Mia wished people would stop talking in riddles.

Fiona rolled her eyes. "Jeez, Mia, whenever we go anywhere, men trip over themselves when you walk past."

Now it was Mia's turn to roll her eyes.

"You might be clueless, but I'm not. Last week, when we were in town for lunch, there was a group of men walking out of Rinaldi's when we were walking in." Mia jumped as Fiona smacked her hands together. "They crashed into each other to get a look at you. It was like a four-car pile-up on the expressway!"

Mia knew she wasn't the awkward girl who felt inferior to her beautiful sister anymore. Her looks had matured, she'd lost weight, and she'd accomplished many things. But she wasn't experienced with men. She just wasn't. "You don't understand."

The more she thought about it, the more anxious she was about spending any time with Adam at all.

And the panic had only escalated once she'd done her research.

Adam wasn't just a football coach at a small college. He was famous. No. Mia rethought that... *infamous* was a better word. A quick search had yielded more than she ever wanted to know about him. There was information about his career, but even more on his personal life—dirt on the women he'd dated, the party scene he'd frequented, and the crash to earth. Adam was a bad boy. He was handsome and charming—a rich, successful, risk-taking, professional athlete.

Fiona cleared her throat and Mia wiped her eyes. She didn't mean to take the emotional side trip; it was just that the more she thought about the simple lunch and shopping expedition, the more she panicked. If their outing was 'a date', she was in trouble.

"This is really bugging you, isn't it?"

Mia answered with a nod.

"Why? You have everything going for you. He'll be eating out of your hand."

"No, I wasn't even nice to him."

"What happened the other night? Is there something you're not telling me?"

"Not really. I got defensive, and nervous, and I turned into a total bitch. I have no idea why he even wants to be around me, except that he probably thinks he's rescuing Ben."

Fiona wrapped an arm around Mia's shoulder. "You were scared as hell about Ben. It's understandable if you weren't at your best. I doubt you were a bitch." Fiona paused and tilted her head. "Do you even know how to be a bitch?"

"I was horrible. When he mentioned his family's connection to the library, I turned to stone. Swear to God. I had no idea what to say."

"Well, then look at lunch like a fresh start. A chance to be charming."

"Charming, right." Mia shook her head. "This is going to be a disaster."

"Mia, oh my God. He's just a guy. It's just a date!"

She turned and faced Finn, who was obviously losing her patience, and it was easy to understand why. Slim and gorgeous, Fiona possessed a self-confidence that came from years of being told she could do anything. Years of growing into herself.

Mia, on the other hand, was still figuring out where she fit in. Her college years had been unremarkable because she never got out from under her sister's suicide. Originally, Mia had gone to school to study acting and voice, and her first two years at NYU had been amazing. She gained confidence and started to spread her wings socially. But when Sara died, it devastated her. Her parents were grieving, Ben was just a little boy, and Mia felt guilty being so far away from home. At some point, being with her family was more important than being on stage. So, she left NYU and finished school at a university closer to home, focusing on literature, classics, and library science. It was a comfort to be home, but she folded back into herself, preferring her books to people.

And men, forget men. She was so out of the dating loop, the thought of her lunch with Adam just about triggered a full-blown panic attack.

"I don't know how to go on a date, not that this is really

a date or anything." Mia was so embarrassed by the admission, she felt physically sick. She'd built her life, her reputation, on her confidence and her ability to make people believe she could handle anything. In most cases it was true, but when it came to men, Mia wasn't sure of anything.

"I don't know what to do," she whispered.

"Oh, my God." Fiona was beginning to understand. "You're *scared*."

"Of course, I'm scared! Let's look at this…" Mia stuck her hand in the air and started to count off. "First, I can count on one hand the number of actual dates I've been on in the last ten years and still have fingers left over. Two, a guy like Adam Miller is totally out of my league. My recent experience is limited to computer geeks and engineering grad students, and not even the cute ones. Third, he was a pro athlete… one with a pretty bad reputation. And fourth, I haven't…"

Mia couldn't even bring herself to think about number four. She pulled her fingers into a clenched fist. It was humiliating.

"What?" Fiona searched her face for some kind of clue. The question hung in the air until Mia screwed up her courage and blurted out her confession.

"I can't remember my last date—it was sometime in grad school. And I haven't had a second date with the same guy in over five years."

"Whoa. Seriously? I mean—I figured you'd have been

seeing people since grad school."

"That was the plan." Mia leaned back into the soft cushions of the sofa. "It took me a long time to come to grips with Sara's death. She had so much going for her, and she blew it, and then she checked out, leaving all of us to raise the baby she left behind."

"I can't even imagine," Fiona said while copying Mia's posture and leaning back.

"After I received my library degree, I planned on saving so I could get an apartment and move out of my parents' house. I was ready to start having a real life. Then my dad was killed, and my mom—who was never that maternal—decided to move away. Alone. That's when it got ugly. Apparently, my mother had been spending money like crazy, and there was a lot of debt. When she sold the house, there wasn't much left over. Fortunately, my father had life insurance, including a policy just for Ben. After it was all settled, I deposited the money that was left to Ben in an account to take care of his needs. You know, child care, medical care, I invested money for college... I bought a car so I could drive him places." Mia poured herself another glass of wine. "I took care of him full time. He's my whole life, and I'm okay with that, but there has been no dating. No nights out with friends. There hasn't been much of anything."

"So, there's been no, you know...?"

"Sex? Are you kidding? Not for a really, really long time.

Hell, I haven't been seriously kissed since I was twenty-one."

Fiona's hand wrapped around hers. "You never said anything."

Mia shrugged. "What was I going to say? It's humiliating."

The emptiness went clear to her toes. It wasn't that Mia just wanted sex, although that would be a step up. What she wanted was the chance to find the love that went along with it. Mia had never been in love.

She'd never felt the exhilaration, the euphoria, the soul-stealing, all-consuming excitement that only happens when another person captures your heart. She'd never kissed in the rain, she'd never made love in the morning, she'd never known the touch of a man who considered her the center of his universe. Mia was fully aware of what had been missing from her life. All the emotion, the lust, the longing… she'd missed out completely.

And she almost cried at the thought of it.

SATURDAY MORNING, MIA wandered through the village of Compass Cove still feeling like a bit of a tourist. The area by the waterfront was nearly the same picture postcard it had been when she spent summers here as a kid. Sailboats dotted the water, gulls circled overhead, and New England could be seen off in the distance.

The day after Ben ran off, Mia had done some research and found a fall baseball league with some openings. She hadn't hesitated—she'd made three phone calls and signed him up. It wasn't football, but he was thrilled. Unlike a lot of mornings when he fought getting up, today Ben bounced out of bed for an early practice.

That left Mia with a couple of hours to herself, and she had to think about what she would do with the time. She stopped at Rinaldi's Cafe, picked up a latte, found a bench by the dock, and settled in to gather her thoughts.

Since her confession to Fiona, Mia had been dwelling on her poor excuse of a social life. She'd been in a book club here, taken a class there, but she'd never truly made an effort to make herself available. Her friendships revolved around work, and she'd given herself little opportunity to socialize. Sure, she had it tough raising Ben on her own the past two years, but there were a lot of single parents in this world and they didn't make excuses. There were probably a load of reasons why she wasn't dating. With enough therapy, a good psychologist could probably set her right. But that was something else she didn't have time for. Ever since she'd had to take care of Ben on her own, she didn't make any decision without thinking of him first.

She sat, gazing at the deep greenish blue water. There were a few sailboats and some kayakers out for a morning on the bay, and it felt familiar. Her family often rented a house on Maryland's Eastern Shore, and there had been many mornings that she and Ben had taken walks and seen a collection of boats and kayaks, just like here. Even before he was her responsibility alone, they'd had a special relationship. The memory of his little hand in hers warmed Mia from the inside out. But now that she and Ben were settled, maybe it was time for Mia to make her own memories. Maybe it was time for her to start having a life.

Behind her, a row of shops were opening. There was a neat little antique shop, a bookstore, and a very upscale salon. A thought ran through Mia's head and she looked at her watch. The coaches respectfully asked the parents not to stay around for practices the first few weeks, so the kids could acclimate, and that left her with over two hours to kill. Tentatively glancing at the ends of her hair, she realized she could use a trim. It had been ages since she indulged in a little personal pampering.

Tossing her empty cup in a nearby trashcan, Mia made her way to the salon, which called itself *Visions: a Day Spa.*

The owner had created a lovely environment. Getting inspiration from the area, the salon was decorated in a palette of soft cream, brown, blue, and beige. One wall was actually a waterfall. Sheets of water flowed over the stone surface, creating a stunning visual effect. Plush chairs and the sound of running water provided a relaxing area for clients to wait. The receptionist was on the phone and looked up at Mia when she finished her call.

"Can I help you?"

"Ah, yes. I want to have my hair trimmed."

The woman tilted her head. "Do you have an appointment?"

"No, I was taking a walk and decided at the last minute. I could make one and come back next week."

"Let me see what's available." Her fingers clicked on the keyboard. As she examined the screen, a petite woman with shoulder length black hair walked from the back of the salon.

"What's up, Kris?"

"Just looking for an opening." The receptionist looked up. "I have a one o'clock?"

"I can't do one." Mia frowned, but the dark-haired woman whose skin glowed like warm bronze leaned in and pressed a couple of keys on the computer.

"I'm available."

"Oh," Mia said. "Are you sure?"

"Positive. Come on back."

She extended her hand, so appreciative that they were willing to accommodate her. "I'm Mia DeAngelis."

The stylist froze, her mouth dropping open, before tears welled up in her eyes. "Mia? Oh, my God. I can't believe it's you?"

Mia looked at the woman closely. *Hmmm.* Button nose, unrealistically long black eyelashes, deep chocolate brown eyes, wide smile... it was familiar.

Her heart jumped to her throat when she saw the dimples. "Oh, my God," she said on a breath. "Lilly!"

Without a moment's thought, the women were clutching each other, and Mia could not have been more thankful to whatever power had brought her into this shop. She and Lilly Vasquez had been inseparable whenever Mia visited Compass Cove. The girls had sleepovers, days at the beach, and endless hours in one or the other's backyard. They'd lost touch when they hit their early teen years and Mia didn't make as many visits.

"I can't believe it's you!" Lilly rubbed her hands up and down Mia's arms.

"You two know each other?" the receptionist asked.

"We were summer friends. Gosh," Lilly began, "it was so long ago."

"Our grandparents were friends. I think Lilly and I met when we were around five or six."

Lilly nodded and gave Mia another squeeze. "I was so sorry to hear about your dad."

Mia nodded, appreciating the kindness but not surprised. That was Lilly. Sweet and kind. She hadn't changed.

"Okay, well, let's get you started," Lilly said. "You can tell me everything you've been doing while we're making your hair gorgeous."

TWO HOURS LATER, Mia emerged from the shop with her hair cut in long, flippy layers, a fresh manicure and pedicure, and a small bag of cosmetics.

Allowing herself to be fussed over her was just what she'd needed. While her nails were drying, Kiki, the resident make-up artist, gave her a mini-makeover and guided her in the purchase of eyeliner, blush, and lip-gloss. For her skin, all Mia needed was some moisturizer with a sunscreen; clear mascara would accentuate her already long lashes. No fuss. Just the way she liked it.

It turned out Lilly was the salon's owner. She'd left Compass Cove right after her high school graduation and worked in Beverly Hills, making a name for herself as a hair stylist. But she'd hated the cut-throat nature of the business, especially in the high-end salon where she'd been employed. She'd come back to Compass Cove a year ago, and now her salon was filling a niche for a younger clientele who didn't want the same bouffant hairstyles favored by their grand-mothers. It was pure chance that Mia had walked in there that morning.

Not only happy she'd finally done something for herself, she'd reconnected with one of the people she'd missed all these years.

There was a mirror in the nearby antique shop window and Mia was startled when she caught her reflection as she passed. Her hair, which was still long, had a glossy shine she'd never noticed before. The way it framed her face made her features appear just a bit more refined, and her eyes, which were now lightly outlined in jade, stood out dramatically.

No doubt about it. Lilly was a genius, and Kiki wasn't far behind.

The changes were subtle enough that most people wouldn't notice, but Mia noticed. If she could just muster some confidence, and stop hiding who she was on the inside, she might find a way to be happy. Really happy.

Moving along, Mia stopped at the main intersection in town, which charmed her every time. The ornate clock in front of the bank where her grandfather used to work still kept perfect time, and the florist on the opposite corner had decorated the sidewalk with red, orange, and yellow mums. But it was the compass rose that adorned the center of the intersection that gave the downtown its special character. Commissioned years before, the simple design was inlaid in the pavement as a tribute to the hamlet's nautical past. Mia turned and realized she was right in front of Jennings Brothers. The compass shop, which also made custom watches and jewelry, had been in business for almost 300 years. Mia loved the story her grandmother had told her, about the young widow who brought a broken compass that had once belonged to her husband to the shop to be repaired. She and the compass-smith had fallen in love and they'd credited the broken compass for bringing them together. Most families in Compass Cove kept a compass in the house as a reminder how true love brings people together.

"Morning." A tall man stepped out of the shop, bearing a crank to extend the blue awning. His smile was wide and his blond hair fell in a mess across his forehead. He might have been thirty-five, but he had the air of an old soul.

"Good morning," Mia said. "I was admiring the window display. You have so many beautiful pieces."

"Thank you. Would you like to come inside?"

Glancing at her watch, Mia nodded. She had a few minutes. Not being able to remember the last time she'd been inside the shop, Mia eagerly walked in as the man held the door for her.

It was an old building, but instead of feeling simply old, it felt like there were stories here. Inside, the shop sported dark wood shelves which went from floor to ceiling. Glass cases and antique tables dotted the floor, but there weren't just compasses and watches adorning them. The place was a treasure trove. Hand-blown crystal and glass, jeweled boxes, and the most exquisite handcrafted jewelry were also on display.

"What's your name?" he asked.

"Mia," she said, still taking in her surroundings.

Stepping to her side, he smiled, picked up an adorable small glass cat, and settled it in her palm. When she held it up to the light, a rainbow of colors sparkled on the inside. "I'm Liam Jennings."

Shaking his hand with her free one, Mia couldn't help but smile. "This is an amazing place. I came in with my grandmother once or twice, years ago, but it's so different now. Did you make this?" she asked about the cat. "It's gorgeous."

"There's a local artist nearby who blows glass. She opens her studio a few times a year. It's amazing to watch her work."

Mia would love to see that. She examined the cat once more before handing it back to him.

"You're new in town?" he asked.

"I just moved here to take a job at the college. But my grandmother has lived here for almost sixty years. So, like I said, I've visited."

"Who's your grandma?"

"Janet Lang."

His mouth dropped a little. "Seriously? I had her for tenth grade history."

Mia shrugged. "You and half the town."

Walking around, she stopped at a glass case that held a very old, tarnished compass. There was an engraved plate mounted below it that said:

Lucy and Caleb ~ m.1750.

"Is this…?"

"It is," he said. "Want to see it?"

"Really? Oh, my gosh! Yes."

Playing up the drama, Liam took a key from his pocket, opened the case with a flourish, and removed the antique compass. He held it for her inspection, and Mia couldn't believe she was looking at the town's history, its heritage. The researcher in her was fascinated; the romantic in her was giddy.

Taking her hand, Liam placed the compass in her palm. She was surprised that the brass compass case wasn't cold against her skin, but warm. Within seconds, the needle started to wiggle, and then swing wildly back and forth. "Why is it doing that?" she asked. "Did I break it?"

For a few moments, she and Liam watched as the compass went wild in her hand.

"Oh, boy," Liam whispered. He brushed a lock of hair off his brow and leveled his gaze at her. "From time to time, it's said the compass behaves strangely. I've never actually seen it until now, but it usually happens when it's held by someone looking for their 'true north'."

"True north?"

"Geographically, it's the direction towards the North Pole. But metaphorically, it seems to apply to those whose hearts are lost and in need of direction."

Mia felt a tingle crawl up her spine. She'd come to Compass Cove for a chance at a better life, but was her heart looking for something? Was she lost?

"According to what my father told me—he's here during the week if you want to stop back—the last time this happened was maybe sixty years ago."

"Sixty years? Wow." She was frozen, staring at the face of

the compass and the swinging needle.

Finally, Liam took it from her, gently placing it back in the case. "Is your heart searching for something, Mia?"

"Yes. No." God, she was confused. "Maybe a little."

Liam faced her, and shoved his hands in his pockets. "Then I hope you find it."

Mia stared at the compass for a long time, then looked at Liam, at a loss for what to say. She was always searching, always hoping that life would give her the love story she wanted.

The love story she wondered if she would ever have.

ADAM WENT OVER the game plan again. They needed everything to go right if they were going to win. They also needed a shitload of luck.

One of his receivers was worried that there was too much loose fabric around his middle, giving their opponents something to grab on to. But Kelvin, his potential superstar, sat in the corner of the locker room, wringing his hands and mumbling. Praying. Not a bad idea. Maybe he'd find a quiet spot and have some words with the Big Guy himself. Although, Adam was pretty sure he'd used up all his requests when he was trapped in his crushed car.

His goal for the game was to make a good showing and come away with all his guys in one piece. If they won, he'd start believing in miracles.

Adam closed his eyes and tried to relax.

Instantly, she was there. His mind kept drifting back to Mia. He was genuinely looking forward to seeing her and Ben tomorrow, and that had him shaking his head.

He didn't know why it was important to him that she liked him, but it was. He got the feeling there was a lot of depth beneath that guarded surface, and she was so damned adorable.

So adorable.

Yeah, he was in trouble.

AT THE PARK, Mia stood next to another woman and watched Ben snagging grounders at second base like he'd been doing it since birth. He was smiling and talking to other boys on the field with ease. He was part of the team.

He was happy, and Ben hadn't been happy for a long time.

Glancing to the right, she smiled at the woman who was eyeing her curiously. "You're a new face," the woman said.

"Ah, yes," Mia replied. "We just moved here."

"Which one is yours?" the woman asked, her strong New York accent more apparent with the question.

"The boy at second base."

The woman nodded approvingly. "He's a good ball *pla-*

ya. I'm Donna."

"Mia." Time to jump in, she thought. "From what I understand," Mia began, "the league asks each family to do some volunteer work. Do you know who I would see about that?"

The woman pointed out a man holding a clipboard. "You need to give a few hours. Bobby Della Rocca is in charge of volunteers."

"Thanks," Mia replied. Walking toward Bobby, Mia knew it was time for her to become part of the team, as well.

Chapter Three

ADAM FUMBLED WITH the delicate china teacup and glanced over the gardens that surrounded the flagstone patio. September was rewarding them with perfect late summer weather. Surrounded by flowers that were still lovingly cared for, Adam relaxed, as he always did when he was here. It was just after eleven in the morning, he'd already coached his pee-wee football team to their first win of the season, and he had an interesting afternoon planned. If he left by 12:30, he would make his lunch date with Ben and Mia without a problem.

His hostess, easily one of the people he loved the most in the world, fussed over a piece of pastry. She always wanted everything to be perfect for him.

"Grandma, it's fine. I don't need chocolate. I'll have jam."

His eighty-two-year-old grandmother, Anna Miller, frowned. She treasured their Sunday morning visits and always made sure she had all his favorite foods. Except coffee. He could never persuade her to brew him a nice strong cup of coffee to go along with all the cookies, cakes, and pastries she made available, so he learned to make do with tea.

The house in Jennings Cove was the same as ever. Infused with his grandmother's spirit, the gardens bloomed with life. There was an energy surrounding the grounds that he could only attribute to the generations of Millers who'd lived here. This place was about family, about the connections he'd avoided for years. Visiting her did more than make her happy, it allowed Adam to reconnect with the part of himself he lost when his celebrity began to matter more than people.

"I'm sorry about that, dear."

"It's fine."

"But you like the chocolate croissants. I asked for them, specifically."

"Don't worry about it." He took the plate from his grandmother's hand and smiled.

"So, how was your first game yesterday?" she asked.

He grimaced. "We lost, but not as badly as I thought we would."

"You'll bring those boys along. Be patient with them." She dropped a lump of sugar in her tea and stirred gently.

"I'm trying." He thought about how their pathetic play in the first half yesterday would have tried the patience of a saint. He broke off a small piece of the croissant, spread some jam, and popped it in his mouth before fishing for information. His grandmother was a very active member of the library board of trustees, and he knew she'd met Mia.

"How are things at the Library?"

"Oh, wonderful. The fundraiser for the music collection is going well and the new librarian is settling in nicely." Grandma stopped stirring, and placed the spoon gently on the saucer.

That was the opening he was waiting for.

Of course, when Mia popped into his head, his body responded. Damn.

He was with his grandmother, for God's sake—this was not okay. His groin tightened and Adam drew a deep breath as he tried to rein in his lust, tried to get her out of his head. The last three nights she'd been part of some very hot dreams. He hated his lack of control, but since he wanted to prep for his date, this was the perfect opportunity to fish for some information.

"You know," he said casually, "I met her a few days ago." Grandma looked over and asked him the wordless question—her eyes were that intent. Adam was hoping she'd say something, give him some little bit of information, but all he got was the stare he remembered getting when he was a kid, the one that told him to spill his guts before she had to start asking questions. "Her nephew got lost over near the practice field. He hung out with me while he waited for her to come and get him. Nice kid."

"Really? Well it's a good thing he found you." She leveled her gaze at him. "What did you think of Mia?"

Adam sat back in his chair. What didn't he think about

Mia? "I don't know. Nice enough. It's too soon to form an opinion." *Liar.*

Now his grandmother's look became intense. Her eyes narrowed and she grinned. "Don't hold out on your old granny, Adam. Tell me what you thought of her."

He chuckled. "She's serious, a little shy, but I'd like to get to know her better." *In bed. I'd like to get to know her better in bed.*

His grandma smiled, and he knew she'd like the rest of his answer. "In fact, I'm taking her and her nephew to lunch today, and then we're going shopping for a bicycle for him."

Gram brought her hands together in approval. "That's my boy. You remember what I taught you."

Adam remembered. She had schooled him in all the social graces. He knew how to treat a lady, not that he always treated his women like ladies. But he'd pull out all the stops for Mia. Grandma always told him that the little things were what mattered. His grandfather, James Miller, made a point of doing the little things that kept his grandmother happy for the fifty-four years they were married. His father and mother were the same way. When his grandfather died, part of his grandmother died, too. She'd lost her best friend. Adam was still waiting to meet a woman like that, a woman who would appreciate the little things.

"From what I understand, she's had some difficult times."

"What do you mean?"

"Well, Fiona Gallagher told me Mia hasn't had it easy. Apparently, her nephew's mother, Mia's sister, died when he was a baby, and Mia's parents were in a terrible accident two years ago that left Mia the responsibility of raising him on her own."

Adam was stunned. "Ben is ten and Mia doesn't look like she's even thirty."

"She isn't. She's technically been the boy's guardian since she was twenty-one. She left college in New York to finish near her home in Maryland."

"Wow." That was sobering. When he was twenty-one, Adam was shotgunning beers, playing football, and screwing around. Mia was being a mom. No wonder she was so serious.

"You be extra nice to her, Adam. She's a good girl, not one of your floozies."

Adam leaned over and kissed his grandmother's cheek. "I'll be nice, Grandma. Just like you taught me."

MIA CHECKED HERSELF in the mirror one last time, singing along with the Barry Manilow her grandmother had playing in kitchen. Why she was so worried about this afternoon, she didn't know.

Her hair swept softly over her shoulders and a pair of silver hoop earrings peeked out when it moved. Her floaty, pale blue skirt and fitted white top were stylish and neat without being fussy. She'd pushed up the sleeves and then surveyed the neckline. Too much cleavage. Damn. Even with the weight she'd lost, the boobs and the butt just wouldn't get smaller. She'd be like a size eight if those two parts were proportional to the rest of her. Instead, she was nowhere near what her mother considered "ideal". And no matter what she did, she had to worry that "the girls" would make a showing every time she wore a low-cut shirt.

"That's a lovely outfit," Nana said, leaning against the wall near Mia. "And take it from a skinny, flat-chested woman—you fill out the top beautifully."

"I'm presentable." Mia tugged at her shirt again.

"Oh, dear God. Mia, you're a knockout. Women spend thousands of dollars to have boobs like those."

"Shhhhh," Mia hissed. "Ben's right outside."

"Oh stop. If I were twenty years younger, I'd go buy my-self a pair." Nana pulled her t-shirt away from her body and looked at her profile in the mirror. "How would I look?"

"Mom would tell you to get a breast reduction."

"Your mother would kill to be shaped like you. Is she still giving you a hard time?"

Considering her mother asked her at the beginning of every phone call if she'd lost any more weight, Mia would say, yes, Mom was giving her a hard time. You'd think a near death experience would soften a person. Not her mother. Mia adjusted her shirt again.

Squeezing her eyes shut, Mia fought back the familiar feeling that she wasn't good enough. When she opened her eyes, Nana looked at her in the reflection. "Just be yourself."

She nodded and drew a deep breath.

Throwing a light sweater around her shoulders, she hoped it wouldn't get too warm and slipped her feet into some pretty sandals to finish the outfit, even though Adam would tower over her. There was no denying that she found him attractive. He was handsome, built like a god, and could use words with more than two syllables. But there was more. Something in the way he shook her hand, and looked at her—the way he spoke to her on the phone—whatever it was, it made her stupid.

And Finn was right, it scared her. To death.

"You know," Nana said, "You never told me your friend's name."

"He's not my friend," she shot out, but the disappointed look on her grandmother's face made her tone down the attitude. "Adam Miller."

There was silence. Total. Silence.

To say Nana was stunned would have been an understatement. She was speechless.

"What's wrong?"

Her grandmother grinned. It was a knowing smile, and something about it put Mia on high alert. "Nothing," Nana said. "I'm going to make myself scarce. Have a good time."

"Wait…" But Nana had scooted away at light speed.

Mia was on her own.

Just then, Ben came banging in the front door. He'd been shooting baskets in the driveway for the last twenty minutes, trying to be nonchalant about the afternoon, but Mia knew he was bursting. "He's here. Are you ready?"

"Yes, I'm ready." She glanced over at Ben and down and noticed his foot was bouncing. Sometimes he could contain the hyper, other times he couldn't. "It's very nice of Coach Miller to do this, so be on your best behavior."

He nodded nervously. "I know. I will."

She ran her hands over his shoulders and once again was reminded of how tall he was getting. But he was still a boy. Young, naïve, scared. "Remember, manners matter. We'll probably have lunch first, so you know what I expect."

"Okay, okay."

She heard Adam's footfalls on the stoop and looked up to see his smiling face at the screen door.

"Hi," she said. Reaching for the door handle, Mia noticed how his black truck dwarfed her little compact in the driveway. "Come in."

"Thanks. Hey, Ben."

"Hi." Ben held the front door. "Cool truck."

"It gets me around. Here." He handed Ben the keys. "Go have a look. Just don't drive off, okay?"

Ben laughed and ran outside, leaving Mia alone with a very sexy Adam. Being close to him was exhilarating and terrifying, and Mia couldn't ever remember being so tuned into every sense, every feeling.

He was wearing tan shorts and a marine blue polo that spanned his broad shoulders and chest. A wisp of hair peeked out near the collar. His arms and face were tanned, and even though he was clean shaven, she could see the faintest shadow of a beard. What got her was the smell of him. It was a musky, fresh scent—like standing on the beach after a storm. Mia had to fight the urge to lean in and inhale.

"You changed your hair," he said. "Pretty."

"Oh, ah…" She smoothed her hand over her hair and felt her cheeks flush. "Thank you," she said quietly.

God, he was handsome. Not pretty, like a waxed and oiled-up male model, but in a more rugged sense. His face was strong, angular; his body was big and muscular. This man oozed testosterone, and this type of attraction, this strong physical pull, was new for her. After a few seconds of staring at him like an idiot, Mia saw him glance away, and when he looked at her again, he smiled. And she died.

"Are you ready?" he asked.

Mia snapped back to reality, regaining her power of speech and willing her knees not to buckle. "Oh, yes, let me get my bag."

Note to self, she thought. Don't let your mouth hang open. Don't stare. He's going to think you're a lunatic.

Walking out to the car, Mia was deep in her own head. She was a grown woman. She could handle this. She could handle him.

Of course, on the ride to town, she barely said anything. Being with Adam apparently turned her brain to jelly. Ben, on the other hand, sat in the back seat, pushing buttons and chattering.

"Does he ever stop?" Adam asked, his eyes wide.

"Sometimes. But he's very excited. He hasn't stopped talking about you since Thursday," Mia said with a chuckle.

Adam laughed. "Got it."

"Where are we going to eat?" Ben asked.

"There's a nice place near the water. It's casual, has great food."

"Awesome," Ben said, finding another gadget to interest him.

"Is that okay with you, Mia?" he asked. Adam certainly wasn't living up to his reputation. He was the perfect gentleman. He opened doors, asked if she was comfortable, if she liked the radio station, if she was agreeable to his choice of restaurant. No man she'd ever met, including her own father, was this consistently considerate.

"Mia? Dock's End, do you know it?"

Perfect—she'd zoned out again. "I don't, but that sounds fine."

His mouth turned up at the corner, making her heart speed up. Not since high school, when her crushes were unrequited and her dreams of romance were unfulfilled, had anyone had this effect on her.

Watching Adam made Mia feel like the sixteen-year-old

nerdy girl all over again.

ADAM SWUNG INTO the parking space and made the quick move around the hood of the truck to open the door before Mia had the chance. She graciously accepted each and every courtesy, smiling and making him feel like a clumsy teenager. His grandmother was right about her. She wasn't like any of the women he'd dated in the past fifteen years, which meant he was totally out of his element.

But he made the extra effort because she seemed to genuinely appreciate it. She smiled bashfully when he opened her door, and let him help her out of the truck. When he took her hand, her fingers curled around his and he warmed immediately. Her hands were slender, her fingers long and tapered, and Adam imagined what those hands could do.

Ben shot ahead, and Mia called him back. It was at least ten seconds before they realized they'd started walking toward the dock and their hands were still joined. She looked at him and bit her lower lip, sending his system into shock. Goddamn. When she wiggled her fingers out of his grasp, he missed her.

What the hell was going on? He was a hand on the ass kind of guy, not a hand holder.

Mia locked eyes with him again and his heart twitched in a way it had never done before. Generally cautious, knowing the difference between a causal relationship and something more serious, Adam had kept things casual with women for years. But with Mia, it wasn't the same. This woman had power, and it scared the crap out of him.

Adam watched as she surveyed the block, the marina, everything in the immediate area, as they found a table on the deck. He enjoyed the way she drew things in and took time to process her surroundings. "It's so pretty here. I've always loved the way everything in Compass Cove is centered around the water."

"I know what you mean. It was my life growing up." He pulled out her chair, then sat next to her under the large umbrella that sheltered their table. He pointed to his left and drew her attention to the marina. "I spent three summers piloting tenders at Roosevelt's."

She smiled. "Really? My grandmother used to take my sister and me to the Italian ice stand that was right there."

"Vinnie's? Great place. His grandson runs it now."

She looked up from the menu and turned to him. "Did Vinnie finally retire?"

"No," he said softly. "He passed away."

"Oh. Oh, that's sad." Her mouth twisted a little and her eyes glanced in the direction of the stand. She was genuinely sorry he was gone. "Did you know him well?"

"I went to school with one of his grandsons, so yeah. Compass Cove is that kind of place. You tend to know everyone."

She nodded. "That's why I jumped at the chance to move here."

"You have family here? Right?"

"Just my nana. My parents grew up here, but Dad and my mother didn't come back too often. Dad was in the navy, and Mom never liked it here. According to her, 'The place smothers you.'"

As obnoxious as that sounded, he could almost relate to her mother's feelings. "There's some truth to that. I hesitated coming home when my career ended."

"Why?" At this point, Mia folded her arms on the table and leaned forward, revealing even more cleavage. Adam's eyes were drawn right to her glorious chest, which was now offered up like a meal. Shit. He needed to focus on the woman, not the package.

"I'd lived in cities for a long time." Adam set his gaze on a boat in the harbor. "It was fun, always something to do, and I could be somewhat anonymous."

"I've been anonymous my whole life. I'm done with it." Mia said. As she did, she leaned back, and Adam wondered how many more of his brain cells she was going to fry today. "And the city isn't that far."

"I'm still getting used to being back in a place where everyone knows what I'm doing all the time." Where the scrutiny made it harder to hide screw ups.

Mia looked off into the distance, maybe looking at the same boat he'd been staring at a few seconds before. When she returned her gaze to his face, Adam felt like he was going down for the third time. He wasn't sure what it was, but her eyes said there was a story she wasn't telling. "I guess that could be a problem, but it's better than no one caring about you at all."

Yeah, definitely a story there, and maybe some baggage. A long silence gave both of them a chance to regroup, and let the tension between them ease… but Adam was curious.

Ben was fidgeting with the place setting, typical ten-year-old behavior. But watching the kid, Adam could see what was motivating Mia. He was a good kid, and based on what he knew so far, he guessed Ben's very pretty aunt was at the heart of it. "So," he said to Ben. "What do you think you're going to eat?"

Ben shrugged and looked at the choices.

"Hungry?" Adam asked.

"Starved," Ben said. "Why couldn't you come at twelve-thirty?"

"Ben," Mia's voice was quiet, but firm. "Remember what I said about manners."

She had a look on her face that reminded Adam of the thousands of "don't-screw-with-me" looks his mother had given him. "I was with my grandmother. I wasn't sure if I would be ready by twelve-thirty."

"Oh. Is she sick or something?"

"No," Adam said. "I go to see her every week when I'm in town."

"My grandma moved to South Carolina, after Grandpa died," he grumbled.

There was a long pause as Adam processed the information. "That stinks. Do you miss her?" The boy shrugged again, and right then a waitress came by to take their drink orders and rattle off the specials.

It took him a second to notice Mia was staring at him. The corners of her mouth were turned up ever so slightly. "You visit her every Sunday?"

"When I'm around. She still lives in the family house in Jennings Bay."

"She lives there alone?"

"There's staff, and my mother lives in a cottage on the grounds." Adam wondered if he should say something and then just gave in to the impulse. "Grandma sends her regards, by the way."

"Excuse me?" she said. "Her regards? Do I know your grandmother?"

Adam laughed. He'd surprised her a little, and that was always a good thing. "Yes, you do."

Mia looked away for a second and then back at him. It didn't take long; she figured it out. "Your grandmother was at my first interview."

"Give the lady a prize."

The waitress returned with water for Adam, iced tea for Mia, and a glass of chocolate milk for Ben. Once they ordered their food, Ben went back to the puzzle he found on the menu, and Adam and Mia settled back into their conversation.

"So, how did I come up while you were with your grandmother?"

"She's a very active member of the library board. I was asking her about her week and she mentioned that the new librarian was settling in."

"That's when you mentioned to her that you knew me?"

"Not initially." He took a drink of his water and leaned in. "Although she did mention that you are a lovely young lady." Mia blushed, looked down into her glass, and started to play with her spoon. Adam liked that he could fluster her, but then watching her chew on those gorgeous lips flustered him pretty good too. Damn. "When I told her I was seeing you today, she was happy, and reminded me to mind *my* manners."

Mia took a breath—it almost sounded like a sigh—before meeting his gaze head on. Her eyes were so dark it was like looking into the night sky, and it took Adam a little while to breathe.

"Please tell her I said 'hello'," she said.

He felt himself smile. "I'll do that."

ADAM COULDN'T DENY he was having a good time, even though he had no idea why. It was the antithesis of every date he'd been on over the past fifteen years. And if he wasn't misreading her, Mia was enjoying the afternoon, too.

One thing he had to say about the woman, she had her priorities straight. And at the top of the list was her nephew.

Ben should have been enough reason for Adam to run from Mia DeAngelis. But, for some odd reason, the part of her that was a mother was one of the things Adam found most appealing. He didn't want to like her or be attracted to her. Quite honestly, she represented a lot of work.

But when he looked at her, his fight or flight reflex kicked in, and instead of giving in to the urge to bolt, Adam wanted to fight.

For her.

Talk about a wake-up call. It shocked him to think that at his age he might actually be growing up. It had taken long enough.

After lunch, they went to the bike shop, where he watched Mia help Ben decide between a blue mountain bike or a silver one. She asked him questions and let him make the evaluation himself. She was good at helping him feel independent. After they chose the bike, and Ben was beaming, they picked out some accessories—a light, a small saddlebag with a tool kit, a lock, and a helmet.

Aunt Mia had done her homework.

Adam loaded the bike in the truck and secured it, all while Ben watched. "You're sure it won't fall out?"

"Positive," said Adam. "I'll take it slow on the way to

your house if it will make you feel better." Ben nodded and Adam grinned at Mia as Ben climbed into the cab of the truck.

"He's excited," Mia said quietly.

Adam nodded. "I know exactly how he feels."

At Mia's house, Adam watched from the living room window as Ben showed off his new bike to the kids on the block. There was nothing like a new toy to make a kid part of the group. Ben would have to stay there on his own, but a really cool bike was a way in.

Mia was in the kitchen getting them something to drink. No matter how uncomfortable she was around him, she wouldn't let him go without making the offer. She was all about making other people comfortable.

Her new home was in the hamlet of North Harbor, which used to be a place where people from Brooklyn and Queens could buy little summer bungalows just a short walk to the beach. Now, it was occupied year-round. The classic Victorian where Nana lived was one of the bigger homes in the area, with a large, wrap-around front porch and a decent backyard. Looking out the front window, Adam could see clear across to where he lived in Gull's Point.

The living room was what his grandmother would call cozy—filled with large, comfortable furniture in soft greens and blues. The tables were also oversized and functional, having loads of storage, and around the room shelves filled with books took over the wall space. There were fresh and dried flowers all around, and framed pictures on the walls and tables. Knowing this was her grandmother's house, Adam was able to get a sense of the family history.

Many of the pictures were of Ben. There were photos of people who could have been Mia's parents and a series of pictures of two girls together from the time they were small children until they were young adults. One, the older of the two girls, was a striking blonde who looked like a thousand other striking blondes he knew. The other girl was chubby, awkward, barely looking at the camera, and definitely overshadowed by the blonde.

He looked again.

No.

But there it was. No doubt about it, the hair color, the shape of the face... yup. It was Mia.

Adam couldn't believe it. Talk about a transformation. The shrinking violet had bloomed.

The girl with Mia in all those pictures must be Ben's mother. When he looked closer, he could see the resemblance right away. He wondered how she'd died.

Moving toward the kitchen, he passed a piano that held more pictures. Her grandma sure loved her family.

Stopping in the kitchen doorway, his eyes found Mia immediately. She was standing at the counter, singing softly to the Stevie Wonder song playing in the background while stirring a pitcher of fresh lemonade. Her hair tumbled down her back in soft curls and her feet were bare. Adam could have watched her forever if Mia hadn't noticed him and jumped.

"Oh!" She drew a hand to her chest. "You startled me."

"Sorry." He stepped into the room and walked toward her. "Can I help you with anything?"

"No… I think… I…" She stammered like a schoolgirl and Adam found he was charmed. *Charmed?* Since when did he get charmed? *Since Mia*, he thought. He leaned his hip into the counter and watched, enjoying the fact that he made her nervous and trying not to think about how she affected him. And she affected him plenty.

"There are a lot of pictures out there. Big family?"

"Not really. Sara was my only sibling. My mom has a brother who's married with two sons, and a sister who never married. My dad was an only child." She was still stirring as she talked, but glancing at him from the corner of her eye. "My uncle and his family live in Massachusetts, so we rarely saw them, but they come to see my grandmother, or she goes there, every other month. Aunt Regina is my uncle's twin. She taught at Virginia Tech for years and just retired, she doesn't live too far from my mom. I like her. She's fun, but I don't see her much. I'm sure the pictures helped Nana feel closer to everyone since we were all so far away."

Something caught the sunlight; he reached out and took a small brass compass from the shelf directly in front of her. He grinned because even though it was something he might expect to find in any home in town, somehow finding one here made sense. Never had anyone fit Compass Cove like Mia. Her family obviously had a lot to do with that.

"That's my nana's compass. Grandpa gave it to her when he proposed. She loves the story of Lucy and Caleb. Told it to me over and over when I was little."

Adam placed the compass back on the shelf. "Don't forget the ghost," he said, referencing the legend.

"She never forgot the ghost." Angling her body toward him, her chocolate colored eyes warmed as she continued. "I met Liam Jennings yesterday. I had no idea the shop still had the original compass."

"Yeah. People say it does all kinds of weird things. I don't know if I buy all the stuff about it helping you find your soul mate, though.

Mia stirred the lemonade dreamily. "Finding your true north."

"Ah," Adam said. "You're a romantic."

Mia's eyes turned up to his and she squinted. "I'm a girl. Of course I'm a romantic."

He laughed and nodded. He didn't believe that stuff for a second, but he loved how she did. Mia had had such a rough time, but she still had enough optimism to dream about the happy ever after. "Tell me about your Nana."

"Ah, okay." Mia placed the spoon on the counter and faced him. "What do you want to know?"

"Where was she from? How did your grandparents meet?"

"Well, she grew up on the Upper East Side. Her family was very wealthy." Adam watched her drift into the tale. "Her father was a builder, and the one thing he wanted was for all his children to be well educated, even the girls. My grandmother enrolled at Barnard when she was sixteen."

"Wow, that's young."

"Yeah, she's brilliant. Majored in History, Classics and Ancient Studies." Mia examined her fingers. "She met my grandfather, whose family was from Queens, during her senior year. She was just nineteen; he was a twenty-three-year-old former Navy pilot, and a student at Columbia."

He nodded and started to wonder about the brains in Mia's pretty head. Obviously she was smart... she was a college librarian, but she came from some serious academic stock. She paused to take two glasses from the cupboard and continued. Adam found himself soothed by her sweet voice. It was soft, musical—almost like a caress.

"Nana was engaged to the son of some equally wealthy family friends, but once my grandfather set his sights on her, it was all over. He pursued her relentlessly, and she fell for him. The family was scandalized when she broke the engagement, and my great-grandmother didn't speak to her for two years. She and my grandfather married the day after she graduated from Barnard and my mother was born nine months later. Nana never regretted her decision."

He folded his arms and smiled at the way she told the story. "Your grandfather sounds like he was a man with a mission."

"That he was." Unexpectedly, Mia's hand took a small frame from the same shelf as the compass.

"Is that him?" he asked.

"Uh-huh. He used to take us fishing." The gentleman in the photo was standing in a Boston Whaler, clutching two smiling little girls close to him. The picture captured a perfect moment, and Adam watched as Mia ran her hand over the image. "I miss him. I miss both of them."

Adam wondered what it must be like to feel so intensely. He was only now learning to let his guard down with his family, but she seemed to give everything she had to whatever she did.

"When did your grandparents move here?"

"Nineteen-fifty-seven. My grandfather got a job with a small bank. He became president eventually. They were married for fifty-one years, and I think he loved her more every day." He watched as she put the frame down and braced her hands behind her. "I'm sure that's more than you ever wanted to know about my family."

"Not at all. You learn a lot about a person from their family. My grandparents sound similar to yours. They had a great relationship. I was close with both of them."

"Was?"

"My grandfather died about eight years ago. It was very tough on my grandmother. On all of us."

"My grandfather, too. It wasn't too long after we lost

Sara. Nana keeps busy though. She still works and goes to exercise classes and book groups. She likes to travel. I hope I have her energy at seventy-nine."

"My grandmother is eighty-two and does more in a day than I do in a week." He stepped toward her and pulled a lock of her hair between two fingers. "It's nice that we have that in common."

She nodded, her breathing picked up, warmth came off her skin, and Adam planned. There was quiet now, and the only thing he heard was the gentle sound of the beach in the distance. As he inched closer, Mia's eyes locked on his, and he looked deep into them—soft brown with a darker rim—like a bowl of rich chocolate frosting. Her hair still floated between his fingers and a blush rose in her cheeks.

"I hope you like the lemonade," she said. "I tasted it, but I always worry that I make it too sweet."

He cradled her face in his hands and let his thumbs brush her cheeks. "I'm sure it's fine." Adam could only smile as he nuzzled her hair and took in the smell of her, a mix of flowers, the sea, and the sky. God help him.

"It seemed okay to me," she said, her breath catching and her voice so soft it was like a puff of air.

What was it about this woman? What made her this irresistible? She was so nervous she was trembling, and Adam had to admit, something about Mia made his own insides a little jittery. "You have the most beautiful hair. And your eyes, the way you look at me…"

"What are you doing?" she asked, barely able to get the words out.

Adam was done teasing, and talking was way overrated. He looked straight into her eyes when he answered. "Research."

He lowered his head and their lips touched. From that day on, any time Adam smelled or tasted lemons, he would think of Mia. Her lips held the sweet and tart taste of the lemonade and something that was uniquely hers, something that made him want to kiss her forever. Adam took little sips of her lips, then coaxed her mouth to play with his. When her hands settled on his waist, he knew she wasn't going to pull away. At least not yet.

A little hum came from her throat, something that sounded like a cat's purr, and that urged him on. Sliding his hands down her sides and around that beautiful behind, he lifted her up and sat her on the counter facing him. He kissed her again, this time more deeply, enveloping her completely in his arms as he continued to taste that gorgeous mouth. She smelled like heaven and felt like a cloud wrapped up in silk. Pressed against him, her body was a complete contrast to his—she was soft and supple, and Adam found he was losing himself in the feel of her. At one point Mia pulled back, hesitated, looked into his eyes, then gazed at his mouth. She studied it, and when she ran one finger over his bottom lip, Adam didn't know how he held himself together. It was sexy, it was innocent, and inside he felt a tightening in his gut that scared the crap out of him.

He leaned in and kissed her again, holding her so close he could feel her heart beating. She inhaled, stealing his breath, and then she whispered his name. Hearing that was unexpected, intimate, and Adam felt like he'd been given a gift. A very dangerous gift. This woman and her sweet kisses should come with a warning label. She was addictive, and he would never, ever have enough. He tried to clear his head, but rational thought was gone—all that was left was Mia.

The front door slammed and Adam pulled back quickly at the sound of overlapping voices. He could pick Ben out of the mix, but there was a woman, too. Her grandmother, no doubt. Mia looked at him and took a deep breath before easing herself from the counter. He felt completely disconnected, standing there when he wanted to make love to her right on the kitchen floor. Leaning against the refrigerator, he watched Ben charge into the room, followed by Mia's Nana. She was small and slender, with long, thick salt and pepper hair pulled into a tight pony tail... *holy shit.* The sight of the older woman twisted Adam's stomach in a knot; *he should have realized.*

Adam straightened himself. This was the curse of small towns. He knew Mia's grandmother. And she knew him.

Ho-ly shit.

Chapter Four

"I CAN'T BELIEVE you knew him, and you didn't tell me!" Mia was furious. After sharing the hottest kiss of her life with Adam, Nana walked into the kitchen, and Mia watched her date all but swallow his tongue. He'd gone into shock, and it wasn't from the kiss. "You didn't say anything about teaching him! How could you?"

"I didn't think it mattered. It was almost twenty years ago."

"Didn't matter? Oh, my God!"

"Mia, calm down." Nana turned on the music and Bobby Sherman started belting out "Easy Come, Easy Go."

How ironic.

Sinking into the kitchen chair, Mia couldn't shake the picture of Adam practically running out of the house. He'd engaged in a little small talk with Nana and then bolted. What a disaster.

Mia let her head drop to the table.

Her grandmother's hand left a light touch between her shoulder blades and Mia couldn't help but wonder why she couldn't have a normal life.

"What's wrong?" Nana asked.

"He looked, I don't know, spooked." Mia rubbed her hand under her hair and across the back of her neck. She was warm. He did that to her.

"I don't know. He might have seemed surprised, but I don't think he was that *spooked*." Nana was trying to make light of the whole situation, but Mia was still trying to make sense of what had happened. "I guess you had a nice time?"

Mia closed her eyes and nodded. The best time ever, she wanted to say.

"And I got the sense," Nana began, "That Ben and I interrupted a private, um, *conversation*."

"You could say that." It was only the understatement of the century. God, how had she let things get so out of control? And Ben! Thank God the only thing on his mind was riding his new bike.

Mia ached. She couldn't get over the way her body lit up when he touched her. The response had been automatic and intense. And then it was over, and even though Mia barely knew Adam, there was an ache, a void when he stepped away. What did it all mean?

A light breeze wafted in the back door, and Mia rose and walked toward the coolness, hoping it would steady her. She may not have been the most experienced person when it came to matters of the heart, but the way she felt was more than simple lust. Without a doubt, Adam was a gorgeous specimen. But there was more.

"Sweetie? Did something happen?" Nana walked over, stood next to her and laid a hand on her back, making small circles.

It was a kiss, she thought. *Just a kiss.* But as she let herself relive it, her body—her heart—reached out for Adam, and never had anything been more confusing. Mia could only shake her head, hoping against hope that her grandmother wouldn't ask any more questions.

She didn't, but her hand stayed on Mia's back, circling, always trying to soothe. "When I met Grandpa, I had no idea my reaction to him would be so visceral."

Mia turned, amazed that her grandmother always knew what to say.

"I was so young, barely twenty, and I had no experience with boys. When I met him, well…"

Nana was lost in her own memory, bringing her fingers to her lips, remembering her own kiss. "The first time he touched me, it was so innocent, but still…" She paused. "After that, I was lost to him."

"Oh, Nana…"

"I'm sorry I didn't say anything about knowing Adam. I should have."

"It's okay."

"For what it's worth, he drove me crazy, but I always loved that kid. He was a good boy, challenging, but good. Probably one of my favorite students. I think he's a good man."

Mia nodded. "You don't think he's going to be all weird-ed out because we're related?"

"Maybe at first, but in the long run, I don't think so," Nana said.

"I mean you know him, and he knows you and…"

Nana laughed. It was an honest to goodness belly laugh, and Mia wondered what was so funny.

"You're right about that," Nana chuckled. "But that's true of a lot of people in town. You can't avoid it here."

"I guess."

"Oh, Mia, you'll get used to it. You were brought up with a certain level of separation. Compass Cove has none. I taught for over thirty years. Thousands of kids passed through my classes, and you'll be hard pressed to find someone here in town who isn't connected to me somehow. It's one of the things your mom hated."

Mia nodded. "He looked pretty freaked out. I don't know."

"He'll be back." Nana was trying to contain her chuckle. "Adam Miller is many things, but he's not stupid." She was the second person who'd said that about him.

As they continued to stand quietly by the back door, Mia recalled the kiss, thinking about how Adam had touched her. It was gentle, intimate… like he knew her. When she looked in his eyes, she could tell he felt as off balance as she did, but he didn't stop kissing her until there was no other choice.

"He was nice?" Nana was back to questions.

She nodded. "Very."

"Ben seems to like him."

Mia smiled. "He's so great with Ben. I mean, he has a pretty bad reputation. I thought he'd be… I thought he'd be different."

"Not what you expected?"

Mia shook her head. "He broke the arrogant jock stereotype I'd been warned against all to pieces." She drew a breath and shrugged.

Nana examined her face, looked at her close, like she was searching for information. Then her eyes widened. "You *really* like him."

Crap, crap, crap. She really had to practice that poker face. "I liked spending time with him. We got along very well, but I can't imagine I'll be able to hold his interest."

Nana stood, and started to gather fixings for salad. It was another quiet moment and Mia wondered if she could use the break in conversation to make a getaway.

"You know," Nana turned to Mia, her normally bright eyes now full of concern. "You always sell yourself short. I did the same thing." She started to peel leaves off the head of lettuce. "Part of the reason I wouldn't go out with Grandpa at first is that I thought it was some cruel joke. I mean, why would he want me?"

"Grandpa adored you, Nana."

"I know," she said. "But it wasn't always easy to believe that." Her grandmother put the lettuce in the bowl and closed the gap between them. "You don't know who's going to be your love story, Mia. It may be Adam, it may not. But don't be so afraid that you close the door before you have a chance to find out."

THE BURGER WAS done perfectly, and Adam chased the bite he'd just taken with a taste of his favorite local beer. It was his second meal of the day at Dock's End, but this time he was by himself. The breeze off the harbor forced him to throw on a jacket, but the weather was just about as perfect as his burger. The waves slapped at the pylons holding up the waterfront deck and the gulls made their familiar squawking sound overhead. The evening couldn't have been scripted better. Okay, so he didn't like that he was alone. That pretty much sucked.

He should have just picked up a pizza and gone home. Sitting near the bar, staring at the table where he'd had lunch with Mia and Ben a few hours earlier wasn't helping him erase the memory of that kiss.

And it certainly wasn't helping him forget his former history teacher walking into the kitchen. It was the last thing he expected, and it completely kicked his ass.

Then Mia came into his head. That sweet, gorgeous girl fried his brain cells every time he saw her, and he had no explanation for his reaction.

"You are so full of shit, Miller," he grumbled to himself. The explanation was simple. He liked her. She was funny, smart, and down to earth. Not uptight or cold like he originally thought. Sure, she was reserved, but she was honest and she had no expectations. Because of that, Adam found he could relax around her. Couple that with some good old-fashioned chemistry, and she became a girl he could dream about.

He took another pull on his beer and thought about how she felt in his arms, fitting against him perfectly. Adam always wanted his relationships simple, and the reaction he had to Mia was way more complicated than anything he'd experienced before. *Damn chemistry.*

He flipped open the scouting report for the following week's game and tried to concentrate on something that didn't have to do with Mia, but he couldn't get her out of his head. He couldn't get the *feel* of her out of his head.

"What are you doing here?"

Adam looked up to see one of his assistant coaches, Drew Griffin, approaching him with a beer and a basket of ribs. Drew was a hometown boy who'd stuck around, landing a job teaching English at Compass Cove High and coaching at Jennings. He was probably one of the smartest guys Adam knew. Drew and Mia were around the same age. They'd probably hit it off.

Which would suck, because then Adam would have to kill one of his best assistants.

Drew raised his beer in salute as he sat down at the table. "How was your bike expedition?"

"Successful. Got the kid a kickass bike."

"How was the librarian?" Drew took a pull on the bottle. "As expected?"

"She's all right. Nice enough." *And she tastes like heaven.*

"Yeah? I got a look at her the other day. *Damn.*"

"What's that supposed to mean?" Adam heard his voice drop a whole octave, coming out in a growl. He freaking growled. Like a wolf protecting his territory. *Shit.*

Drew froze with a rib just touching his lips. "She's good lookin'. That's all."

"Yeah. Right. She is." That ended the conversation for a few minutes. Drew ate his ribs, and Adam devoured his burger.

"So, I guess you had a good time?" his assistant asked.

Adam took a drink from his own beer and nodded. "Yeah."

Dropping a rib in the basket, Drew leaned back in his chair. "Yeah? You practically rip my head off for saying she's hot, and all you can say is '*Yeah*'?"

"What? Do you want me to share my feelings or something?"

"No, but what's up with you? Women don't usually have an effect on you. At all."

"Who said this one did?"

"Uh, the whole alpha dog thing you just did."

Adam took a breath and looked at Drew. He never talked about this stuff, but then again he'd never reacted to a woman like this before. "I like her. She's gorgeous, that's a given, but that's only part of it. She's smart as hell, sweet…"

"She's got a kid."

Adam focused on his hands folded in front of him. This part was the real kicker. "That doesn't bother me. It should, but it doesn't. She's totally got her shit together."

"Wow. So, are you going to see her again?"

"I don't know."

Drew raised an eyebrow. "*Why?*"

"We were, ah, having a moment back at her house and her grandmother walked in on us. I mean nothing was going on at the time, but it was awkward."

"Nothing was going on?"

"No," Adam folded his arms across his chest and leaned back in his chair.

"Then why is it a problem? I mean, Mia's an adult and… oh, wait a minute…" Adam could see Drew putting the pieces together. "Where did you say she lived?"

"North Harbor. Near the beach."

Drew started to chuckle. "I know where this is going."

Adam finished his thought. "Grandma is Mrs. Lang."

"Damn." Drew's mouth dropped open and the chuckled turned into a full-blown belly laugh. "I can't believe Mia's her granddaughter."

Adam nodded.

"Holy shit." Drew was enjoying Adam's predicament way too much. "It's sobering when you find out teachers have actual lives, isn't it?"

"Yeah, but she freakin' hated me. Constantly on my case. I almost failed one semester."

"Mrs. Lang was always pretty fair. Did you almost fail because she hated you, or because you screwed up?"

Adam looked out at the harbor. Of course he'd screwed up. He didn't stop screwing up until he almost killed himself in that car accident. Adam had always thought he was untouchable, but Janet Lang didn't buy it, or take his crap. Other than his family, she was one of the few people in his life who wasn't afraid to call him on his bullshit. He wished he'd listened to her more.

"Mia looked like she wanted to crawl in a hole," Adam said. "I'm sure she's gotten a full report on me from Grandma by now."

Drew laughed again. "I wish I could have seen your face."

"It's not funny." Adam ran his hands through his hair. "Mrs. Lang wanted to talk, and 'catch up'. I kept thinking, what am I supposed to say? 'Hey, nice to see you. I was just groping your granddaughter.'"

"Groped? Tell me you got your hands on the librarian's ass. That booty is a freaking miracle."

Adam had no intention of telling Drew anything about Mia's ass, because he'd already said too much. Only now, with that comment, he had to control the urge to throw Drew right off the deck.

"Sorry," Drew offered nervously.

Without responding to the apology, Adam dropped some money on the table and stood. "I got the check."

Drew nodded his thanks and took a last drink from his beer before standing himself. "Look, if you like her, see her again. What do you have to lose?"

Adam thought about what Drew said as he left the table, and for the first time in his life, he knew there was a lot to lose. Mia was the kind of person who could wreak havoc with his emotions and his nice safe existence.

Yup. A lot to lose.

But he also thought about what he might lose if he didn't at least try to see her again.

Aw, what the hell.

He took out his phone and opened a text to Mia. *Had a great time today. See you soon.*

He started toward his car, apprehensive about what he'd just done. The phone buzzed in his pocket almost immediately. When he saw the response, Adam breathed a little easier.

Me too. :)

Chapter Five

"YOU NEED TO calm down and tell me what's bothering you."

Janet Lang stared into her teacup and wondered if she should be telling Lina what had happened with Mia and Adam. But she was worried, and the only way she was going to get over the worry was by talking it out with a friend. Lina Rinaldi had been her best friend for over fifty years; she could trust her with this. She needed to.

Staring out of the front window of Rinaldi's Café— Lina's family business and the center of all things important in Compass Cove—Janet sipped her tea. The morning bustle was just beginning; the street filled with more cars, and more customers ambled into the café looking for their morning sustenance. Her friend was waiting for an answer. While Janet wondered if she was overreacting, she also wondered if Adam Miller was a bad idea for her granddaughter. She had no doubt he was a good man, but Mia was so inexperienced in situations like this, Janet didn't know how it was going to go.

"Janet? Mother of God! It can't be that bad."

"They were kissing."

"Who?"

"Mia and Adam," Janet said. "Kissing, like… I don't know. They were pretty involved."

"That must have been something to see." Lina bent toward her and smiled. "Was it hot?"

"LINA!"

With a chuckle and a wave of her hand, Lina sat back, but Janet couldn't dismiss it as easily. Yes, Mia was an adult, but she was new at this, and Adam was, well, Adam. That was enough.

"He was all over her and she was not shy about her part in it. Fortunately, Ben didn't see them. That's when we doubled back and went around to the front of the house. I figured if I slammed the door loudly enough, we could avoid embarrassment."

"Did you?"

"I don't know. I think they were both mortified."

"So, little Mia and the football star. Who'd have thought it?"

"Not me." Janet ran her fingers over the edge of the mug, and shook her head.

"Nor I." A third voice chimed in. When Janet looked up, she saw the very polished, poised, and concerned face of Anna Miller.

Anna motioned for Janet to scoot into the booth, and she sat down with the kind of familiarity that came from growing old with people. "I want him to find a nice girl, but I don't know about this. Am I a horrible person that I'm more worried for Mia than my own grandson?"

Janet cringed. "This isn't making me feel better."

The waitress brought Anna a mug, hot water, and a selection of teabags. "He's come so far, but still…"

Lina threw up her hands. "Oh, for crying out loud!"

Both Anna and Janet lifted their heads and stared at her.

"They're both adults, and the two of you have to stop acting like this is going to play out like Romeo and Juliet!"

Janet shook her head. "But Mia—"

"Is an intelligent woman who is no pushover. Look at what she's been through. And sure, Adam has had his tough times, but who hasn't? Stop this. You don't even know if they like each other."

Janet huffed a little, rolled her eyes. "Trust me, they like each other."

Lina smirked. "I guess all the passion skipped a generation in the family. Mia sounds a lot like you."

That's what she was worried about. "She's definitely not her mother. They couldn't be more different, but I don't know if I want her to be like me. I tend to act before I think."

"You've done alright. People love your impulsiveness, your passion." Lina took a mouthful of her and grinned. "I seem to remember a party, right before Tom died, when I caught the two of you smooching in the coatroom."

Janet felt herself smile and blush at the thought, but the tingles that started around her heart spread right through her. Thoughts of Tom always did that. She wanted that for Mia, she did, but she fretted about it anyway. "She's so inexperienced."

"So were we," Anna said. "And Lina's right. It's too soon to know anything."

That was the truth. Hadn't they all been swept off their feet? The three of them had married young, had babies young, and been lucky enough to have husbands who were not only the loves of their lives, but gave the three women all the room they needed to be who they wanted to be.

"Janet, you have to trust her," Lina said. "She's a smart young woman. And she's tougher than you're giving her credit for."

"I know. I'm just worried about her. So many things have changed recently. This is her first shot at a real life."

"I guess I can understand, but he's not a womanizer," Anna said in Adam's defense. "Well, not anymore."

What could Janet say? She wasn't really worried about Adam. At the core, he was a good man, and she knew that. It was the intensity of what she saw. Her memory drifted back to the moment when she approached the back door and saw their embrace. It was intimate, familiar, and she wished she hadn't seen it.

"I know it was just a kiss, but the way they looked at each other...I never expected that. Not on a first date." Oh, sure. She'd tried to soothe Mia's fears afterwards, but Janet understood why her granddaughter was unnerved. "I don't know that anyone else will ever have that effect on her. It's what I've always wanted for her, but it's so fast."

Lina patted her hand. "You don't have a say in the matter. Things will unfold the way they're supposed to."

Anna drew a breath. "I guess we have to wait and see."

With so much swimming around in her head, Janet couldn't stop the most unsettling thought from the past few days from flying right out of her mouth. "I think he's the one. Am I crazy? She may circle around this, but I really think he's it for her."

"You don't know that," Anna said quietly. There was a hint of worry in her voice, because her old friend knew Janet was never wrong about these things.

Recalling again what she saw, Janet nodded. "Oh, yes. I do."

WITH A BAG from the campus deli in his hand, Adam walked down the path to the library with a purpose, scanning the quad, and looking for any sign of Mia. His original intention was to take her out to lunch, but by the time he waded through his messages and e-mails, and actually called her, she'd already left the library. Fortunately, one of her coworkers gave her up, and told him that on nice days she ate at one of the tables outside.

As mid-September days went, this one was perfect—sunny and warm, without being too hot—it seemed like everyone on campus was taking advantage of it. The Great Lawn was crowded with students playing Frisbee, reading, or just hanging out. The president of the college had donated about fifty Adirondack chairs, which were situated all around campus, and every one was occupied.

The stone terrace was on the side of the library nearest the administration building, and if you didn't know it was there, you'd miss it. The flagstone patio was a quiet spot with large shade trees, bordered by low shrubs and large planters filled with flowers. The view of the sloping rear lawn, the formal gardens and Long Island Sound in the distance was spectacular and the patio had been set up with wrought iron tables and chairs to encourage people to take a break and enjoy their surroundings. Without a doubt, it was one of the most picturesque spots on campus.

Adam followed the path around the library. Halfway down the steps to the patio, he saw Mia, just where he thought she'd be, sitting at one of the tables facing the water. The breeze lifted her curls, and her soft mocha-colored dress floated and fluttered around her legs, giving him glimpses of skin that made his blood run hot.

The only problem with the scene was the tall guy standing near the table, smiling at her.

And Mia was smiling back.

Who was this guy?

He wore khakis and a blue button-down shirt, with the sleeves rolled halfway up his arms. About the same height as Adam, he had the lanky build of a runner, but his glasses, messy brown hair, and the battered leather briefcase identified him as an academic.

Their voices were low, but happy, and the man's hands were moving as if he were telling her a story. Mia was laughing, completely at ease. Adam hesitated for a split second, and then moved forward.

He set his bag on the table, and both Mia and her friend's eyes shifted.

"Adam! What are you doing here?"

The man she was talking to folded his arms, and clenched his jaw, obviously pissed that they had been interrupted. Yeah, well, screw him. Adam wasn't about to make it easy for another guy to move on Mia, so he leaned in and kissed her on the cheek. It could have been seen as a platonic kiss, but he and Mia knew there was nothing platonic about what had happened the other day. The blush rising in her cheeks sent the same message to her friend.

"I wanted to take you out to lunch, but when I called, someone inside told me you were already out here, so I grabbed a sandwich." He glanced at the guy and then back at her. "Is that okay?"

"It's fine. Oh, gosh." She motioned with her hand. "You two don't know each other. Adam, this is Noah Connolly.

He's in the English Department. Noah, this is Adam Miller."

They shook hands, but it wasn't at all friendly. "You're the football player?"

Adam smiled. "Used to be. I coach now."

"Ah." There was something obnoxious about the way he said it. Something superior. *Asshole.*

Pulling the chair closest to Mia away from the table, Adam sat and proceeded to stare the guy down.

It didn't take long.

"I'd better go," Connolly said. "I'll see you, Mia. Nice to meet you, Coach."

"You too, Professor."

When he was out of eye shot, Adam turned his attention to Mia, who was twisting her fingers nervously. Maybe this was a bad idea.

"I'm sorry if I interrupted something."

"Oh," she said, smiling, "You didn't. Noah and I have gotten to be friends; we're both new here."

"I understand. Still, you seem surprised to see me."

She bit her lower lip and he felt the blood in his head rush south. "I am, a little. You left kind of quickly the other day."

He leaned back in the chair and rubbed the back of his neck. "Yeah, I never expected to see Mrs. Lang in your kitchen. I'm sorry."

"I figured. I had no idea she knew you. She left out that part when I told her who was taking us out."

He laughed because they'd both been blindsided. "So, did she tell you what a pain in the ass I was in school?" Adam unwrapped his sandwich and opened his bottle of water.

"No," she said, taking a bite of her salad. "She told me you were one of her favorites."

Adam froze letting her words sink in. "Really?"

Mia nodded. "Really."

He took a bite, glad he didn't have to say anything right away, because he was still processing what she'd told him. Either Mrs. Lang was bullshitting, or he wasn't as big a screw-up as he'd thought. He noticed a paperback sitting to Mia's right and he picked it up, turning it over so he could see the cover. He expected she would be reading some classic, or something more academic, but there, staring him in the face was a shirtless man with breeches and boots clutching a very well-endowed woman, in a low-cut, white ball gown. The man's mouth hovered by the woman's ear and her hands gripped his biceps. The models looked in serious lust.

"*The Duke's Secret Bride*?" he asked.

Mia let out an impatient breath. "Are you going to pick on me?"

"No." He hesitated. Then felt himself smile. "Maybe a little. Romance novels, huh?

"I *love* romance novels," she said, grabbing the book back from him. "But that shouldn't be a surprise. We established the other day that I'm a romantic."

"We did," he said. "I guess I expected your taste would

be more literary."

"I have a master's in Comparative Literature. After I finished that, I went to Library School. I've had my fill of the depressing stuff. I like happy endings."

"Okay." The romance novel was such a small thing, but suddenly she was more accessible, more normal. Pointing at the book, he couldn't resist asking, "Is it hot?"

Mia swatted at his arm and he grabbed her fingers and held on. "What?" he protested. "Look at her!"

Mia chuckled softly. Her hand was small, warm, and soft in his, and he'd keep it there as long as he could, but the talk about the sexy book cover couldn't go on or he'd lose control right there in public. "How's Ben? Loving his new bike?"

"He's fine, and yes, he loves the bike. He'll be here in a couple of hours."

"Here?"

"Yup, our sitter learned last week that she's pregnant, and she doesn't want the added burden of another child to watch right now. She has two of her own, and number three is already giving her trouble."

"So, just like that you have no sitter?"

"Just like that. Found out yesterday." Mia waved her hands, dismissing it. "It hasn't been easy from the beginning. Ben's been here more than he's been with her."

This kind of problem would have leveled some women, and Mia may have been thrown by it, but she handled it. There was no panic, no blaming. She just handled it. "Ben must be bored stiff."

Mia shrugged. "There's nothing else I can do. I thought I had everything under control, and less than two weeks into school, I'm scrambling. Fortunately, the bus brings him right to campus, or I don't know what would've happened. I'll have to find someone else."

Adam had an idea, one of those thoughts that hit him in the head and he should've kept to himself, but didn't. "He could come to football practice after school. That will buy you a couple of months to find someone you're comfortable with."

"Practice?"

"Sure. I could give him jobs, he'd get to know the team, do guy stuff."

"Guy stuff?" Mia drummed her fingers on the table, a smile teasing at her mouth, waiting to hear his answer.

"Yeah, guy stuff." He tucked a piece of hair behind her ear. "Talk about women, smoke cigars. We'll teach him how to burp the alphabet."

Mia giggled and light shot into her eyes from the gentle teasing. "He'll be schooled in the proper execution of the fake fart?"

"I'll bet that's already been mastered, but yeah." His hand drifted down her arm and Mia sighed. He could tell she wanted to say yes, but as much as she may have liked him, she still had reservations. "You don't know me well, I get that, but since I was one of your grandmother's *favorites,* that has to mean something." He tried to coax another smile out of her, because he loved her smile, but where Ben was concerned, he knew she was dead serious.

"It does, but I don't know. He can be a handful."

"He's a boy. He supposed to be a handful. But cooped up inside, he's going to drive you nuts."

Examining their linked fingers, she nodded. "Okay."

"Yeah?" The gesture, that she was willing to trust him with Ben, caught him right in the gut. "Maybe Kelvin can bring him over. He's usually here before practice, right? Ben talked about him a lot the day we got his bike."

"That's a good idea. I'll tell Ben tonight," she said.

"I'll give Kelvin a heads up."

Mia caught his gaze and when she finally smiled, Adam lost his breath. He wanted nothing more than to kiss her, but remembering the flash of heat when they kissed last time, he didn't think that would be a good idea with the whole campus watching.

Mia must have been thinking the same thing, because her eyes were locked on his mouth. But like him, she made no move.

"I have to go in," she said softly, still staring at him, still making his blood rush. "Thanks for having lunch with me."

Her chocolate brown eyes were addictive. He could fall right into them. "You're welcome."

"I'll talk to Ben tonight." Pushing back from the table, Mia gathered her things and stood. "Are you sure about this?"

"I'm sure," he said, standing with her. "I'll see him to-morrow."

Nodding her appreciation, Mia slipped inside the library and left Adam wishing he'd gone in for that kiss.

MIA WATCHED AS Ben finished his second helping of chicken, rice, and salad. The way the kid ate, she was surprised he wasn't 300 pounds. But instead of growing out, he grew up. He didn't have extreme growth spurts, but he grew steadily, and based on what the pediatrician said about his hands and feet, he was going to be a very big boy.

"Do we have dessert?" he asked.

Mia nodded. "I bought ice cream last night. Do you still have room?"

Ben leaned back, patted his stomach and laughed. "Tons."

Mia smiled and rose as he cleared his plate and hers from the table. He put the items right in the dishwasher and sat down again, waiting for his dessert. Nana stood at the island and scooped out three bowls of chocolate chip ice cream. "So, I saw Coach Miller today."

"Where?" Ben's head popped up.

"You did?" Nana asked.

"He stopped by when I was having lunch."

Both Ben and Nana's eyes were focused on her and she couldn't wait to drop the surprise on them.

"Does he want to date you or something?"

God, she hoped so. "It didn't come up, but we did talk about you."

"Me?"

"I'm confused," Nana said.

Mia raised an eyebrow as she took the bowls and put them on the table, sitting across from him. "He wanted to know if you would want to go to football practice after school instead of spending your time in the library."

Ben froze with a spoonful of ice cream right in front of his mouth. "Really? That would be, like…" He took a breath and continued, "That would be the best."

"I thought you'd like it. He said you'd have jobs. You wouldn't just be goofing off."

"I can go?"

"Yes. Kelvin will walk you over in the afternoon. Nana or I will pick you up."

For a few seconds, Ben didn't say anything. When he reacted, he dropped his spoon in the bowl and went to her, throwing his arms around her neck. "Thank you for saying yes."

"Well, I'm saying yes with a condition. You have to keep up on your schoolwork. That comes first. Understand?"

"I will. I promise." He was in his chair again, digging into his ice cream. "This is going to be awesome."

Nana came up from behind, put her hands on Mia's shoulders and kissed the top of her head. Then, she sat down and grinned like a cat in cream.

It was good, and despite her earlier misgivings, Mia felt like she'd gotten this right.

MIA LAY IN her bed that night and thought about the day's turn of events. Ben was over the moon about spending time with the team. She was still second guessing the decision because it was going to throw her mother over the edge, that much was certain. Ben was the only thing left of Sara, and although Mia had been left alone with him in Maryland when her mother moved south, Mom still thought she had a say in how Mia raised him, never really seeing her as his mother. After meeting with the lawyer in a few weeks, Mom would know how serious she was about being a mother to Ben.

That didn't solve her problem with Adam, though. He got to her. She didn't know what to think or what to do about him. Mia wasn't easily impressed, and she had no love for jocks, so the attraction was rooted in something other than his persona. He was handsome, no doubt about that, but he was funny too, and seeing him with Ben the other day set all her girl parts tingling. Around him, her biological clock wasn't just ticking, the alarm was going off.

The gentle knock brought her back to reality.

When the door opened, a sliver of light and Nana's smiling face entered the room. Her grandmother was truly beautiful; and seeing her like this, illuminated from behind, she looked almost angelic. "You awake?"

Mia nodded and propped herself up in bed while Nana assumed the lotus position opposite her. She sat perfectly erect, her long silver hair falling to her waist, and her big brown eyes flashing with life and amusement.

"So," she began. "He's going to football practice every day?"

"That's what I said."

"What brought this on?"

"My babysitting dilemma came up while we were having lunch and he offered."

"Interesting." Nana paused. "What made you say yes?"

"He made a good point about Ben needing to be outside. Sitting in the library is fine occasionally, but he needs activity."

"This is a huge about face for you."

"I know, but I have to do what's best for him. Not what other people think is best." Now Nana was grinning. "No matter what instructions Sara 'left,' or what Mom wants, I have to do what's best for Ben."

"I agree, but you knew I would."

"I know."

"So what's bothering you?"

This situation was complicated, and putting her finger on what was bothering her wasn't easy because it was more than one thing. "I'm not looking forward to telling your daughter about this."

"This will make Ellen crazy, so be proactive. Tell her before Ben does. Then you're informing her of a decision, not defending yourself."

Nerve-racking as that was, it was a good idea. "Okay."

When she didn't volunteer anything else, Nana drew her own conclusions.

"Let me guess—Adam's the other part of this?"

Breathing deep, Mia nodded. "I like him. But he's such an unknown. This could go south in a heartbeat."

Nana shook her head, reached out, grabbed one of her ankles and extended her leg in a stretch Mia hadn't been able to do since she was nineteen. She had to start doing yoga. "Mia, you're projecting. Why do you always think something is going to go wrong?"

"Because it usually does."

"Stop it."

"It's not that easy. I mean, look at who he is. Why shouldn't I be worried?"

"Why did you say yes then?" Nana asked.

"I don't know. Maybe shouldn't have."

It was times like this that Mia saw the tough side of her Nana, the side that had taught teenagers for over thirty years. "You're being unfair, and basing your opinion on gossip, not fact. Here's what I know. Adam is close with his family. He adores his grandma and has done wonders for the college. He volunteers his time, donates money to good causes, and has changed his life for the better. Don't judge a book by its cover. Your mother does that all the time. Is that who you want to be?"

Having been judged plenty because of outward appearances, often by Mom, Mia shook her head.

"Look, I think you're worried more about how you're going to deal with Adam. He's not the kind of man you believed you'd be attracted to, and I understand your trepidation, and this whole *thing* with him has happened pretty fast. You've barely had time to settle in. But you need to face that you aren't really worried about Ben. Ben is going to do great. This is about you."

Leaning back into her pillows, Mia thought about a rebuttal, but she gave up. There was no use in even arguing the point when it was the truth.

Chapter Six

THE PLAN WAS dinner and a movie. It was simple enough until Mia and Fiona entered the Dock's End and hit a wall of people.

"Oh, my God!" Fiona exclaimed. "Are they giving away food?"

"Crab leg special," one older woman said. "The wait is almost an hour."

"An hour?" Mia said. "If we want to make the movie we're going to have to find fast food."

"Mia!" Turning toward the voice, Mia saw Lilly waving at her from the end of the bar. The two of them started moving toward each other at the same time, with Fiona following Mia and a tall blonde following Lilly.

"Hey!" She grabbed her in a hug. "How are you?" Lilly asked.

"Great, except for the wait. Is it always like this on a Thursday night?"

"No, they advertised some special, and everyone went crazy," Lilly said before turning. "This is my friend Jordan. This is Mia, we were summer friends back in the day."

Noticing Finn behind her, Lilly smiled.

"Finn Gallagher. I work with Mia."

"Hi. You guys are going to be here forever." Lilly was thinking out loud as she scanned the crowded waiting area. "Wait. I have an idea. Let me check on something." She went toward the hostess and spoke to her briefly, thanked her, and came back looking triumphant. "We're next."

"Lucky you," Fiona said.

"No, all of us. I hope you don't mind, but I told her we were a bigger party. It worked out because the table they're clearing seats four. Now it's a full table."

"I guess we will make the movie," Mia said, both grateful and happy at Lilly's quick thinking. Something about reconnecting with her old friend was incredibly comforting. The other good side to all this was that, with two other people in their party, Fiona wouldn't question her endlessly about Adam.

Fiona liked people who were quick on their feet, so she was very grateful. "Thanks for doing that. You're sure you don't mind?"

"I don't," Jordan stood up from the bench where she'd been sitting. "The more the merrier."

Within minutes the hostess sat their group, and a friendly, but harried, waitress took their drink orders. They kept it simple with a carafe of wine, and as much as Mia adored Finn, she loved that they were now part of a larger group. She hoped this would be the start of some new friendships.

Exchanging information about their jobs and families, Mia learned that Jordan was a third grade teacher at the elementary school. She loved it, but working and living in the same town sometimes had her students a little too close for comfort. It made her recent broken engagement that much more awkward.

"So," Fiona began with a raised glass, "Since we're all friends now, let's share. Mia, why don't you tell us how your week went?"

Fiona was dramatic, if nothing else, and Jordan and Lilly leaned in, curious.

"Good," Mia mumbled.

Nope. This wasn't going to be a relaxed evening.

"Good? Is that how you'd describe your recent close encounters with a certain football coach?"

Aw, shit. Why did she do that? Mia drank her wine, and feigned indifference. "Nothing to tell." *Lies, lies. So many lies.*

Lilly was immediately interested. "Football coach? The formerly famous, uber hot coach at Jennings? Is that who we're talking about?"

Mia glanced around at the bar and the packed tables. "I cannot believe how crowded it is in here."

"Stop trying to change the subject," Fiona said. "I've been dying to know what happened with you two all week."

"If you're seeing Adam Miller, there's a whole pack of women who want the inside scoop," added Jordan. "Including me."

"There's not that much to tell," Mia said. "He helped on Sunday when I bought my nephew a bike, and he came and had lunch with me on Tuesday. He's been very sweet."

Lilly almost spewed wine across the table. "*Sweet?* Honey, no one has ever described Adam as sweet."

"He has been, though. Really." Mia felt the warmth spread to her cheeks and the memory of the kiss in the kitchen jolted her into tingly awareness. This had to stop eventually. Didn't it?

"She's lying. Look at her face," Jordan said with a knowing smirk.

"I'm not lying!" Mia protested. "We all had a nice time on Sunday, and Tuesday was innocent. You should know that, Fiona, since you were spying from the copy room window."

Fiona raised an eyebrow. "There was handholding and you two seemed very familiar."

"Oh, God," Mia dropped her face in her hands. "Do you three want gory details, is that it?"

"YES!" They all exclaimed loudly enough to get heads to turn nearby.

"Shh." Now Mia was embarrassed.

"Oh, stop." Fiona waved her off. "It must have gone really well. You had one date, and an impromptu lunch, and now he's got Ben at football practice every day."

Jordan piped in. "Who's Ben?"

"My nephew," Mia said. "I'm his guardian."

Satisfied, Jordan rested her chin in her hand and waited for Mia to continue.

"You're going to have to tell us something," Lilly said.

Mia sat up very straight and thought about what to say. The goal was to give away as little as possible, because talking about it made it feel like something. She couldn't let it feel like something. "I… I like him. We get along well, and he's great with Ben, and—"

"For Pete's sake!" Fiona squeaked. "Get to the good stuff. Did he kiss you? Was it hot?"

Mia froze. Her back was still straight as an arrow, her hands were folded in her lap, and everything inside her flared up at the thought of Adam's hands on her. His mouth. The memory of how he smelled and tasted came rushing back… finally, she couldn't take it anymore. She gave up and as her muscles relaxed, her answer just spilled out. "Oh, my God. It was so hot."

"Seriously," Jordan said. "Wow!"

"Hallelujah!" For a second, Mia thought Fiona might pump her fist, but she didn't, thank God.

It was Lilly who was quiet. Her childhood friend was the one who'd known Adam the longest, and her silence had Mia a little worried. The fact that she hadn't commented wasn't lost on anyone at the table. When she finally fixed her eyes on Mia, she smiled. "The best thing you can do regarding Adam is not listen to rumors. Gossip thrives on him, and while he's no angel, he doesn't deserve what people say about him."

"I was wondering about that." Wondering was an understatement. Scared to death was far more accurate.

Reflective now, Lilly gave Mia's hand a reassuring squeeze. "He's one of the best people I know, and I hope you get to find that out for yourself."

Mia had a clear view of the boats moored at Roosevelt's Marina. She thought about young Adam, the Adam Lilly knew so well, and wondered if finding that part of himself again had anything to do with why he'd returned to Compass Cove. Was he hoping to reclaim the person he used to be? Was he safe from his past when he was here?

Thinking about him had become a habit. Ben had started talking about the game on Saturday, and Mia wondered if she should take a leap and go. She wanted to show support for the team, and seeing Adam would have been fine with her. Mia wanted to take Lilly's advice; she hoped she did have the chance to get to know him better, and if more bone-melting kisses were in her future, that would be even better.

ADAM SAT IN his office Friday night, going over the game plan for the next day. He was worried about his young team, as he always was. He wanted them to play well enough to gain some confidence but more than anything he didn't want anyone to get hurt. The Massachusetts team was bigger, stronger, and more experienced. But they had some injuries, and that meant his boys might actually have a chance to win.

There was a knock and Adam looked up to see Kelvin standing in the doorway. "You wanted to see me, Coach?"

"Come on in, Kelvin. Have a seat."

Poor kid looked nervous. Little did Kelvin know, Adam was about to make him very happy.

"Everything okay, Coach?"

"Yeah. How are you feeling? Getting comfortable with the system?"

"Yes, sir. I really like working with Coach Griffin."

"He's pretty happy with you, too. Told me you're one of his hardest workers, and you learn fast."

Kelvin smiled but Adam could see he was trying not to get too puffed up. In truth, Kelvin deserved a lot more praise than he was getting.

"So, all that considered, how would you feel about starting tomorrow?"

"Excuse me? Seriously?"

"I don't kid about that, Kelvin. You've done well, and you deserve a shot."

"Thank you, Coach Miller. Thank you." Kelvin was smiling ear to ear, and Adam was almost as happy as he was. This was a good kid.

"I won't let the team down. I'll bring everything I got."

"I know you will. That's why you're starting."

"Thanks again, Coach. I guess I should call my mom."

Adam grinned. Kelvin had no idea Adam had arranged for Kelvin's mother and younger sister to come to the game. "Absolutely, you take off and make that call. I'll see you tomorrow. Get some sleep."

Kelvin stood and made his way to the door and Adam stopped him. "Hey Kelvin, how did Ben seem to you this week?"

"Much happier since he started comin' to practice."

That's exactly what Adam wanted to hear. He'd seen Ben the last three days, but he'd been helping all the coaches and the athletic trainer. Unfortunately, Adam hadn't spoken to him at any length. "Good. That's what I was hoping."

"He's going to try to come to the game tomorrow. He has a baseball game in the morning, but I think Coach Rand told him to come right after."

Adam nodded. He liked the idea of Ben coming to the game. He was part of the team and, of course, if Ben was there that meant he would probably see Mia, and that wasn't a bad thing. "I hope he makes it."

Once Kelvin left, Adam continued to think about Mia. It seemed whenever he had a free moment, his mind drifted back to her, and now he was thinking about how he hoped she would be at the game tomorrow. Time had gotten away from him since lunch on Tuesday and he hadn't talked to her at all. When she picked Ben up at practice, Adam was always so involved with the team, all they did was wave at each other, and now he worried that he should have made more time for her. He grabbed his phone and keyed in the text, not wanting to leave anything to chance.

Hope to see you at the game tomorrow. I have a team shirt for Ben.

Leaning back in his chair, Adam blew out a breath. "Damn," he muttered to himself.

"You're either pissed or horny. Which is it?" When his younger brother, Jack, landed in his office, that meant the family wanted information.

Adam should have known this was going to happen.

It was well meaning, he knew that, but sometimes having his family in such close proximity got to be too much. When he turned in his chair, Jack, who was an FBI agent, approached, and dropped a big paper sack on his desk.

"So, which one? Horny or pissed?"

"Neither." That wasn't completely true. He wanted Mia so bad he could taste her, but his frustration wasn't just about wanting sex.

Jack looked skeptical. "Glad I caught you."

"Just going over my play book," Adam said. "We might actually win tomorrow. Are you coming?"

"Uh huh." Opening the paper bag, Jack put a sandwich and a large Coke in front of Adam and pulled the same out for himself, as well as a bag of salt and vinegar chips which his brother tore open for them to share. "Nobody's heard from you in a couple of weeks, except Grandma. Mom gets crazy when you don't call."

"Is that why she's left me fifty voice mails?"

"Call her back, would ya? You're lucky it's me who's here and not Doug. He'd just kick your ass."

"He could try," Adam said on a laugh. Of course, he knew his forty-year-old brother, who was a Marine Corps officer, would do exactly that.

Jack also laughed, but not for the same reason, and took a healthy bite of his hero and a drink of his soda. "What's new?"

Adam's phone vibrated and before he could pick it up, Jack grabbed it and read the text. "Look at that," Jack raised an eyebrow. "You got a text from Mia. Awww, isn't that nice."

His brother was grinning like an asshole. Adam tried to decide by what means Jack would die.

"She said they'd be here as soon as possible tomorrow, and wants to know where to drop off Ben."

"Give me the phone, Jack." Adam decided that a good old-fashioned beating would be most satisfying. He'd need towels, though, because there would be blood.

The phone buzzed again. "She's looking forward to it."

Adam stood just as his brother slid the phone across the desk.

"Who's Mia?"

Adam thought about lying, but eventually he'd have to come clean, so he decided to tell the truth out of the gate. "She's new on campus. Nice. Pretty. We went out once."

"And?"

"What? She's nice, pretty. Nothing else to tell." That was a lie. "She's a librarian."

"A librarian? You?"

Shit, what was that tone? Yeah, his brother needed a beating. "You want to explain what you mean by that?"

"You've dated models and actresses, bro. A librarian is definitely a little, ah…" He hesitated. "A woman like that isn't your usual style."

"My style?" Adam snapped. "What's that supposed to mean?"

Jack put down his sandwich, leaned back in his chair, and raised a single eyebrow. His expression was someplace between 'are you kidding' and 'are you stupid'? "Well," his brother began. "For one thing. I'm guessing she has a brain."

"Yeah, so?"

"And I assume she's never been a lingerie model."

Adam bit his tongue before answering. On one level, he was pissed because Jack was insinuating Adam now had to date down. On the other hand, his brother had never seen Mia. "That's a shitty thing to say." Adam took a long swallow of his drink. "Besides, the librarian's hot."

"A hot librarian? Seriously?"

"The freshman boys on the team are stupid in love with her. She's working with the team academic advisor, so they all keep their grades up."

"So, how'd it go? Your date, I mean."

"Okay."

"Then what's got you so uptight?"

What was he going to say now? He was starting to sound like a fifteen-year-old. Shrugging as casually as he could, he said, "You're right, she's not my usual type. She has a kid."

"That must be the Ben she mentioned. She's divorced?"

"No. She's his aunt. His mother was Mia's sister. She died." Adam scrubbed his hands over his face. "Ben's hanging around the team, and because of him I feel like I have to be careful. I don't want anyone to get hurt."

Jack chewed and took a long swallow of his drink. "Sounds like Mia matters to you. Like they both do."

"It's a little early to say *that*, but I'd like to see where this goes."

"Take it slow."

Adam grumbled and took a bite from his sandwich. How did he explain the explosive attraction between him and Mia? That taking it slow didn't seem like much of an option. He had no understanding of a woman like her, or the lack of control he experienced when he was around her. He looked his brother straight in the eye and gave himself up. "She's gorgeous, and when I say gorgeous, Jack, I mean she's a goddess. I kissed her and I damn near died. I couldn't stop myself. If Ben and her grandmother hadn't walked in, I would have taken her right on the kitchen floor."

"So much for going slow, but I don't understand the problem here. She's an adult." Jack relaxed, balancing on the back legs of his chair like they did when they were kids. "She's hot and willing. Normally men consider this is a good thing."

"You're really being a dick, you know?" Adam got up and paced the area behind his desk. "She's not like that. I caught her totally off guard with the kiss, but man she just gave it up to me."

Jack eased his body forward and grinned. "Again, how is this bad?"

Not bad, but definitely complicated. He thought about how they fit. How her ass filled his hands, how she felt pressed against him, and how all that beautiful hair felt when he ran his fingers through it. But mostly, he remembered her mouth, that amazing, generous mouth that not only tugged at his libido but made his heart stop. Adam blew out a breath as he dropped into his chair.

"What's stopping you?" his brother asked.

Adam leaned back and scrubbed his hands over his face. Jack was going to love this.

"Well, for one thing her grandmother is Mrs. Lang."

"No." Jack practically choked on his sandwich. "Seriously?"

Adam nodded and Jack burst out laughing. Too bad this wasn't funny.

"You drove Mrs. Lang nuts," Jack said.

"Yup." Adam met his brother's gaze. "There are so many ways for me to screw this up, Jack. Mia is right here in town.

She works for the college. Hell, our grandmother was one of the people who hired her!"

"Ah, this one's close to home. If there's a problem with the relationship—"

"The whole town is going to know."

Adam shook his head, crumpled a napkin, and tossed it into the garbage without ever looking back at his brother.

"So, let me get this straight. You like her, but you're afraid you're going to screw it up?"

"Yeah." That simple admission changed everything. Adam realized it wasn't just lust anymore. It wasn't about getting her into her pants. He really liked her.

Jack rolled his eyes. "Pussy. Grow a goddamn pair, would you?"

"Thanks for your support." Adam should have known better than to expect Jack to understand. His brother had no idea what being in the public eye had done to him. He'd already screwed up publicly when he had the accident; he didn't need to do it again. "I'm trying to keep my head down. Not attract a lot of attention."

"Then you should have built yourself a cabin on some deserted mountain." Jack stood and walked around the room, looking at the depth charts Adam had pinned to the wall. "Haven't you figured out that real life is the toughest thing you're ever going to face? Real people—your family and people you've known your whole life—are more challenging than the biggest, baddest defensive tackle, and a pretty librarian will take you out at the knees faster than a super model."

"Great."

"What you seem to have forgotten is that this town protected you, too. When the media was sniffing around, everyone circled the wagons so you could recover in private."

"I know. I guess I'm trying not to be the self-centered asshole I used to be. I'm thinking about her first. She's sweet, you know." Rubbing out the tension in his neck, Adam swore. "You're right, though. I'm being a candy ass about this."

Jack smiled. "She must be something to have you so worked up. I've never heard you describe any of your women as 'sweet'."

"None of them ever were. She's different, and I don't know what the hell I'm doing."

"Welcome to the club, man. If you aren't tied up in knots over a woman, it doesn't really count."

Adam brought his forearm across his eyes and groaned. If that was true, this thing he'd started with Mia was going to count a whole lot.

MIA'S FINGER HOVERED over the screen of her cell phone as her mind processed the number on the caller ID. Her mother. Her mother was calling her back.

She tried to do what Nana suggested, and call first to drop the "Ben is playing sports" bomb, but Mom was too busy with her weekly lunch with the ladies to take the call.

She could still hear her mother's clipped, mid-Atlantic English coming over the phone. *Really, dear. You know I golf and have lunch at the club on Fridays. Just let me do the calling.*

There was no avoiding what she had to do, so Mia answered the call. "Hi, Mom."

"I would appreciate, if in the future, you could keep my weekly schedule in mind before you make a call, Mia. The phone rang right when Louise Johnson was telling a lovely story about her daughter's honeymoon in Europe."

"How nice," Mia said. "I'm sorry I interrupted."

"So, how are you and how is your job?"

"Everything here is fine. Being with Nana has helped the transition, and Ben and I have been making friends."

"Your grandmother is too attached to that little town. Just remember there's only so much you can do there, and at that college. I also doubt you'll find a husband in a place like that."

"It's really a wonderful place to live. It's diverse, and the schools are wonderful—"

"Speaking of schools, have you found Ben a proper private school yet?"

"No, Mom. He's going to public school."

"We've discussed this. Private school offers so much

more."

"Public school, Mom."

"Mia, really. Think of the children he'll be associating with in public school."

"I do, and it's a great environment. He has friends right on the street. If I thought a private school was the right place for him, he'd go, but he's fine where he is."

"I don't agree. At all."

Normally, that's all it took. Her mother's disapproval didn't have to be boldly stated, one simple sentence or two usually did the trick. This time, however, Mia knew her mother was wrong.

"Mom, you of all people should know that the schools here are excellent. His class is small and it's the same school you and Daddy went to. It's good that Ben experiences that tradition."

"I suppose." Just as Mia suspected, hitting someone like her mother with the "tradition" argument killed the discussion. At least for now. After spending years as a headmistress at an all-girls prep school in Maryland, Mom's prejudice wouldn't die easily.

"How are you doing? I'm guessing your back is better since you're playing golf." Her mother had been pretty badly hurt when she'd been hit by the car. It was one of the reasons she decided that when she moved south, she wouldn't be taking Ben.

"Physio therapy twice a week. Probably forever. I have

pain, but I muddle through."

It was never a simple answer with her mom. Still beautiful at fifty-eight, her mother couldn't wait to retire from education and settle into her new life near Charleston. It was what she'd been planning for, once her father retired, but when he died, it pushed her mother into that life a little sooner. A life that didn't include Ben or Mia, and in truth, it probably wouldn't have included her father.

Yeah, there was a lot she didn't understand, especially her mother's need to micromanage every aspect of Ben's life. She didn't want to raise him; she moved far enough away that she'd only see him a few times a year, but yet, she still tried to exert control.

Not this time.

"School aside, how is Ben doing?"

"Wonderful." Mia wanted to throw up. Why couldn't she have a warm, fuzzy mother? Someone loving and supportive? "He likes school and has made some friends. He's very busy."

"Busy with what? I doubt there's much for him to do. There never was."

Annoyed more than scared now, Mia let the first shoe drop. "He's playing baseball. I got him into a league, and he couldn't be happier."

If Mia didn't know better, she would have thought her mother had hung up, but she heard breathing. Slow, steady, unhappy breathing. "Team sports? We've discussed this. I wouldn't mind if he were taking golf or tennis lessons, something he'd play the rest of his life, but—"

"I didn't call to get your approval, Mom. It's done. He's my responsibility and I'll do what I feel is right."

A low chuckle came over the line. "You sound just like your grandmother. Was the baseball her idea? A little dig at me, perhaps?"

"No, Mom, it wasn't. Nana doesn't spend her time thinking of ways to get at you."

Again, her mother laughed. The relationship between Nana and her mother was never good, but since Sara's death it had become downright hostile. "You keep believing that."

After a brief silence, Mia heard the click of a lighter before her mother continued. Whenever she was tense, Mom smoked.

"So, is that why you called?" her mother asked. "To tell me he's playing baseball?"

"Mostly."

There was quiet on the line. It was her mother's way of telling her to keep going. It was an intimidation tactic and Mia stepped right into the trap. "He's been busy after school, too. My babysitting fell through and Ben is helping a friend of mine on campus until I can make other arrangements."

"Well, spending time on a college campus isn't a bad thing. What's he doing?"

"He's working with the football team."

A quick intake of air told her everything she needed to

know. There was no response at first, but then the low, throaty words came through. "Have you lost your mind?"

"No, and he's doing really well. The coaches keep him busy with jobs and he's learning a lot about goals and teamwork."

"I don't have any words for you."

"Mom, you have to trust me to do the right thing for him. It's football, he's not robbing banks."

"I don't trust you with *anything. Anything.* I can't believe I trusted you with my grandchild. That you would dishonor all of us, most of all your sister, by allowing that leaves me speechless."

"Mom, don't turn this into something it's—"

There was a beep and then silence. Her mother had ended the call.

Once again, in her mother's eyes, she was a failure. She shouldn't let it affect her because it was nothing new. Relationships between mothers and daughters in her family had never been good. She thought about the contentiousness through the generations, and Mia vowed if she ever had a daughter, she'd break the cycle. Never, ever would she make her own child feel like a failure.

But while her mother's words stung, for the first time, Mia didn't question her own decisions. That was, most definitely, progress.

Chapter Seven

SATURDAY MORNING WAS clear and cool. Mia sat in the bleachers watching Ben's baseball game, wishing someone would say something to her. Ben had been to four practices, and this was their second game. By now the other parents were getting to know them, and while she was getting the occasional hello and wave, no one talked to her. God, this was going to be tough.

Ben was doing great, and she absolutely loved watching him play. Her heart swelled every time he got up at bat or made a play in the field. She was proud of him. Proud of how hard he worked, how he interacted with his teammates, and she was amazed at how good he was. He'd been catching during practice, but this was his first game playing at the position and he seemed instinctively to know what to do. He improved every time he took the field, and the other kids really seemed to like him. He fit in with the team, and even with only a couple of games under his belt, Mia could see he was a natural leader.

When the last pitch had been thrown, Mia rose from her spot in the stands and watched her boy with his friends. This had been good for him. Allowing him to become part of a team, a part of something bigger, had been the best thing she'd ever done for him. Her mother could throw all the tantrums she wanted, nothing was going to change Mia's mind. At that second, Ben turned, smiled, and waved to her.

Yeah. It was absolutely the best thing.

Mia watched for a few more minutes, and was startled out of her proud mama place by a small, smiling woman who actually spoke to her.

"Hi," the woman said. "You're Ben's mom?"

Mia returned her smile. "His aunt, actually, but I am his guardian." She extended her hand and the woman took it happily. "Mia."

"I'm Susan Rand. My son is Gabe." She pointed to a very tall boy sitting on the bench in the dugout, his long legs extended and a hat pulled over his eyes. "Ben is very good."

"He loves to play. He loves anything with a ball."

Susan chuckled. "I wanted to let you know that we have a few tickets left for the team trip to next Wednesday night's Mets game." She tilted her head to one side. "Would you and Ben be interested in going?"

"He'd love that, and I'm off on Thursday, so that's perfect."

"Excellent. Where do you work?"

Mia smiled as she watched Ben walk over. "Jennings College. I'm a librarian."

Susan's mouth dropped open and Mia wondered what

she had said that made such an impression.

"You're the librarian?"

"One of them, why?"

"My husband works at the college, too. He's one of the assistant football coaches."

"Oh, that's..." Mia stopped and watched the other mom's stunned expression bloom into a knowing smile. Susan knew about her, and her day with Adam. "It's a small world."

"It sure is." Susan was still grinning as she said it. "So, can I put you down for two tickets?"

"Absolutely. Ben will love it."

"YOU LOOK LIKE one of the students." Never one to mince words, Fiona's commentary on Mia's outfit took no prisoners.

"I do?" The outfit she'd chosen for the football game was a variation of the one she'd worn to Ben's baseball game that morning: jeans, flats and this afternoon instead of a red T-shirt she wore a navy blue Jennings T-shirt. Mia didn't want to stand out like a sore thumb, but she was hoping for a better reaction than that.

"You're adorable, but you probably made Adam feel dirty."

"I don't know about that. I walked into a coaches meeting when I dropped off Ben and he was polite and all, but he ushered me out pretty fast." Mia was trying not to let the brush off bother her, but she just couldn't shake all the stereotypes about professional athletes that she'd been force fed over the years. "It's fine. I guess he figured out he's not into me."

"It could be something else," Fiona said.

Something else? "Like what?"

"Like he was *busy*. That field house is locked down like a vault on game day. I'm surprised you didn't need a secret password to get in."

"I don't know…" Mia's deep-rooted insecurity wouldn't allow her to let go of her doubts. In her mind, it was already over, so she didn't want to dwell on it. Watching the field, she saw Ben come out with a few of the coaches. He was listening to everything they were saying, and when Drew Griffin leaned closer to talk to him, Ben paid close attention. It was like witnessing a miracle.

Was Sara watching and wondering what the hell she was doing? Was Mia doing the right thing? After the hang up yesterday, she knew her mother's opinion. There'd been radio silence since then, and she expected she wouldn't hear from Mom for at least a week. Mom's silent treatment used to be torture, but now, by not talking, she was doing her daughter a favor.

But regardless of the note Sara left her, and her mother's interpretation of her sister's very vague instructions, there was one thing Mia knew. Ben wasn't going to conform to some set of rules that were laid down before he could walk. Mia had to do what was best for him now.

Adam may not be interested in her, but being around the team was good for Ben. That's what mattered most.

As she and Fiona looked for seats, Mia soaked in the atmosphere, enjoying the buzz in the stadium. It was a gorgeous day and the stands were filling up.

"God, I love it here." She turned to Fiona who nodded. "I can't understand, for the life of me, why my parents didn't want to live here."

Fiona tilted her head. "Your dad's work I'm guessing, but let's face it...could you see your mom in Compass Cove?"

Fiona made sense. As much as her mom disliked the town, the town never liked her mom either. Her mother was too aloof, too distant, preferring to spend time with her grandmama, Nana's mother, in the city. Compass Cove was about closeness, about being in everyone else's business and supporting each other. That was not her mother.

Mia watched the players doing calisthenics and drills. Their white jerseys were accented by blue and gold numbers; they moved in military precision one moment, and played like little boys the next. She recognized more than a few of the names stitched across their backs. Many of the boys frequented the library and that made her happy to be here. They were her students, and supporting them was important.

Mia finally spotted Adam on the sidelines. He wore a dark blue polo with a Jennings logo, khakis, and a pair of aviator sunglasses. He was big, powerful, his face hard-edged and battle-worn. Seeing him this way, in his element, cemented what she already knew. Adam wasn't a pretty boy. He wasn't polished or refined. He was rugged, physical—a warrior, a man who would protect what was his.

Despite the activity around him, Adam was focused, writing notes on a clipboard, conferring with the other coaches and shouting directions to his team. For a second, she stopped thinking. All that filled Mia's head was how it felt when he held her. She hadn't seen him since earlier that week, but the memory of the kiss left her breathless. In his arms, Mia had felt totally safe and completely happy. Nothing could have prepared her for the contented feeling that settled over her when he touched her. For the first time in her life, her guard dropped, and Mia let someone reach inside and touch her heart. She had no control over it, and she wondered if she should stop trying. Mia drew a breath and took him in. No matter how hard she tried to deny it, Mia knew she could fall in love with him.

He turned toward the stands and smiled wide when he saw a group of boys hanging over the rail, waving. Mia recognized Gabe Rand and two other boys from Ben's baseball team. Adam acknowledged them with a wave and called Ben over so he could say hi to his friends. When Ben saw his teammates, he dashed toward the stands. Adam stood by and watched, his mouth tilting slightly at the corner, and if Mia ever wondered about this man, the doubt about his character vanished with this one small act. He may not be interested in her, but the gift he'd given Ben was invaluable.

Adam gave him belonging. He wasn't just the new kid. Ben was part of the team at Jennings, and that would make things easier as he found his way in this new place. Mia's heart was happy, and turning her eyes back toward Adam, she saw he was staring at her. His eyes made her think about his gentle touch and soft kiss, but it was his kindness that meant the most to her. This warrior had a gentle heart, the heart of a father, and Mia was almost overcome as their eyes held. All she could do was mouth a simple *"Thank you."*

There was an almost imperceptible nod, and he turned back to the field, calling Ben to walk with him. Mia, no longer able to stand, sank into the seat. Fiona dropped down next to her.

"Are you still going to tell me he's not into you?"

Finally breathing again, Mia shook her head. "I don't… I, um… I don't know what to think."

Fiona wasn't going to let up on her, that much she knew. "Maybe you should stop thinking."

"I agree, thinking is way overrated."

Turning, Mia found herself staring into the grass green eyes of Noah Connolly, who'd taken a seat on the bench next to her. He grinned like a little boy, and handed her a bag of popcorn from the concession stand. Ever since Adam had interrupted their conversation the other day, Noah had been more of a presence. She thought a nice friendship was developing with him, but over the last few days she saw his intentions were a bit more personal.

Too bad for Noah the only one Mia wanted to get personal with was the coach. But with him running hot and cold the way he did, she still wasn't sure if he felt the same way.

ADAM HAD SPENT more time than he should paying attention to what Mia was doing during the game. Never letting anything distract him while the game clock was ticking, he just couldn't help himself. He was especially interested when the professor joined her in the stands. Talk about spoiling the view. Mia looked so damned cute in her Jennings gear and her bright smile, and then he'd get an eyeful of Doctor Dork chatting her up. This whole jealousy thing was new for him, and he didn't like it. It was time for this quarterback to rush.

After giving the team their post-game talk, he passed Joe and his wife, Susan, in the corridor by the offices. A tiny thing with a big personality, Susan managed her husband and three sons with military precision. He liked her. She was no bullshit, but had a romantic streak a mile wide. Based on the way she constantly tried to fix Adam up with different women, and the way she was eyeing him, he could see she was itching to talk to him now. That was fine. If he was going to keep Mia's attention, he needed an advantage.

"What are you looking at?" Susan asked, grinning.

Adam planted his feet apart and folded his arms. "I need information."

"Do you? You could always go to the *library*," she giggled. "That is their specialty."

And here came the jokes. "I could, but I need information from you. Tell me about Noah Connolly."

Susan raised an eyebrow. As an administrative assistant in the Provost's office, she would have reason to know things about the professor. Adam wasn't fishing for anything confidential, but he always felt it was best of you knew your competition.

"He's in his early thirties. Just got his Ph.D. Very charming."

Charming? He could be charming. "Anything else?"

"He's very interested in Mia and hasn't made a secret of it."

"What else can you tell me?"

"He's considered quite the catch, and he doesn't like to lose. I overheard him offer to take her and Ben to the movies."

That made Adam a little crazy. Two weeks ago he and Mia were in her Nana's kitchen, and she was melting into his arms, tasting like lemons and hot sex. She was soft, supple, and just waiting for him to take her. Connolly and his movie dates could go to hell. Adam didn't like to lose either.

That did it. He couldn't take this slow even if he did spook Mia. There was no time to take it slow. "Joe told me that Gabe's baseball team is going to the Mets' game."

"We are! It's going to be a nice family day."

Adam's wheels were turning. "Sounds like fun. I love baseball."

Susan looked at Joe, who was holding back a laugh, and then back at Adam. "We have one ticket left."

"One?" This was perfect, Adam thought.

"Just one," she said quietly.

"I'll take it."

Chapter Eight

"OPEN YOUR MOUTH, Mia. Let the sound escape."
Mia pushed through the note as she was instructed.
"That's better."

Mia focused on the instructor's voice and let the tones come from inside. It had been ages since she'd had a voice lesson and it felt good, cleansing, to sing her heart out, even if she was only doing warm-ups and scales.

With luck, Professor Salica would take her on as a student. She knew he had a full load of students from the college, but he indicated he might take her on privately.

That would make her very happy.

It had been so long since she'd been able to focus on singing. In her heart, she was belting out songs on the Broadway stage; in reality, she was helping students with papers, and faculty members find criticism and data to support their research. She was not living the life she thought she'd live, that was for sure.

"You have a lovely voice," he said. "It has a wonderful sound in the upper range. Not at all shrill."

"Thank you." Mia stepped toward the piano as Professor

Salica started to pack his briefcase. "It's been a while for me."

"I could tell." He put another music folder in his bag and Mia felt the disappointment descend. Professor Salica's face was impossible to read. "I can't give you a set time every week, but I suppose I can work you in based on your schedule."

Mia clapped her hands together. "Oh! That's wonderful! Thank you, professor! Thank you!" She shook his hand.

He smiled warmly. "You may not be thanking me when I ask you to sing something for the fiftieth time."

Mia was so excited she practically danced out of the studio. She'd could take her time walking back to her car, go pick up Ben from school, and then get ready to take him to his first major league baseball game.

She stepped out of the music building and started down the long path to the library. The weather was perfect, and on this part of campus the view across the bay was spectacular. There was a vacant bench, and Mia took a moment to collect her thoughts. A light breeze, just right for the sailboats she saw in the distance, scooted around her and coaxed the leaves on the trees into making their own music.

It had been a good day so far. She'd had lunch with Noah, hoping she hadn't misjudged his intentions. He was smart and sweet, and took a sincere interest in who she was and what she did. Yes, he was criminally good looking, but when he left her outside the music building with a light kiss on the cheek, Mia realized she might be leading him on, and that was the last thing she wanted to do.

It turned out his parents and her mother belonged to the same golf club in South Carolina. Her mother made a point to mention him during their last phone conversation, along with the fact that he would be a 'suitable match'. "You could marry him," she'd said nonchalantly. "He's brilliant, and you'd have gorgeous children."

Suitable, sure, but he did nothing for her. Noah was exactly the type of man her mother would want for her—well-educated, attractive and completely predictable. Sure, he was nice, and he tried to be funny, but it was hard for Mia to see Noah as anything but a friend. There was just no spark. Adam, on the other hand, provided lots of sparks, but she had no idea what expect.

Rising from the bench, Mia headed for her car. Ever since they'd arrived in Compass Cove, good things started happening. The town was like medicine for her and Ben. Everything felt better.

The changes began when she signed him up for baseball, and bought him the new bike. In just a few weeks' time, there were kids in and out of her yard looking to play. Additionally, Mia couldn't discount the role Adam and the team were playing in Ben's life. He'd made friends, he was taking on responsibilities, and as a result, these last two weeks of school were much better than the first.

She didn't get one call from the principal.

There was one big decision Mia was tossing around in

her head, and it was the kind of change that would make her mother nuts. It would upset her more than the move to Long Island. Mia had decided that she was going to talk to an attorney about officially adopting Ben. It was something that she'd mentioned from time to time, but her mom and dad felt that it would be disrespectful to Sara's memory. Mia thought it was practical, and more than anything else, she knew it was the right thing to do.

She was Ben's mother. If not biologically, in every other way. Every decision she made, every choice in her life, was done with him in mind. She loved him more than anything or anyone in her life. Because of that, and because of the way people saw her, Mia saw no reason not to adopt Ben.

The drive home was pretty, as always, but signs of fall were starting to pop up everywhere. Cornstalks and pump-kins decorated the front porches on her street, and Nana's garden was no longer filled with pastel summer flowers, but deeper, richer autumn blooms.

Ben was in his room, getting ready for the game, and just listening to him Mia expected him to explode. He was beyond excited. Mia, on the other hand, was nervous. It was going to be an interesting evening. Ben would want to sit with his friends, and that would leave her with the other parents who she was still getting to know. The group of adults was predictable. They were married, friends for years, and most were at least ten years older than she was. If she was lucky, it would only be slightly awkward.

"Ben, are you ready?" she called. "We have to meet everybody at the school in ten minutes."

He came tearing out of his room, down the stairs, and slid in his stocking feet halfway across the living room floor. He smiled when he stopped right before crashing into the couch.

"Jeez! Slow down," Mia said. "I want to go to the ball game, not the emergency room!"

"I'm ready," he said. "This is going to be so much fun." Ben hopped around as he pulled his sneakers on.

Mia hadn't ever seen him this enthusiastic about anything. She shoved some snacks in her bag, grabbed their sweatshirts, and headed for the door.

When they got in the car, and Ben was all buckled in, Mia tossed him a brand new New York Mets cap. Ben whooped with enthusiasm and they pulled out of the driveway.

ADAM MANEUVERED HIS truck between two SUVs in the school parking lot. Hordes of parents and kids were milling around and he tried to stay focused on the reason he was there. Mia was making him crazy, and he was having a hard time making sense of what was going through his head. He was jealous, borderline possessive, and he had no right to be. But there was a proprietary feeling when it came to her, like she was his, and no other man should have her. He'd seen her having lunch with the tool professor earlier in the day, and he'd had to leave Rinaldi's before he hurt someone. He'd almost bowled Mrs. Rinaldi right over getting away from the counter. He could still hear her yelling after him that she was going to talk to his grandmother about his bad manners. There were a few choice Italian words in there as well.

Just as he had always been a free agent, he expected the women he got involved with would be the same, preferring a no strings existence. What was worse, he still couldn't figure out what it was about Mia that turned his brain into Silly Putty. She was pretty, but he'd had more than his share of beautiful women. There was something else. Her hair swept over her shoulders and flowed softly down her back, her skin was flawless, and she had curves where girls were supposed to have curves. Yeah, and they were spectacular curves. Adam still had dreams about exploring every one of Mia's curves.

His attraction to Mia was powerfully physical, but it wasn't the usual lust that made him want to screw a woman brainless. No, he wanted to take Mia to bed and make slow, sweet love to her. He wanted to feel her warm against him, to know she was happy and satisfied and safe.

And he knew he was in serious trouble. Because he didn't know how to be the kind of guy he sensed she needed him to be, and his head hurt just thinking about it.

He looked around as he walked toward the group. It was going to be a nice night. The weather was still on the warm side and a few high clouds dotted the sky.

He found Joe, said hello to him and Susan, and watched as the kids and parents interacted. This was all new to him. Families were a strange entity that Adam never thought about much. Lately, though, he thought about families all the time.

That was another kick in the ass.

Then his mood perked up as Mia's little Honda pulled into the parking lot.

Immediately, he pictured her face as he'd seen it mid-kiss the day they'd gone out. The way her eyes fluttered shut, her flushed skin, her rosy lips—all of it was burned in his brain. Adam shook off the fog brought on by the sight of her and decided he'd better go over and say hi before she saw him first. The last thing he wanted was for her to run again.

He screwed up his courage and walked toward her car. God, he hoped this wasn't a mistake. Ben had just taken off to be with his friends and Mia was standing by the open back door. She bent over to retrieve something in the back seat just as Adam walked up. He got a fine view of her ass and then a wonderful view of her eyes when she stood up and met his gaze head on.

"Adam!" She brought a hand to her chest. "What are you doing here?"

"Goin' to the game."

Her face was a mix of shock and confusion. Her eyes darted around and it looked like she was looking for a way to escape. Obviously, he made Mia a lot more nervous than he thought. Lucky for him, she was trapped. But in the interest of fairness, he explained. "Susan had one ticket left, and she offered it to me."

"Of course she did." Mia shook her head, seeing the set up plain as day. Lucky for Adam, now that the shock had worn off, she looked happy to see him.

"I was glad. I've wanted to spend some time with you."

She closed the car door, engaged the alarm, and nodded, seeming to regain her composure. "You did? You could have called."

"I know, but every time I sit down to call, it's too late." She nodded and Adam couldn't tell if she believed him or not.

"Your team must be flying from the win over the weekend."

"Yeah. The boys worked really hard for it." He walked with her toward the group of parents and tried to read her mood.

"Kelvin's been on Cloud Nine since Saturday," she said. "He's such a nice kid. I really like him."

"I agree. Nice family, too. His mom is something special."

"I don't know his mom," she responded. "But I imagine she is quite special if she was able to do such a good job with him under such difficult conditions."

Like you, Adam thought, imagining how difficult it had

been for Mia raising her sister's child on her own. He didn't know anything at all about her parents, other than what he'd been told, but from his vantage point, Mia had been flying solo for a while now, and the kid was lucky to have someone who loved him so much.

A few people walked by them, and said hello, but he could see she still wasn't completely comfortable. This had to be hard. Feeling protective, he was glad he came. Sliding his hand to the small of her back, they started moving toward the bus.

"You don't mind that I took the ticket?"

Just like the other day, her body turned ever so slightly and pressed into his. It was the smallest amount of contact, nothing more, but Adam couldn't help thinking she wanted to be close to him. Her eyes met his at the same time she bit her bottom lip, shook her head.

"Not at all," she said quietly.

Adam felt like he'd hit a home run.

MIA CLIMBED UP the bus steps after Ben, who bolted to the back with his friends. She continued down the aisle, found a pair of unoccupied seats and settled in next to the window with Adam right beside her. How did this happen? One minute she was nervous about being the odd one out, now she had an impromptu date with the most gorgeous man on the planet.

She'd been thinking about him constantly, even with all of Noah's attentions. She thought about the way Adam kissed her, touched her. The romantic in Mia, the person who lived in the fantasy worlds found in books and movies, always wished to be swept away on a wave of passion. Adam did that. The one kiss—that one long, beautiful kiss—finished Mia off. If he prodded her even a little bit, she would have done anything he wanted.

Staring out the window as they pulled out of the school parking lot, she had to get her imagination under control. If she didn't slow down, she'd be planning an imaginary wedding.

"Mia?"

He was leaning back in his seat and smiling at her. He looked perfect in his jeans, T-shirt and open, button-down shirt. It was like he walked out of J. Crew, and the miracle of it was he was sitting there smiling at her.

"Hey," he said. "Nice side trip?"

"Yeah, sorry." She stared down at her hands and began twisting her fingers. Yup, she was nervous. "I was thinking about Ben," she lied.

"Really? I was hoping you were thinking about me."

Mia's eyes flew open wide. Did he read minds, too?

"I… well, I was surprised to see you, so naturally…"

The look of amusement in Adam's eyes made Mia want to crawl under her seat. She was no good at this and he made her so nervous. But here she was with Adam, who seemed to enjoy watching her make a fool of herself.

"I should have told you I was coming. I'm sorry."

"It's not a problem. It's nice to have someone to hang out with."

He rewarded her with a grin that was sexy and playful, and a little bit dangerous. Mia felt her insides go all squishy when he took her hand in his.

She needed to talk about something or she might just melt in the seat. There had to be something she could talk about so she could stop thinking about the way his fingers were winding around hers.

"Someone at work said the pitcher on the Mets who's starting tonight grew up in Compass Cove."

Adam nodded. "Sam Lucas. He was a few years behind me in school. Got an arm like a cannon."

"Wow. Your high school produced two professional athletes?"

"More than that. There's a catcher on the Cubs, who played in high school with Sam. A couple of guys made it to the NHL, and there have been a few Olympic hopefuls."

"Jeez! Is it in the water?"

He laughed. "You aren't the first person to ask that."

There was a break in the conversation, and feeling a little more relaxed, she brought up another topic.

"You know what? I saw your grandmother. She was at the library for a board meeting." That was what they needed—some common ground. And, with luck, she'd get to tease him a little.

"She mentioned it." He kept her fingers securely in his. "Did she grill you about our date?"

"I wouldn't call it grilling. She wanted to know if you behaved yourself that day we went to lunch." No matter how hard she tried, Mia hadn't been able to call it a date.

Mia chuckled when she saw Adam's eyes narrow. The things she could have told his grandma.

"What did you tell her?" he asked.

"Wouldn't you like to know?"

"Yes," he said. "I would."

Mia giggled again, took her hand from his, and said nothing. She could have some fun with this. And she discovered, much to her surprise, she could flirt.

Adam ran a hand through his hair and stared at her. She decided to try to ignore him, but even when she wasn't looking his way, she could feel his gaze. Skimming a book she'd brought along for the ride, she glanced up every once in a while. His eyes were piercing and so very blue, Mia had to fight the urge to let herself get lost in them. Happy for the distraction, she went back to her book.

Of course, Mia hadn't factored in that Adam was better at games than she was. He'd had a lot more practice. He let her pretend to read for a minute or so, then he leaned in and began whispering in her ear.

"Did you tell her what happened in the kitchen? When

we were alone?"

His voice was warm and intimate. *Oh, God.* Her heart jumped to her throat and fluttered uncontrollably.

"Did you tell her how I touched you? How I kissed you?"

Every inch of her was on fire remembering how it felt to be held like that, kissed like that. She remembered his strength, how he tasted, and she remembered how aroused he was and how it felt pressed into her.

Mia sighed, and this time he was the one who was amused. Adam not only knew how to play games, he knew how to play dirty.

Drawing in a long breath to compose herself, she tried to shake the images out of her head. But then, as if to say he didn't want her to forget, Adam took Mia's hand. She looked first at their hands and then at him. His eyes were fixed on their linked fingers, and he was concentrating on the slow, gentle circles he was tracing with his thumb.

"I lied. I told your grandmother you were a perfect gentleman." Mia could barely hear her own voice.

"I know. She told me." He locked onto her eyes and smiled. His dimple seemed more pronounced and the sparkle in his eyes was just another way of letting her know he had the upper hand. Mia decided she would throw him off the bus for being a sneak, if she could get away with it.

"And, by the way," he said. "She knew you were lying."

The realization that he'd played her made Mia shake her head and laugh once again. "I hate you."

Adam touched his lips to the top of her head. "No, you don't," he said. "That's why this is so damn scary."

ADAM WAS SURPRISED the nosebleed seats weren't so bad. They were toward the front of the upper level, so everyone had a good view. The kids sat in the front rows with parents at each end and rows of adults behind them. Mia managed to get a seat almost directly behind Ben and Adam claimed the seat next to her.

The ride to the ballpark should have taken an hour, but with the traffic it was over an hour and a half. They had a nice conversation on the way in and he discovered she'd led a pretty interesting life. She also had a lot of nerve, although he guessed she didn't think so.

Coming back to the seats, he hoped she wasn't angry with him for buying her food. She was Miss Independent, and here he was carting back half a dozen hot dogs, three with the works, drinks, peanuts, Cracker Jack, and a plate of garlic fries.

But hell, she needed to eat and so did Ben, and there was nothing like eating hot dogs at a ball game. He scanned the crowd and saw Ben having a great time with his friends, and one row back was Mia sitting quietly, reading the program, and occasionally exchanging a few words with Susan.

He took a long look around and wondered why he didn't

come to games more often. He loved the whole scene. The food, the music, the way the park smelled and sounded was something that just screamed "good time".

Adam made his way down the aisle and Mia smiled when she saw him coming back. It turned him inside out. The more he thought about it, the more he realized he liked her. If he got involved with her, he knew it wouldn't be easy and casual. It would be work, it would be real, but he didn't doubt for a second she would be worth the effort. It was more than just a physical attraction between them, and it was the *more* that had him so edgy.

He couldn't decide if it was her vulnerability or the sweetness that had gotten to him first. Then again, maybe it was the strength he saw in her, the intelligence. Maybe it was all of it.

She liked him well enough, and unless he was blind she was attracted to him, but she didn't trust him, yet. Which was probably why she was still hanging around with the professor. He wondered what he could do to change that. Then he looked at her again, and the way her tongue was gently playing over her lips, and he realized trust or not, he still wanted to get into her pants.

A few other women were watching when he sat down with Mia, with Susan taking special interest. His former celebrity status kept people interested. It pissed him off. Every year or so, he turned up on a *People* magazine list, or an old picture of him with some model popped up. He ignored most of it. Adam knew he wasn't the same guy as the one being reported on in the tabloids. But it still bugged him that some people were more worried about his life than their own.

"Did you buy enough food?" she asked, surveying the pile he had in his hands.

He examined the tray himself and nodded. "I think so." He nudged Ben's shoulder and handed him a hot dog with the Cracker Jack. The kid's eyes lit up and he said thank you.

"He has a drink already?" Adam asked.

"I just got him something. You didn't have to buy all this."

"Uh, yes. Is it a problem?" He hesitated, then handed her a hot dog and a lemonade...and waited for the reaction. Mia pressed her lips together when she looked at the plastic cup, then she blushed and smiled. Yeah, that's what he wanted. He wanted her to think about the last time they were together. God knew, he thought about it all the time. *Compete with that memory, professor.*

"Umm, are you sure you don't want the lemonade?" she asked.

The smokiness in her eyes and the parting of her lips sent a shot of electricity through Adam's body. If he had flustered Mia at all, she'd regrouped and had gone on the offensive. Removing the straw from the wrapper, she popped it into the cup, wrapped her luscious lips around the straw and pulled the drink into her mouth. She licked her lips again and glanced up at him through her lashes. Was he drooling? He had to be drooling.

"It's good," she said softly. "Not too sweet."

"I'll have a taste later." *Holy shit.* Their exchange was pure seduction and all they talked about was lemonade. Did she know what she was doing to him? Time to change the subject. He cleared his throat and focused on the tray in his lap that was now doing double duty hiding his hard-on.

"I didn't know if you liked ketchup or mustard, so I brought you both." He held out the small foil packets.

"Thanks." She took the ketchup. "What did you get for yourself? A case of indigestion?" She paused and looked at the pile of seasoned potatoes he'd been looking forward to all day. "What is that smell, by the way?"

"*That smell* is the aroma of garlic fries."

"Garlic fries?" She looked again and took a sniff. "Are they good?"

"Heaven. A ballpark staple out west. Although they give them a different twist here. Never had them?"

"My parents didn't let us have any kind of junk food, and we never went to baseball games. Anywhere." Turning her gaze toward him, she smiled. "Aside from that, I never had the nerve, or the desire, for that much bad breath."

He grinned as he picked up one of the fully loaded dogs and took a healthy bite. He pointed to the tray in his lap. "You want one of these?"

"No, thanks." Mia took a bite of her hot dog and the

two of them settled into an easy silence while they watched the teams take batting practice.

MIA'S HEART WARMED as she watched Adam guide a very sleepy Ben to the car. There went her ovaries again—*pop, pop, pop.*

It was almost one o'clock in the morning and all the kids were wiped out. The game was four and a half hours long and went fifteen innings. Thank God, the Mets won and both she and Ben had the day off tomorrow.

Her boy slumped against the door when it closed and went right back to his dream world. He looked so content. It was a good night on a lot of levels.

With his hands shoved down into his pockets, Adam approached her. Cars were pulling out around them and Mia knew she should say thanks, get in the car, and go home. Instead she folded her arms and held her breath.

"I think he's gonna sleep for a week," Adam said.

"He was so into the game. I had no idea he'd love it so much."

He edged nearer to her. "What about you? Did you have a good time?"

Mia looked away. His question had so many answers. The game was fun. Meeting new people was fun. It was the Adam part of the evening that made her dig a little deeper.

Did she have a good time? The answer wasn't that hard. "Yes, I did. I'm glad you took the last ticket."

"Yeah? I really wanted to see you."

"Really?"

"Yes. I'm sorry we haven't talked. I get distracted with team stuff."

"It's okay, I think you made up for it." There was no doubt that he had. Making such a big effort to spend time with her and Ben was more than she ever expected, and he'd been so sweet. He taught her how to keep score, and they had conversations about food and books and their lives. It was one of the best times she'd ever had. Even now, with the shadow of a beard and his clothes rumpled from the long night, he made her heart flip.

Adam took another step closer, crossing into her personal space. "Did I? It wasn't torture?"

"It wasn't that bad."

"Good. Let me take you to dinner Saturday. Just the two of us. Can you get a sitter?"

"I think so," she whispered. Hopefully, Nana was around. If not, she'd go through her entire contact list to find a sitter.

He was standing so close she could feel his warm breath. It was getting to the point in the goodbye that she needed to decide what she wanted, and Adam's eyes were asking how this was going to go.

Mia knew exactly what she wanted. Her insides churned

at the thought of his touch. It was all she'd thought about for weeks. This time though, instead of backing away, Mia pressed into him and let her hands feel the hard muscle of his torso as they moved slowly and settled on his chest. The heat from his body chased away the chill in the air, and thawed a heart that had been cold too long. Mia had hoped the feelings would go away; she didn't want to get caught up in a situation that was hopeless. But she couldn't help herself.

Adam took her face in his hands. He was being so gentle, Mia almost cried. First, he dropped a kiss on her forehead, then her nose and then he softly kissed her lips. He took it deeper, reaching around and pulling her close. His mouth moved over hers, consuming, taking everything she would give him.

"God, you taste so good."

"Adam," she purred as his lips nipped at her neck, then moved along her jaw. He stopped just below her ear and nuzzled. Mia didn't know she was capable of such lovely sounds, but apparently, she was.

"This scent here, this sweet scent, is all you. I dream about it." He kissed her just behind her earlobe.

Mia was dizzy and just about to lose her balance when Adam turned her, putting her back against the car. His hips pressed against her and Mia felt him. He was big, hard, and the tension in his body told her that he wanted her, which was completely surreal. His one hand laced through her hair and gently held her head, and his other hand slipped around her waist and settled on the skin at the small of her back.

Even though he was more man than she could handle, Mia fell into the moment. They were standing under a lamp post, which allowed Mia to see all his features clearly, including his slightly crooked nose, a small scar on his chin and his eyes, his gorgeous eyes that were dark and focused on her. This time there was nothing sweet about the kiss—it was mind-blowing. His mouth covered hers and his tongue played, drawing Mia into the heat. He held her close and she completely surrendered, losing herself in the smell and feel of him. His hand slid into the back of her pants and the softness of his touch was too much. She had no thoughts in her head, all she felt were his hands, his lips, his tongue, and his body pressed against hers. Mia clutched his shirt and held on, afraid she would fall, as every part of her went soft and pliant.

When he broke the kiss, Mia could feel his heart hammering away under her hands and she was barely able to catch her breath. This was what she'd been missing. This mind-numbing, sense-stealing passion was what had been absent from her life. Everything burned. *Everything.* Good Lord, how did people survive this?

Resting his forehead against hers, Adam blew out a breath. "Still hate me?"

Mia felt a smile pull across her face as one of her hands came up and touched his cheek. They locked eyes and Mia felt her heart trip and fall. "More than ever," she whispered. "More than ever."

Chapter Nine

WHEN HE'D GOTTEN the message from his old teammate Greg Rhodes that he was interested in having a look at Kelvin, Adam never thought he'd follow through. Greg recruited from big D-1 schools, and Jennings had a good program, but it was small potatoes for a superstar agent like him. But his old friend had a way of surprising people. And there he was, walking down the field like he owned it.

Greg smiled, winked at a couple of women who were at the front of the stands, and Adam was thankful that Mia was sitting a little farther back, out of Greg's line of fire. There was a part of him that was glad to see his college buddy, but that didn't mean he wanted Mia to meet him.

Now Adam had to wonder what was going to happen with Kelvin. Greg wouldn't be here unless he saw big money possibilities, and since Kelvin was a freshman who had started one game, it was a little early to know how things were going to go. But Greg was one of the best sports agents out there, and he didn't get to be the best waiting for things to happen.

"I can't believe you moved back to East Bumblefuck,

man," Greg's voice boomed, as always, and Adam hoped all the kids who were around didn't hear him. "I'd forgotten how isolated this place is."

Adam took his friend's outstretched hand and was quickly pulled into a bro hug, Greg giving him three hearty slaps on the back. "Damn, it's good to see you, Miller."

"Same, man. Never expected you to show."

"I hear your kid has wings on his feet. You think I'm passing that up?"

"He's still green, but yeah, he can run. I'm warning you, though, don't push it. He's not going to make a move without talking to his momma."

Greg laughed. "Well, I'll just have to charm his momma, then."

"Coach Miller?" Adam looked down and saw Ben holding some papers. "Coach Rand wanted you to have these." Ben handed off the papers and looked suspiciously at Greg.

"Thanks, buddy. Ben, this is Greg Rhodes. He also played pro."

Ben shook Greg's hand, still not sure what to make of him. One thing Adam had learned about Ben over the past couple of weeks was that the kid had a first-class bullshit detector. This close to Greg, the alarm bells were probably screaming. "This is Ben DeAngelis. He helps out around here."

"Cool. You play ball, kid?"

Ben shook his head. "No. I want to, though."

Adam patted Ben's shoulder. "Why don't you head back to Coach Rand."

Once Ben was out of earshot, he filled Greg in on the story. "His aunt is his guardian and she's a little skittish about football."

"Ah, well someone should let Auntie know she can't put the kid in a bubble."

"I'm working on it."

Coupled with a wicked grin, Greg's eyebrow shot up. "I bet you are," he said.

"Look, I gotta get inside," Adam said. The team was on their way off the field.

"I'll catch you after the game." Greg shook his hand again. "We can grab a beer."

The invitation caught him by surprise but thinking about it, one beer he could do. Adam wasn't picking Mia up until eight for their reservation, and having a long chat with his old friend was a in order. "Meet me in the field house after the game. I'll introduce you to Kelvin, and we can take off from there."

Greg smiled and waved before making his way toward the stands. There were so many things he'd cut out from his old life, and Greg Rhodes, who'd been a good friend, was one of them.

He'd almost said no when Greg had suggested to go out, mostly because Greg was never about one beer. But he had to find out what the guy wanted from Kelvin. Before he left the field, Adam turned and caught sight of Mia. She was sitting with her friends, and Noah Connolly was there, but he wasn't concerned now like he was just a week ago. Not since they'd spent all that time at the baseball game the other night. Hell, not since the kiss they shared in the parking lot that left them both staggered.

Adam planned on stealing plenty of kisses from Mia tonight, and if he was lucky, maybe more than that.

AFTER FIGHTING OFF wave after wave of humiliation, the text finally came at 8:45.

Adam wasn't coming.

Oh, he felt bad, according to one message. There was an agent there scouting Kelvin. An old friend. He had to put his player first.

Adam said he was sorry. Again.

That he wanted to watch out for Kelvin wasn't the problem. Canceling their date wasn't even the problem if he was that concerned about the situation with the agent.

It was the way he treated it. He was late, and he dismissed her in a text message.

A text message.

Mia wondered if she was being naïve? Was she being too sensitive? This was their official first date, and maybe she was overreacting, but it felt wrong.

Nana kept poking her head in the living room, asking if Mia needed anything, but what was there to do? She'd been stood up. If there was anything more embarrassing, she didn't want to know what it was.

Realizing that sitting in the living room stewing about it wasn't doing her any good, she kicked off her killer heels and went to the kitchen. There was a bottle of Sauvignon Blanc in the fridge calling to her, and once she had the bottle and the glass in hand, Mia retreated to her room.

Thank God Ben wasn't home. He'd been invited to a baseball team sleepover at Gabe Rand's house, so he didn't have to see his aunt fall apart over someone who wasn't worth it.

"Asshole," she muttered, thinking about Adam and his buddy. "You could have called."

Pouring a glass of wine, she set the bottle on her dresser and slipped the black silk dress over her head, flinging it without much care. It landed in the corner, leaving her staring at her reflection in the mirror. A few days ago, she and Fiona had gone shopping, and without saying why, she'd splurged on new bras and panties because she discovered she enjoyed having frilly things next to her body. She liked that she was starting to feel confident enough to put on things that were so girly, so pretty. So sexy.

But as she looked at her breasts pushing over the top of the bra and her soft belly and thighs, Mia heard her mother's voice scolding her foolishness, and picking apart her appearance. Once again, she felt anything but pretty, and she wondered what she'd been thinking.

Taking a large gulp from the glass, Mia blinked back the tears that burned her eyes. She would not cry. She would not be weak. *He was not worth it.*

If Adam was going to be a jerk, screw him.

But she couldn't help it—the first tear slipped down her cheek, and then another and then another, but to her surprise the emotions weren't what she expected. Frustrated with herself, angry that she'd allowed herself to be drawn in by the handsome face and the hot kisses, Mia decided right then and there that she was done being a doormat. Dabbing at her eyes, she vowed things were going to change. Her mother, Adam—the whole damn world for that matter—no one would ever treat her like she didn't matter ever again.

PINCHING THE BRIDGE of his nose, his head throbbing, Adam made his way to the kitchen door. Calming the dog as he walked. He had no idea who was knocking at the butt crack of dawn, but there was a good chance the person was going to die.

More knocking. "All right. I'm coming. Calm your ass down."

Adam grabbed the dog's collar and opened the door to the smiling face of his mother.

Shielding his eyes from the bright sun, he realized it wasn't as early as he thought. Bubba pulled, and knowing the dog was probably ready to burst, Adam let him go into the yard. "Mom?"

"Good morning, handsome son." She kissed his cheek as she stepped into the kitchen. Something was up. Linda Miller managed her family like a pro. She had a reason for being here on a Sunday morning, with what looked to be a bakery box from Rinaldi's Café.

"Good morning." He cringed at the bright light that flooded the kitchen when she pulled open the blinds covering the large kitchen windows. "What a surprise."

She grinned and turned on the coffee maker. "Oh, bullshit. You should have known I'd show up. I want to know how your date went, and I don't want to hear it through the old lady grapevine. I want to hear it from you."

"My date?" Why was this happening? He could only imagine how the news had travelled regarding his date with Mia. The date that never happened.

Adam rubbed his temple. What had happened was that he'd had way too much to drink and his head was throbbing. His mother, God love her, and the sunlight weren't helping. But she wanted to talk, and when mom wanted to talk, he listened. *Damn.* Adam always liked a good time, but he couldn't remember ever having a hangover like this. He must be getting old. It was like there were a thousand little librarians smacking him upside the head with big fat reference books.

"So?" his mother said while popping a coffee pod into the brewer. "Did you have a nice time?"

"You know," he teased. "If I'd had a really nice time, you could have interrupted something."

Mom froze. Blushed. "Oh." She bit her lip and looked around. "Is she here? Should I leave?" she whispered.

"No. It ended up that we didn't go out. But you have to promise me you'll never do this again. It's awkward."

"Well, if you called me I wouldn't have to stop over." She put down the box. "Why didn't you go out?"

Her voice rang with disappointment, and he could totally relate. He'd wanted nothing more than to have Mia all to himself.

Adam took a seat at the island and opened the bakery box. He needed sugar and starch to help his head. "Greg Rhodes came into town. Do you remember him? We played at Notre Dame and were drafted the same year. He's an agent now and he was looking at one of my players." He took a bite of the best bear claw he'd ever had. "Mrs. Rinaldi should be canonized for this pastry."

"Adam, he was your roommate for three years. Of course, I remember him." She fiddled with a dishtowel that was folded on the counter. "I don't understand. You cancelled?"

"Yeah. Greg and I went out for a couple of beers and time got away from me."

His mother moved toward him, setting a cup of coffee on the granite in front of him. "You didn't stand her up, did you?"

"Nah! No. What kind of guy do you think I am? I sent her a text. It's fine."

"*Fine?*" She folded her arms and waited. His mother, who was a social worker by profession, was never at a loss for words, but she appeared to be struggling. "You texted her? Is that what you said?"

Uh oh.

Adam took a healthy swallow of his coffee and realized this might not end well. He'd broken dates before. Things happened. But something was swirling around his kitchen, and he was starting to smell a little bit of crazy on his mom.

"It's not a problem. I told her why, and she said it was fine."

"She actually said the word 'fine'?"

Adam nodded and wondered, suddenly, if he'd missed something big. "Am I in trouble?"

"Oh, yeah. Fine is not fine. Fine is bad."

He took another bite of the bear claw and watched his mother's face. Mia would tell him the truth, wouldn't she? "Isn't that whole 'fine' thing kind of a cliché?"

His mother was stirring sugar into the coffee she was holding. "Now that you're back in the real world, Mr. Quarterback, you will realize that not all women consider your attention a gift from above."

"That's not fair…"

"Oh, it's very fair. I love you, Adam. You're a good man, but if you want a real relationship, you have to learn to give more than you take. Cancelling a last-minute coffee date is different than a Saturday night dinner date. Much different. When did you let her know?"

He groaned. *Shit.* "A half hour after I was supposed to pick her up. No. Forty-five minutes."

Mom took a seat at the island, tapping her index finger against the mug. Her cold stare said everything. "So you left her sitting at her house, waiting for you to show, and then, without even the courtesy of a call, cancelled."

He nodded. *When she said it like that…*

"You stood her up, and you did it by text message. You're lucky you even got 'fine' in response."

"I didn't think."

"No kidding?"

"I did things the same way I've always done them. It didn't occur to me that…I don't know. Like I said, I didn't think much about it."

"You didn't think about *her*, that's for sure." His mother broke off a piece of a croissant in the box and popped it in her mouth. She wouldn't look at him. Wouldn't make eye contact. After a long minute, she pushed her coffee away. "I have to go."

"You just got here."

Without saying a word, she eased herself off the stool.

There was nothing quite as intimidating as his mother's disapproval. Never one to pull punches, she loved without hesitation, and gave her family everything she had. She'd endured the loss of her husband at a young age, and raised four children without a thought for herself. He saw a lot of the same qualities in Mia.

"People deserve your best, Adam. For the record, you're too old for the '*I didn't think*' excuse. I raised you better than that."

He couldn't disagree. He'd been cut a lot of slack over the years, and it seemed that if he were going to turn the corner, he would have to do better. "I'm sorry, Mom."

She'd taken her jacket from the hook by the back door where he'd hung it, and kissed his cheek before pulling open the door. "I'm not the one who needs an apology. Good luck."

The dog ran in from the yard to bid his mother a proper goodbye, rolling over by her feet so he could get his belly rubbed. Once Bubba was satisfied, she turned toward Adam, who waved to her from the door and patted the dog's head when he ran inside the house.

Closing the door, his mind went in two directions. On one hand, he didn't need his mother meddling in his relationships. He was thirty-seven years old and he'd been taking care of himself for a long time. On the other hand, he hadn't done too good a job with his life on his own. Sure, he was successful, well liked, but what did that mean? Letting it run through his head, it became obvious that this wasn't only about his broken date. Adam needed to rethink how he did things, how he treated people.

"I have some work to do, Bubba," he said to the dog. "Think I can fix this?"

The dog lay at his feet with a moan and a heavy sigh.

Not the answer Adam was looking for.

MIA LEANED BACK in her chair and gazed across her desk at Adam, who, along with being gorgeous, was obviously certifiable. "You want to go out next weekend?"

"I feel bad about canceling. I figured I could make it up to you."

"You don't have to do that," she muttered. "I'm sure you're busy." *Way to sound pathetic, Mia.*

"Not too busy for you." He'd turned on his charm, full force.

She could not be affected by him. *Be angry. Remember how you felt the other night.*

"And it's a bad idea."

"We get along great. How is it a bad idea?"

Was it possible that he had no clue?

"You're angry about me cancelling. I had to deal with the agent…"

Mia waved him off. "Adam, it's not why you cancelled,

it's how you did it.

He was stalking the room like a nervous cat, and after some extended pacing, approached her desk. The closer he got, the more she felt her stomach tighten. "I'm sorry. I didn't think…"

"That's obvious."

"Jesus, Mia. Was I supposed to call you? I was in the middle of a crowded bar."

"Yes, you were supposed to call. You should have stepped outside well before you were supposed to pick me up and let me know what was going on. That's what you *should* have done. It would have been the considerate thing to do." Pausing because she didn't want her hurt to show, she added, "I would have understood, you know? You were looking out for one of your players, and I would have understood."

Adam sat on the corner of her desk and leaned in. Now Mia could smell him, and she was angrier with him for making her want to jump him than she was for being so obtuse. How could he do this? Kiss her the way he did, make her dream about him, and then humiliate her. The bigger question was, why was she surprised he'd pissed her off? He was behaving in character—like an arrogant, self-serving jock.

"You're right."

"I am?" *Holy shit.*

"Yes. I don't know how else to apologize." He reached out and skimmed his fingers over her check, cupping it with his hand. "Give me another chance, please?"

Oh, God. Why did speech leave her now? Just that simple touch warmed her nerves, set her senses screaming. She rested her cheek in his palm like a needy kitten.

Adam's jaw was set, his eyes fixed on hers. He was so much man. She swallowed hard and could only imagine what he had in mind—she wanted to know. And that was the problem. As pissed as she was at him, she wanted him. Taking a deep breath, Mia refocused and pushed his hand away.

"No. You had your chance." *Keep going, don't break,* she was thinking. She wanted to get some distance between them, but there was no place to go. "I can't imagine what made me think I could date someone like you."

"Like me?" His eyes narrowed. Yup, that struck a nerve. Adam now knew he couldn't charm her, so he started losing his patience. "I've made mistakes, Mia, but I'm not a criminal."

"I know, but I think it's obvious we come from two different places. Maybe I'm overreacting, because like I said, I do understand why you wanted to stay and talk to the agent. But you shouldn't have dismissed me the way you did. I deserve better."

Maybe she was weak, because when she looked into Adam's deep blue eyes, all she wanted to do was to give him the chance he was asking for; she wanted to be with him more than anything, but she knew he wasn't safe. Especially for her.

He was thinking, probably trying to figure out a way to get her to give in. "What about Ben?"

"What about him?"

"Did you tell him? Is he still allowed to come to practice?"

Mia drew a shaky breath and exhaled, wondering why it was always so hard to breathe while he was around. "Yes, he is. I didn't think it was fair to let the situation between us affect him."

It was a decision she hadn't come to lightly. It would have been easier on her to tell him what happened, it would have kept her from having to see Adam, but what would that do to Ben? He had to learn to trust other people, and he and Adam had built a strong relationship in a short time.

She thought about this morning, when he was ready for the school bus a full ten minutes before he needed to be. Mia asked him about it and the response was telling. *"Coach says 'If you're on time, you're late.' So I'm trying to be ready for everything a little earlier."*

This was a more mature and responsible response than she'd ever expected from a ten-year-old, and it was Adam's doing. Getting homework done, the good manners, the neat room, were all part of the influence he was having over Ben.

"I'll look for him at practice, then?"

She hesitated. Nodded. "He'll be there."

"And what about you? Are you sure I can't make it up to

you?"

Mia couldn't even look at him. If she did, she'd cry, and the last thing she wanted was a guy who felt emotionally blackmailed.

"Why don't we just forget about it," Mia said quietly.

"I don't think I can do that."

"We'll be friends; it's fine. Probably better, in fact."

Mia looked up and saw a million questions in his eyes, more than likely the same questions she was asking herself. She shrugged. She was a coward. She knew that, but there was no way Mia could assume the risk he represented.

His expression told her that wasn't the answer he was looking for. Maybe he wanted to kiss her into a coma again. "*Friends?*"

"Is there a problem with that?"

"Well, yeah. I want to fix things between us..." he said.

Mia stiffened her spine as Adam edged a little closer. There was no way she could put herself in a relationship with a guy with his reputation, or his track record. It wasn't like she hadn't given him a chance. If he wanted more, he could have just followed through, called her, done something after their first two "dates" other than blowing her off. Standing her up was the last straw. He was treating her like a convenience. And even though she was naïve about men and relationships, she wasn't going to be a convenience.

"You know, we've known each other about a month. The fact that things already need to be fixed isn't good. I think being friends is better for both of us."

"I said I was sorry. I really am."

"You might be sorry, but I'm not going to be treated like an afterthought, and that's what you did. You made me feel foolish, Adam. In my mind, I think being friends is a pretty good offer."

He stared at her, his posture shifted, he looked down and then back at her. It occurred to Mia that this may never have happened to him before. It was entirely possible a woman had never told Adam Miller '*No*'. Finally, his face told her he understood. "Okay then," he said quietly. "I'll see Ben later?"

"I'll send him over with Kelvin."

They stared at each other, not knowing what to do. Mia liked Adam way too much for her own good. She loved looking at him, loved talking to him, and loved the feel of him, but she wished he would leave. It took a half a minute of awkward silence before there was a knock at the door and Noah popped his head in. He'd called that morning to see if she was free for lunch.

"Oh, sorry." Yeah, Noah didn't look sorry, but smug. Adam, on the other hand, got more pissed off. *Perfect.* "Are you ready, Mia? I have a class around two."

The testosterone swirling around the room was making her dizzy. Adam looked like he could do real violence, but Noah, bless his geeky heart, stood his ground. Smiling.

"How are you doing today, Coach?" Noah asked.

Adam's head whipped away from Mia and he directed

his intimidating man-gaze right at Noah, but it wasn't working this time. Mia thought she might have seen an actual vein pulsing in Adam's neck; he was jealous. He was so jealous he was ready to explode. It was impressive and thrilling as hell. Maybe this friend thing was a mistake.

Trying to act casual, Mia realized she was still holding her breath as she grabbed her purse from her desk drawer. Adam was watching, waiting, and then, without a word, he rose from the edge of her desk and stalked out of her office.

Thankful he'd finally left, Mia could allow herself to breathe.

Chapter Ten

"ARE YOU REALLY going to sing?" Lilly was smiling ear-to-ear as Mia walked back from putting her name on the karaoke list.

Nodding, and taking a sip from her third beer, Mia figured she should slow down her drinking if she didn't want to slur the words of the song. Fiona had no such hesitation as she headed toward the bar and said, "She's going to kick ass."

Thinking about it, Mia knew she'd do a more than respectable job.

Her three years at NYU may have been cut short, but her time there wasn't wasted. In fact, there was a good possibility, she'd be banned from ever singing karaoke in town again. But this was going to be fun. Other than the voice lessons she'd just started, she hadn't had time to sing in ages, so tonight she was going to indulge her inner diva.

Feeling happier than she had in a long time, Mia surveyed her surroundings. McGinty's Pub had been around for over a hundred years in this very location. Originally, it catered to the town's fishermen, buying the local catch and becoming known for its seafood chowder. Now, it was still a gathering place for the locals, but more for a fun night out with friends or a quick bite to eat of the simple but delicious fare they offered.

The pub also hosted karaoke night once a week, and so, for the first time in years, Mia was having a true girls' night out and she intended to make the most of it.

"Okay," Fiona said coming back to the group. "I've been hit on by the same guy five times. It's getting annoying."

"Who?" Mia looked around. "Is there something wrong with him?"

"He's seventy-five."

Mia, Lilly, and Jordan tried to suppress the giggles that were building, but it was no use. Fiona, who was fiddling with her drink, leveled her gaze at them and rolled her eyes as they laughed.

"Are you all done? Because if you aren't, I'm going over to that group of hipsters and tell them you three are totally hot for guys with big horn-rimmed glasses."

Jordan savored her martini, and glanced in the direction of said hipsters. "At least they wouldn't need oxygen after…"

Again, Mia couldn't help but laugh. Nana was getting a big hug and a kiss for pushing her out the door, because if she hadn't Mia would have stayed home, and once again would have lost out on a fun evening. It was good to have friends.

Ever since the evening that the four of them had dinner together, the friendship had developed quickly. They had a lot of common ground and their personalities, while different, all seemed to mesh.

Jordan ordered another chocolate martini when the waitress came by and winced as the latest karaoke superstar made a fool of himself singing a lounge lizard version of "Do You Think I'm Sexy".

"I don't know what's more terrifying, the singing or the bad hairpiece?"

Mia leaned her arms on the table and grinned. "Definitely the hairpiece. It's like a small animal."

Jordan clinked her glass to Mia's in agreement. "I'm glad Lilly talked me into coming out tonight. I guess I can't wallow at home forever. Lord knows, Chase isn't hiding."

Chase, Jordan's ex-fiancé, came from a very prominent family, and he'd been caught the day before their wedding screwing his secretary. It was such a cliché, it made Mia wince, but for Jordan it meant taking a stand and walking away from the wedding of her dreams and what should have been a life of relative ease.

Chase was humiliated, but that didn't stop him from taking the secretary on the honeymoon. Supposedly, they were now engaged.

"You shouldn't be thinking about Chase."

"Honey, it's hard not to when I'm the one who's being blamed for the whole mess. You know, I'm the one who *overreacted,* and called off the wedding."

"Not everyone blames you." Mia smiled and Jordan returned a weaker version. It was hard to imagine what she was going through; it couldn't be easy, especially since her fiancé's family had lived in Compass Cove for three generations. But her own grandmother had heard plenty of gossip about the cancelled wedding, and the consensus was that Jordan got out in the nick of time.

"I'm really glad you moved here," Jordan said. "It's nice to meet someone who doesn't pass judgment on me."

"I bet there are more people in your corner than you think."

Sighing, her friend nodded and took another drink. "I hear you are very popular, my new friend. First Adam Miller, and now you and the new English professor are an item?"

Mia thought about Noah. They'd been out four times and date number five was tomorrow night. He'd been over to the house a couple of times, and for all intents and purposes, they *were* an item. If there was any doubt, it had been vanquished when one of his colleagues in the English department sent out invitations to a literary themed Halloween party. They'd been invited together.

They became a couple in two short weeks.

As soon as the invitation had come, Noah came to her house with a list of ideas of famous romantic pairs from literature. Tristan and Isolde? Lancelot and Guinevere? Daisy and Gatsby?

Scarlett O'Hara and Rhett Butler from *Gone with the Wind*, were Mia's first thought. She loved the idea of wearing a big flowery gown and Noah would look dashing as a Confederate soldier. But he decided that was "too commercial." Mia wondered what made a couple acceptable, since he seemed intent on finding the perfect match. Again, he asked her for suggestions from something she'd recently read—and that's when Mia, who considered herself very well read and was highly educated, horrified her academic boyfriend by telling him the last ten books she'd read were romance novels. The look on his face was *priceless.*

If Noah weren't young and healthy, she was sure he would have had a heart attack. Once he started breathing again, it seemed he took her revelation as a challenge, scribbling titles of books she might like.

Of course, he was stunned when Mia told him she'd read them all.

Mia shouldn't have been surprised to find out that Noah was pretty stuck up in general. Food, wine, movies... everything. And unlike his awkwardness, there was nothing endearing about him when he became a pompous ass. By the end of the evening, he'd decided they'd go as Hamlet and Ophelia, which disturbed her more than a little since Ophelia's story didn't end so well.

"Mia, I think you're up next."

"What?" Mia looked at the stage, realized she was going to be singing after the lounge lizard, and the familiar butterflies returned to her stomach. Some people hated the nervous feeling, but for Mia, the nerves came on just before the shot of adrenaline, and the rush of being on stage was something she'd love forever.

Putting down her drink, she turned toward the stage and glanced toward the door. She felt her pulse race because standing there, staring at her, was Adam.

And God, did he look good. Even in the dim light of the bar, she could see his flashing blue eyes, the slight shadow of his beard, and the bands of muscles in his forearms.

The slight buzz she was feeling from the beer and the crowd was giving her more nerve than was wise, especially with a man who could melt every female heart within a hundred feet of him. But there he was staring, smiling a little. And then a tall blonde woman walked toward him, took his arm, and the two of them found seats at the bar.

Glancing in his direction just as Adam turned his head, Mia cringed when he caught her looking. *Crap*. He grinned, and that just pissed Mia off even more. But at the same time, the tingles which started around her heart were crawling down her midsection and made her more aware than ever of how much she still wanted him.

Awesome.

It wasn't like he needed the ego boost. He certainly had enough attitude without her help. *Asshole.* He was an asshole. He'd treated her like crap and ignored her. She should be taking comfort in the fact that she had nothing to do with him. Even though there had been a brief window in which he'd been nice, and he was giving Ben something to do in the afternoons, he'd probably saved her a lot of grief by blowing her off. Looking back in his direction, she caught him looking this time, but he didn't think anything at all of staring. He smiled—and that got her seriously pissed off.

The DJ who was running the karaoke finally got her attention and Mia knew she was about to completely humiliate herself. Well, if she was going to go down, it might as well be in flames. Glancing for a third time at Adam, who was still looking her way, Mia headed toward the platform that acted as a stage. Originally, she'd planned to sing something pretty and light, but now she wanted to show off.

A lot.

"You know," she said to the DJ, "I think I might like to sing something else."

He glared at her, annoyed. "Seriously?"

Mia turned on her charm, giving him a girlish smile. "Please?"

He asked what she wanted to do and then nodded just before Mia stepped onto the platform to face the room.

SHE WAS GOING to sing? He noticed she was with her friends and was drinking a bit. Drunk? That could be interesting, and he'd certainly take the opportunity to tease the crap out of her. No one who sang during karaoke could expect any less.

Mia stepped to the mic and gave the audience that pure, sweet smile that undid him every time. Then she floored him when she set her eyes right on him. Damn.

The intro was a familiar wailing sax and twanging guitar. Unlike the other performers so far, Mia didn't look awkward or uncomfortable as she swayed to the thumping bass. The song was familiar, and had the potential for all kinds of embarrassment. But when Mia opened her mouth, the notes she belted out rocked the noisy bar.

Holy. Shit.

It was a classic female anthem, a staple for drunken bar patrons and wedding guests, and while Adam's musical knowledge was usually crap, he was blown away at what Mia's voice was doing to cover it. On top of the vocal gymnastics, Mia wasn't just singing, she was *performing*, and it didn't take long for her to get the crowd with her. Less than a verse in, and the women were bouncing up and down, clapping over their heads, and the men were probably wondering what they could do to get her into bed.

By the time she hit the first chorus, she owned the place. Adam decided, right then, there wasn't anything she couldn't do.

The entire bar was moving, but the only thing Adam was totally aware of was the rushing sound in his ears and the pounding in his chest. The burn through his body was intense and the memories of how she felt pressed against him—warm, soft, and his—intensified with each note.

Adam couldn't take his eyes off her. She was sexy, confident, and he felt like he took a hit to the chest when she looked right at him and sang. He didn't realize how intensely he was staring at her until he got an elbow in the ribs.

Lisa, his date, was not happy. At all.

"Who is she?"

"She works on campus."

"You know her?"

He should have told Lisa that Mia was a friend, but he couldn't get the words out. He could have told her that he'd been an ass and stood Mia up, but Adam simply nodded, and kept his attention glued to Mia.

Sure, he knew he should have been paying more attention to his date. That would have been the nice thing to do, but Adam didn't.

It wasn't long, maybe two minutes into Mia's song, when Lisa turned on a wicked high heel and left the bar. He didn't even call after her. Yeah, he was a real prize.

Turning back toward the bar, he'd been joined by Joe and Drew, forgetting that they were coming here to watch the game.

"You'll have to tell me your secret to charming women," Joe said.

"Fuck you," Adam said, still completely mesmerized by Mia's voice.

"You know she's still seeing the professor, right?" Drew added.

Adam grumbled at Drew's question. Mia made sure he

knew when she sent those lines in his direction. He'd pulled in every favor out there to get information on the English dork and what he found out he didn't like. He was a poster child for the good guy award. Adam couldn't even say he was a wimp, because he'd found out that the guy was an Academic All-American in lacrosse when he was at Yale.

Yale. Of course he was an Ivy Leaguer. That made him perfect for the whip-smart Mia, but Adam knew he was still getting to her. That's what the declaration of female independence was all about, and that made him wonder if Dr. Dork was good for her in other ways.

"Adam?" Joe gave him a shot to the ribs.

Coming out of his trance, he looked at the stage and at Mia, whose eyes were closed as she belted out the final notes of the song, finishing even bigger than she'd started. The crowd was going crazy and her friends were screaming their approval from the table. She smiled wide as she finished— once for her audience and once for him—and Adam felt his insides collapse. Less than two months in town and she'd made this place her very own. This girl was amazing.

And at that moment Adam realized how badly he'd fucked up.

"Do you think you'll get another shot with her?" Joe asked. The way his friend read his mind was almost eerie, but considering Adam was probably looking at Mia like he wanted her to bear his children, it was understandable.

Turning toward the door to leave, Adam shrugged. "I don't know. I just don't know."

Chapter Eleven

WHEN HE WENT to football practice, Ben never knew what he was going to be asked to do. Sometimes he just held things for the coaches or players. Other times he'd get water, or help the equipment manager. He helped the trainer sometimes, too. The best part was he got to be around football, and every day when practice was over, Coach taught him something new.

They always worked on throwing, but Ben also learned how to receive a snap, about the different positions, and sometimes Coach wanted him to receive. That was a little scary. Ben would run downfield and Coach would throw a bomb that Ben didn't think he would catch, but he always did. He never missed. Ben was relieved that Aunt Mia had changed her mind a few weeks ago and allowed him to keep working for the team. If she hadn't, he'd never have found what he was good at.

Coach Miller would bring him home or back to the library most days, but sometimes Aunt Mia would come by before practice was over and watch. She was trying to learn so she could understand why it was so important to him. On those days, she always talked to Coach.

They thought he was asleep after the baseball game. He'd fallen asleep on the bus, but when Coach had gotten him in the car, he only pretended to sleep. That's when he saw his aunt and the coach kissing. And it wasn't like one of those friendly kisses. It was gross.

Coach's hands were on Aunt Mia. Ben knew they liked each other. He was only in fifth grade, but he could see it by the way they acted at the game. Coach paid a lot of attention to Aunt Mia when they were sitting together that night. Sometimes he held her hand, or his arm would be on the back of the seat. Every time he looked at her, his eyes got all soft and mushy.

Aunt Mia acted all girly when he was around. She'd play with her hair or bite on her lip. She always smiled when she was with Coach, and even though she pretended that he was annoying, she really liked him.

At first, he thought Aunt Mia was letting him hang out with the team so she could keep kissing the coach. But something changed, and now she was seeing Noah all the time and Ben got really confused. Ben didn't really like him, and Aunt Mia didn't either. Oh, she acted like she did, but Aunt Mia liked Coach Miller. He could just tell.

Kelvin picked him up in Aunt Mia's office to walk to the field. Ben really liked him. Kelvin was cool and smart and he was a good football player. He could run faster than anyone Ben had ever seen. But what he liked best about Kelvin was that he treated Ben like he was just one of the guys.

It was drizzling a little as they walked down the road toward the field house. He didn't really care, because he had a lot on his mind. When Ben looked up, he saw Kelvin was looking at him.

"You seem worried, man," Kelvin said.

"I do?" Ben wasn't really worried, but he was thinking about a lot of things. Mostly about the coach and Aunt Mia.

"What's up?"

Ben took a deep breath and blurted it out. "I think Aunt Mia and Coach like each other."

Ben looked at Kelvin and saw he was smiling, even laughing a little. "Yeah, I would say they do."

Ben's face dropped. "I don't want him to hurt Aunt Mia's feelings."

Kelvin patted his shoulder. "I think they're still figuring it out."

"Right. Figuring it out."

Kelvin took a step in Ben's path and turned to face him. Ben stopped and Kelvin asked him the question, "You know something, pal?"

Ben had been hanging out with the team for a while, and he'd known Kelvin even longer. He felt like he could tell Kelvin anything. So he blurted it out. "Remember the baseball game I went to and Coach was there?"

"Yeah." Kelvin folded his arms and nodded. "Did something happen?"

Ben nodded. "You should have seen the way they kissed. If they don't like each other, there's gotta be something wrong with that."

Kelvin laughed. "Is that so? Well I guess you better have a talk with Coach Miller then. You are the man in your house."

That made Ben think. "You think I should? I don't want him to get mad at me."

"He won't get mad if you're respectful. He likes honesty."

"Okay, and what about that teacher guy? Should I talk to him too? 'Cause he's hanging around."

"Is Doc Connolly trying to kiss your aunt, too?"

"He's trying, but I think the only one Aunt Mia wants to kiss is the coach."

Kelvin nodded. "You better talk to Coach Miller."

Ben took a deep breath and decided Kelvin was right. He needed to find out what was going on.

ADAM LOOKED OVER at Ben, staring out the passenger window. Usually the kid chewed his ear off, but today he was unusually quiet. Something was bothering him. Kelvin told him there was something on Ben's mind, and from Ben's posture Adam could see that was true.

He called Mia and told her he'd drive him home. He

knew she got off work at four that day, so this way she didn't have to wait around for practice to be over. A couple of times she came by and watched. He'd seen her across the field, bundled against the wind that constantly whipped around the field in the late afternoon. Every time he looked at her, he wanted her a little bit more. He wondered if he'd ever get the chance again.

Adam was just about to ask what was eating him when Ben spoke. His voice was low, but level and very firm. "You have to be careful with my aunt," he said. "You can't hurt her feelings."

Talk about being blindsided. Stopped at a light, Adam shook off the shock before answering. "Okay."

"I mean," he said, facing Adam, "I know you like her."

What did this kid know? "Well, yeah. We're friends."

Just saying the word "friends" reminded Adam of the major way he screwed up.

Ben didn't budge. His face hardened, and Adam saw something eerily familiar in the set of his jaw. "You kiss all your friends like you kiss her?"

Forget blindsided. Adam just stepped on the mother of all emotional landmines. Yep. Ben knew something. There was a short toot from a horn and Adam saw the light had gone green. He stepped on the gas and realized he had to open up the conversation. "Did Mia say something to you?"

"No. And she doesn't know I'm talking to you about this either." Ben took a breath. "I saw you kissing after the baseball game, by the car. You thought I was sleeping. *I wasn't.*"

Adam still had dirty dreams about that kiss, about where they should have ended up if she hadn't needed to take Ben home. His hands had worked their way under her shirt and caressed the soft skin on her back. His mouth took hers in every way possible. She'd been so responsive, Adam didn't know if anyone would ever be able to match Mia's passion.

"You were awake?" Adam saw Ben nod. There was nothing he could think of to say. He did like Mia. But beyond that? That was the hurting territory Ben was talking about. Did he want to go there? Did Mia?

"Ben, sometimes adults, well, we like kissing. It doesn't mean—" He stopped. "People can kiss without—" He could see by Ben's expression that this was going no place good. "It's hard to explain."

"You aren't allowed to make her cry. She doesn't cry a lot, but I hate when she cries."

Adam had to admire the kid's protectiveness. He had a message and he made sure Adam received it—loud and clear. "No crying. Got it."

"She likes you, Coach. I think she likes you a lot more than Noah."

That made Adam happy, but Mia had been seeing the English geek pretty regularly since he'd blown off their dinner, and the more Adam learned about the professor, the less he liked him.

"Why do you think she doesn't like him?"

Ben screwed up his face. "Well she doesn't hate him or anything. He's okay, but he talks to me like I'm stupid. He's kind of a tool." Adam had to fight back the shocked laughter. Ben was being serious, but hearing him call Noah Connolly a tool made Adam's day.

"I just think she likes you better."

They lapsed into a long silence after that. Adam thought about Mia and Ben, and how much having them in his life had become important over the last month and a half. He didn't want to hurt either of them. Knowing that told him how things were going to go, but he'd have to tread very carefully, especially with Noah Connolly in the picture.

As they pulled in the driveway, Ben finally spoke.

"Are you mad at me, Coach?"

"Mad at you? No, not at all. I like the way you're trying to take care of your aunt. It's a good thing."

"She takes care of me. My parents weren't there for me, but Aunt Mia was. I guess it's my turn."

Adam nodded. He shouldn't ask the question that was on his tongue, but he had to, and he expected Ben was more in tune with what was going on than anyone thought. God knew he talked like he was forty; the backbone in this kid was amazing.

"What do you know about your parents, Ben?"

"Not too much. My mother killed herself when I was a baby. My grandparents always said she 'went away', but I asked Aunt Mia what happened." He took a deep breath and Adam continued to listen. "I never knew my dad and I don't think he knows about me. All I do know about him is that he played in the NFL."

"Really? Wow." That explained a lot. Maybe the expressions he saw that were so familiar was because Ben reminded Adam of someone he knew. Someone he played with or against. It creeped him out a little. And how would he feel, he wondered, if he had a kid out there who didn't know him?

"Yeah." He grabbed hold of his backpack and pulled the door handle. "Thanks for the ride, Coach."

"Hang on, Ben." Adam turned the key in the ignition and opened the door. "I'll come in. I want to say hi to Mia. I haven't seen her in a while."

Ben grinned. "She'll be happy to see you."

Adam hoped he was right.

THE BACK DOOR was open and when they stepped in the kitchen, he saw the table was set for dinner. There was something in the oven and then Adam's ears picked up. Music was coming from the front of the house. He looked at Ben who had stopped to listen as well. The boy smiled.

"She's taking singing lessons again. And piano."

Adam followed Mia's voice and stopped at the kitchen

door to watch her. She sat at the piano, her back to them, and he held a hand out to stop Ben from entering the room and interrupting her. She was playing and singing. Her hair flowed down her back and moved as she put all she had into the song.

Adam had seen Mia at work, and she was very good at what she did. The students trusted her and the faculty was beginning to respect her abilities as a researcher. Mia was wicked smart and there wasn't much she couldn't handle, even from the most pretentious Ph.D.'s. But watching her play, hearing her sing, was watching Mia do what she was meant to do. He knew it when he saw her at the pub, and he knew it now.

He was frozen, listening to her sing about love and heartbreak. Her hands moved furiously over the keys. Adam played the piano himself. Technically, he was good, but he could never match the ability that seemed to come to her so naturally. And then there was her voice. It was pure and as clear as the message of the song she was singing.

Just like the night at the pub, Adam saw a side of Mia that left him speechless. This quiet, demure woman was a star that had never had a chance to shine. He looked down at Ben and suddenly grasped that when Ben's mother had so selfishly taken her own life, she'd stolen Mia's too.

When Mia finished the song, she rubbed her hands, turning when she heard Ben's backpack hit the wall. Her eyes widened when she spotted Adam and he couldn't say a word. He was so awed that he stood there, staring at her like a love-struck twelve-year-old.

"Hi," she said. "I didn't expect to see you."

He nodded. "I figured." He walked toward where she sat at the piano and crouched next to her. "Now I know why you're always a little bit sad."

"Excuse me? Sad?"

"You're always a little sad, Mia. Like you're missing something."

She squeezed her eyes shut and pressed a finger to her lips. Emotion was taking hold and Adam could see the music came from her core. "It's important to me and I don't get to sing very much anymore."

"And now I've heard you twice. I will say, I like this song better." He couldn't help teasing her—watching her react was like an addiction. It was his only defense, since being around her affected him in a dozen different ways.

Her face flamed red and she focused now on her hands, lying in her lap. She knew he was referring to her slap at him during the karaoke performance, and her inherent sweetness didn't let her hang on to any of the attitude she'd shown the night she sang. "Sorry about the bar. I was a little buzzed and, well, you know."

"Don't worry about it. I deserved it, but I can't get over your voice. It's beautiful. What I heard was…" He stopped. "I don't even know what to say."

Mia looked around. When she saw Ben had left the

room, she reached out and touched Adam's face. "I think you're a little sad, too."

"Why do you say that?" He brought his hand over hers without thinking.

"I think you miss playing football the way I miss music."

She was right, he did miss it. He missed it every day. And even though his career would have been winding down by now, it bothered Adam that a stupid decision on his part ended it early. His sadness, if that's what it was, came from disappointment in himself. "It's different, but I think we understand each other better."

She smiled. "I think we do."

He nodded and looked at her hands, which he now knew could do amazing things. "Next year, you have to let Ben play football. There's a really good youth league based in town and he's born to play." Adam lifted her hands and glanced at the piano. "Just like you, Mia. And from what he tells me, it's in his blood."

Mia looked at him and nodded. Clearly, Ben had told him about his father. "You'll tell me when sign up is for the league?"

"I'll tell you."

"Will you promise me he won't get hurt?"

"No. You know that's not realistic." Adam stood and pulled her to her feet.

"Will you stay for dinner?" She smiled at him sweetly, and at that moment she could have asked him to put a roof on the house and he would have done it. "I made lasagna."

"Yeah? I love lasagna." He hesitated. "Am I forgiven?"

She nodded. "I'll set another place at the table."

Before she got too far, he reached for her hand again. "Wait. Is your grandmother going to be around?"

Her eyes went wide and her lips parted slightly—she looked startled at the question. Confused. Worried. "She's closing the bookstore tonight. It's just us."

Nodding, Adam released her hand. "That's too bad. I would have liked seeing her."

The smile that broke across Mia's face was blinding, and internally, he celebrated. Adam knew if she was willing to give him another chance, he had to accept her place in this town and her connections to him and everyone here.

Mia left him in the living room while she went into the kitchen, and as Adam looked around the large space, taking it all in, he realized he wanted this. He wanted a home like this. He wanted the kids and the wife and as he looked toward the kitchen, where Mia added a place to the table, he realized he wanted her. The problem with that was he didn't know if he deserved her.

MIA STACKED THE dishwasher, perfectly content to let Adam help Ben with his homework. Nana always offered to help, and if it was reading or writing, Ben couldn't have been in better hands. But tonight, math was giving him fits, and Adam seemed to have a good handle on it.

When he surprised her earlier, she was a little embarrassed about the impromptu recital; but his reaction, showing so much respect for her music, tugged at Mia's heart. He wasn't supposed to be like this, so kind, so understanding. He was supposed to be arrogant, shallow, and not too bright. Adam was none of those things. He was so much more.

When the phone rang and the caller ID told her it was Noah, she regretted her acquiescence earlier to his suggestion that he come over to watch a movie. She reached for the phone to get it over with.

"Hello?"

"Hey, Mia, it's Noah."

"Hi, Noah, how are you?"

"Good, we still on for later? I'll bring the popcorn."

"You know, I'm a little tired. Would you mind if I took a rain check?"

His silence told her he was disappointed. She felt bad, but she had no interest in seeing him.

"Oh, okay. I'll call you on the weekend. We can get together then."

The man had no read on her. Mia was starting to wonder if she was really waiting for a spark with him, or if she was settling.

"Yeah, sure," she said, a little guilty. "That's fine."

"Night."

"Night."

Mia stared at the phone after she hung up and felt a little guilty for lying to him. But she wanted to spend time with Adam, and she didn't know how she felt about Noah yet. He was nice enough, but there was something about him that conveyed a sense of superiority. She'd dealt with just that kind of snotty attitude from her mother her whole life; she didn't need it in her boyfriend.

She turned to see Adam standing by the kitchen door. He had his jacket in his hand.

"Oh, are you leaving?"

"I heard you on the phone with Connolly. You're tired. You don't need me underfoot."

Mia panicked. She'd told Noah not to come over so Adam would stay, not leave. God, that was bad, but she wasn't going to jump him or anything. "Oh, no," she started. "I'm fine, I just—" She pointed at the phone. "He'd be here every day if I didn't set some boundaries."

"So, you want me to stay?"

Mia nodded and Adam moved closer to her. The heat started building as soon as they made eye contact, as soon as he realized she wanted to spend time with him, and not the guy she was dating. But hey, they were friends. She should be able to spend time with her friends. Even if this particular friend tended to throw her system into a complete meltdown.

"Ben doesn't like him."

"Noah?" Mia shrugged and twisted her fingers as Adam stepped into her personal space, and did what he always did when he got so close. He played with her hair.

"I don't like him either," he said.

"Why?" Mia's voice came out on a breath and she closed her eyes to keep from catching Adam's gaze. She knew why he didn't like him. It was a territorial male thing.

"Ben said he's a tool."

"He called him a tool?" That surprised Mia. She'd never heard Ben use the word in that context, and he'd never said anything to her about it. "Why is Noah a tool?"

Adam grinned and kept his eyes locked on hers. His fingers twirled a lock of her hair and Mia's insides jangled in response.

"Because I don't think he gets you. From what I know, he's not a bad guy, but don't get your hopes up."

"In theory, we should be perfect for each other." Mia brushed a piece of invisible lint off Adam's shoulder and glanced up for a quick second.

"I'm no expert, but relationships don't always follow rules."

"His parents and my mother are friends. They belong to the same golf club in Charleston."

"I get the pressure, but it isn't about them. Do you like him?"

She looked away and he turned her face back toward his,

but she still averted her eyes. If she looked at him, he'd know. "You aren't sixteen, Mia. You can make your own decisions."

"I know, but it's not like I have all these men banging down my door." Finally, she straightened her back and looked in his face. "I don't have much luck with that, and he calls when he says he will. That should mean something."

Adam stepped back and leaned his hip into the table. He knew they weren't talking about Noah anymore, they were talking about him. "I guess. But I'll ask again—do you like him?"

That was the big question, and the answer wasn't easy. She liked Noah well enough, but the more time she spent with him, the more she realized what was missing. "So far it's been okay, but there's no, no—" She stopped. Did she want to go there?

"No what?"

"No chemistry. No spark. He's nice, but—"

"You're not feeling anything?"

If Mia had a bigger ego, she probably would have thought Adam was happy about that. He certainly looked happy. Too happy.

After the confession, there was silence. They both avoided eye contact, and for her part, Mia couldn't believe she'd just opened herself up like that. If she were a gambler, she'd bet he was enjoying her embarrassment a little too much, but if he was, his face didn't show it. However, he did look a little nervous.

"Look," he said. "I hate to bring this up, but Ben had a talk with me today."

"A talk?"

"Yeah. He said he knows we like each other and he warned me that I was not allowed to hurt your feelings and that I was not allowed to make you cry."

"Oh. Wait. What?" Mia shook her head and walked in a circle. What made Ben say that? What made him think it was possible? "Why did he say that?"

"After the baseball game. We thought he was asleep in the car. He wasn't."

He wasn't asleep. He wasn't asleep and he saw Adam kiss her within an inch of her life. Did Ben see what Adam's hands were doing? What her hands were doing? "Oh, my God."

Mia leaned her head against the wall. "Oh, my God."

Adam came to her, laced his fingers with hers, and she looked up. "It's not the end of the world."

"How do you explain something like that to a ten-year-old?"

"He's a lot savvier than you give him credit for." Adam held her hands and made her sit at the table. "He tried to be the man in the house. He wanted me to know if I hurt you, I'd have to answer to him for it. He wasn't upset about the kiss, but he wants to protect you."

Mia looked at their joined hands. "And this is when you

talked about Noah?"

"Yeah, he doesn't like Noah. And I think if Ben has the opportunity, he'll tell him."

"Oh, boy." What a man she was raising. Just when Mia thought she was making a mess of everything, Ben showed her differently. "Noah won't respond like you did. He won't take Ben seriously."

Adam took her face in his hands and dropped a sweet kiss on Mia's lips. She'd never been so grateful to be in a chair, because the way her bones had just melted, she wouldn't have been able to stand.

"The thing the professor doesn't understand is that if he hurts you, he's not only going to have to answer to Ben, he's going to have to answer to me."

She sighed. An honest to goodness sigh escaped and Mia fought back the tears. They were good tears, but tears nonetheless. With her emotions pouring out, she felt more vulnerable and confused than ever.

In a move that she was sure would stay with her forever, Adam dropped to one knee and wrapped her in his arms, holding her like she meant everything to him. It was like this whenever he held her. Safe. Secure. Perfect.

"Shhhhh. It's going to be okay." His hand went gently up and down her spine, and she wished he could hold her like this forever. "You're going to get me in trouble with Ben if you cry."

A watery laugh escaped, along with a sniffle, and Mia was

able to gather herself. "You know, you have to stop kissing me."

"I do?"

Mia nodded and after a few seconds, reluctantly, Adam agreed. "Okay."

"We're still friends, right?" she asked.

"Oh, yeah," he said. "Friends."

Chapter Twelve

"PASS THE ONION rings," Lilly said, grabbing the basket that came her way. "I swear Mrs. Rinaldi should go to heaven just for these rings."

"And the mac and cheese," Mia added. "It's a dream, even though I'm sure it won't look like a dream on my ass."

"Your ass is perfect," Fiona said. "Stop bitching about it, or I'm going to have to hate you."

"Since I've sworn off men, I couldn't care less about my ass. It's liberating." With that, Jordan bit into her house special burger. Mayo and ketchup slipped out the back of the monstrous sandwich and Jordan rolled her eyes in delight as she slipped into a food coma.

Looking around the table, Mia couldn't remember consuming more food, all of it rich and fattening, or having a better conversation. Her mother would have a heart attack if she'd been there, but not before she reminded Mia of what the calories would cost her. Which is why hearing a comment like Fiona's was different for her. Mia had never been the pretty one.

But what mattered more was feeling like she belonged.

She had her family, she had friends—in short, Mia had a life. Ben had been her first consideration when she'd made the move to Long Island, but Compass Cove had been good for both of them. The mid-week lunch with the girls was such a treat, and it helped take Mia's mind off the fact that she had a meeting with the lawyer that afternoon about the adoption.

Mia took a bite of her mac and cheese and stopped mid-chew when the door to the café opened. It was the middle of the lunch rush and she shouldn't have noticed yet another customer walk into the busy restaurant, but this guy was something. He was tall, broad, and so gorgeous it should be criminal. Six-two and with muscles that screamed to be touched, he was wearing khaki cargos, a plain white t-shirt that spanned his chest, and his biceps bulged out of the sleeves. The face was a work of art. All clean lines and great bone structure, he had dark hair, dark eyes and the most wonderful scruff. If something was off in the picture at all, it was that the man was using a cane, which made Mia think he might be military.

All she could do was sigh. "Oh, my…"

"What's wrong with you?" Fiona wondered. Then she turned and her eyes locked on the guy, who was talking with a table of old men. "Good Lord. I think my ovaries just exploded."

"Right?" Mia said. "He's a god."

Lilly, who'd been concentrating on the onion rings, looked up—and within seconds was out of her chair and hurtling toward the man. At first, he was stunned to get an armful of excited woman, but once he recognized Lilly, his embrace became warm and familiar. And if he wasn't good looking enough before, he smiled, and Mia felt her toes curl.

Lilly linked arms with him and walked Hot Guy back to their table. Fiona probably should have wiped the drool off her chin, Mia was reminding herself to breathe, and Jordan ate her burger in big messy bites.

"Girls, this is Nick Rinaldi. Nick and my brother Luca were best friends in high school. Nick, my friends, Mia, Fiona, and Jordan."

He smiled again and nodded his greeting and then focused his eyes on Jordan, who had barely looked up from her lunch.

"Good burger?" he asked.

Jordan, her mouth full, finally swallowed. When she looked up into Nick's face, everyone could clearly hear her intake of breath. Yeah, she was impressed. "Uh, yes. It's excellent. Very good."

There was a blush creeping into her cheeks, and Nick grinned. Even embarrassed, and eating like a trucker, Jordan was stunning. Tall, lean, and blonde, her Northern European roots could not be denied. Neither could her embarrassment when Nick reached out, picked up a napkin, and dabbed at the corner of her mouth.

"You have a little mayo right there."

There was more blushing from Jordan and more grinning from Nick.

Snatching the napkin from him, she finished the job herself. "Thank you. I got it."

At that point, there was nothing left to say. The hormones circling the table had rendered all of them speechless, Jordan most of all.

"Nice to meet you, ladies," he said. "But if I don't find my Nona soon, she's going to box my ears."

Lilly gave him one more hug. "I'm glad you're home. Call me soon."

Returning the affection, Nick kissed her on the cheek. "I will."

Watching him walk away was almost as much fun as looking at his face—the view was phenomenal.

"My God," Fiona said. "He's—I don't have words."

Jordan had folded her arms on the table and rested her head there. "I made a fool of myself. He laughed at me."

Lilly laughed. "I think he thought you were cute. Oh, and you have a fry in your hair, right there..." She went to grab it and Jordan slapped her hand away.

"I can't believe this."

Fiona leaned in. "Since you've sworn off men, it shouldn't be a problem."

Jordan groaned, and that's when Mia thought about Nick's story. "What happened to him, Lilly?"

"Nick was a navy doctor. When he graduated he did his internship, went on to specialize in pediatrics, as well as trauma and emergency medicine. His last stint was at a military hospital in Afghanistan."

"He's hardcore," Fiona said.

"Totally. He's done four tours overseas and two on ships. This last one, when he was wounded…" Lilly paused. "The first report we got was that they didn't think he was going to make it."

"How was he wounded?" Jordan asked.

"He was helping some Red Cross volunteers who were administering vaccinations to local children when an insurgent burst into the clinic and started shooting." None of them said a word and Lilly continued. "Nick was in a rear treatment room, and instead of getting out a back door, he grabbed his gun and ran up front to help. He got the shooter, but not before the bastard killed six people, and shot Nick."

"He saved them," Jordan whispered. "Like an honest-to-goodness hero."

"Yup," Lilly said. "A hero. He had a ton of surgeries, was in and out of the hospital and rehab for the last six months. He's recovering well, as you could see. The only thing he's still dealing with is his hip and the emotional toll. Four children died before he could stop the guy. But ten others survived because he was there."

"Those poor babies," Mia said. "That poor man."

Mia thought about men like Nick and wondered what made them tick. No doubt he was a special breed, but at his core, he wasn't so different from Adam. Physical, confident, protective. While Adam wasn't running after armed insurgents—there was no comparison there—Mia had no doubt he'd protect those he loved without having to think about it.

"Mia?" Lilly snapped her fingers in front of Mia's face. "Jeez! Daydream much?"

"Sorry. I was thinking."

"About?" Fiona said.

"Men like Nick. Who will risk everything for what they care about, what they believe in."

"The kind of man you want to marry," Jordan said wistfully, glancing at the kitchen door where Nick had disappeared. "Not like the self-centered mama's boys who don't think about anyone but themselves."

Once again, all of them were silent. Jordan's comment certainly applied to her broken engagement, and Mia thought about Noah. While he certainly wasn't as bad as Jordan's ex, he didn't think about much outside his own little world, and for her it meant acknowledging that he didn't particularly care for Ben. There was no overt dislike, but he didn't connect with him, and when she told Noah she was seeing the lawyer about an adoption, he didn't understand the need. He didn't get it.

He didn't get her.

MIA FELT GOOD when she arrived back at campus from her visit with the lawyer. Sort of. On one hand, she was happy at how easy the adoption would be since she was Ben's legal guardian. Sadly, because her parents were never mentioned as custodians, there was no father, and her sister had passed, Mia was all Ben had. Legally adopting him wouldn't be a problem.

When she called her mother before she left the lawyer's office, she knew there would be some upset. Before the accident, her father had suggested the adoption, treating it as an almost inevitable step. Her mother, however, had an entirely different opinion. The call confirmed nothing had changed; her mother flipped. Mia had tuned out most of what Mom had said because she had no intention of changing her mind, but her mother's final words were that Mia was causing her to relive Sara's death all over again. Didn't she understand that Mia lived her sister's death every day? Raising Ben was a constant reminder that Sara was gone. The adoption was for Ben, for the child Sara left, so he could have a more normal life.

And on that level, Mia should be happy. Ben wouldn't have to explain why he lived with his aunt and his great-grandmother; he wouldn't have to answer questions about his mother. She would be his mother, and that would be it.

Driving over to the practice field, she wondered about Ben's time with the team. He'd been going for over a month and she knew everything was going fine, but she liked watching the team. She liked watching how Ben was a part of things.

When she emerged from her car, which was once again parked next to Adam's truck, Mia wondered where the sun had gone? It had been a nice day. Now—not so much. Making her way over to the small set of bleachers, she climbed to the top and settled in, spreading out a towel she'd found in the back seat of the Honda. It was 5:30, which meant there was another half an hour of practice. There was a fine drizzle falling, and the darker clouds rolling in from the west told her it was going to get worse.

Trying not to think about the storm that was coming, Mia took in her surroundings. She'd spent more time sitting in the stands the past month than she had in her whole life. Between baseball practice and games, and the college's games, Mia was getting comfortable at athletic events. She even liked going. She liked the camaraderie and the excitement. But more than anything, she liked seeing Ben happy.

Of course, going to games also meant Mia could see Adam.

A rush of guilt washed through her. Noah was coming over tonight to have dinner, and she was thinking about Adam. When didn't she think about Adam? The man was like a disease. He'd gotten into her system and she didn't know what she could do to get him out. She had wanted to give things with Noah a chance to develop, but Adam, and the effect he had on her, was always in the back of her mind.

And here she was watching his every move.

The communication between the team and their coach was impressive. There were times that it was almost wordless, other times she heard Adam's voice clear as day, and times when his team gathered around him and she could see him instructing. Ben was next to him the whole time, holding his binder and listening intently. He was as much a part of the team as anyone else. There was a pat on the back from one of the players; he was asked to hold something for a coach, and he was as willing as she'd ever seen him. He needed this. He needed a man in his life. Watching Ben get high fives and fist bumps as the players left the field, Mia realized he had fifty men in his life, and the one that was about to toss the football around with him was making a huge impact.

Adam caught sight of her, then motioned to Ben to hold on before he jogged in her direction. He looked like such a jock with his nylon windbreaker, shorts, mussed hair and dirty knees. Mia's heart flopped around in her chest, unable to find a steady beat. He smiled as he got closer and set one foot on the lowest row on the bleachers.

"Hey," he said, his deep voice warming her skin like a gentle caress. "You mind if we throw a few?"

"Nope. I'll wait."

Adam nodded and smiled again. Mia melted. She envisioned herself turning into a puddle of Mia-goo right before his eyes. God, she was pathetic. She stayed where she was and watched as Adam directed Ben. On Adam's count, Ben took off down field. Adam dropped back, set his feet, and threw the football. It launched from his hand, spinning in the air in a rising arc. It was like a missile heading right for Ben's back. Mia inhaled sharply—and then at exactly the right moment, Ben cut to his right, turned, and plucked the ball from the air. His hands wrapped around it and he never missed a step. When he didn't get clocked with the ball, Mia felt her body relax, and then she stood in awe.

Adam was only focused on Ben and smiled at him as he ran toward him. Damn. He really was good at this. The two of them retrieved a half a dozen balls and then Adam ran down the field. He was about forty yards away from Ben, and one after another, Ben threw the footballs at Adam's moving target. He was dead on every time. Adam threw a few of the balls back, which Ben caught easily and stuffed in a big mesh bag. Ben, looking bigger than she ever remembered, looked up, and let her know with one contented look that she'd done the right thing.

ADAM SHOULD HAVE waved and walked away. But no. As much as he willed himself to go back to his office, he found himself crossing the field and climbing the bleachers, taking the steps two at a time.

It didn't help that she looked so freaking cute. She was wearing a short, belted jacket, a bucket hat, and she carried an umbrella. Her hair looked curlier than usual and there was something about her face that looked both sad and totally kissable at the same time.

"Hey," he said. "Get off work early?"

"No, I had a meeting with an attorney, so I took the day off."

That got his back up. A lawyer? "Is everything okay? Why do you need a lawyer?"

Mia bit her lip and looked at him through her lashes. He felt some minor explosions rip through his system as he looked in her eyes.

"I'm not in trouble, if that's what you're asking." She shrugged and leaned in like she was letting him in on a secret. "I'm going to adopt Ben."

Adam felt his heart creep to his throat. Up until recently, he could barely take care of himself, and this woman was going to officially become a mother to a boy on the verge of puberty.

"Seriously?" He adjusted his body and stretched his arm out behind her. "That's..." He hesitated, "I don't know what to say."

"It will make everything easier, mostly for Ben. He won't have to explain me anymore. I'll just be his Mom."

And everyone will think she was a single teenage mother, but somehow, he doubted that mattered to Mia at all. "How does he feel about that?"

Mia smiled softly. "He's happy about it. He always

wanted to call me Mommy when he was little, but my mother freaked out about it. She's not too pleased about the adoption."

"Why not?"

"Mom said it's like making her relive Sara's death all over again."

Adam whistled softly through his teeth. "That's a heavy guilt trip."

"She'd better get over it. The adoption is right for Ben. That's all that matters."

Once again, Adam saw the motivation for everything Mia did. Ben. The kid had her heart and soul, and Adam couldn't get over how she was so focused on doing what was best for him. She'd rearranged her whole life, and not just once, but over and over. Could he have done that? Could he have been that selfless? He doubted it. It had taken him thirty-seven years to become a guy who was worthy to talk to her. "You're doing right by him. He's happy."

"He loves being here. This and baseball make him very happy. I'm glad the meeting went well, because when he left for school this morning he was pretty angry with me."

"Why?"

"He has a make-up game on Sunday, and I have to work from ten to three. My friend from work is going to watch him, we trade babysitting when one of us has to work, but she has two little kids and can't take him to his game."

"What time?"

"It's at 2:30."

"I could take him." Adam spoke without thinking.

She was stunned at his offer, and Adam liked that he could throw her off her game a little. "I couldn't ask you to do that."

Adam smiled. "Why not? I don't mind."

"Adam, you don't have to. Having Ben here in the afternoons is great, but really, it's already above and beyond."

Now Adam was quiet as he to understand what was going on in her pretty head. He couldn't decide if she was too independent to take his help, or if being around him still made her nervous. They'd definitely had a moment when he'd had dinner at her house the other night, but she was still trying to keep him at arm's length. He really did want to help, and he had to find a way to let her know that.

"I don't mind," he repeated. She was looking down and fidgeting with her umbrella, and it bothered Adam that she was still hesitating. "You don't believe me, do you?"

"It's not that. I just don't understand." She looked at him with eyes that were almost liquid. Something was swimming around in there, and he wanted her to know that she had no reason to worry about him. "You're going to be tired from the week. You'll probably go see your grandma, I mean why…"

"Why do I want to do it?"

Mia chewed on those gorgeous lips and his desire surged. *Damn.* Either he had to learn to control himself or she had to stop doing that. *Focus*, he thought. "Look, I like Ben." He paused so he could think this through. "I like you. We're friends. And…" He took her hand in his and fell into those beautiful brown eyes. "Friends help each other."

There was a little whoosh of breath and then he heard an audible sigh. He'd gotten to her. Did he really want to do this? Did he want to keep her from getting serious about Noah, because at that moment he knew he could. If he were honest, Adam knew he wanted her for himself, but what he didn't know was if he had the nerve to be the guy she needed him to be. He just didn't know. All he was sure about was that he didn't want to hurt her.

"Thank you so much. I don't know what to say."

He squeezed her hand. "Tell me what you need me to do on Sunday."

MIA AND ADAM hashed out the plan for Ben's time with him on Sunday. It was a lot for her to take in, and even after being in Compass Cove for a few months, Mia was still experiencing a bit of a culture shock. People around here were so nice. Everyone helped each other, and the guarded city girl in Mia was having a hard time making sense out of all this small-town kindness.

But Adam was the enigma. On one hand, he treated her like she really mattered to him, like he cared about her, and about Ben...but she still hadn't forgotten how she felt the night he stood her up. As Adam sat with her going over his day with Ben, she saw her nephew emerge from the field house. Whatever Mia thought about Sunday's new plan, Ben was going to love this.

He ran across the field and bounded up the bleachers in a few quick steps. Adam wasn't holding her hand anymore, but his fingers found a way to brush against hers, and his thigh was always pressed close, giving off intense heat. God, she had to clear her head. Clear *him* out of her head. Whenever Adam was nearby she couldn't do anything but think about him, about how he felt under her hands...

"Aunt Mia? Did you see the lawyer?"

"Huh?" Ben was talking. Crap. "Uh. Yes. I did."

"Is everything okay?"

"Fine," she said. "Perfect. The adoption won't be any problem. He's filing the paper work in the next few days."

Ben smiled and looked at Adam. "Did she tell you?"

"She told me. You're a lucky kid."

Ben nodded, and as Adam reached out and patted the boy's arm, he broached another subject. "So, I hear you have a baseball game on Sunday."

"Yeah, but I can't go." He put his head down and tried not to let his disappointment show. "It's an important game."

Adam looked at her and nodded, pushing Mia to tell him.

"Ben, Coach said he would bring you to your game on Sunday. I'll meet you there when I get off work."

"Really?"

"Yeah," Adam replied. "Is that okay with you?"

Ben nodded. He was struck dumb by the idea, but Mia could tell he was more than okay with it.

"Thanks, Coach. That'll be awesome. Thanks."

"No problem." Adam rubbed his hands together and smiled. "So, are you guys hungry? We could grab some dinner."

Mia felt her heart break a little at his request, because she had to tell him no when she wanted to tell him yes. "Adam, I have plans tonight." Her voice came out on a hoarse whisper. She never expected this to sting the way if did.

He nodded, and when he looked in her eyes, he seemed to understand. "No problem."

"I'm sorry, I–"

Adam stood and pulled her to her feet, then placed a finger on her lips. Looking to his right, he saw Ben had left the bleachers and was on the field.

"Mia, I messed up with you. Don't apologize."

She looked down at their hands, which were still joined. She hated that he messed up. He scared her to death, but she still would rather be scared with him than safe with Noah. He seemed to sense what she was thinking, because when she looked up he was grinning at her.

"But if you *want* to break your date, I won't complain.

I'd love to take you out."

Once again, her breath hitched. He had that effect on her. God, how she wanted to call Noah and tell him not to come over. She wanted to be with Adam, but she also had to be realistic. "Will you mess up again?"

His face froze and his eyes locked on hers. After what felt like an eternity, Adam's hand came up and his thumb gently grazed her cheek. "I like you a lot, Mia. More than I should, probably, but I don't know how to do this thing." He motioned back and forth between them. "I don't want to hurt you, and I could."

Mia nodded, the disappointment weighing her down. After a few seconds, Adam let go of her hand. "Have a good time tonight."

"Thanks." She took a step down the wet bleachers, and her little leather flats betrayed her; her foot slipped. But before she fell, Adam's arms wrapped around her waist, and he hauled her up. It was only seconds, but she went from nearly falling down the steel bleachers to being pulled against his chest and enveloped in his arms. She'd dropped her umbrella, and now that it was really raining, the two of them were getting drenched. Adam didn't move, but his eyes searched her face until he fixed his gaze on her mouth.

He wanted to kiss her. And Mia would let him do it without any objection.

The warmth coming off his body was messing with her head, and Mia couldn't stop herself from pressing into him.

It was pouring now, the rain coming down in buckets, when a crack of thunder finally brought them both back to earth.

"Oh, my God," he said. "You're soaked."

Not giving her time to object, Adam scooped her up and took off toward the field house. Ben had sheltered himself under an overhang, and he laughed as Adam ran across the field with her in his arms. She was sure she squealed as he cut around the biggest puddles. He was fast, and holding her extra weight didn't seem to slow him down at all. Drinking in the way he smiled at her when they were finally under some shelter, Mia realized she was falling for him. She was already halfway there.

Adam looked at Ben, who was smiling himself. "Go inside and get a few towels, please."

He lowered her to the ground and Mia found she couldn't catch her breath. Looking up at Adam, his eyes sparkling, his smile wide and water dripping off his hair, Mia didn't even try to stop herself. Without thinking, she launched herself at him, kissing him like she'd die if she didn't.

If Adam minded the kiss, he didn't show it.

He dove into it with the same hunger she did, pulling her against his wet body, letting his lips and tongue explore, and that's when Mia heard herself moan. She gave in completely, because he made her feel so good. He pulled off her hat and his hands plunged into her hair. When he said her name, Mia stood on her tiptoes to get closer to him.

"God, you're all wet," he said against her hair.

"You have no idea," she whispered back, and as soon as she said it she froze, opened her eyes, and looked at Adam's very amused expression. "Did I just say that out loud?'

Grinning, he kissed the corner of her mouth, and then nibbling her lower lip so seductively it tied her insides in knots. "You sure did," he crooned. "Now what should we do about that?"

Mia stepped out of his arms and backed away. He was too hot, too much for her. "God, I go crazy when you're around. What's wrong with me?"

Giving her a long hard look, Adam leaned against a pillar that was supporting the roof of the entryway. "I'm glad I'm not the only one. But for the record, you kissed me that time."

Mia turned and saw Ben standing by the door. He was holding clean white towels and looking at the two of them like they were out of their minds. Mia focused on Adam, who turned his head and smiled at Ben. "Thanks for bringing those out, pal. Why don't you go help Lou with the equipment for a couple of minutes?"

Ben handed her a towel and then handed one to Adam. "Are you two okay?"

"Fine!" she shot out. "Just fine."

"Go help Lou."

Ben turned and went inside, leaving her alone in the rain with a big, sexy, wet man. A man who turned her brain into mush. Mia pressed her back into the wall and covered her face. "Oh, my God. I'm a slut."

"What?" His face screwed up and disbelief flashed in his eyes. "How do you figure that?"

"I told you! When you're around I go crazy. When you touch me I—I—" She stopped and looked away. "I can't control myself. I can't. All these years, and who knew? I'm a slut."

Adam came to where she was standing, and settled himself against her. She could feel the bulge in his shorts and she had to remind herself not to touch him. Adam let his thumb brush the wetness off her cheek. "Take it from a man who's been around, you are no slut, Mia. And I can't control myself around you either."

"But even *you* said you're not a good bet. Why do I act this way around you?"

He laughed and continued to brush his thumb over her cheek. "Your skin is so soft. All of you is soft. It makes me nuts. But you're involved with someone else, and I should stay away from you."

With that, he kissed her again, this time sweetly. And Mia melted into him. He held her and whispered in her ear, "I know who I am. I've spent years coming to grips with it, but just because a guy has an Ivy League Ph.D. doesn't make *him* a good bet."

Looking down, she nodded.

"And you aren't a slut. Not even a little. Okay?"

"Okay."

Chapter Thirteen

I F EVER THERE was a perfect fall day, this was it.

Cool and crisp, the sky was blue and everywhere he looked, the trees blazed with October color. The park, which sat on acres of waterfront land, was probably one of the best kept secrets on Long Island. He had no doubt that if more people knew about the ball fields and soccer fields that boasted a water view, real estate in the hamlet would sky-rocket in value.

Adam sat in the bleachers with Joe, Susan, and the other parents from Ben's team, and rather than feeling awkward, as he expected—the single guy among the families—he was completely at ease. When he arrived, no one even raised a brow when he walked over with Ben. The fathers engaged him in conversation as they stood near the backstop, watching the kids warm up, and the moms asked after Mia.

He liked feeling as if he were part of Mia and Ben's family, and the thought drove home how important she was to him. He hoped she felt the same, because while he respected her right to make her own decisions, after what happened between them the other day, he was going to do his damnedest to make sure Noah Connolly was nothing more than a blip on the screen.

Connolly seemed like a decent guy, but he wasn't right for Mia. She had too much fight for Noah, too much raw energy.

Hell, Adam didn't know if *he* could deal with it, but he wanted to give it a shot.

Looking around, he remembered when he played baseball as a kid. Always in the spring, because fall was reserved for football, he recalled seeing his family in the stands cheering him on. After his father died, his family made sure someone was there for each kid when there was a game or event. Someone was always in the audience or in the stands and he, his brothers, and his sister knew that security their whole life.

Understanding what his mom went through was part of what drove him regarding Ben. While he was sure Mia's nana was a help to her, he could see why Mia hesitated asking for help. What he'd learned from Ben was that the family was all about self-reliance. Mia had only started to realize it was okay to lean on others since moving to Compass Cove.

Spending a Sunday afternoon with Ben was no hardship; knowing Mia would be by soon made things even better. She was so much more than a friend to him, and the kiss outside the field house a few days ago sealed the deal for him.

Looking down at his folded hands, Adam acknowledged,

for the first time in his life, that he wanted someone in his life. Someone to share things with. Someone who was more than just a warm body.

Joe sat next to him and handed him a cold can of soda from the concession stand. His friend had been quiet about his relationship with Ben and Mia, but Adam wanted to know what he thought, and Joe would never volunteer his two cents without being asked.

Unless it was about football, Joe didn't give unsolicited advice.

The game was in the third inning, and when he last checked the time it was almost three. Ben's team had just taken the field and Adam saw he'd donned the catcher's equipment. This morning, when Mia dropped him off, he sat on the floor with the dog and some hot chocolate and told Adam about every kid on the team and about the positions he played—which seemed to be everything but pitcher and right field.

"Ben's good," Joe said.

Adam nodded and let the cold drink slide down his throat. "I think that kid can play any sport. He's a born athlete."

"Is Mia adjusting to life with a jock? I know there were some reservations."

Adam let out a breath and leaned back on the riser behind him. "I think she wants to do what's best for him. She's pretty relaxed about the sports thing."

"Relaxed is good. Susan likes her a lot. All the women do." Joe leaned toward Adam. "I think they wanted to hate her cause she's so freakin' gorgeous, but they can't. Susan said she's 'sweet'."

Adam agreed with the assessment, especially since he'd used it himself. "She is."

Then, for some reason, Joe chuckled under his breath.

"What's funny about that?"

"Well, she didn't look real sweet when she was grinding against you during that kiss the other day."

Adam's stomach rolled. If Joe had seen that, other people probably did too. And with just a mention, he was suddenly reliving the way Mia had felt during that kiss. Her whole body molded to him, and every move she made, every touch, turned him on.

He didn't know if she was grinding against him, though. She was stuck to him pretty good, and her body did this little wiggle thing. Breathing out, Adam avoided looking at his friend. Okay, so maybe she was grinding. All he knew was that the kiss was hot, and if he didn't want to take her to bed fifteen kinds of ways before, he did after.

And he knew he didn't want Noah Connolly's hands on her.

Adam struggled to shake the vision and the feel of Mia from his head and drag his attention back to something safe, the game. The other team's slugger had gotten a triple and was leading off third.

The kid was a gorilla. Ben was big for his age, but the locomotive-posing-as-a-kid who was on third was freaking huge. The players in this division were ten and eleven years old—this one looked like he could vote.

The count was three and one, with one out, and the boy at the plate was small and skinny, with thick, coke-bottle glasses. No one would take him for a dangerous hitter, but apparently, he had a knack for placing the ball exactly where he wanted it.

Adam trained his eyes on Ben, who moved with such fluidity, even in the bulky equipment, that he made playing the game look easy. Unlike a lot of boys his age, gangly and uncoordinated, Ben had command of his arms and legs, his movements were precise.

The pitcher wound up, delivered, and there was a crack. Watching the flight of the ball, it looked like it was going to drop in for a neat little single and bring the runner at third home. But in a flash, Gabe Rand, who was playing center-field, moved like lightning, stuck out his hand and snagged the ball right before it hit the grass. Joe was on his feet screaming and beaming like a proud dad.

But in a split second, everything changed. The runner made a snap decision to tag up at third, and even though his coach was motioning for him to hold up, the kid ran toward home.

Gabe reacted in a way every coach hopes a kid will react and shot the ball at Ben, who instinctively blocked the plate.

At the same moment Ben caught the ball, the giant running from third base barreled into him.

As the boys made contact, everything seemed to go in slow motion. People jumped from their seats, kids reacted in the field, helmets flew and dirt clouded the air. It was like a scene from a movie, wordless and quiet.

There was a loud *crack,* and a blood curdling scream. What Adam saw after that would be burned in his memory forever. Ben was on the ground, screaming, his upper body thrashing around and his legs—his legs seemed dead—moving only because they were attached to the rest of him. The coaches and umpires surrounded him, and without another thought, Adam jumped from the bleachers and ran to Ben's side.

He'd seen pain like this. Pain so raw and so new that the person couldn't process what was happening. But seeing Ben like this was a whole new kind of terrifying.

Adam crouched down next to him, reaching out to brush some dirt off his face, the contact letting Ben know someone was there for him.

"Ben, try to calm down. Don't move."

Ben nodded and hissed a breath out through his teeth as he lay back and closed his eyes. He was quiet for a second, and when a small sob escaped, Adam's heart lurched.

One of the coaches called 911 while another folded a jacket and put it under Ben's head. The goal, until the EMTs arrived, was to keep him still and calm. Fortunately, the firehouse wasn't far from the ball field.

"I want my mom," Ben whispered.

Stroking the hair from his forehead, Adam didn't know what to say. The kid was asking for his dead mother. The pain must have been blinding.

"Is she on her way here, Coach?"

"Huh?" Adam examined Ben's face, and he realized he was talking about Mia. His mother.

Someone had to call her. Just as he took his cellphone out of his pocket, the ambulance arrived.

The EMT's made quick work of Ben's pants and when his leg was visible, it was obvious that it was bad. Adam had seen his share of injuries, and if he had to make a guess this one was surgery worthy. Ben's leg was deformed and the only good thing was that the bone hadn't broken through the skin.

Joe was next to Adam as Ben was examined and carefully put on the stretcher. "Do you want Susan to call Mia?" he asked.

It would be so much easier to let someone else call, but Adam couldn't do that to her. She was going to freak out, regardless, but he had a feeling he could keep her a little calmer if he called himself. He wanted her to know he'd take care of Ben 'til she arrived. That her son would be safe.

Safe with him.

"I'll call her."

With his phone still sitting in his palm, he slid his fingers over the touchscreen, wondering what he was going to say to her. How was he going to keep *her* calm?

Then her voice was in his ear.

"ADAM, I'M JUST walking out of the library I should be there in about ten minutes."

"Mia." All she heard was him exhale, and it put her instantly on alert. Something was wrong.

"What is it?" The tone in his voice was one thing, but suddenly, she could feel it.

"Ben's been hurt. He's going to be okay, but he's going to the hospital."

"Oh, my God. What happened?" Visions of him getting hit in the head, of brain damage, flooded her mind.

"He broke his leg, and it's pretty bad."

On the move now, she mentally made a checklist of what she needed to do. Did she have her insurance card? Probably. She'd have to call people, but first she had to get to Ben and make sure he wasn't scared.

"Where should I meet you?" Going into crisis mode, Mia knew she'd be fine. She'd be fine until the crisis was over, and then she'd break.

"They're taking him to Harbor Hospital. Honey, I think he's going to need surgery."

Harbor Hospital. Surgery. *Shit.* Calm, Mia. Breathe. Focus on the problem at hand. "Do you know a good orthopedist?"

"The best. Want me to call him?"

She sniffled and whispered, "Yes."

"Okay. I'll take care of it." He paused, and she could tell he was worried, too. But Mia had to admit that as scared as she was, she knew Ben was in good hands. Adam was with him and she wasn't as worried as she could have been. "They're putting him in the ambulance," Adam said. "I'm going to jump in there with him."

Mia felt a tremor in her stomach as she thought about her child being so badly hurt, he needed an ambulance. "Take care of him, Adam."

"You know I will. You'll probably beat us. See you when we get there."

When the connection was broken, Mia let out a shaky breath. Broken bones. Ambulances. Surgery. She had to remember to breathe. It seemed every time she turned around, something changed. Two months ago, she was dealing with Ben having fights at school, now he was hurt. Badly. When she looked at her phone, there were three text messages from different team parents offering help in whatever way was needed. Nana would be a rock, as she always was. They'd get through this.

Just as she slid the key into the ignition, her phone rang. Her stomach turned when she looked at the caller ID and saw Noah's name.

"Hello?" Her voice was short, but who could blame her?

"Hi, have you given any thought to dinner?"

"Dinner?"

"We have a date, right?"

Holy crap. He didn't know what happened and she forgot about everything. "Noah, I have to cancel. Ben was hurt at his game. I'm on my way to the hospital."

There was a long pause. "Oh, oh, well, that's fine."

Fine? She thought. Of course it was freaking fine, her son was severely injured. "Yeah, I have to go."

"After you get him settled, call me, maybe we can get a late supper."

Mia knew this wasn't right. This was one more example of why her relationship with Noah was going nowhere, and she couldn't let it go any further. He was nice, he was smart, and he was good-looking and charming, but he was never going to be the guy for her. "Noah, I won't be calling tonight. Ben is probably having surgery and I'll be with him."

"I just thought... I mean..."

"Noah, no."

"No?"

"How can you expect a call when I'm going to be taking care of my son?"

"I don't know. I just thought... I'm sorry."

"Look, we are just not on the same page here. It's not you; I don't doubt you're a great guy, but I have different priorities."

"Wow, a variation of the 'It's not you, it's me' line."

"I don't know what to say. I know a lot of people thought we were perfect for each other, but my heart isn't in this, and I don't think yours is either."

He sighed. "You're probably right about that."

Impatient, Mia still tried to be polite. "I have to go, but I am sorry."

"Take care of your son, Mia. I hope he's okay."

"Thanks."

As she pulled out of the library lot, Mia's thoughts returned to where they belonged—with Ben.

Chapter Fourteen

ADAM SAT IN the ambulance wondering how Ben was holding it together. Remembering the pain he'd been in after his car accident, he was amazed the kid wasn't screaming his head off. God knows, he did. He was a grown man and he wailed like a just-smacked newborn. But Ben was lying there, oxygen mask on his face, breathing slowly and forcing his eyes shut to defend against the pain. He was trying so damned hard to be brave, but there was that lone tear track that let Adam know Ben was scared to death.

"We're almost there, pal." Adam touched Ben's shoulder and he nodded, opening his eyes and revealing every emotion.

"Is Aunt Mia…"

He barely got the words out, but Adam was quick to reassure him. "I talked to her. She's meeting us at the hospital."

Ben nodded again and looked around as the sensation of the ambulance slowing and then stopping got his attention. A small lurch made Ben wince, but the telltale beeping made it clear they had arrived at the hospital and were backing into the bay. Adam had never been so relieved in his life. All he wanted was for Ben to get treated. Seeing him in this kind of pain, this afraid, and not being able to do anything about it was torture.

When the doors flew open and he had a second to adjust to the light, he saw Mia, her hair being lifted by the breeze, her knuckles white from the tension, and still looking more beautiful than she should, considering she was probably scared out of her mind.

He hopped out of the ambulance and went to her, wordlessly letting his hand settle softly between her shoulder blades. Mia didn't hesitate, she turned into him and rested her head on his shoulder. That was the only signal Adam needed; he folded her in his arms and held her as the EMTs readied Ben for the move out of the back. Her body curved against his and all Adam wanted to do was take away her pain and worry.

"He's going to be okay," he said against her temple.

Of course, right then, Ben cried out, and Mia broke toward the ambulance. "I'm here, Ben."

Desperate to get to him, she wasn't paying any attention to what was happening. Dropping his hand on her shoulder, Adam guided her a few steps away. "Mia, honey, step back so they can get him out."

Mia stepped away momentarily, only to bolt to Ben's side once the stretcher was on the ground. Adam watched as she looked him over, stroking the hair from his face, looking at the cut by his brow, and finally settling on the splint wrapped around his right leg. After taking it all in, Adam watched her quiet her own fears and give Ben the comfort he needed. She looked in his eyes, touched his cheek, and whispered in his ear. Ben nodded, and when Mia smiled at him softly, Adam felt the grip around his heart tighten.

The EMTs took their places alongside the stretcher and Mia followed as they brought Ben into the emergency room. Standing back, Adam looked toward the parking lot and to the harbor beyond, leaning against the cement pillar supporting the overhang.

Why was he in knots over this? He'd been to this hospital with injured players over the past few years. He'd waited until family could get here so some kid who was away from home wouldn't be alone. He knew the drill.

Once Mia arrived, he should have relaxed; but unlike when the patient was a kid on his team, there was no way he was going to leave. Mia and Ben were too important to him. And while he'd fought these feelings his whole life, there was no denying he was falling for her. Fast and hard.

There were so many things running through his head, he didn't realize how much time had passed until the ambulance crew came out with the empty stretcher.

"You still here, Coach?" The EMT who sat in the back with Ben walked over when they'd finished putting away the gear.

"Yeah, figured I'd wait around a bit." The truth was, Adam didn't know what the hell he was doing, but he didn't want to leave.

"They were going to take the kid to x-ray, and the doc said something about a C-T scan since he got his bell rung."

All he could think was that Mia must have been out of her mind, and truthfully, Adam was more worried than he'd ever been. He extended his hand to the tech, who was still standing next to him. "Thanks for everything."

"No problem. Let us know how the kid's doing."

Watching the ambulance pull away, he figured he'd do what he said he was going to do—set himself up in the waiting room in case Mia needed anything. Dragging his hand across the back of his neck, Adam turned and almost ran over Mia.

"What are you doing out here?" she asked.

Was she going to tell him to leave? He tried to read her meaning, but the look on her face didn't convey anger so much as fear. Fear and something else.

"I was just heading to the waiting room."

"Waiting room?"

"Yeah. Do you need something?"

Mia took a breath, grasped his hand. "I need you," she whispered. "Please come back there with me?"

Adam felt the air leave his own lungs as he saw the panic in her eyes, and instinctively, he circled her with his arms. "He's going to be okay."

"They think he might have a head injury, too."

"He was conscious and talking the whole way here. That's a good sign."

"I know," she sniffled. "But, but…"

He held her as she struggled to be brave, struggled to stay calm, understanding there wasn't anything he could say. He could only be with her, offer her comfort. "Come on, let's go back and wait for him."

"You'll stay?"

Adam held her head gently in his hands and locked eyes with her, hoping he could give her some extra strength. "I'll stay."

The relief that washed across her face was so complete, Adam had a hard time keeping his own emotions in check. Whatever any of this meant, it was obvious that he and Mia were a lot more than friends.

NOT KNOWING WAS the worst part. Janet sat restlessly in the waiting room with a few of the parents from Ben's team, wishing she had some news. But she didn't, and she was worried sick.

The last she'd heard from Mia, Adam had called, and Ben was in an ambulance on his way here with a broken leg. He'd been hurt at his game and the break looked bad.

She'd seen Mia for a split second while Ben was having x-rays, but that was it. What surprised her most was that

Adam was nowhere to be seen. Especially considering the way things had been developing between him and her granddaughter.

Technically, she supposed, Noah and Mia were a couple, even though they sure didn't act like it. However, the way Adam looked at her, touched her, joked with her, well, that's what intimacy was built on. Maybe it was good they were trying to be friends. Their comfort level made everything easier between them, while the professor's silly formality pretty much doomed him from the get-go. More than one person had said it: Noah was a very nice man, but they just couldn't see him with Mia.

The only person who disagreed was Mia's mother, and Janet shook her head wondering how a woman could be so out of touch with her child.

"Goodness, what's taking so long," she whispered.

The waiting was grating on everyone, though, and while she sat there, she wondered if she should call Ellen and tell her what happened. She decided against it. There was no way she wanted to catch the crap for Ben playing sports. And her daughter's argument would be crap. Mia was doing the right thing, and Ben was happier than she'd ever seen him.

"Mrs. Lang?"

Janet looked up and standing before her was a smiling, young nurse. "Your granddaughter wanted me to come and get you."

"Oh?" Gathering her things, she didn't question. "Lead

the way." She felt her stomach clutch in response to her nervousness as she followed the nurse through the double doors.

"How is Ben doing?"

"Not bad, considering, and your granddaughter is nervous, but she's been better since her husband got here."

Janet stopped in her tracks. "Her husband?"

The young nurse nodded. "What a gorgeous couple, and he's so great with Ben."

They rounded a final corner, and entered a cubicle. That's when she saw she had no need to worry.

On a stool, situated by Ben's left shoulder, sat Mia. And on the other side of the bed, straddling a chair that was pulled right up to the bedrail, was *her husband*. Adam.

Wow.

"Here they are," the nurse sang. Good lord, Janet thought. It must take a lot of energy to be that young and chipper.

"Your grandmother was chewing off her fingernails, Ben."

"Hey, Nana." Poor baby's voice was weak and sad. "They're taking me to surgery soon."

"Surgery?" Janet looked from Mia to Adam and back to Ben. Not wanting to scare him, she waved off the worry. "And once it's all healed, your leg will be as good as new. Did you meet your doctor?"

"Yes," Ben nodded. "He's one of Coach's friends."

Janet looked to Adam, who filled in the blanks. "Ryan McAndrews."

She recognized the name immediately—another one of her former students. And he was, more than likely, the best orthopedic surgeon in New York. Ben was in good hands.

"You know him, Nana?" Mia asked.

"Yes, and he has a stellar reputation."

"Aww, gee thanks, Mrs. Lang." The deep, gentle voice hadn't changed in twenty years. Ryan had been one of her best students, and now he was going to use those brains and that talent to reassemble Ben's leg.

"You take good care of my great-grandson, doctor."

Ryan smiled the same way he did when he was a kid. Big, warm, and full of confidence. Then he turned that smile on Mia.

If the situation wasn't serious, Janet would have laughed watching Adam squirm as the handsome doctor made moves on her granddaughter.

Remembering her student history, Adam and Ryan had been friends and teammates in high school, but there was always underlying tension. A rivalry. Ryan was the do-good, super-student; a star athlete who found his way to Harvard. Adam was more laidback, a bit of a slacker, and more inclined to find trouble. He didn't lack intelligence, but he knew that while Ryan could have gone anywhere on his academics alone, Adam needed sports to get into a top university.

Now, watching Ryan talk to Mia and Ben from his spot on the opposite side of the bed, Adam looked uncertain. She wondered if he realized how much Mia cared for him. Mia might have been dating Noah, but her heart belonged to Adam.

Janet inched over to him and put her hands on his big shoulders. "I'm glad you were here with her. I was worried."

He looked up into her eyes, and that's when Janet saw the truth. *Holy Schemoly.* There was no denying it. Adam was in love with Mia. He may not have realized it yet, but it was all over his face. Less than two months and this big, tough, hard-living jock was head over heels for her girl.

Nothing could have made Janet happier.

Adam's big hand came up and covered Janet's. He was worried, too. For all his experience, the injuries he'd had, he was scared for Ben—and she suspected, for Mia as well.

But somehow, Janet didn't doubt that it was all going to be okay.

"You ready to take a ride, Ben?"

Unnoticed, a nurse and an orderly had slipped into the cubicle and were getting Ben ready for the move to the operating room.

A knot formed right in her belly.

Adam stood next to her and laid his hand on her back. There was kindness in his touch along with genuine concern. Things she always knew were inside the tough kid, but he was reluctant to show. Traits that made him one of her favorite students, even when he tested every limit.

They both leaned forward and while Janet kissed Ben's forehead, Adam simply patted his shoulder.

"You hang in there, buddy. We'll all be here when you wake up."

"Thanks, Coach. See you later."

Mia walked alongside the gurney and Adam hung back, taking a deep breath and watching as they moved toward the elevator.

"It's going to be a couple of hours for the surgery, but he's going to be fine. I already told Mia, the break looks clean." Ryan looked confident and calm, and that should have reassured her; but this was her great grandson, and logic had left the building.

"Where can we wait?" Janet asked.

"The O-Rs are on the fourth floor. There's a waiting area up there. Mia will be there once we take Ben in. We'll let her stay with him until then."

It was about all Janet could do to nod. "I'm going to tell everyone out in the waiting room what's going on." Turning to Ryan, she continued, "Thank you. I feel better knowing you're taking care of him."

Ryan smiled and gave her a big hug. "I'm glad Adam called me."

"Me, too."

ADAM WATCHED MRS. Lang scoot back to the waiting room before he turned to Ryan. "Thanks again for coming, man."

Ryan took Adam's outstretched hand and nodded. "So, ah, I have to ask… you and Mia?"

Adam thought about the question, wondering if his friend was just curious or if he wanted to make a play for Mia himself.

"Nothing official, but she matters to me. They both do."

Ryan nodded. "Yeah, that's kind of obvious. Good for you."

That was a shocker. "What? No joke? No crack about how she's too good for me?"

Ryan let out a laugh. "Nah, I think you've earned a reprieve. Besides, it looks like she has you on your knees, so that's a big plus in my book."

"That she does."

"I'll talk to you later."

Turning, Ryan left and Adam thought about what had just happened. Since he'd come back to Compass Cove, everything in his life—his priorities, his goals—had changed. Neighbors were kind, protective, and simply knowing a guy like Ryan McAndrews could accept him with someone like Mia proved that people didn't see him in the same way anymore.

He never would have believed it, but coming home had saved him in more ways than he ever imagined.

Chapter Fifteen

AFTER SEEING BEN wheeled into surgery, Mia went to the waiting room, where she found a slew of people waiting for her. There were some parents from the team, Nana, and sitting in a corner was Adam. He locked eyes with her immediately and Mia felt calm, safe. It was centered in her heart and spread through her. God, she was in serious trouble.

Right then she knew jettisoning Noah was the right thing to do. There was no way she should date anyone else when she felt this way about Adam, and unless she was blind and stupid, he was feeling the same.

Without missing a beat, Susan Rand grabbed Mia's hand and dragged her over to the other parents. "What's happening?"

"He's going to be in there a couple of hours. We just have to wait."

"You poor thing. Are you hungry? I can get you a sandwich or…"

Just then, she felt a familiar tingle and warmth. She didn't have to see him to know that Adam was there. His hand settled on her back and he pulled her close.

"Susan, let Mia settle down a little. One of us can get her something later."

"Are you sure, I don't mind..."

"I'm not very hungry right now, but thanks."

Taking charge, Adam led her toward her grandmother, putting a little distance between her and the crowd. It wasn't that Mia didn't love all the support, she did, but she was never one to expose her feelings publicly. Once she sat, Nana's arms looped around her shoulders and Mia leaned in.

"Are you calling your mother?"

"No," Mia said. "I'll call after he's in his room. There's no use in setting her off prematurely."

Nana nodded, understanding full well that this was going to unleash a tirade from her mother, and Mia wanted to avoid it as long as possible. If she could avoid telling her altogether, she would.

"Did the doctor say anything else?"

"Just that it was going to be a long recovery." Now she was questioning everything and turned to Adam. "He's the best, right? You said he's the best."

"He's the best. Ben couldn't be in better hands."

Satisfied with that, Mia turned her attention to what actually happened at the field. All she knew was that there was a collision.

Just the thought of it made her cringe. "I can't imagine how hard he was hit for him to be so badly injured. What happened?"

"It never should have happened, and the other coach was very apologetic. The kid took it on himself to make the run home. He had at least forty pounds on Ben. It was like a truck hitting him."

"They should assign kids to leagues based on height and weight. Age means nothing at this stage."

"You're probably right. I'll bet the kid who hit him is shaving in a year."

Mia tried to laugh, but the whole situation was too scary. Her baby was injured. Badly injured.

"Ben planted his feet and got into position to protect the plate. When the other boy made contact, his leg just snapped."

"Oh, God."

Putting his arm around her, Adam tried to be of some comfort, but it seemed even he wasn't sure what to do. "He's tough. He'll come through fine. And to top it all off, he can tell everyone that he made the out."

"He what? He made the out?"

Adam smiled. "He did. Held onto the ball, which I'm going to bet is one of the first things he asks when he can think clearly."

Smiling herself now, Mia nodded. "You're probably right."

"He's got a lot of spirit. He's going to be okay."

"Listen to Adam, Mia. He's right," urged Janet.

She nodded and thought about Ben's face when he came off the ambulance. She hated that he was in pain, but remarkably, she wasn't second-guessing her decision to let him play. Six months ago, she would have been doing just that, but now she chalked it up to him being an active boy. Yeah, the kid who hit him needed some discipline, but overall, being on a team had been great for Ben.

Adam was the other really good thing.

The silence between them was a little awkward, and she guessed it had something to do with their close encounter after practice the other day. Mia hadn't been able to get the kisses out of her head, and she wondered if Adam was feeling the same thing.

"So, ah," he began. "Is Noah meeting you here?"

"No," she whispered. "He's not." He fixed his gaze on her, one of his eyebrows shooting up. Mia could tell he had questions, but he wasn't going to ask.

However, Nana had no problem asking. "He's not coming? Why?"

"We decided to part ways. It wasn't working out."

"No kidding," Nana mumbled.

"Nana, he's very nice. It's just…"

"Just what? That you two were completely wrong for each other?"

"I don't know about *completely* wrong." At this point she saw Adam was listening, but trying not making it obvious. There was a tiny, self-satisfied tilt at the corner of his mouth.

But it was Nana's piercing stare that got her attention. More explanation was required; unfortunately, Mia didn't have much. "He doesn't get me."

"Doesn't get you?" her grandmother repeated.

"No, and we are done talking about this. Especially here. I get that you're trying to distract me…"

"No, I'm not. I just want to know." Nana folded her arms and shot a quick glance at Adam. "He doesn't *get* you?"

Now she could see Adam was fighting an even bigger smile, because he'd just those words to her not two weeks before.

"Nana!"

"Okay, I'm sorry. I was curious."

"I don't know exactly what I mean, but it wasn't going to work. He's not a bad guy, but… I don't know."

Nana smiled and patted her hand. "It's good you figured that out before it went too far."

"Hmmph. Going too far wasn't the issue." *Crap.* Mia hated when she did that. There was no reason to say certain things aloud, and she did anyway. Nana was stifling a giggle, and Adam was looking away. Mia had just blurted out information about her sex life, or lack of it, and now she wanted to crawl under the chair.

Until she looked back at Adam and the softness of his expression made her heart jump. It was the same face he wore after he kissed her. His eyes smiled, and the curve of his mouth reminded her of how she felt when he touched her.

Immediately, she could feel the stroke of his hands, the gentle pressure of his lips, the sweep of his tongue, and Mia gasped. Right out loud, she gasped.

Adam's smile widened, and her grandmother watched each of their reactions, turning her head side to side, and finally grinning herself. God, Mia hated when she was outnumbered. But just as quickly, Adam's face dropped. Walking toward him was an older woman—a tall, striking brunette with blue eyes and a gentle smile.

"I heard you were here." The woman extended her arms, and when Adam stood, they wrapped each other in a strong hug.

What the hell?

"Hi, Mom."

Mom? This was his mother?

"You promised you'd come and see me, you brat. Do I have to drop in next Sunday? Really early? I'll bring donuts."

"I'll come over." He smiled and shrugged and even winced a little when she slapped his arm. But the whole exchange was playful and lovely, and it made Mia smile.

"So why are you here?" she asked.

Adam ran his hand through his hair and looked at Mia. "That's a little complicated." He stepped around Nana and brought Mia forward toward his mother. Holy shit, was she meeting his mother? She had a kid in surgery and now she had to meet Adam's mother?

"Mom, this is Mia DeAngelis. Her nephew has been

hanging out with the team." He watched his mother's face, and added a little more to the story. "Ben was hurt at his baseball game today. He's in surgery."

"Oh, you poor thing!" Adam's mom came to her instantly, grabbing her hand and sitting down with her. "You must be worried sick. I'm Linda, and if you need anything, let me know."

"Mom is the patient advocate here."

Mia's head was spinning. *Respond, Mia. Say something.* "Thank you. Everyone has been so caring."

"Good to hear. I'll check in with the OR and see if there's any information."

"Oh, you can do that?" Mia looked from Linda to Adam and back.

Patting her hand, Linda stood. "Honey, I can do anything I want. Be back in a few minutes."

ADAM HADN'T EXPECTED to see his mother at the hospital and it wasn't the way he'd thought she'd meet Mia, but she could give them information about Ben, so any discomfort was a moot point.

"I appreciate your mother's help." The way she was twisting her fingers, Adam could see Mia was still fighting waves of panic. Any information his mother could give her would help, but it wasn't going to be enough.

Adam stuffed his hands in his pocket and stood close. He was ready, because Mia was on the verge of breaking.

Once she slumped forward, her elbows on her knees, her head propped in her hands, Adam moved. It was the sniffle and the tremble in her shoulders that sent him to his knee.

Crouching before her, Adam pulled Mia into his arms and held her as the emotions flooded out.

The tears didn't come hard, but softly, and he knew this wasn't about anything except being scared.

"It's going to be okay. It's all going to be okay."

"I know. In my head, I know that. But there's so much I don't know. What's he going to need? How's his recovery going to go? There are so many things I have to think about."

Adam leaned back, but his hand stayed on her shoulder, moving up and down her arm in a gentle motion. Her grandmother was sitting next to her now, rubbing her back.

"You do things one at a time." He grabbed a tissue from a box that was one the table next to her, and blotted at her face. "Don't try to plan it or figure it out all at once."

"Sweetie, Adam's right. Get through one thing at a time."

"I know, but it's not how I work."

"That's how it has to be," Nana said. "Ben's going to look to you for comfort. If you're a basket case, he's going to know."

Mia nodded. Adam released her face and took her hands

in his. They were small and so cold. Fear was swamping her, and the best he could do was offer a shoulder and support. "Try not to worry," he said. "You aren't alone here. You have friends and family to see you both through this."

"I'm not alone," Mia whispered.

"No, you're not." With her grandmother's gentle touch reassuring her and Adam holding her hands, Mia relaxed as the realization set in. Knowing she didn't have to cope with Ben's injury by herself made all the difference. And as the tension drained, her tears stopped.

"Thank you. Thank you both."

Adam made a last swipe near her eyes, and as the wetness touched his fingers, he knew he was going to a place he'd never been with a woman. He'd certainly never expected Mia to have this effect on him when she walked into his office six weeks ago.

Never in a million years.

"Well, I have some news." His mother. His mother was right behind him, and after this was all over he was going to have to tell her everything.

He stood and turned around, making quick eye contact with his mom. He hoped his expression told her not to ask too many questions. Not now. Not today.

"How's Ben?" Mia was on her feet and stepping around him to face his mother.

"Dr. McAndrews said it's going to be a while yet, but everything is going as expected. There are no surprises."

"Okay. That's good."

"The break is bad and needs to be dealt with carefully since Ben is still growing."

"He mentioned that. Okay." Mia glanced over her shoulder at Nana and Adam, looking relieved. Turning back to his mother, she grasped her hand. "Thank you so much."

"My pleasure. I'll check in on you in a little while." His mom took a step away and turned back. "Adam? Could you come with me for a minute?"

"Sure." And like the good son he was, he followed, readying himself for the questions he'd hoped to avoid. Once they were a safe distance away, his mom turned and folded her arms. Yup. She was going to grill him.

"Well?"

"Well what?"

"What's going on with you two? She's lovely, by the way."

"She is."

"You didn't tell anyone you were seeing her again?"

"We're friends. That's all."

"Friends? Adam, honestly. You expect me to believe that?"

"Mom, I swear, until today she was dating one of the new professors at school."

"They broke up?"

"Today."

"Considering the way you two look at each other, that's

probably a good thing."

He took a breath and ran his hand across the back of his neck. He had no comeback for that; the chemistry between him and Mia was undeniable.

"I care about her. I don't know what's going to happen yet."

"Don't screw it up like you did last time."

"Mom…"

"Adam, you don't get a second chance with the love of your life every day. Don't. Screw. It. Up." She poked him in the shoulder for emphasis.

"Love of my life? Mom–"

"Don't be an idiot. I need more grandchildren."

When she kissed him on the cheek and patted his shoulder, he realized his usual excuses weren't going to work. He'd have to tell her the truth.

"I don't know if she'll have me."

"Honey, based on the way she looked at you, she's half in love with you already. All you have to do is let yourself love her back."

His mother walked away, leaving him with something to think about, just like when he was a kid. Then, he was too young and stupid to appreciate her wisdom; now, he took it to heart.

His eyes drifted to Mia, who was in a conversation with Susan Rand and Gabe. His heart squeezed tight at the sight of her.

Love her back. Just love her back.

Chapter Sixteen

A DAM DIDN'T THINK it was possible, but Mrs. Lang had gotten Mia to leave the hospital to go home and get a few hours of sleep. Ben had been out of surgery for about five hours, with the procedure going exactly as planned. When the nurse gave him some medication that would help him sleep through the night, Mia's grandmother, who was a night owl by nature, volunteered to stay with him.

It was a fight, but Adam knew getting her out of there, even for a few hours, would be a good thing. They stopped and had a bite to eat at a diner that was open late, but Mia was so distracted he figured what she needed most was sleep.

He had to stop at home to feed the dog and get some clothes before he took her back to her house. That he didn't want to take her home and wanted to tuck her into his bed was a problem.

He pushed that thought right out of his head with an attack of conscience. He shouldn't be thinking about sleeping with her when she was so distraught. He was never the guy who'd take advantage of an emotionally compromised woman, and he wasn't about to start now. Especially when the woman in question was someone he cared about.

She let out a heavy breath and Adam saw her hand come to her eyes.

"Almost there," he said.

She nodded. "Thank you for... for... everything, Adam. I don't know what I would have done without you there."

"I'm glad I could help."

"Ben was happy to see you when he woke up."

Adam smiled. "And the first thing he said to me was?"

"Coach, did I make the out?" Mia giggled. "Just like you said."

The silence that settled over them was comfortable and Adam loved how he could feel her calming down, even though there were no words.

When they pulled in front of the house, Mia sat up and stared. "This is your house?"

He looked at the well-lit, artfully landscaped cape, and then back at her. She was smiling. "It's beautiful, Adam."

"It was my aunt's house. When she moved to Arizona, I bought it."

"It's perfect." Mia stepped out of the car and walked to the white fence that surrounded the yard. "Do roses bloom on the trellises?"

The trellises and arbors were part of the house's architecture and gave it a lot of charm. Adam was lucky he had a great pair of landscapers to help with the upkeep.

"My aunt was an avid gardener. There are millions of

flowers. You need to see the place mid-summer."

"I can imagine. Is the inside just as pretty?"

"Let me show it to you. I think you'll like it."

Her eyes were still shimmering, but she smiled again when he laced his fingers with hers. Walking into the house holding her hand felt right, and it was one more thing that told Adam he and Mia were on the verge of starting something life-changing.

As soon as they stepped onto the side porch, Bubba started making noise. The damn dog was better than any alarm system. His big nose was pressed to the glass and his entire body was wiggling.

Okay, so he wasn't going to attack anyone, but he sounded fierce.

"Oh! I love dogs!" she said. "I was never allowed to have one when we were younger because Sara was allergic."

The dog almost jumped in her arms as soon as he opened the door.

"Bubba, down," Adam commanded.

"Oh, he's great. Did you call him Bubba?"

He nodded and the dog finally sat long enough for Mia to stroke his head and coo at him. Adam smiled as he watched Mia make his dog fall in love with her, and after a minute she stood and looked around the kitchen.

His house was deceiving. On the outside it looked like a charming, quaint little cape. But because the lot sloped in the back, down to the harbor, the house was big and open on the side that faced the water. The back wall was all windows and French doors, and tonight the reflection of the moon off the water was spectacular. Mia walked toward it and pressed her hand to the glass.

"This is incredible. I used to climb into the attic at Nana's to get a look at the water and you have it right here."

"I'm lucky, I know. The house is too big for one person, but I'd never leave it. It's home now."

Funny, it felt more like home to him with Mia there.

AFTER TODAY, MIA knew she'd found her place. The hospital had been a steady stream of people checking on her and Ben, offering to bring food and volunteering to help her. Apparently, a dinner schedule had already been figured out so Mia wouldn't have to worry about feeding Ben for the first few weeks. These people cared about her and there was nothing phony or calculated about anything.

It was about friendship.

Adam flipped on the overhead kitchen light. When Mia turned to face him, he looked at her, really looked, and it was in his fathomless blue eyes that she saw her future. She'd never seen anything like that with Noah. Had never seen the possibilities. But with Adam, she saw everything.

At the same moment, they started moving toward each other, coming together in the center of the open space.

Without any hesitation, her arms slipped around his waist, and Adam held her so close she wondered how she was breathing. Soon, they were matching each other breath for breath, and Mia understood that there was no one else who would ever make her feel this way. And even if it were hopeless, she'd rather take her chances with Adam than have a sure thing with someone else.

"I'm sorry," he whispered.

"Sorry? Why?" Mia tilted her head back, looked into his eyes.

"I should have left well enough alone. I shouldn't have offered to take him to the game, but…"

Mia stopped the stream of words when she pressed a finger against his lips. "Don't you dare take this on yourself. You did a wonderful thing, and if you've taught me anything about Ben, it's that I have to let him be who he is if he's going to be happy. He's an athlete, and yes, he could get hurt, but he could also get hit by a bus."

Adam chuckled. "Well, let's hope he doesn't."

Mia laughed too. "I agree, but no one is to blame for Ben's injury except for an over eager eleven-year-old boy who didn't follow directions. And honestly, I can't even be mad at him."

Everyone had been very impressed when Cole, the bull moose from the other team, came to the hospital with his dad and apologized. Adam had been so focused on Ben at the field, he didn't see Cole break down when he realized he'd really hurt someone. Apparently, the kid was a monster physically, but emotionally he was a marshmallow.

Without thinking, Mia's hand reached up and cupped Adam's cheek, much like he'd done earlier. "I love how much you care about him. I…"

Mia felt herself tremble as she realized that, heart and soul, she was lost to him.

This was one of those moments of reckoning a person hears about. Her whole life could be set on a new course with a single decision. But at this moment, with this man, there was only one path, one direction, and they had to go there together.

Going up on her toes, Mia pressed her lips to his. There was a spark inside her. Faint and perfect. Then she kissed him again, and again, each time longer, and deeper, giving more of herself each time their lips touched. The spark flared, and burned, pushing Mia to finally tell him what she wanted.

"I don't want to go home tonight," she sighed. "Let me stay."

Adam didn't move, his eyes were closed, and for a second she didn't know if he'd heard her.

When he finally looked at her, his eyes held a sheen of purpose, a longing. And there was a question. "God, Mia, what have I done to deserve you?"

"You get me, Adam. You understand me better than I understand myself."

There was so much more she wanted to say, but caught up in the moment, Adam's mouth came down on hers. His lips were warm and firm, just like the other times they'd kissed, but this time there was more, there was a hunger behind his kiss that pulled Mia into a sweet and perfect place, a place where the world dropped away, and nothing mattered except being with him.

Wrapped firmly in his arms, Mia's head dropped back and Adam moved to her neck, nipping at the skin and sending the most amazing shocks of pleasure right to her core.

"Mia…" His words were nothing but a groan. "I don't know if we should."

This man was all she'd dreamed of, all she wanted, and there was no way she was going to let him stop doing anything because he was having an attack of conscience.

"Why?" she asked, already knowing the answer.

"It's been a long day, emotional. I don't think—"

He was such a good man, and once again, this was proof. He put her first. He always thought about her first. That was how she knew being with him was exactly the right thing to do.

"Adam." Reaching up, Mia tilted his face toward hers. She wanted him to see how sure she was. "I'm a grown woman, and while I may not be very… experienced… I know what I want. And I want you."

"Mia…"

"Take me to bed, Adam."

Never in her life did Mia think she could be that forward, and based on the stunned look on his face, Adam didn't either. But then, the shock began to fade to a soft kind of amusement and his mouth turned up playfully.

"Not a lot of experience, huh?"

Mia shook her head. "Just a little, and it was a long time ago."

"I see. Well, that is a problem."

Seeing the way his eyes were skimming over her, she knew he was all hers. "I figured you had more than enough experience for both of us."

He chuckled quietly. "That's true."

"So, my lack of experience coupled with your, ah, excessive experience makes for a good balance."

He brushed a kiss across her temple. "Makes perfect sense."

"I know." The scent of him was seeping into her and Mia felt a tingling rush through her system as they shut out the rest of the world.

"You're sure?" he asked, even as he swept her into his arms.

Before she even had a chance to nod her response, he was walking toward the front of the house, eventually going down a long hallway that ended at his bedroom. Mia was happy to be safely in his arms because once she wrapped her head around what was happening, she was certain she wouldn't be able to walk.

She heard the voices of her mother and sister rattling around in her memory, telling her she was wasting her time, that Adam could never be the man she wanted him to be. Finally, Mia told the voices to shut up. She'd been listening to those voices for her whole life, and the only time she was really happy was when she trusted herself. Her inner voice, her heart, was telling her to trust Adam.

She couldn't deny that she was falling for him. She'd known it weeks ago. And while he kept her cradled in his arms, safe and secure, Mia couldn't think for a minute that this was a mistake.

"Promise me that if you change your mind, you'll tell me."

"I won't change my mind." She wouldn't.

He was serious about the question and stopped right next to his bed. The moonlight was streaming into his room, giving the space a magical bluish glow. But Adam wasn't looking at the moon, he was looking at her. "Mia, promise me."

She nodded. "Promise."

ADAM'S LIFE HAD been filled with aggressive women who knew what they wanted, and what he expected. Here was Mia, strong, sensible, and yet so much more vulnerable than anyone he ever knew. He didn't know what made her this way, but she wasn't with him for any ulterior motive. The desire between them was pure, they wanted to please each other, and that moved Adam more than he thought possible.

For the last month and a half, since she walked into his office, he'd imagined getting his hands on her, taking her to bed and enjoying every inch of her. They'd gotten past the initial combustion, and settled into a safe friendship. Now that was going out the window, and he wondered if they would ever be able to step back once they crossed the line. Would they want to?

His hand cupped her cheek and while Mia gazed up at him, he kissed her soft mouth. Satisfied that Mia knew she could say no, he set his mind on making sure she wouldn't want to. He could only guess at what she meant about her inexperience. While he didn't think it was likely, he considered the possibility that Mia could be a virgin.

She'd spent the better part of the last nine years raising Ben, and if she was the late-bloomer she claimed to be, there was a chance he was her first.

And that possibility was the scariest damn thing he'd ever faced in his life.

He set her gently on the bed and leaned over to turn on the light on the bedside table.

Just as quickly, she reached up and turned it off.

He turned it on again, and when she reached out to shut it off, he took her wrist and held it over her head.

"Adam, the lights…"

"What about them?"

Mia lay on her back, her hair fanned out behind her, and Adam hovered over her, one knee on the mattress, his hands now cuffing both of her wrists. From this angle, the rise and fall of her breasts was spectacular.

"I think I'd like the lights off."

Lowering himself down to steal a kiss, he shook his head. "I won't be able to see you."

There was silence. Mia took a shaky breath and when she looked back at him, tears pricked at the corners of her eyes. *Shit.* Adam eased himself next to her and then pulled her into his arms. "Don't, honey, don't."

"I don't want you to see me."

"Why? You're beautiful." He didn't hesitate or think about his response. "Your *body* is beautiful and I can't wait to touch it…" His hand skimmed over her hip. "To taste it…" He left a kiss on her collarbone. "And then I can't wait to be inside you."

By this point, her eyes were fixed on his and she took a deep breath. The tears were still there, but barely. That, at least, was a good sign.

"You're beautiful," he whispered. "Soft and beautiful."

Not being able to wait, he slid his hand under her sweater. There was light heat coming off her skin and her breathing was becoming more rapid. There was a flush in her cheeks now, and Adam knew the key here was to keep talking.

Being inexperienced was one thing, but also being insecure about her looks was making Mia more scared than she needed to be. If only she realized, he was a goner. A total goner.

"You're sure about this," he asked again.

"Yes," she said. "I want you. I'm just nervous, and I don't know why."

Scared. He didn't need her scared. He needed her to relax.

"I don't want to embarrass you, but I have to ask…" He took a deep breath. "Will this be your first time?"

Mia shook her head no. Okay, not a virgin, but still nervous.

"It's been a long time," she said.

"How long?"

"Uh, nine years," she said quietly.

"Oh." *Holy shit.*

"He was my boyfriend at the time. It didn't last long, and it was awful."

"The relationship or the sex?"

"Both." Now she was embarrassed. Seriously embarrassed.

"I don't mean to pry, but I want to make sure I'm careful with you." His hand was making lazy circles on her back and Mia burrowed into him. He had to make this good for her.

"You aren't going to take me home?"

Now he understood why she was terrified. Rejection. "Only if you want me to."

She sniffled again. Shook her head. "I want to stay."

It didn't take much to change her position so she was on her back again, gazing up at him with her eyes still bright from the tears. Propped on one elbow, Adam drew the fingers of his other hand from her collarbone, over her breasts, across her belly, and finally settling on her hip.

She shivered at his touch.

"You have to tell me if I'm going too fast, or if something hurts, okay?"

She nodded.

"I also need to know if you like something." He leaned in, kissed her, nuzzled behind her ear, and for that he was rewarded with another sigh. "Because if there's something in particular I'm doing that you like, I'll make sure I do it again."

She giggled, and when that small thing made him happy, he knew it was going to be different with her. It was going to be something special. Something intimate.

Yep. A goner, for sure.

"I won't hurt you. I promise—"

He was stopped when Mia's hands came up and held his face. She gazed at him with eyes that melted him right to the core.

"Adam, I trust you."

"You do?"

"Yes. Now stop talking and kiss me."

He smiled. "God, you're bossy."

Grabbing the front of his shirt, she grinned back. "You'll get used to it."

Chapter Seventeen

NEVER HAD BEING with someone meant so much or carried such risk. He kept hearing "nine years" in his head. *Nine years?* She'd been twenty or twenty-one when she'd last had sex. It never occurred to him that when she became Ben's guardian she didn't just give up her career goals—Mia gave up her life.

His one hand still rested on her hip and the other eased her sweater up and over her head. With every touch, Mia breathed out. Her skin was warm, flushed, and already had a light sheen of sweat. Her scent, something combining perfume, heat, and aroused woman, was getting him so hot, Adam had to make a conscious effort to rein in his baser instincts to take her.

"Sit up," he instructed. She did as he asked, looking at him through a cloud of eyelashes, and that gave Adam the opportunity to pop the clasp on her bra, removing it in one move.

Holy God. He couldn't breathe. Mia, naked from the waist up, was heart-stopping. She was beautiful, and sexy, and… he leaned in and kissed the top of one breast, then the other. Her head lolled back and Adam eased her back into the pillows. He let his hands run over her, teasing her, and loving her responsiveness.

"Adam, oh my God. It feels… it feels…"

"It feels good, doesn't it? I want you to feel good."

"I do, but it's more." She arched a little, pressing against him. "I want… I want…."

He smiled. "Soon enough. Let me take care of you. Okay?"

She nodded and he unbuttoned her pants. She'd already slipped off her shoes and he had no trouble guiding the pants down her legs along with the little wisp of underwear, and tossing both on the floor.

Lying on his bed like that, she was a vision. Never in his life had he been with a more physically beautiful woman, and that he cared for her so much made this all the better. Her body was all softness and curves. She was shapely and rounded; from her breasts, his eyes traveled down and took in the gentle tapering of her waist, the tiny, soft mound of a belly, and the curve of her hips. Her legs were long and smooth. There was no defined ribcage, no knobby knees. She was, in no uncertain terms, a goddess.

And she was his.

Adam's hand slipped between her legs and she gasped, trembled. "Oh…"

He kissed the corner of her mouth and enjoyed the reaction when he slid a finger over her lush folds. Watching her face, he realized a climax wasn't going to take much. She bucked a little as he played with her a bit more, stroking and teasing the wet heat, and when he moved his mouth to one breast, sucking ever so slightly, Mia exploded.

Her back arched as she fisted her hands in the comforter and although her mouth opened, no sound escaped. He'd never seen anything like this. Every nerve ending within her must have fired.

Mia felt everything, responded to everything. Her body was waiting for his touch. Nothing about this was routine, there was no detachment. He was totally in control of the situation, of the pacing, but this was still all about Mia, and that she trusted him so much made him want to make it even better for her.

This was what he'd been missing. He'd had the groupies, the gorgeous celebrities, and a lot of hot sex, but he'd never had a connection to any other human being like he did with Mia. With her trust, she gave him everything. And when she reached up and pulled him close, he realized he'd never want anyone else again. This was a commitment of the heart, and it was clear she owned his.

Mia looked up and smiled, still breathing heavily, still twitching from one of the most intense orgasms Adam had ever witnessed. How incredible would it be when he finally made love to her?

He was surprised when he felt her hands between them, and Adam realized she was working at his buttons. When she'd released them all, her hands ran up his torso to his shoulders and pushed his shirt over and down. He pulled his arms from the sleeves, then watched as she touched and studied his chest.

"My God, you're perfect," she said. Then her hand reached for his fly, unfastening the button and easing down the zipper. Slowly, she let her fingers graze over his erection and he gasped.

"Mia…"

She moved again and this time her hands glided around his waist and slid into the back of his jeans, over the muscles of his ass and again, her touch elicited another sharp intake of breath.

"I love that I can finally touch you like this. I've wanted to since the first time you kissed me. I wanted…"

Adam couldn't take it anymore, his mouth covered hers and he took her into a kiss that wasn't gentle or tentative—this was a kiss meant to arouse and possess. It was a kiss to let her know that he didn't just want her, but needed her. Needed her touch, her kiss, her whole body.

Adam rolled away from her long enough to shed the rest of his clothes and find a condom. When he came back to bed, Mia sat up, her hair falling all around her like some classical painting, and her hands made a hot path over his skin. Linking her arms around his neck, she pulled him down on top of her.

"Make love to me, Adam." Her voice was as soft as a

tropical breeze and just as seductive.

Adam stroked the hair away from Mia's beautiful face, kissed her again, and then did as she asked and loved her.

MIA AWOKE AT three in the morning, curled against Adam. His arm was looped around her waist and he was snoring very quietly in her ear. Mia wondered what had brought her to this place, and the more she tried to attach a reason to it, the more she didn't really care.

But even though Mia would like nothing better than to stay snuggled in bed with Adam, her mommy instinct had kicked in, and she had to find out how Ben was doing. Wiggling away, she managed to get up without waking him.

He moved a little, rolling onto his back and settling back into a restful sleep. Looking at him, Mia couldn't help but think about what else they could do together in that big bed. The throbbing between her legs seemed incessant when Adam was around. She couldn't help but want him; no matter what happened, she would always want him.

Her clothes in a tangle on the floor, Mia looked about for something to wear. On a chair by the picture window was a basket of folded laundry. Picking through it, she found a T-shirt and made her way to the bathroom. The shirt was a little snug around her chest, but it fit, and hung nearly to her knees. Looking in the bathroom mirror she smiled. "Property of Notre Dame Football." Her boyfriend the football player. Who'd have thought it?

Mia couldn't remember ever feeling happier. Even though she had an injured boy on her hands, and she knew she was going to catch fallout from her mother about it, she felt happy down to her toes. This thing she'd started with Adam was good and right.

Tiptoeing out of the bedroom, she found her purse and her cellphone and settled on one of the stools in the kitchen to make her call. Bubba greeted her with a big sloppy kiss and a wagging tail.

"Hey, boy." Mia smiled. The dog was a mess, but she loved him already. He circled by her feet and plopped down in a heap, groaning for good measure. She checked her messages before calling the nurses' station.

"Hi," Mia said when the voice came on the line. "This is Mia DeAngelis, I was just wondering how Ben is doing?"

"Hi Mia, your grandmother told us you'd be calling."

"I'm sure she did." If nothing else, the people who loved her knew her very well. "He's okay?"

"A little restless, but that's understandable. The cast is going to take some getting used to. But he is sleeping and he's not in any pain."

"That's good. Nana's okay?"

"She's playing checkers with Ben's roommate."

That sounded like Nana. Ben's roommate was also re-covering from a badly broken leg, but he'd gotten his in a car accident that had also severely injured his mother. The poor boy. It was no mystery why he wasn't sleeping. "Thanks for the update. I'll be there in the morning."

"Get some sleep," the nurse said. "He's fine."

Mia ended the call and relaxed a little. The moon was just setting, and the sight of it hitting the water on the horizon was spectacular. As she stood at the French doors, looking outside, a pair of arms slipped around her waist from behind. Adam's body enveloped hers and she'd never felt so completely protected.

He kissed her neck and looked outside with her. There were no words exchanged and they just enjoyed the silence for a little while.

"Ben's okay?" he finally asked.

She nodded. Leaning against him, Mia relaxed immediately and almost started to doze off. That is until her stomach growled. And it growled loudly enough for the dog to cock his head and prick his ears. Adam laughed.

"Hungry?"

"I guess I am. Sorry."

He turned her in his arms and Mia felt her insides go warm and squishy at the sight of him. He wore only a pair of athletic shorts. His chest was bare and Mia let her hand rest on the soft mat of hair in the center. He was muscular, strong, but not bulky, and when he pulled her close she could feel the erection in his shorts. What kind of miracle was at work here that he wanted her again?

"You've had quite a workout," he said. "I guess I could feed you."

"I'm not the only one." Unable to help herself, Mia's hands trailed down Adam's sides and around to the small of his back. His skin was tight, smooth, and she left a soft kiss in the center of his chest just because she could. His eyes closed and held her away from him, obviously trying to keep his own hunger under control.

Mia didn't want him in control. In fact, at that moment she wanted Adam more than she wanted food, so she kissed him again. And again. And again. Finally, he lifted her up and set her squarely on the kitchen island.

Tapping her forehead, he smiled. "You have a very bad girl living in there."

"Who'd have thought? Is that a problem?"

Slipping his hands under the T-shirt, he shook his head. "Hell, no. God, I love how you look in my shirt."

Now that she was more eye-to-eye with him, Mia decided to press her luck. Leaning forward while he caressed her bare skin, she kissed his neck, his ear, and his temple all while letting her hands explore.

"You're playing with fire, Mia. Much more of this, and I'm going to take you right against the wall."

That she could get him this crazy, this aroused, was something she'd never even dreamed of. Okay, maybe she'd dreamed about it, but she'd never thought she'd have this kind of power. Wrapping her legs around his waist and kissing him long and deep, Mia sent Adam a pretty clear message.

His tongue invaded her mouth, and when he kissed her back, she truly felt as if she were being devoured. One of his big hands was between her legs and the other was kneading her breasts, and instead of pulling back from him, she pushed her hands deep into his shorts, which ultimately dropped to the floor. His eyes were dark, hungry. There was no sign of the blazing blue, just black heat.

"Fine," he growled, grabbing for her. "Hang on."

As he lifted her again, Mia linked her arms around his neck. The next thing she knew, her back was against the wall nearest the big windows, and Adam entered her. Mia cried out, loving the invasion, the feeling of fullness. Her body stretched to accommodate him in this new position. It took Adam a second to catch his breath, but then he adjusted his grip on her and started to move.

There was nothing soft or romantic about this joining, it was about lust, and satisfying it as quickly as possible. Every thrust went deeper and deeper, touching her, driving her a little higher, a little closer to heaven. Mia felt Adam's breathing quicken and his body heat up. She held him because it made her feel safe, and because he seemed to need it. Keeping her lips pressed to his neck, she whispered his name. There was something desperate about the way he was holding her. Something possessive. And whatever it was that was making him feel this way, Mia was willing to let him use her body for whatever he needed.

She held him tight as the rolling sensations built inside her. Heat, incredible heat, spread out from her center. She was headed toward release, and feeling his shoulder muscles bunch under her hands, she expected he was too. It wasn't long.

In a moment that was almost primal, Adam let loose, thrusting one last time and spilling himself inside her. His sounds were rough and violent as his body spasmed. He screamed her name and Mia held on even tighter.

Everything was trembling, and in the seconds following his climax, Mia had her own. It came on slowly, in waves, but then her body shattered, over and over. Her heart broke open and everything inside came pouring out. Shuddering in Adam's arms, holding on, Mia understood the depths of her feelings for this man. The love.

Mia loved him.

And there was nothing she could do about it.

THE WOMAN WAS a cookie junkie.

After their wild kitchen sex, Adam grabbed a container of chocolate chip cookies his grandmother had sent home with him, poured two big glasses of milk and nudged Mia back to bed.

Settled on top of the covers with their snack, he watched

her devour the sweets like a starving ten-year-old, while Adam gave himself a silent beating. What the hell made him lose control like that? He took Mia right against the kitchen wall. There was nothing gentle or tender about what he did to her, it was a hot, sweaty fuck.

That's not to say Mia didn't enjoy it. It was amazing. From the way she screamed, he was pretty sure she saw stars, but that didn't excuse him. He should have controlled himself. He should have treated her more gently.

And on top of it all, he didn't use any protection.

They ate and drank in silence, and when he put the glass on his bedside table, Mia surprised him by crawling up and straddling his lap. She faced him, used her thumb to wipe the corner of his mouth, and then she looped her arms around his neck.

With her soft body settled right on top of him, of course, he got hard again. She was addictive.

"Do you want to tell me what's bothering you?" she asked.

"Why do you think something's bothering me?"

"Because you haven't said five words to me since we came back to bed, and I'm wondering why. I have a theory, but I'd like to hear it from you."

"I don't know what you mean." How did she know he was bothered? On top of everything else, his girl had ESP.

"Okay, I get to try? Fine. I think you feel bad because, well, things got a little wild there."

"I was more than a little wild. It wasn't okay to treat you like that."

"It wasn't?"

"Mia, I should be more careful with you."

"I'm not made of glass. I won't break."

"Still, I should have…"

"Done exactly what you did. It was incredible, and I love that I can drive you crazy. It makes me feel beautiful, sexy… powerful. And I've never felt powerful."

Looking in Mia's eyes, he lost himself. The deep, luminous brown was drawing him right in. "You are all those things, and so much more." He was in awe of her, simply in awe of her generous heart. "You weren't scared?"

"God, no. Scared? Of you? How can you even think that?" Her hands stroked his face and Adam felt his feelings for her well up from the pit of his stomach. She was so sincere, so open with him.

"I didn't use any protection."

"It's okay," she said. "I went on the pill a couple of months ago."

That made him smile. "Planning ahead?"

She froze, turned red. Damn, it was so easy to make her blush. "I guess I was hoping things would change, yes. Is there anything you need to tell me about?"

"There's nothing. I'm healthy."

Her voice softened and her lips brushed over his. "Then stop this, okay?"

He nodded and smiled at her. This beautiful creature was amazing, simply amazing. "So, we should plan on kitchen sex on a regular basis?"

Snuggling into him, she laughed. "I think you have a lot to show me. Be creative."

Taking that as an invitation, Adam pulled off the T-shirt she was wearing and admired the now naked woman settled in his lap. Her breasts alone were an absolute feast. Mia licked her full, beautiful lips and Adam could feel his heart pounding out of his chest as he touched her. "What do you want to know?"

Mia reached for his shorts, inching them down over his erection, and smiled shyly. "Everything."

Then she wiggled her sweet spot against him and he groaned. *Oh, God.*

"Show me," she whispered.

Damn. Adam didn't think he was going to survive her, he truly didn't. But if he did, he pretty much figured he'd be Mia's slave forever.

Not a bad outcome.

Chapter Eighteen

MIA DASHED AROUND her grandmother's house gathering clothes for Ben. It was six-thirty in the morning and neither she nor Adam had had much sleep, but she was running on adrenaline. Adam on the other hand, was slumped over the piano.

"Where are you getting your energy?" he asked. He was two cups of coffee ahead of her and twice as tired.

"I don't know. I guess it's just the rush of Ben coming home and…everything else."

He picked his head up when she said, 'everything else' and smiled. "Everything else nearly killed me. I don't know how you can even walk."

She inched over to him and rubbed his back. "I'm sorry if it was too much. I couldn't get enough of you."

He made a low, guttural sound in his throat and grabbed her, pushing her against the piano. "Don't tease me or I'll show you that it wasn't too much."

"No, we'll be late!"

"Exactly. Let's see how you explain *that* to Nana."

"Meanie," she snipped.

He sat at the keyboard and fiddled with the keys, and that caught Mia's attention. It actually sounded like something. "Do you play?"

"I took lessons for ten years." To show her he did an impressive run up and down the ivories.

"Wow." She smiled and hoped she didn't seem too shocked that he had other layers. "I had no idea. Play something."

"Nope."

"Why?" Mia wanted him to play. Badly. This was a whole new side to Adam, and she wanted him to show her what he could do.

"I haven't really played in about twenty years. My repertoire consists of Christmas carols, which I get roped into playing every year when we trim the tree. So, if you want," he cracked his knuckles, "I can play Jingle Bells."

Mia laughed and hugged him around the neck. "We'll play a duet sometime."

"Deal," he said on a low chuckle. "Tell me something—how did you go from majoring in musical theater to being a college librarian?"

Mia sat next to him on the piano bench and started fiddling with the keys herself. "When I was in high school, there were two places outside the classroom I felt comfortable. The theater and the library." She began to play something simple to give her hands something to do. "I was a bit of a wallflower in school, and those were my sanctuaries. So, when my dreams of the Broadway stage went south, I went to my other safe place. I got my graduate degree in Library Science."

"It must have been hard for you, giving everything up."

This was something Mia never talked about. Her mom never considered that she would do anything less, and being the dutiful daughter, she *did* give up everything that she'd been working toward. But those early years were a blur. "Honestly, when Sara first died, that's what consumed me. My sister was dead. I had this baby. Ben was about a year old when it happened, so I didn't think about much of anything. I went to school. Then I went to graduate school for what seemed like forever. I earned two master's degrees in record time. The responsibility of it all didn't really hit me until after I had come to grips with Sara's death. When my father died, and my mother moved, that's when I realized I was frozen in place. I was stuck. And my mom didn't care."

Adam took her hand, giving her his full attention.

"I had an okay job, a small apartment in the city, but no family close by. The few friends I had from high school or college were single and didn't have to worry about child care."

"I guess moving here with your nana was a no-brainer."

"I guess." That made her think. "Does that make me seem like an opportunist?"

He squeezed her hand. "No, it makes you smart."

"My mother would send us to my grandparents for a

month or so every summer. Her parents and my father's parents. Once we were out of school for the summer, she didn't know what to do with us. But I loved coming here. It was the best part of my year. I had friends, I had family... and I wanted Ben to experience that. To live in a place with good schools, and parks, and streets where he could ride his bike."

Adam smiled when she mentioned the bike.

"I mean, Nana babysits occasionally, she gets mad when I don't ask her, but I can also afford a babysitter if I want to. I have a better job and there are teenagers on my block who want to babysit. Who I can trust!"

Mia reflected on everything she was telling him. This could be enough emotional baggage to send Adam running for the hills, but so far, he was sticking, being supportive, being him.

"You have roots here, what kept your family away?"

"Oh, my mother hates it here. Anything east of the Midtown Tunnel, except for maybe the Hamptons, was off her radar. Said Compass Cove was stifling, boring, limiting. Pick an adjective. Once she left for college, she rarely came home. When I told her I'd made the decision to move here, she said it was just one more thing she could add to the list of why I'm her—" Mia sucked in a breath, and her eyes started to burn as she thought about what she was about to say. God, this hurt.

"What?"

"—why I'm her greatest disappointment."

She'd never said that to anyone, even Nana, and soon big, fat tears were falling and she couldn't get them to stop. Hearing herself say it out loud made it so much more real, made the rejection and disapproval that much more palpable. She had never been good enough for her mother. No matter how much she did right, or how much she accomplished, Mia was never good enough. There was nothing quite as awful as knowing your own mother didn't love you.

"Oh, my God..." Adam cradled her head against his shoulder and she cried harder than she ever had. The pain from her childhood, her adolescence, every dig about her weight, her shape, her lack of social life—all of it came flooding to the surface. Forget being the favored child; all Mia craved was to be loved equally.

"Oh, Mia. Oh, baby, I'm so sorry."

"She has no idea what's happened to Ben. I don't want to tell her because she'll just use it to berate me. The thing is she won't care how he is; it will be all about me screwing up."

"How did you screw up?"

"Sports are the big no-no. Ben's father was an athlete, and he abandoned my sister when she was pregnant. So as far as my mother is concerned, that means all athletes, and sports, are evil. She didn't want him raised with the same 'mindset'. I tried to honor her wishes, but..." The tears were still falling and now Adam was using the end of his sleeve to wipe her eyes. "It's so stupid! How can I keep the child from being who he is? That's just wrong."

"You're doing the right thing. Don't think for one minute that you aren't."

"It's hard sometimes. I've always been too fat, too quiet, too emotional… the list goes on."

He didn't say anything because, really, there wasn't anything left to say. He held her, soothed her, and now he knew more about her than anyone else. People in Compass Cove knew Ellen DeAngelis was difficult, but no one knew this side of it. Mia had always kept quiet. "I always tried to figure out what was wrong with me. I mean, if my own mother can't love me, there has to be something, right?"

"There's nothing wrong with you. Nothing. This is all on her." Adam wasn't letting go. His arms kept her securely against his chest as he gently dropped kisses on the top of her head.

"We need to go get Ben," she said quietly.

"Are you okay? Do you need a minute?"

She shook her head and hugged him one last time. With that, she stood and went to get her purse and the bag of clothes they were bringing to the hospital.

"Mia?"

She turned and saw Adam was still sitting on the piano bench.

"If your mother thinks you're a disappointment, then she knows nothing about the extraordinary person you are.

Nothing I can say will fix that, but you've changed my life in ways you can't imagine."

There were no words. All Mia could do was walk over and kiss him. Holding his face in her hands, she kissed him, and kissed him. This man was everything, and Mia didn't know what she'd done to deserve him.

BEN HAD A session with the physical therapist to learn how to use his crutches, but in truth the kid wasn't going to feel like doing much the first few days. The anesthesia alone was going to knock the hell out of him. Adam helped him maneuver from the wheelchair to the front seat of his Mercedes where there was more than enough room for a bum leg. He didn't drive this car much, but with four doors it had the space they needed to get Ben home.

Mia was going to drive her grandmother's car home since Mrs. Lang had been up all night, and that left Adam alone with Ben. The poor kid looked wrecked. He may have slept, but it wasn't a good sleep, and he said breakfast was crappy.

"Before I head to practice, I'll hit the store and get you whatever you want. Junk food, snacks. I can grab a pizza from DiRaimo's for lunch."

"Thanks, Coach."

"Everything okay, pal? I mean, I know injuries are the worst, but anything else?"

"I'm going to miss the end of baseball season. I can't go to practice anymore with you, and now Aunt Mia won't ever let me play anything again. I'll be lucky if she lets me out of the house."

He had to ask. "You're jumping to a lot of conclusions, aren't you?"

"It's the truth. Aunt Mia worried about me playing, and look what happened." He motioned to his casted leg. "This sucks."

"You know, she and I were just talking about this. She's more concerned about your grandmother going crazy, but she knows who you are and she respects it."

"Really?"

"Really. And as far as the baseball team goes, go to games. Sit on the bench, keep score, cheer on your teammates. You can still be part of things even though you're hurt. You can still come to football games and sit on the sidelines."

"Aunt Mia won't mind?"

"Like I said, she's more worried you *won't* do those things. She's also worried about how your grandmother is going to react."

"Grandma hates sports, unless it's golf or tennis. She definitely won't like you."

Adam laughed. "Well, that will be too bad for her, because I'm not going anywhere."

There was silence for a few minutes and then Ben spoke

again. "Are you going to date Aunt Mia since she broke up with Noah?"

"How did you know about that?"

"I heard Nana on the phone with Zia Lina. She was pretty happy about it."

He couldn't imagine Mrs. Lang just blurting that out in front of Ben, and then he remembered the baseball game. Or rather, after the baseball game.

"Were you pretending to be asleep again?"

Ben smiled. "Yeah. It's the only way I find out anything. So, are you dating her?"

There was a lot more than dating going on, but he sure wasn't going to mention that to Ben. "Yes."

"Finally! You guys took long enough. Just don't kiss in front of me. It's gross."

Adam grinned. This was actually getting funny. "You know what? If she wants to kiss me, I'm going to let her. Someday you'll understand. For now, you'll adjust."

Ben grumbled a little but Adam guessed he was happy about the development. Ben's approval was good news. That was going to make Mia feel more comfortable with everything, maybe even about her mother.

AT NINE O'CLOCK that night, Adam pulled into the driveway at Mia's and saw the lights on in the kitchen. He'd left them at about two in the afternoon before going to practice, and then a meeting with admissions and all his coaches about next year's recruits. He was wiped—unsurprising, since he only got about ten minutes of sleep the night before.

Not hesitating, he went to the kitchen door and let himself in. This felt like another home to him because Mia was there. Wherever she was would be home. It was a new feeling for Adam, and he liked it.

However, when he stepped into the kitchen, the only one there was Mrs. Lang. His old teacher was standing barefoot at the sink, in Yoga pants and a t-shirt, washing dishes. On the iPod was the old Neil Diamond song, "Forever in Blue Jeans" and she was swaying to the music. She turned when she heard him step into the room and smiled. Adam should have felt welcome, but the smile made his stomach lurch, and he went right back to high school. The last time he saw that look, he got lectured.

"Adam, I'm glad you're here."

Oh yeah, he was going to get it. Some things didn't change. *Shit.* He dropped into one of the kitchen chairs. "What did I do?"

Grabbing a dishtowel and drying her hands, she laughed and took the chair adjacent to his. "What did you do? Is there something I need to know?"

"No. Maybe. I don't know."

"Okay," she said and patted his hand. "I do want to talk to you."

He relaxed a little. A very little, because he figured she probably wanted to talk about Mia. Adam was ready and blurted out the first thing that came into his head. "I care about her. I really do."

Mrs. Lang smiled and nodded. "I know, and I know you care for Ben, too. But this is new for her. Be mindful of that."

"This is new for all of us." Both he and Mia were in uncharted territory.

"I don't want her to get hurt, Adam. She's been through so much." There was a crack in her usually cheerful veneer, and he saw the fear, the worry. This whole family had been through hell.

There was no hesitation; Adam took his teacher's hand, seeing her for the first time like a person, not the woman who busted on his ass about homework.

"I don't plan on it, and I'll protect them from anyone who tries."

"She's taken a lot of hits over the years, my poor Mia."

"Yeah, from people like your daughter." The comment shot out like a bullet. Damn. Watching her reaction, he knew it was something he should have kept to himself, but it was out there now with no way to take it back.

"I know. I've tried to be a buffer, but it's not always easy. Ellen is a force of nature and I don't mean that in a good way. She's very hard. Very aloof. She's a lot like my mother. Mia's more like me, and like her father, Ted. He was a good man."

"Someone needs to talk to her, and if that has to be me, fine."

"I've had more than one talk with her," Mrs. Lang said. Now he was getting a different look, one that was more serious. "I didn't know she'd told you about her mother."

More than she told you, he thought. "Look," he began, "I don't know how a parent could be so cold toward their own child. Especially someone like Mia. I was a complete asshole and my family stood by me, so be sure—I will not let her unload on Mia. About anything."

"Did Mia tell you very much?"

"She told me enough." Thinking about her this morning, about how distraught she became when she talked about her mother, made him want to protect her. Just from that short conversation, Adam knew Ellen DeAngelis was toxic.

Still, he was surprised when Mrs. Lang lunged at him, hugging him fiercely. "You go to the head of the class, Adam. Thank goodness. Someone needs to stand up to Ellen. I don't know why Ted never did. He was a lovely, intelligent man who served his country with honor, but he needed to grow a pair."

Huh?

"Really? Did you just say grow a pair?" Not what he was expecting.

She smiled. "I did. My daughter walked all over him. It made me sad. Ted deserved better."

When she looked at him, he saw tears pricking the corners of her eyes. Jesus, he thought, what did I do now?

"Adam, I know you always thought I didn't like you, but deep down I knew you were a good kid. A pest to be sure, but a good boy."

"I think pest is too nice; I was a pain in the ass."

"Maybe so, but you've grown into an exceptional man, and I'm so happy you and Mia found each other."

There were gifts, and then there were unexpected gifts that meant everything. Mrs. Lang's approval fell into the latter category. "It took me a long time to get here, and I still don't think I'm good enough for her."

"You got here exactly when you were supposed to, and as long as Mia thinks you're good enough, that's all that matters."

He had to remember that, because as long as she would have him, he wasn't going anywhere. And he wasn't going to let anyone make her feel inferior. His concern was Mia; nothing mattered more than she did.

And considering that a few years ago all he cared about was himself, coming to this point was a big deal.

The last twenty-four hours had been full of moments like this. Big and small. Mia had changed his life for the better, but now he had to bring it back to something practical. He'd remembered they were all supposed to go to Massachusetts, to Mia's uncle's house for Thanksgiving and even though it was over a month away, traveling with Ben in his condition wasn't a good idea. "I talked to my grandmother tonight and she wanted me to invite all of you for Thanksgiving. It's not going to be easy to travel with Ben, and she'd love to have everyone."

"Oh, honey, that's sweet of her. It sure would make everything easier."

"We'll talk about it as the time gets closer, but..." He rose and she did the same. "Right now, I'm going to check on Ben and see Mia for a few minutes."

"I think they're both asleep, but regardless, they'll be happy to see you. I couldn't believe Mia crashed the way she did." Adam stopped by the kitchen door and looked back at Mrs. Lang, who had an honest to God gleam in her eye. "You'd think she didn't sleep a wink last night."

Adam barely managed to keep himself from smiling. The woman still knew how to push his buttons.

Chapter Nineteen

EARLY THANKSGIVING MORNING, Mia rose and went to the kitchen, hoping that doing some baking would get her mind off her nervousness. Focusing her attention on something other than the knot in her stomach had to be a good thing, right?

They'd been together for a little over a month, and now she was spending Thanksgiving with Adam's family. His whole family. His grandmother, parents, aunts and uncles, assorted cousins, brothers, sister and some nieces and nephews. He told her it would be a crowd, maybe close to forty people, and that she should prepare herself. He made the gathering sound like a scene out of a screwball holiday comedy. Even as nervous as she was, Mia was excited.

Her family holidays tended to be very quiet affairs. She'd never had the big, noisy family gatherings. Her father was an only child and her mother said they needed "their own traditions", so they didn't get together with her grandparents or other family. Unfortunately, their family tradition usually meant the four of them at home, or going to a friend's home where there were other people who lacked big, extended families. The day consisted of elegantly prepared food and quiet conversation.

No cousins. No noise.

This year, as always, her mother had opted not to be with family. Not wanting to travel on such a busy holiday, instead she was having dinner with friends from their golf club, all retirees without families in the area. *People just like her mother,* she thought.

Happily, Mia wasn't facing another lonely Thanksgiving, and it certainly wouldn't be a stuffy one. Her mother was a dignified lady, but Mia didn't want dignified.

Adam had what Mia had always wanted: noise and chaos, people arguing, and football games on the front lawn. And she always thought holidays should have kids. Lots and lots of kids. According to Adam, there would be plenty of children there, and Mia couldn't wait.

On the counter behind her, Mia had the ornament she'd found at the antique shop by the harbor. The Millers decorated their Christmas tree on Thanksgiving Day, and Mia knew she couldn't go to a tree trimming without an ornament. The delicately engraved blown glass angel was so exquisite, Mia almost kept it for her own tree. Almost. But Anna Miller was an angel, so it seemed most appropriate with her.

Opening the recipe box she'd taken down from a shelf, Mia thought about desserts. Her first thought was to make dishes that were sophisticated—the kinds of desserts she'd grown up eating—things with delicate crusts and fillings. Then she thought about the little hands that would be grabbing at the sweets, and she changed her plan. She'd make one, decadent flourless chocolate cake, but the other desserts would be kid friendly—dark chocolate brownies and chocolate chip cookie bars. She'd asked and there were no nut allergies to worry about, so she pulled out a bag of walnuts to throw into half the brownies.

But first, breakfast. Holiday breakfast meant fresh cinnamon rolls. She'd made the dough and the filling the night before, so it was just a matter of putting them together.

As she rolled out the dough, Mia thought about all the things she had to be thankful for. Ben was thriving in his new home, and if Mia had ever worried about the move, those doubts were gone. He was her greatest gift. Seeing him happy and doing well was what any mother wanted for her child. He was still recovering from the broken leg, but as with most things, Ben bounced back.

Then there was her own life. Adam had affected a major change there too, and now Mia didn't have to wonder if she would have a love story, only if this one would last. Since they'd gotten together, Adam had done everything to make Mia feel special. For a guy who hadn't done the romance thing, he had it down pretty good, from helping her with Ben, to quiet nights at home, to romantic dates.

That brought back a memory from the past weekend. She'd had Sunday off, and Adam showed up at her door.

Without any warning, he'd whisked her off to New York City. She figured he'd pulled out all the stops and sprung for a Broadway show, but to her surprise they ended up strolling through the collections and exhibits at the Metropolitan Museum of Art. Mia hadn't been there since her parents took her when she was a child, but there she was, holding Adam's hand as they looked at the collection of Impressionist paintings and enjoying a quiet afternoon.

There was nothing flashy or pretentious about the outing. He didn't spend a lot of money or try to impress her.

They found a deli for a late lunch.

Walked around midtown for a while.

And after it turned dark and got cold, he drove them back to his house, where he made love to her.

Mia had never been happier.

A familiar bark from the yard brought her back to reality.

Rising from the table, Mia went to the back door and pushed the curtain away. There was Bubba, standing on his hind legs, his massive nose pressed to the glass. Behind him, Adam stood with two cups of coffee. He must have smelled the cinnamon buns.

She unlocked the door and smiled as he walked to her and planted a sweet kiss on her cheek.

"How are those cinnamon rolls coming along?"

Mia stepped aside and Adam and Bubba entered the kitchen. "Did you get up early and drive all the way over here for cinnamon rolls?"

He grinned and Mia felt her insides go all jittery. "Yeah, pretty much. But ahh…" Adam leaned in and kissed her lips lightly. "There is that."

Mia stepped back from the door and hoped against hope that how she felt about him wouldn't be completely transparent to his family. It was hard enough keeping her feelings in check under normal conditions. In the middle of a big holiday celebration, when all kinds of good family feelings were overflowing, Mia feared she'd do something to slip up and show all the people who loved him that she did too.

He kissed her again and held out the cup from Starbucks. "Rinaldi's was closed, but I got you this… Caramel Brulee Latte." Mia reached for the cup, but Adam pulled it back. "I'll trade it for a cinnamon roll."

Games. It was always a game with him. He was such a guy.

"Oh, I guess," she said.

Triumphant, Adam smiled and when he offered it again, Mia wrapped her hand around the cup. This time her fingers lightly brushed against his and heat curled deep in her belly. God, what he did to her. She could jump him right then and there.

"It'll be a few more minutes."

He nodded, grinning because he knew she was having dirty thoughts, and sat at the kitchen table. Mia gave herself a quick look. At least she'd showered the night before, because she wasn't exactly painting a pretty picture in her old plaid pajama pants and T-shirt. But Adam didn't seem to care. He liked her the way she was, and Mia mentally pinched herself. She had this wonderful person in her life, someone who was a great influence on Ben, and had given her more romance in two months than she ever thought she'd have in her life. He was her friend. He was her lover.

He was everything she'd ever wanted. Watching him pet the dog, there was no doubt.

"Have you decided what you're making for today?" he asked.

"A really great cake, and then I decided to keep it simple. Cookie bars and brownies. I'm sure your grandma will have plenty of fancy desserts."

Adam nodded. "The kids will love you for it."

"How many kids?"

The dog had laid his big head in Adam's lap. Running his hand over Bubba's head, Adam gave her the rundown. "A ton. My brother Doug has three kids, all girls. Nine, seven, and four. My cousin Rob has a five-year-old girl and his wife is pregnant. The girls are gonna love you." He smiled. "My cousin Mark and his wife have four. A boy who's around Ben's age, twin girls who are eight, and a two-year-old boy. I think my cousins Cathy and Linda will be there too. They have eight kids between them, ranging from a newborn to a really snotty thirteen-year-old girl."

Mia laughed. "She's thirteen. 'Snotty' is a job requirement."

He nodded. "I shouldn't be too judgmental; her dad's been out to sea for the past ten months. He's a Navy pilot."

"Having gone through that, she has her reasons. Deployments are hard on everyone."

The timer let Mia know the cinnamon rolls were done. Adam was right at her side when she pulled them out of the oven.

Grabbing a spatula, she transferred the mass of steaming, gooey rolls from the pan to a plate and threw the tool into the sink. Adam's hand reached out, ready to pick one off the plate, but Mia slapped it back.

"They're too warm and I still have to ice them."

"Fine." He turned around and leaned his back into the counter while he watched her work. Mia had gotten used to having Adam in her kitchen. She'd pretty much gotten used to him, period. "Ben still sleeping?"

"Mmm hmm." There was something on his mind, though. This visit wasn't just about cinnamon rolls or stolen kisses; Adam had something to tell her. His face was tense, his eyes worried. Inside, panic welled up, but she had to ask. "Are you going to keep stewing about whatever it is that's bugging you, or are you going to tell me?"

Blowing out a breath, he looked at her and grinned. "Man, you really are inside my head, aren't you?"

Mia felt herself smile.

Adam straightened his back, and pulled her closer, keeping hold of her free hand. "My grandmother called me late last night to let me know that a couple of old friends of mine are in town, and will be joining us for dinner."

"Okay, that's nice—isn't it?"

"Yeah, Greg, he's the agent who talked to Kelvin. He and I go way back, but umm, Pilar..."

"Pilar?" Knuckles white as she gripped the spreader, Mia took a deep breath and wondered why he felt the need to tell her about Pilar. This couldn't be good.

"She and I were together for a long time. A couple of years and, uhhh... when I had my accident, I cut off all contact with people from my old life."

"Including Pilar."

"Yeah. It was the only way I could recover, but it left it kind of unresolved between us. At least from her point of view."

"I thought you said you never had a serious relation-ship?" Her voice cracked. *Crap. Breathe, just breathe.* "That sounds pretty serious."

"Not because I saw her as my girlfriend or anything. She was, I dunno... convenient." Knowing how he sounded, Adam closed his eyes. "I can't believe I said that."

"Me either."

"I know, and I wanted you to be prepared. She's the type of woman who'll think we can just pick up where we left off, because that's how it was between us." Adam took the spreader from her hand, placed it on the counter and turned her toward him. His hands rested on her shoulders and he leaned in to look in her eyes. "She won't care if I'm there with you. She'll think she has rights to me."

"I see. So, tell me about her."

"Uhh…" Adam hesitated. He'd been dreading the questions, because the answers would play into every one of Mia's insecurities. "What do you want to know?"

"What does she do? How did you meet her?

"We met in a club VIP room in LA. She's a model."

"Figures." Stepping away, Mia crossed the room. She went to the big window that faced the backyard. She was thinking. The girl was always thinking.

Adam stubbed the toe of his sneaker against the floor. "I'm sorry. I know we were invited to Fiona's if you'd rather, we can go there—"

"No, you should be with your family on Thanksgiving." One eyebrow shot up. "Should I go to Fiona's with Ben?"

Jaw tightening, he ground out a response, angry that it even had to come up. "Absolutely not."

"Can I ask why she was invited?"

It would be so easy to lie to her, but she deserved to know what she was up against. It was the only way they could put up a good fight. "Greg called my mother to tell them he was in town, so she and Grandma invited him to dinner. He didn't tell them Pilar was with him until yesterday."

"Greg was the friend you were with the night you cancelled on me, right?"

Shit. "He needs a favor from me."

Mia tried to smile, but the attempt was weak. "He wants to sign Kelvin?"

"Yeah."

"So, he's bringing your ex-girlfriend? Why? *A gift?*"

He crossed to her and Adam felt a pounding in his chest. Taking her face in his hands, his only concern was Mia. This entire day had the potential to ruin what they'd started. "She's not like anyone you've ever met. I don't want you hurt."

Mia covered his hands with hers and came up on her toes to drop a kiss on his lips. "Then don't let her hurt me."

RUNNING AROUND IN her bedroom four hours later, Mia had changed her clothes three times. As she looked at the most recent outfit, she finally felt like she'd gotten the look she was going for. It was festive, not too dressy and a little sexy. She hadn't been going for sexy originally, but with the model coming, Mia was willing to give it a shot. She'd only bought the push up bra the day before. Thank God. Not that the girls needed much help, but what the hell, Adam would be happy. She liked it when she caught him looking at her, when she saw the desire in his eyes.

Mia gave herself another onceover. The shapely sweater dress was the perfect shade of spicy brown, and had a nicely scooped neckline. She wore black leather boots with very high heels, a pair of gold hoop earrings, and if she could get the damned clasp to work, a nice chunky necklace. Mia was showing off more cleavage than usual, and while she liked how she looked, thinking about Adam's family, she wasn't sure it was appropriate.

"Goddammit!" The clasp didn't close right again, and Mia had to catch the necklace before it hit the floor.

As soon as she'd said it she regretted it. She never swore, and hated setting a bad example for Ben. Of course, her son was hanging around a college football team, she was sure his vocabulary was growing every day.

There were footsteps in the hallway and a tapping on her bedroom door.

"Come in."

The door opened and Adam stepped in the room while she struggled once again with the necklace. He came to where she was standing by the dresser, and positioned himself behind her. He gazed at her in the mirror, and gently took the necklace from her hands. Without a word, he reached around, fastening the clasp. Then unexpectedly, he looped his arms around her waist and left a kiss on her neck, just near her ear. They locked eyes in the mirror, and when Adam smiled, Mia felt her heart kick into overdrive.

"You look beautiful."

"No, I don't. I look... *fat.*"

Adam's eyes narrowed. Annoyed. "How do you figure that?"

"Look at me." Mia looked down and wrapped her arms over his. She couldn't remember the last time something had been this important to her. She wanted his family to like her, to accept her. Spying the swells of her breasts peeking out of the neckline, she changed her mind again. "I should change. The dress is too tight."

"Mia, shh." Pressing his lips to her temple, Adam held her close. "You look amazing."

"No, I don't. My ass is huge, my boobs are... I don't even know..." A hitch in her breath told her it wouldn't be long, and a lump formed in her throat. Adam turned her toward him and pulled her close. Mia pressed her face into his sweater taking comfort in his warmth. "I'm sorry. I'm a mess, and now your ex-girlfriend will be there, and she's famous and gorgeous and sophisticated and I'm a... I'm a nobody."

Adam leaned away and looked down into Mia's eyes. "You will *never* be a nobody. Fame doesn't make you important, Mia, substance does. I learned that the hard way." One of his hands came up and he stroked her hair away from her face. "You're one of the best people I know. You've made a life for yourself and Ben, you make a difference in the lives of the students, you're incredibly talented,

315

and I've learned how to be a better person because of you." He kissed her forehead. "Don't judge yourself against a woman like Pilar. There's nothing beneath the surface. No depth. She's beautiful, sure, but even in that department, she has nothing on you."

"How can you say that? She's a lingerie model, and I'm a librarian!"

"Honey, I might regret saying this, but I've seen you both naked. Trust me, you win." He raised an eyebrow and grinned at her. "Fix your make-up, but don't you dare change the dress. I love the dress."

"Okay," she whispered.

"I will give you one tip about my family. It gets embarrassing, but they like to sing. They love music. My grandmother has three pianos in the house."

"Really?"

"After dinner, prepare to be recruited. You could be the new accompanist for Christmas carols while we trim the tree."

"You're sure?" She sniffed and smiled because she knew the answer.

Adam grabbed a tissue and dabbed at her eyes. "I'm more than willing to give it up so you can show off."

Mia laughed and hugged him close one more time. Three months ago, she didn't know she could feel this way about another person. Now she couldn't imagine ever losing it.

Chapter Twenty

MIA'S MINI-MELTDOWN HAD put them behind schedule. They'd be making an entrance, which is exactly what Adam wanted to do when he heard about Pilar and Greg dropping in for Thanksgiving.

When he talked to his grandmother, he found out that while his mother happily invited Greg, no one had any idea Pilar would be part of the deal until it was too late. He knew Greg was angling at the opportunity to recruit Kelvin, but he wondered why he'd be bringing Pilar. Mia's observation, as sick as it was, was the only explanation. Did he really think he could offer up a woman for a favor?

More than likely, he did, which pissed off Adam. This is what some people still thought of him. Looking to his right, he thanked God Mia didn't. He couldn't believe how upset she'd gotten earlier, all because she didn't think she was anything special, because she didn't think she was good enough to meet his family.

She was so pretty, but he'd finally figured out that while her outer beauty was extraordinary, it was her inner beauty that made his heart trip. There was this light inside her, this goodness that spread outward to everyone she loved. Adam wanted to be one of those people.

He knew his family would love her. Gram already did, and his siblings were dying to know more about her. One of the things Mia always said she missed out on was having was a big noisy family; now Adam worried that his big, noisy family would scare her off.

The realization had been slow in coming, but it all hit this morning, when he had to tell her about Pilar flying in. He knew she'd feel threatened, that she'd feel inadequate somehow. There was no way to explain to her how he felt, so he'd have to show her.

He couldn't lose her, because she was his best part. His very best part.

They pulled into the road that was the driveway to his grandmother's house. He could see how nervous she was, her knuckles were pure white. She looked terrified, and if he thought it would help, he would turn the car around and head back to Compass Cove. But as they approached the front of the house, Mia perked up. The kids were outside playing soccer, and it seemed to Adam as soon as kids were involved, she felt better. It only took one look from her, one smile. When their eyes met, Adam had to fight the urge to tell her he'd give her as many children as she wanted.

Relatives clamored around the car before they even got out, and that included a horde of kids. He looked back at Ben and saw he was a little nervous, too. But Ben was a survivor. He was tough, and Adam guessed he'd have friends in ten minutes.

He opened the car door and got out, and Mia did the same. As expected, every male over the age of sixteen stopped and stared at her, and Adam hoped Mia noticed. Not just because he wanted her to see how proud he was to be with her, but also because her ego most definitely needed the boost. Ben, who'd been taken off crutches only yesterday, eased out of the back seat, letting his booted foot lead while Adam rounded the car to them. Her hand was warm as he took it in his, and led her to the crowd that had gathered.

"Hey, everybody. I'd like you to meet Mia and Ben." She was trembling, unfortunately, and he hated that there was nothing he could do to ease her nerves. She'd have to handle the situation on her own. "Mia, Ben—this is, well, everybody. You'll have to figure it out as you go along."

Adam could see she was still apprehensive, and he guessed it had more to do with meeting Pilar than meeting his extended family. Ben's boot became an immediate topic of discussion and the kids whisked him away without much thought. He quickly became part of the group.

The small tug on his jacket was most welcome. Looking down, he saw his four-year-old niece, Rosie. She had magnificent dark hair and eyes, and the attitude of a pissed-off pixie. She glared at him and gave Mia and assessing glance. When she reached out her arms to be picked up, Adam obliged.

Rosie didn't miss a beat. Grabbing Adam's cheeks, she planted a noisy kiss on his lips and he could see Mia was enchanted. "Happy Thanksgiving, Rosie."

"You're late, Uncle Adam."

"I know, I'm sorry about that. The crazy frog people had me trapped."

His niece closed her eyes, shook her head, and slapped a tiny hand against her forehead. "Frog people? Do I look like I was born yesterday?"

In a way, she did. Rosie was a tiny little thing, only her attitude was big.

"Is this your girlfriend?" Rosie gave Mia a good onceover, and Adam saw how quickly Mia tried to prepare herself for his clarification of their relationship.

"Actually, Rosie, it is." Adam turned his niece toward a very shocked Mia. "Rosie, this is Mia, my girlfriend. Mia, my niece, Rosie."

Rosie nodded and wiggled her way down before Mia could say a word. "Well, then you two better get inside. I think your *old* girlfriend is driving Granny crazy."

Without a second thought, Rosie took off to annoy the big kids, and left Adam to worry about what he'd find inside. Mia should have been a nervous wreck, but she'd stepped away and gazed up at the house.

Three stories tall, the white clapboard house had dark green shutters, stone and a tile roof. While the overall design was simple, a large front portico, sun porches, and massive windows created an elegant look. But, elegant or not, the house would never be mistaken for anything but a home. Set on over six acres, there was a guest house and a six-car garage, gardens, and a waterfront the size of a small public beach. The stable had been converted to a caretaker's cottage, and the couple who took care of the house and grounds lived there with their two children. It was one of the most impressive properties in the hamlet, just smaller than Harborside, the massive estate owned by the Hardt family.

"What a beautiful home," she said. "I can see your grandmother here."

Adam smiled. She was right, and his grandfather had said the same thing—that the house reflected Grandma, through and through. "My great-grandfather commissioned the house in the thirties."

"What a place to grow up."

"We lived in the guest house. We moved in right after my father died; I was going on ten. My mother still lives there."

"Four kids in a guest house?"

He laughed and understood why she'd say something like that. "The guest house is about 2500 square feet."

"Seriously?"

He nodded. "I'll give you a tour later. You can see where Jack and I used to sleep, but right now we should go inside. Are you ready?"

"I guess." With her hand firmly in his, they started toward the front door.

"Hold onto me, okay?" He kissed her for good luck, and then again because he couldn't help himself. He planned on kissing her again later with the hopes she'd forgive him for putting her through all this shit.

THE MILLER HOMESTEAD was stunning. She could only absorb so much on a first glance, but the entry foyer and grand staircase had more hand carved woodwork than she'd ever seen in her life.

People lived like this, in homes with servants' quarters and guest cottages, with big Kennedy-like families. Mia grew up comfortably middle class, and while her mother acted like a pompous snob, this was a different world altogether.

Adam kept hold of her hand as they made their way through the house. They passed two parlors, one that held a large evergreen tree ready for decorating. At the far end of that room sat a baby grand piano. The house, while elegant, was also comfortable, and that was something not lost on Mia. This was a family home, and she hoped the people Adam cared about accepted her. Maybe if they did, he would find a way to take the last step and love her.

It seemed like an endless walk to the kitchen, but she could hear the noise, the mix of voices, and with each step, Mia's nerves ratcheted up. Adam squeezed her hand a little harder as the voices got louder. The distinctive cadence of one voice set itself apart. The English was flawless, refined, but it was not a member of Adam's family.

Had she ever been this scared? Maybe when she left home for college, or when she realized she would be raising a child on her own. Those were her life changing moments and this one, with Adam's family, was right up there. Get through this for him, she told herself. That's all you have to do.

The kitchen was an enormous room filled with dark wood cabinets, granite and stainless steel. Savory smells from the food being prepared surrounded her; there must have been twenty people packed in the space, and all of them stopped when she and Adam crossed the threshold.

Before any of his family could greet them, there was a screech from across the room. Charging at Adam was Pilar Manheim.

Her black hair was pin straight, her clothes were expensive, and she was thin; God was she skinny. She wore a lot of make-up and her perfume was tinged with the smell of cigarettes. She might have been a million-dollar model, but everything about her felt phony. Mia couldn't imagine what Adam had ever seen in her, and suddenly Mia wasn't so worried.

Pilar's arms wrapped around Adam's neck and she planted a kiss on him that was worthy of an R rating. It was wet, noisy, and caused the others to turn away in embarrassment.

If the woman wasn't such a caricature, Mia would have been really upset, but she just couldn't get angry over someone like this.

Adam grabbed Pilar's arms and peeled her away. In the same move, the model's hands came up and stroked Adam's face. "Oh, my God. I've missed you so. Let's go somewhere so I can say hello to you properly."

Mia had not moved. She was still next to Adam and her arms were folded, yet Pilar didn't seem to see her. Apparently, she was invisible.

"Ah, Pilar. Wow. This is a surprise."

"No, it's not." She slapped at his arm and looked over at Linda Miller. "Your mama told you I'd be here." She linked arms with him and led him away from the doorway while Mia watched. She leaned her shoulder into the doorframe and wondered how Adam was going to gracefully extricate himself from this woman's clutches. It was funny until she slid her hand over Adam's rear end. Pilar meant business and Mia didn't know how she was going to handle this.

"Mia?" She looked to her left and there stood a beautiful blonde with bright, hazel eyes. "Hi, I'm Emily, Adam's sister-in-law."

Mia was relieved she could focus on someone else and smiled. "It's nice to meet you."

"You too, finally." Glancing toward Pilar and Adam, Emily shook her head. "I'm sorry about this."

"There's no way anyone could have anticipated. Gotta

love the unexpected."

Emily laughed. "That's one way to look at it, because Linda and Grandma are mortified."

The two of them were talking to a man in the corner who looked oddly familiar. She knew she'd never met him before, but Mia felt like she should know him.

Pilar's hand was now making slow circles around Adam's butt and coming dangerously close to forbidden territory. "I swear if she touches him like that one more time, I'm going to take off her hand." Mia had no idea she could be so possessive.

Apparently, Adam's sister-in-law approved. "I'll hold her down."

"You ladies look like you're plotting murder." The deep voice belonged to a tall, dark haired man with just enough grey at the temples to make him distinguished, and even though it hardly seemed possible, he was better looking than Adam.

"Mia, this is my husband, Doug. The oldest of the Miller sibs."

He smiled a thousand watt smile and Mia wondered how any woman could stay standing in his presence. The man was criminally good looking. Doug was the Marine, and he looked every inch of it. "A pleasure, Mia. My brother said you were beautiful, but I think that was an understatement."

Her face flushed at the compliment and then it burned when she looked back at Pilar grabbing Adam. "That's it." Mia straightened and focused on the target. "Time to crash the party. Will you excuse me?"

Crossing the kitchen, she laid her hand on Adam's arm.

He looked at her and breathed out. Relieved. "Hey. I'm sorry. I've been rude." Wrapping his arm around her waist, he pulled her close. "Greg, Pilar, this is Mia DeAngelis. Mia, Pilar Manheim and Greg Rhodes."

Greg shook her hand and looked at her the same way Mia figured she was looking at him—something was familiar. Pilar, on the other hand, folded her arms and stuck her nose in the air. "And you are?"

Mia looked at Adam and could only imagine what her eyes were saying. She was pissed off, truly pissed off at Pilar and at him. He had ten seconds to give the right answer.

"Mia and I are together, Pilar." *Ding! Ding! Ding!* Mia smiled and Adam got a gold star.

"Together?" Pilar sneered. "What does that mean? You're doing her, Adam?"

The entire room went silent, and Mia wanted to crawl into one of the kitchen cabinets, but before she had the chance, before anyone moved, Adam took Pilar by the elbow and led her from the room. He didn't say anything, but the way his jaw was set and the vein in his neck bulged—he was angry.

"Should I follow them?" she asked.

Both Jack and Doug shook their heads, but they also looked concerned. "We'll give him a minute," Doug said.

"Then we'll make sure he hasn't killed her," Jack added. "You'll stay here."

Emily stepped next to her and another woman had joined them. She put a hand on Mia's shoulder, almost impressed by Adam's reaction. "I've never seen him like that."

A petite woman hopped up onto a stool, her long hair in a messy bun and a smudge of flour on her nose. Based on the description from Adam, it was his youngest sister, Natalie. "She's a bitch. I hope he scares the crap out of her. Hi, I'm Nat."

Mia nodded, still embarrassed by the scene.

"Don't let it bother you," Natalie said. "No one here has ever liked her."

"You've met her?" Mia asked.

"Once," Emily replied. "Adam brought her to an anniversary party about four years ago."

"She was snotty and skinny to the point of being scary, not thin, like a runner might be thin, but emaciated. And all she did was tell anyone who would listen how fabulous she was." Natalie popped a small piece of cheese into her mouth. "Adam wasn't at his best, he was living fast and loose. That was about six months before the accident, wasn't it?" She looked to her sister-in-law for a response.

Emily nodded as she spread some Brie on a piece of French bread and handed it to Mia. "It got to the point that we didn't know who he was. The accident was tragic, but it brought him back to us." She glanced at Greg Rhodes, who'd stepped away from the conversation. "In some ways, it saved him."

Mia thought about the man Adam used to be and who he was now. Other than the fierce competitiveness, there was nothing left of the self-destructive celebrity. In all likelihood, even if he gave Pilar the chance, she'd be bored with who he'd become. It kind of stunned Mia that she wasn't jealous or worried about a supermodel stealing her boyfriend. What she hated was that Adam was being confronted with such an unpleasant part of his past.

ADAM GUIDED PILAR through the house and gave her a nudge into the solarium, which was as far away from the kitchen, and Mia, as he could get. The pounding in his head was a sign that he was so angry he could do real harm, so once he had the door closed he put as much distance between them as possible.

Flipping her hair, she started. "You have some nerve, you know? You drop out of my life and then you humiliate me with that woman."

"Have you lost your mind? Who are you to say those things around Mia? Around my family! You have no right, and if you have any hope of staying here another minute, you will treat her with respect."

"Oh, this is about your little girlfriend? What? Doesn't she know about you?"

"She knows."

"Really? Does she know about the things you did, the women you did? Does she know all about your past, Adam?"

"I'm not the same person anymore, and she's part of the reason why."

Pilar sat in a large wicker chair and laughed. She laughed right from her belly, sending all her derision in Adam's direction.

"You're still the same. Men like you don't change. You just found someone new to fuck."

Lucky for him, just as he started toward Pilar, ready to unload ever profane thing he could think of, his brothers stepped into the room. Jack grabbed one arm, Doug, the other.

"Whoa!" Doug said. "Adam, she's not worth it."

Jack agreed. "Seriously, bro. Don't let her get to you. Keep your focus on Mia."

Pilar hissed. "Mia. Pssht. I'm surprised she's not in here, wondering if you're going to leave her. By the way, since when do you go for fat women?"

Adam tensed, barely restrained. He was a good ten feet away, and he would never touch her, but Pilar pulled back into her chair and looked scared. He'd never in his life hit a woman, and there was no way Pilar would change that, but the bitch needed to know she'd crossed the line. Once again, his brothers held on. Just in case.

"For the record," Jack said quietly, "Mia's not worried."

Adam felt like he could breathe when he heard that.

329

Knowing how insecure Mia had been, he couldn't stop wondering what she was thinking about this mess. "She's okay?"

"More than okay," Doug said. "This one, however, is not worth your time."

Adam turned to Pilar, who looked like a piece of tangled wire. Her long legs were crossed and she'd assumed her best indifferent pose, staring out the solarium window toward the harbor.

"Don't cross me, Pilar, and stay the hell away from Mia. You're a guest in this house, and if you insult my family by behaving badly, I will be the one to show you out."

He and his brothers moved toward the door, but her voice stopped them.

"Are you in love with her, Adam?"

He turned and thought about the question. He knew Mia was more important than anyone had ever been to him; he knew he couldn't even think of going on without her; he knew she made him a better person.

He could barely get the words out, but there was no doubt in his mind. "You let me worry about Mia. But if you hurt her, I will make your life a living hell."

Stunned, Pilar sat back in the chair, saying nothing, and Adam turned and exited the room with his brothers.

Doug patted him on the back and Jack couldn't stop smiling.

"Have you told Mia?" Jack asked.

"What?"

Jack chuckled lightly. "That you're in love with her."

"Not yet," Adam said. "I guess I should."

"Yeah," Doug said. "You might want to let her know."

AFTER THE DISHES were cleaned up, and dessert had been served, Mia found herself a quiet spot on the patio with a cup of coffee and her thoughts. This was such a beautiful place. The moon was shining over the cove and someone had lit a fire in the outdoor fireplace, chasing the November chill from the air. Everything here was geared toward comfort, beauty, and being with other people.

This was a crazy family. They were loud, funny, and totally devoted to one another. Mia was a little envious. It was what she'd always wanted. Adam said they could be a little scary, but Mia thought they were wonderful. Every person was warm and open, treating Mia like they'd known her for years, including her in gossip and family arguments, and accepting her with Adam without question.

She'd only known Adam since late September, not even three months. He'd become such a part of her and Ben's lives so quickly that she wondered if any of what she felt was real. How was it that she'd gone thirty years without feeling anything like this for anyone and then BAM! He was the antithesis of what she thought she needed or wanted, and that made Mia wonder… had being closed-minded and judgmental, like her mother, kept her from being happy?

The footsteps coming from inside the house broke her from her reflection. Adam was coming out to the terrace and in one move he covered her in a plush knitted throw. Then, he straddled the end of the chaise she'd settled in and faced her with the sweetest smile ever.

"It's getting cold," he said as he leaned in to kiss her.

"A little." Mia melted into the kiss, which was more than a peck, and definitely hinted at what was to come.

"Did I tell you," he began, "how incredible you were tonight? Not just with my family, but with Greg and Pilar. You've been very…understanding."

Mia didn't respond, but instead focused her eyes on her coffee cup. Adam tilted her face toward his, and kissed her again. Just as he did, Pilar came onto the terrace and lit a cigarette.

"Aren't you two just the cutest." Her tone dripped with arrogance and superiority, causing Adam to hold Mia's hands tighter. Pilar roamed around the terrace, looking at the plants and taking long drags from her cigarette before parking herself on a stone bench. "So, Adam, are you actually going to marry this woman?"

Nothing like humiliation in front of a stranger, especially a stranger like Pilar. There was a long pause and Adam spoke. "Honestly, I don't think with my baggage, Mia would have me."

Holding back her own response was the hardest thing Mia had ever done. She stifled the impulse to leap up and propose to him herself. It could be there was nothing remotely sincere about what he said, other than Adam's intention to spare her the embarrassment. But even if that was his intention, she appreciated it.

Pilar glared at her and raised an eyebrow. "Not interested, Miss Librarian?"

There was something enormously satisfying watching this horrible woman grasp at anything to save face. Taking advantage of the situation, Mia stood and Adam followed. She addressed him directly, not even acknowledging Pilar's question, knowing that the slight would annoy her to no end. "I'd like to say goodnight to everyone. It's getting late."

Adam nodded and without giving Pilar a second look, walked Mia into the house. It was hard to say, but it seemed that Greg and Pilar... more Pilar... took Adam to a place he didn't want to be. Mia was safe. He put his arm around her shoulder and kissed the top of her head. "You're the best, kid."

"I'm trying."

Stopping in his tracks, Adam turned her toward him. Words were unnecessary. His hands came to her face and he kissed her. He seemed to sense what was going on in her head and in her heart. With his hands still cupping her cheeks, he squared up and looked at her. "Stop it," he whispered, kissing her again. "Just stop it."

"I'm sorry. She's been getting to me all day."

"Don't let her." Adam's hand took hers and pulled her along. "She's acting this way because it's all she has. There's no way she can keep up with you."

"You think she's jealous? Of me?"

Adam smiled and kissed her again. "Oh, honey, I know she is."

ADAM BRUSHED A lock of hair off Mia's face.

She was tucked into his bed, sleeping like an angel. Staring at her, Adam wondered what he could do to make her understand she had nothing to worry about.

Mia had put on a good face today, but she was as wired as a nervous cat, and he suspected Pilar's presence had done a number on her confidence. Adam knew he hadn't helped it either that he had spent a lot of time with Greg, and that meant Pilar too. But Mia didn't know that, all that time, all he could think about was her. The woman had stolen his heart.

Greg found Mia attractive—really attractive. From the minute he met her, he kept making comments to Adam about taking her off his hands. Finally, Adam had told him to lay off. It was all to piss Adam off, of course. His friend was doing it to get a rise out of him—God knew he could still push every button.

But now Adam had to figure out what to do about the woman curled against him. He was in love with her. He was so over the top in love with her it hurt physically. Dropping his hand to her soft shoulder, he ran it down her arm and wrapped her tiny hand in his.

Mia's eyes fluttered open and she looked at him, a sweet smile touching her lips.

She brought her hand, the one he was holding, to the side of her face and together they touched her earlobe where a diamond earring glistened. "Thank you for my present," she said quietly.

He'd wanted to get her something special for her upcoming birthday, her thirtieth, and he'd settled on the flawless diamond studs, since he wanted something as pure and perfect as she was. "I'm glad you like the earrings."

"I love them." Pushing herself up on one elbow, the covers dropped away from her breasts and Adam breathed in hard when she leaned in and kissed him. "I love you, Adam." She kissed him again. "I love you."

He closed his eyes tight, because once again she'd been the braver of the two of them. She'd told him she loved him, not expecting anything in return. Simply giving him something of herself, something beautiful.

Adam was going to have to spend his entire life figuring out ways to deserve her.

Mia didn't stop. She wiggled her way on top of him, straddling him while he lay on his back. Her hair had been pulled back in a ponytail, but she pulled out the elastic and let it fall. It tumbled down her back and over her breasts in soft waves and curls, creating a toffee colored cloud all around her.

Leaning down, she kissed him, first on his lips, then at the hollow of his throat and then in the center of his chest. Adam heard the moan come from deep within. "Mia," he said. "My beautiful Mia."

Brushing her lips over his neck, and around to his ear, she whispered, "I love you."

And then with a move as smooth as water, she took him inside her. He almost passed out from the warm moist sensation enveloping him, almost lost his composure when she laced her fingers with his and started to rock. He couldn't do anything but gaze at her. This amazing woman who was everything to him, moved with purpose and grace, taking them higher and higher until finally his body convulsed and emptied inside her.

There were stars and lights behind his eyes, then he watched as she arched, closed her eyes, and cried out. He felt her tighten around him, intensifying what he'd already experienced. Mia collapsed against him, their slick bodies sticking together, and Adam wrapped her in his arms. His. She was his, and once again Mia gave without thought of what she would receive.

"I love you," she said.

Chapter Twenty-One

SATURDAY WAS GREY. No rain, but no sun, and it wasn't expected to come out for days. Ben had hoped it would be a nice day for Mom's birthday.

Mom.

He was still getting used to it, but he was happy that the adoption would be final soon. Then he would have a mother. He wouldn't have to explain why he didn't have one, or why his aunt took care of him—he'd be another kid with a single mom.

And maybe if Coach stayed around, he'd have a dad too. They really liked each other. The other kids at Thanksgiving said they were in love, especially the girls, and Ben thought they were probably right. He saw the way they kissed and he saw the way Coach looked at her. He knew what was happening when they thought he was asleep in his bed and he heard them go into Aunt Mia's room. He wasn't stupid, and guys talked. Guys talked a lot about that kind of stuff.

Coach took him to town to get her a present, and he walked around the fancy store really, really confused. There was so much glass and breakable stuff, Ben kept his hands stuffed in his pockets.

"Ben, come over here."

Looking up, he saw Coach was waving to him. Walking carefully so he didn't bump into anything, he saw Coach standing by a shelf filled with glass animals. Hundreds of them. Ben liked this. He'd find something here. She loved animals and she loved glass. So that was perfect.

"Ben, this is Liam. His family owns the shop." Liam nodded at him, ben thought anyone who had a shop with so many cool things had to be alright. Ben shook his hand, and started examining the display.

He checked every shelf and table, thinking there was nothing that was just right... but then he saw it. Yeah, that was perfect.

"Can I see that one?" he asked, pointing to a figurine on the center of a shelf. The man smiled. Ben opened his hand and took the animal on the flat of his palm. It was a cat. He remembered the litter of kittens under their front stoop in Maryland. Both he and Mom really wanted to take care of them inside, but they weren't allowed to have pets. He thought she'd really like this.

The man said the cat was made of blown glass. It looked like a diamond, but it had these little black eyes. When he held it up to the light, it reflected so many colors. It was perfect. Mom would love it.

He only had one problem. Ben only had ten dollars and he didn't think that would be enough.

"I like this." He extended his hand toward the man. "But how much is it?"

Liam crinkled his eyes. "This is unique. It was made by a local artist." He looked at him again. "How much are you offering?"

"I have ten dollars."

Liam made a face, nodding. "I want this to have a good home, so I guess we can take that."

"Really?"

"Yes, sir," he answered. "Would you like it wrapped?"

"Yes, please."

Liam took his money; when he returned, he handed Ben a little silver bag containing a wrapped box. It was when Ben looked up that he saw the man give Coach his credit card back. They were trying to do it so he wouldn't see, but he did. He almost said something, but he kind of felt like this is what a dad would do for his kid, so Ben kept quiet and enjoyed what having a father would feel like.

MIA SAT IN the living room, reading a book, with strict instructions from Adam and Ben to enjoy the day. She wasn't supposed to lift a finger, cook a meal, make a snack, nothing. They were going to do everything. So, Mia lounged, with a sappy, and somewhat dirty romance novel, in jeans, her favorite soft rag socks, and a Notre Dame

Football sweatshirt she'd stolen from a certain guy's laundry basket.

Just as she was settling into a nice warm daydream, Adam's truck roared into the driveway and Mia watched as her boys made their way to the house. Adam carried her coffee and Ben had what appeared to be a gift bag. They talked and laughed as they came up the path.

What a pair they made. Adam was wearing jeans, an untucked blue chamois shirt, and a brown barn coat. He was so gorgeous her heart was hammering away before he even got in the house. Ben was in his usual jeans and T-shirt, a Jennings Football sweatshirt, and a baseball cap.

Her boys.

Did life get any better?

Bubba charged into the house and leaped on her, wet paws leading. He was up and he was down as quickly as someone could say 'mud'. Adam grabbed him and sent him to lie down in the entryway. Poor dog. He curled up, his eyes wide and his tail thumping wildly.

Adam handed her the Starbucks, to which she was becoming addicted, and kissed her lightly. "Happy Birthday, again."

"Thank you." Another kiss and another. He hadn't shaved yet today and his beard was scratchy, but she didn't care.

"Um, you guys can stop being gross now." Ben was growing impatient.

"Sorry," Adam said. He stepped back. Ben plopped on the end of the couch and handed Mia the bag.

"Happy Birthday, Mom."

Every time Ben said 'Mom', that was Mia's best present. But she took the bag, and before he could put up a defense, pounced on him and gave him a big kiss on the cheek.

"Ah, man," he complained.

Mia smiled, sat back, and pulled her legs up. She held the bag in her lap and carefully removed the pretty package. The box was wrapped in delicate cream-colored paper and tied with a brown satin ribbon. It was almost too pretty to open. But open it she did, and she had almost as much fun watching Ben's face as seeing what was inside the box. Pulling the tissue aside, Mia gasped when she saw the delicate object.

The tiny cat sat in the palm of her hand and seemed to be staring right at her with the tiny black eyes. It was perfect, and she recalled holding this figure when she stopped in the compass shop a couple of months earlier. Ben had his own smile now, and she guessed it was because they were thinking about the same thing.

"The cats by our front porch," she said. He nodded and Mia felt the tears well up. "You wanted one of those kittens so badly, and I just couldn't keep them in the apartment."

"You wanted one, too," he said.

She hugged him, then wiped her eyes. "I love it, and I know the perfect place for it." Mia got up from the couch and walked to the mantle. It was filled with pictures, including one of Mia and Ben taken when he was about seven on the steps of the Smithsonian. The crystal cat was placed right next to the photo. Mia looked at her son and smiled.

She thought it would be hard to think of him like that, to transition into his mom, but it was the most natural thing in the world. Just as she started to mist up, the doorbell rang. Looking out the front window, there were a pack of boys ranging from eight to about twelve. One of them was holding a football. Ben's friends.

They'd come by every day since he got off his crutches, wondering when he could play. And even on this grey, chilly day, these boys were outside doing boy stuff. She'd been saying no to Ben, worrying about his leg and what he could do to it if he didn't take it easy, but it was getting harder and harder. The poor kid was so bored.

Ben hobbled to the door, threw it open, and just looked at her. That's all he had to do.

"Why don't you guys play in the yard, okay? But Ben, you have to ref. I know you're getting better, but that boot is not meant for football." She loved having a backyard that was big enough for them to play. Ben smiled, and started to go outside—but then stopped, ran back, and gave her a hug. "Stay out of Nana's bushes."

"Okay." He grinned. Then he ran, or hobbled, outside.

She heard the boys charge around the side of the house and Ben couldn't stop smiling. That smile was why she'd moved.

But now she had to prepare. In about half an hour, she would have a pack of muddy, hungry boys in the kitchen, and she knew she'd better see what she had for food.

Adam watched her as she rose and he grabbed her hand before she took a step. His eyes locked with hers and he pulled her to him. His arms circled her waist so easily, Mia wondered what she'd done to deserve feeling like this.

"I'm going to have to steal my sweatshirt back."

Mia's mouth formed itself into a pout. "No, I like it."

"You can keep it, but I need to wear it. I don't want to leave that many boys playing outside without an adult."

Now she was confused. "Why? They're only playing touch."

He rolled his eyes and laughed. "They'll play touch for about a minute and a half." They heard a roar of voices come from the yard; Mia stripped off the sweatshirt and pulled down the ribbed Henley she had beneath. Handing it to him, Adam smiled.

"They're boys; it's normal."

"I'll take your word for it."

Adam pulled the sweatshirt over his head and walked with her to the kitchen. Mia settled onto the window seat and cringed a little when Ben caught the ball where he was sitting and fell onto the grass. He stood and laughed, and Mia breathed out. She was still getting used to Ben being, well, Ben. She'd tried to re-channel the athlete in him, but finally, like any good parent, she realized she had to let her son be who he was.

Perfectly content to be who *he* was, Adam walked out onto the deck. It seemed whatever the role—coach, friend, lover, and maybe someday, husband and dad—he made it work.

"Yo!" he called to the boys. "Are we gonna play ball, or roll around on the grass?"

The boys stopped and Ben smiled.

Mia chuckled as she busied herself finding snacks. So much for not lifting a finger today. She'd baked oatmeal cookies yesterday, so she still had a full container, and fortunately there was a whole gallon of milk. The box of granola bars would be gone, too. She was just about to survey the snack drawer when she jumped. Bubba started to bark wildly and pawed at the back door, frantic to get out.

Mia saw all the boys had stopped playing and were staring in the direction of the fence. Ben broke from the group and Bubba went nuts. When she finally got to the back door, she froze. There, at the back gate, stood her mother and her Aunt Regina. Her mother, holding an umbrella to ward off the sprinkles, was air kissing her muddy grandson. Her aunt, who was far easier going than her sister, was smiling at the scene in the backyard. Finally, her mother looked at the back door and spotted Mia, who was certain her jaw would never find its way off the floor.

Ellen Lang DeAngelis, her very proper, pretentious

mother, had come to visit. She and Aunt Reg had arrived on her birthday while her football coach boyfriend played with her soon-to-be adopted son. Wasn't this a great present? *Woo-freaking-hoo.*

Mia pressed the handle on the door so she could step out and face her mother, who was examining Ben's boot and looked none too pleased. Suddenly, Bubba jumped, and the door flew open with a snap.

Bubba took off around the wet lawn, nothing but a black streak as he ran through two nice big mud puddles. He barked at the boys who laughed, and then made a beeline for Mia's mother. The dog must have decided he had a thing for tall blonde women in white designer trench coats.

There was more barking, a screech, and some laughter from the kids before Adam could grab Bubba and pull him away.

Mia had to admit the two giant paw prints that now adorned her mother's shoulders made quite a statement.

Mom wasn't amused.

STORMING INTO THE house, her mother raged. "Mia Elyse DeAngelis, what the hell is going on?" She ripped off the soiled coat and tossed it over a chair. She turned and glared at Mia, who was passing the container of cookies to Ben to share with his friends. Whenever her mother used her given name, it was going to be a long lecture.

"Sorry about the dog, Mom. He gets excited."

"Forget the dog. I don't care about the dog. What the hell did you do to my grandson?" Her mom sniffed and checked to make sure the kitchen chair was clean before she sat down. "Well?"

"Ben broke his leg. It's healing well and he'll be starting rehab next week."

"He broke his leg? When did this happen and why wasn't I told?" Her aunt had slipped into the kitchen, touching Mia's arm gently in support, and took a spot near the kitchen doorway. Mia loved her aunt. She didn't see her nearly enough.

"He broke it about four weeks ago." Adam came in from the front of the house and stood next to her. "And I didn't tell you," she continued, "because you and I really haven't talked."

Her mother folded her arms. "Well, I've spoken to Ben at least a half a dozen times in the past month. He hasn't said anything. I find that odd."

"You know, he stopped worrying about it after a while. Boys don't really talk about things." Adam jumped in, trying to bolster the argument, but her mother wasn't going to tolerate it from an outsider.

"Somehow, I think he would have mentioned it. Who are you, by the way?"

"Uh, Adam Miller. I'm, ah…" Poor Adam. He hadn't

been prepped for this.

"Adam's my boyfriend," Mia said quickly.

"Your boyfriend? Is this who you dumped Noah for?"

How did she know about that? "No. I broke it off with Noah because of Noah. But we're not talking about that."

"Right," she said. "We're talking about Ben. How did he break his leg?"

Mia didn't answer. She stood there, and then she decided that Ben's injury was nothing she had to hide. Ben was her son and her mother was going to have to deal, so she wasn't vague—Mom got the story with details.

"He broke it playing baseball. He was covering the plate when he and a player on the opposing team had a collision. His leg snapped."

"Oh, my God. Baseball? See. I told you when you signed him up it was a bad idea. There are a thousand ways for him to get exercise. I've always forbidden team sports."

Now Mia was seething. Adam put his hand between her shoulder blades, but nothing was going to calm her down. "Forbidden? You really need to lighten up, Mom."

"We've discussed this. You know what I expect." Her mother's teeth were clenched so tight, Mia thought her jaw might break. But Mia wasn't going to back down. Not this time.

"I know that I'm Ben's mother and you're not. I'm raising him and you're not. That means it's *not* up to you."

"How dare you talk to me like that?"

"Get used to it. I know Ben far better than you do. You up and left me to raise him when you moved south—hell, you did almost nothing while I was in the house. You had plenty of opinions, but you didn't do anything. So now you have to let me handle it. I'm not going to parent by committee."

There was nothing but a clucking of her mother's tongue, a sure-fire sign she was upset. Her mother pursed her lips, narrowed her eyes, and Mia turned to Adam before it got any worse. "Could you go check on Ben?"

"Sure," he said. "You okay?"

"I'll be fine."

ADAM WENT OUTSIDE, and after walking around the house, he found Ben sitting with Bubba on the front porch. He had the container of cookies and was feeding one to the dog when Adam sat next to him on the step.

"I left the dog in the truck."

"He didn't want to be in the truck. He was crying."

"I see." He glanced over and saw Ben had put the leash on. "Okay, well, don't give him anymore of those, he'll get the runs."

"Ewww, really?"

"Yup, but give me one."

Ben smiled and handed Adam the cookies. "Is Grandma

348

pissed at Mom?"

"Oh, yeah." He took a healthy bite of his cookie, tasting the cinnamon and spices. "But Mia's not taking it."

"I hope not. Grandma's a bully."

"Sometimes you need to stand up to a bully."

Ben went quiet and looked at his hands. He was thinking, and Adam found that if you gave this kid enough thinking time, he almost always came down on the right side of things.

"You're right," Ben said, and then he stood.

"Ben, what are you doing?"

"I think it's time to stand up to the bully." And he walked into the house with the dog in tow.

Holy shit.

Adam scrambled up and followed. He got to the kitchen in time to see a smiling Ben go toward his grandmother and his great aunt, and plop on the floor. "Grandma! Aunt Reg! Did Mom tell you about my leg?" He started to unstrap his boot, the sound of the Velcro filling the space. He rolled up his pant leg, exposing the skinny calf with the scars from the incision. "This is where Dr. McAndrews operated. I have two screws."

"Surgery? He needed surgery?" Mia's mother was screeching.

"Aunt Reg?" Mia's aunt was quiet up to this point, but when Ben called her over, she squatted and examined the injury. "The doctor said there was a ton of force that caused my leg to break. Mom said you would understand because of your work."

Adam knew Mia's aunt was a scientist of some sort, and she seemed like a nice woman—very different from her sister. She nodded thoughtfully, listening to Ben talk about his leg. "I'd need to know more, but physics applies to everything."

Mia was watching her mother fume and had to bite back her laughter. Ben was saving the day.

"He needs to get to the city and see someone there," her mother said.

Mia had calmed considerably, and as she watched Ben talk to her aunt, she gave her mother no more than a glance. "He has a wonderful doctor. There's no need."

"But…"

"Mom, there's no need."

Sensing he'd just witnessed a turning point, Adam moved to Mia and took her hand. She smiled up at him, then turned her eyes back to Ben, who was explaining how he got hurt to his grandmother and her sister. The kid didn't flinch.

Mia – 1; Bully – 0.

OF COURSE, THE quiet didn't last. Her mother may have backed off about Ben's injury, but she was getting on her about everything else. The move to New York had gotten five minutes, her job had gotten another five, and now they were on to her weight. Mia was making the bed in the downstairs guest room when they got to that subject. Aunt Regina was settling in upstairs, so there was no buffer.

"I have to say you look good, another twenty-five pounds and you'll be perfect."

"Gee, thanks, Mom."

"And you know, the offer for a breast reduction stands. My surgeon is excellent and I'd be happy to make it a birthday present. It would do so much for your shape if you went down a cup size or two."

Adam walked in just as her mother said the words "breast reduction" and he stopped dead. "Don't you dare," he said. "You're perfect just like you are."

Yes, Adam loved the girls. No doubt a breast reduction wouldn't go over well with him. She smiled.

"I beg your pardon?" Mom did not love the girls, and often spoke of having them taken care of. In her opinion, women of a certain stature were not supposed to be "busty". "Mr. Miller, this conversation does not concern you."

"It does. She's beautiful and she doesn't need to change a thing."

Oh, yes. Mia smiled again. This was her boyfriend sticking up for her, and she loved him.

Adam put her mother's suitcase on a low stand and looked at his watch. "I have to call Sal's and change the reservation."

"Reservation?" Her mother's eyebrow shot up. "Dinner reservations?"

"Yes," he said. "I have to call and let them know we'll be two more."

"Oh, right," Mia said. "I hope it won't be a problem."

"Well," her mother said. "We already have reservations."

Mia turned and faced her mother. "Oh, really?"

"It was a surprise. We have reservations at *Norriture*, at eight."

"Mom, *Norriture*?" Figures. They had to go with the trend. *Norriture* was fancy and expensive and right up her mother's alley. Adam had taken her there the week before because family friends were heavily invested in it. It was nice, but neither she nor Adam thought it was worth the hype. "It's no place for a ten-year-old, Mom.

"Oh, Ben will be fine, but Adam, I'm so sorry, we won't be able to change our reservation. We're meeting other people for dinner, and we didn't know about you."

Mia's locked eyes with his and she could tell he was angry. It wasn't a fury, but a quiet anger that was more about her than anything else. Mia had no intention of going to *Norriture* or anywhere else without Adam.

"I hope your friends won't be disappointed, Mom, but I'm going to dinner with Adam, Nana, and Uncle Rob, Aunt Leslie, and all the boys at Sal's. I hope you and Aunt Regina will come."

"Honey, this is *Norriture*. It's one of the best restaurants in New York!"

"I've been there," Mia said nonchalantly. "Adam took me last week. The place is beautiful, but it's not a place for children."

As her mother started to object again, her aunt entered the room. "Where are we going? Can we cancel that snotty restaurant your mother wanted to go to with her friends? Ellen, I don't know how you keep up this front. It's exhausting."

Mia smiled. She had no idea why her mother moved south to be near her sister. The two of them were oil and water—Aunt Regina took none of her mother's crap. "Mom, I'm going to spend my birthday with the people most important to me. I'm not going to apologize for that."

"I told you it wasn't a good idea, Ellen." Facing Adam, Aunt Reg turned on her best manners. "Adam, if you can change the reservation at Sal's, we'd love to come."

"Regina! You're supposed to be on my side!" her mother screeched.

"Since when?" her aunt replied.

"What about our plans?" Mom pleaded.

"Our plans were to celebrate Mia's birthday. It seems we're doing that."

"Wonderful, just wonderful."

Folding her arms, Mia stared at her mother. She was annoyed, insulted, and truly tired of being treated like a doormat. Maybe her mother should stay in a hotel. Her aunt could stay, but putting her mother off-site was looking better and better.

"What is Sal's—a pizza place?" Ellen was still going. She was like the Energizer Bunny of bitches.

Mia answered her as she moved toward the door, wondering what she'd done to warrant this treatment. "For your information, Mom, Sal's is a very nice Italian restaurant. If there's room, you can come. If not, there's leftover mac and cheese in the fridge."

ADAM FOUND MIA upstairs in her room slamming drawers. He stood back and let her vent until he saw her take a deep breath. She'd handled most of the confrontation with her mother pretty well, but he guessed the cracks about her looks had hurt. Couldn't the idiot woman see the wonderful daughter she had? Going to where Mia stood, Adam took her hand. She was warm. Mia was always warm.

"Don't let her get to you. Don't." He brought her hand to his mouth and skimmed a kiss over the knuckles.

"Lose weight, get a boob job. Shit, what's next? Should I go blonde and get blue contacts, so I can look just like the sainted Sara?"

Adam took her shoulders and turned her to face him. He'd seen her have meltdowns before, but now he knew why. When he looked at her, all Adam saw was this beautiful girl, but the job Mia's mother had done on her self-esteem was bubbling right at the surface.

"The short answer to all of that is no," he said. "The long answer is why would you want to? As I think I've said more than once, you're perfect just the way you are."

Mia's eyes were full of pain as she looked up into his, but surprisingly, there were no tears. He pulled her close and her head dropped onto his chest. Adam's arms fit around her perfectly, just like she belonged nestled against him. Her body was round and supple, her hair was soft, and he often found himself lost in those amber-flecked brown eyes.

"Why does she make me feel like this?"

Families were so hard, especially relationships with mothers and daughters. He'd seen it in his own family and in friends' families, but it had never been anything this blatant, this cruel. "I hate to say this, but you may never measure up in her eyes." Mia's breath hitched, but she held it together, and Adam was happy she wasn't letting her mother win. "But that's her problem, not yours."

Sniffling, Mia wiped a hand across her eyes. "It is if I keep feeling like this. Like somehow I'll never be good enough."

Adam held her tight. "You're good enough. You're better."

Chapter Twenty-Two

THE NOISE IN the house had gone up exponentially once Nana came home with Uncle Rob, Aunt Leslie, and her two cousins in tow. Her cousins Mike and Jason, both teenage boys, commandeered the flat screen in the living room and attached their video game console. Ben loved them, and the three of them spent hours blowing things up and vanquishing bad guys. Her mother complained about the noise, her aunt rolled her eyes, and Mia was happy to have a big noisy family of her own.

Adam had been able to change the reservation to accommodate all the additions, and she was happy that her birthday celebration wouldn't be quiet and dignified. With luck, someone would get nice and drunk.

She sat on the bed in her room and looked at her reflection. Her mother would tell her she looked plump, or busty, or one of the other words she substituted for fat.

Standing, Mia examined herself again, this time in the full-length mirror... and was okay with the person staring back at her. A first, to be sure. Taking a deep breath to calm herself, Mia reached for a pair of dangly earrings, but instead pulled her hand back and grasped the box with her birthday present.

"What did you get from Tiffany?" Mia turned at the sound of Mom's voice. She was standing in the doorway, looking polished and pulled together. And thin. As usual.

Mia took the velvet box and opened it, showing her the diamond earrings. Even her mother seemed impressed, and Ellen DeAngelis was never impressed. "From Adam?"

Mia nodded and took the studs from the box and carefully secured them in each ear. Her mother stepped into the room and walked to the window. "He's very important to me, Mom. I don't know where this is going, but I have a right to find out."

"I don't like it. After what happened to your sister..."

"I'm not Sara and he's not the guy who left Sara."

"But he's... he's a football coach, Mia."

"He's a good man, Mom, and he's been so good for Ben and for me. Your obsession with the sports thing is not healthy. It's extreme."

Her mother sat in the armchair in the corner of the room and gazed out the big windows across the harbor. "I don't like it."

"I know, you said that, but it's not your decision."

There were several bottles of perfume, but Mia reached for the one she'd figured out was Adam's favorite. Spritzing a little behind her ear and a little on her cleavage, she watched her mother cringe. "Something wrong, Mom?"

"The top is a little low cut, don't you think?"

Mia examined the deep V-neck of the soft blue wrap sweater she wore. Her original thought was to layer a cami under it, but with the right bra, it didn't need it, and the neckline flattered her. She loved how he looked at her, loved how his eyes darkened with desire, and never having been a woman who dressed for a man, she found herself doing it more and more often.

"I'm not going to work. This is fine."

"It's too much," her mother said. Mia stopped for a moment and let the words sink in. As she fixed the clasp of her bracelet, and fluffed up her hair, she looked at her mother in the mirror. Her eyes were narrowed, her lips pursed. It was the same tight disapproving sneer Mia remembered from her childhood. Mom never had to raise her voice; she could scold someone with her face. It was something Mia never wanted to be.

Thinking carefully about her response, Mia gripped the edge of her dresser and steadied herself before she turned. This was the face-off she'd been trying to avoid, but if she had any hope of having a pleasant birthday dinner, her mother needed to understand her place. Mia was thirty years old and it was time she acted like it.

Her mother must have sensed that there was going to be a confrontation, because her back straightened and her hands came together neatly in her lap. This was her 'I dare you' pose.

"Too much?"

"Yes. I don't think you need to flaunt yourself quite so much." Mia looked down at the girls and then watched her mother's body language. Slowly, her Mom crossed her arms over her very small bust line. Nana was right.

"Mom, do you sit around and think of the most absurdly mean things to say to me? How is this okay?"

Mia never saw her mother shoot up from a chair quite so fast. "I beg your pardon?"

"I've decided that I like the way I look. You're the only one who seems to have a problem with it."

"If I'm harsh, it's only because I want you to be the best you can be. You have such a pretty face, but…"

"But nothing. My whole life you've made me feel second rate. Stop it."

Her mother sat down and dropped her head. "I had no idea you were so angry with me."

"Well, now you know."

A long, tense silence stretched between them. Would her mother strike out at her, give her the silent treatment, or acknowledge the problem? It was none of those. Instead, she asked a question.

"So, is that why you're with the football player? To get back at me? To dishonor your sister?"

"That's a low blow and totally unfair—to me, and to Adam. I'm not with him to spite you. It has nothing to do with you." She turned away because she felt the emotions welling up. Feelings her mother couldn't, or wouldn't understand. "All you need to know is that I've never been happier, and neither has Ben."

Her mother rose and stepped beside her, making eye contact again in the mirror. "It won't last. He'll leave you."

"You don't know that. But I have to give it a chance. I can't keep worrying about what might happen."

"And Sara's memory?"

"She'll always be with me, Mom, but I can't live my life for her anymore. I have to live for myself and for Ben."

"You work on a college campus. I'm sure there are dozens of suitable men. I don't understand," she sniffed.

"You're right, and how lucky that I found the man who's best for me." How could she possibly explain to her mother how Adam made her feel? How when he touched her everything else dropped away? How when he was nearby, whatever troubles she had seemed less burdensome?

There was another protracted silence, and finally Mia heard familiar footsteps on the stairs. Soon Adam appeared in the doorway, and all Mia's anger melted away.

"Hey, birthday girl." His kiss gently brushed her cheek, and the way he beamed at her melted the tension skittering around the room. Without missing a beat, or thinking about Mia's happiness, her mother was scowling at the scene.

"Mrs. DeAngelis. Looking forward to the evening?"

It took a few seconds for the reaction, but Mia was sure Adam felt the chill as her mother swept out of the room without so much as a glance back.

"I'm sorry about that."

He shook his head. "Eh, don't worry about it."

But she did worry. Her mother created drama. She wasn't warm like Nana, or supportive like Adam's family. No, Mom was all about conflict, and lots of it. Adam wrapped his arms around her and pulled her close, his lips touching her forehead. "I just want you to have a good time tonight. I can handle your mother."

"Really?"

"Really. Your Aunt Regina is a hoot, and I like your uncle and aunt and cousins. It's going to be fine."

She nodded. He was right. Her mother might never come around, and although she could intellectually come to grips with it, emotionally it hurt. Mia made a promise to herself that if she ever had a little girl of her own, she'd never heap that kind of baggage on her. Love would not come with conditions.

A little girl—her's and Adam's. God, what Mia wouldn't do to make that dream a reality. He held her away and examined her eyes, looking for something that might tell him what she was thinking. If he only knew.

The thing was, Adam loved kids. She saw it in the way he interacted with Ben and with his nieces and his cousin's kids. He was a born father, and the image of him holding a baby had her letting out a sigh.

"Are you going to tell me what's running through your

head?"

Mia grinned up at him. "Nothing to tell."

He knew exactly how to get to her, of course; he leaned in and whispered in her ear. His warm breath caressed her skin as his fingers threaded through her hair.

"Fine," he said. "I'll get it out of you later."

Another sigh. She had no control where he was concerned. Now, looking into the blue of his eyes, Mia could tell she'd gotten to him as well. He may not have said it, but it was all over his face.

Adam loved her. And that was the best birthday present of all.

He loved her with her big boobs and round butt. He loved her despite her crazy family. And he loved her son. He didn't have to say it because right there, plain as day, the emotion was on his face.

"Hey," he said. "You look a little dreamy. Are you okay?"

"It's okay. It's really okay." She went up on her toes and kissed his cheek, lingering there for a second because she could. "It's kind of perfect, actually."

When his fingers brushed the hair away from her face and lingered on her cheek, Mia saw everything come to the surface. And when his breath caught, she knew for sure.

"Mia," he whispered. His lips grazed her temple. "Mia, I—I…"

"Shhh." Mia laid and index finger on his lips. "I know. We'll talk later."

He nodded before leaning in to kiss her. And as Adam nibbled her lips, Mia thought what a miracle this was. Three months ago, she was alone, wondering if she would ever feel this way about another person, and here he was loving her back.

There was such tenderness when he kissed her, Mia reached out and let her hands settle on his biceps. She could feel the hard muscle through the fabric of his dress shirt, feel the power he was holding back to be gentle with her. He always thought of her.

"We'd better go," he said. "Or we're going to miss our reservation."

Mia nodded and as if on cue, they stepped back from each other. But Adam reached out and took her hand in his.

When they walked downstairs, hand in hand, Mia watched the different reactions. Her grandmother and her uncle smiled, and so did both her aunts. Her mother still looked irritated, but it was Ben's reaction she most wanted to see—and what happened made her birthday perfect. Ben didn't react at all. He didn't flinch, didn't think anything was the least bit out of the ordinary. In his eyes, she and Adam were together.

"Are we going? I'm starved." Ben hobbled toward her and this, once again, confirmed for her that Adam was right for her.

He was right for both of them.

"WOW," MIA SAID, scanning the packed parking lot. "It's crowded tonight."

Adam kept his smile in check because it was true. Sal's was more crowded than usual, and the reason it was so busy was because he'd filled the place for her birthday.

And he was really hoping she liked surprises.

The Mercedes fit neatly in a nice, close spot, and once they got out of the car, they waited for everyone else to arrive. When the group gathered, Adam let her family move in front of them. He wanted Mia to have the full effect of the crowd when she walked in. There should be at a least forty people there, and he couldn't wait to see her face.

In addition to that, he couldn't wait to see her mother's face.

The scenes he'd witnessed with her mother today showed Adam exactly what Mia was battling. And it sucked.

In his life, Adam had screwed up more times than he could count. He'd ruined his career, let down his teammates, and embarrassed his family. Never once did he doubt their love and support of him.

Here was Mia... smart, talented, and selfless, and her mother treated her like a disappointment. He had no idea how this was possible.

Over the past few months, Adam had learned a lot about the kind of person he wanted to be, and he attributed that to

Mia and Ben. Because of them, he found the best part of himself, and his goal now was to make sure he didn't screw it up.

Her hand was securely in his as they walked in the door behind her uncle and aunt and her two cousins. Mia's family may not have been as unwieldy as his, but not counting her mother, she had some good people in her corner.

A few weeks ago, he talked to his grandmother about the DeAngelis and Lang families. They ran in different circles, but Mia's grandparents were well liked in town. Her grandfather had run the Cove Community Bank for forty years and was a friend to many people. Janet, his grandmother and Lina Rinaldi had been friends for as long as he could remember.

Reaching back, Adam remembered going to the bank with his father and making a beeline for the lollypops that were kept in a decorative wooden box on the bank floor. He distinctly remembered one day when a tall man in a shirt and tie filled the box when he found it was empty.

Adam thought he might have been five at the time. The man squatted down, shook his hand, and let him take two lollipops from the box.

After that day, every time Adam went to the bank with his father, he walked to the big desk and said hello to the man who had given him the lollipops. Grandma told him last week the banker was more than likely Tom Lang, Mia's grandfather.

It was like fate made the connections for them. He had her grandmother for history, and his family endowed the professorship that brought her to Compass Cove. She had family here, ties to the area, and she fit in. From the day she arrived, Mia wove herself into the fabric of the town, and that wasn't going to change.

He held the door to Sal's and Mia smiled. There was nothing better in his mind than to be on the receiving end of one of Mia's smiles. She was still looking at him when they entered the restaurant, and it took a bit for her to respond to the cheers and calls of "Surprise!" But when she did, the shock on her face was worth every bit of planning.

"Oh, my God." Her voice was barely audible as she looked in his eyes. "What did you do?"

"Are you surprised, Mom?" Ben was beaming at her, proud of what he and Adam had accomplished. She reached out an arm and pulled him close. The restaurant was packed, full of noisy people who were surrounding Mia with good wishes. True to form, she was tearing up.

Adam stepped back and let her enjoy the attention. It wasn't something he craved or needed anymore. Lord knew, he'd had more than enough when he was playing pro to last a lifetime. Now he was content to let other people have the spotlight. Especially people who deserved it.

Mia's excitement was so much fun to watch, it took a second to notice that Mrs. Lang and his own grandmother were standing next to him.

"I've never seen her so happy," her grandmother said. "Thank you, Adam."

"Don't thank me. I like making her happy."

His grandmother leaned in and kissed his cheek. "We know, and that's what's making Mia glow like she is. She knows too."

Adam hoped she did.

MIA WENT FROM person to person and thanked them for coming. She was totally overwhelmed by the number of people there. These were her friends, and she'd only been there a short time. Compass Cove really was her place.

She caught sight of Adam talking to Ben, and something in the body language put her on alert. It looked serious for a second, and then Adam's face broke into the wide smile she loved so much. Savory smells filled the air as people munched on appetizers and drank wine. Kids sat together and goofed around, and Mia went to the man who made it all possible for her.

"Hey," he said. As if on cue, Adam looped his arm around her shoulder and pulled her close. Comfort and warmth. And love.

"If my mother's looks could kill, you'd be a goner. What happened?"

"I, ah…" He looked at her mom and then back at her. "I

kind of told your mother to back off."

"You what?" He'd taken on the woman some former students called Dr. Evil.

"I want you to relax tonight. Have fun."

She looped her arms around his neck. It was fun to be able to do that and watch his eyes smolder when she pressed into him. "So you told her to—"

"—to back off." He finished the sentence and glanced at Mia's mom, who looked to be in an uncomfortable conversation with Adam's grandmother. Nice. Grandma would kill Ellen with kindness.

The kiss Mia dropped on his lips was soft and innocent. She didn't need to do any more to let him know how grateful she was. "Thank you for everything."

"You're welcome." Adam nuzzled her hair, and Mia thought this had to be the best birthday present ever.

The moment didn't last. "There's the birthday girl!"

The voice was booming and Mia swore the whole room stopped when Greg Rhodes entered. He pulled her from Adam into a crushing hug. "How are you, darlin'? Have you missed me?"

Mia extracted herself from his grip and reached for Adam's hand. "Greg! I had no idea you'd be here."

"I wouldn't have missed a chance to see you, beautiful."

Adam's grin seemed forced. He pulled Mia closer, and extended a hand to his friend. *Some friend.* "Weren't you out west scouting a prospect? I didn't think you were going to make it."

"I flew back right after the game. I'll be in town a few more days, and then I head back to Chicago."

Mia suppressed a smile as Adam inched even closer. She loved when he was territorial. It was positively primitive, but she didn't care; it made her feel wanted. She liked being his woman.

"Glad you could make it back. Grab a drink and some food. My family is in the other room."

Greg winked and Mia let out a laugh as soon as he was out of earshot. Adam cocked his head to the side. "Are you enjoying this?"

"Oh, yes," Mia said. "If he gets under your skin so much, why did you invite him?"

"Because while he may be an asshole, for a long time he was like a brother to me."

"Okay. Stay close when he's around, though. He gives me the creeps."

"Will do." He kissed her again. Mia felt a tap on her shoulder and looked up to see her Aunt Regina standing next to her. Her face was drawn, worried.

"Your mother isn't feeling well. I'm taking her home."

It was like being slapped, but she wasn't surprised. She understood if her mother was uncomfortable. She even understood if her Mom was angry at Adam, but she couldn't, for the life of her, understand how her mother could justify leaving. "Really?"

She put her hand on her shoulder, because Mia couldn't cover up the hurt. "I know, honey. I'm sorry."

"Alright, I guess I shouldn't have expected any more from her."

"Mia, for once it's not what you think."

"But it's always something, and it's always about her."

Unexpectedly, her aunt hugged her. Aunt Reg was an engineer by profession, who had taught a generation of students. A steady, straightforward woman, overt displays of affection were not her style. She found herself softening as her aunt tightened her arms around her.

"I know this hurts," she said.

Mia hugged her aunt, feeling her warmth and strength. The slights didn't bring tears anymore, but the burn went straight to her heart. She sniffled and her aunt's hand patted her on the back.

"You wear your heart on your sleeve, you always have."

"Is that bad?"

"No, it's who you are. This is who she is, and you're very different."

Mia stepped back, but Aunt Regina didn't let go. She was a kind person. Lovely and sweet, as well as fiercely loyal. "She needs to leave, Mia. She'll tell you why when you get home later."

"Okay." Mia kissed her cheek and as she turned to walk away, Aunt Reg stopped her.

"I know your mom won't agree with me, but I think Adam is a good man."

"Very good." Mia took a step back toward her aunt. "I think Daddy would have liked him."

"I think you're right. Your dad would have admired that he stood up for you. That he didn't care what your mom thought about him, that he only cared about protecting you." At this point her aunt's voice trembled—almost imperceptibly, but it was there.

"Auntie?"

"That's all I've ever wanted for you, sweet girl. Someone who would stand up for you. Be there for you and for Ben. I didn't have that, and your mother never truly appreciated your dad. I'm glad you have someone, Mia."

"Thank you."

Her aunt nodded, kissed the top of her head. "You've done an amazing job with your life, Mia. Made good choices. I'm proud of you. So, so proud of you, and I know your father was proud of you, too."

"Proud of me?"

"Yes, and I'm sorry I didn't tell you sooner. I should have. We *all* should have. See you at home."

It took her a few seconds to recover, because her words left her stunned.

Fiona stepped up beside her and looked at the door. "I saw your mother leave."

"My aunt was just making my mother's excuses."

"What did she say?"

"That it's not what I think."

"It's never what you think."

Mia looked at her friend. Ever since Mia transferred to Maryland to finish her bachelor's, Fiona had been part of her life. They'd gone through graduate school together, struggled to find jobs at the same time, and helped each other with more family issues than she could count. At times, it had felt like she and Fiona had the lock on crazy mothers. Hers was cold and distant, Fiona's was overprotective and meddling. There was no happy medium. But Mia's aunt had surprised her, and given her something to think about. Something she'd never expected.

"She told me that she's proud of me. That she knew my dad would be too."

Fiona's face froze. "She did?"

Mia nodded. "That I've made good choices. She really likes Adam."

"Wow."

"Yeah, I know."

"So, what about Ellen?" Fiona had taken to calling Mia's mother by her given name, while Mia's name for Fiona's was "Mother Gallagher".

"Adam told her to stop dumping on me. I don't think that went well."

Fiona passed Mia the glass of wine she was holding and Mia accepted it, taking a drink of the ruby colored liquid.

"My boyfriend went to head-to-head with my mother.

Stuck up for me."

Fiona took the wine back and finished what was in the glass. "I think that sounds like a good day."

Mia looked at her. "It does, doesn't it?"

"Yup, I also think we need more wine to celebrate." Fiona pointed Mia in the direction of the bar.

Mia agreed. "Let's go find a bottle of Chianti and some chocolate."

Fiona laughed and Mia felt the smile break across her own face. It was a good day.

"WE ARE NOT making out in the car." Mia smiled against Adam's mouth as they sat in his car outside her house.

"Why not? It's dark. No one will see." He pulled her close and let his hand slip under her coat.

Mia made a little sound in her throat and wondered if he would ever stop having this effect on her. Did she want him to? He kissed her soft and slow and there was no way to resist him, no way to hold onto her control when he touched her. And she loved it.

She loved him.

Her heart was so full she didn't know how it didn't burst. Adam's hand stroked her cheek and his eyes shone in the dim light from the house. Everyone she cared about had been with her tonight. They were there to celebrate her birthday, but for Mia it was more about celebrating a change in her life. About being happy.

"I'd better go inside. I do have to talk to my mother."

"Want me to come with you?"

"No, I'll be fine. I'll call you before I go to bed."

He kissed her again and nodded. "Okay. Probably better to let her calm down."

"It doesn't matter, she's never going to forgive you."

"I'm charming. Sure, she will."

"She eats charming for lunch."

Adam laughed and his strength sank into Mia, gave her all the courage she might need to face her mother.

He walked her to the door like a true gentleman and kissed her once more under the porch light. His kiss was strong, passionate, and had a little bit of desperation laced through it. If Mia understood anything, it was that he was just as scared as she was. Scared to try. Scared to fail. Scared of what this could mean.

But in the end, the risk was small compared to the pay-off. To feel like this; to feel so content, so happy, was worth so much. And to have this man, who had given her this... there was no measure for that.

Chapter Twenty-Three

MIA ENTERED THE house, surprised to see it so dark. Only the light from the kitchen spread a thin beam through rooms nearby. Maybe her mother didn't have a reason for leaving or didn't feel Mia deserved an explanation. It wouldn't be the first time her mother had put herself before Mia.

There were just some people who weren't meant to be parents. Mia's mother was one of them. Ellen DeAngelis was brilliant, cool, and distant, not warm and nurturing. Mia, who had could hold her own academically, was really just a big bowl of goo on the inside. She craved closeness and affection. Being a cold, or stuffy never suited her. Once she let her guard down and started acting like herself, everyone was happier. Especially Ben.

Especially her.

A sound from the back of the house made her jump and she realized someone was still up. Probably Nana, since there were times she was positively nocturnal. Moving through the dark, Mia paused and breathed in. She smelled cigarettes? Groaning, there was only one person in the house who would be smoking.

Sure enough, when she walked into the kitchen, her mother stood by the back door blowing a stream of smoke out into the night. There was a glass and an almost finished bottle of wine on the table, along with a lighter.

Mia had no idea why Mom was upset, but there was no doubt this was going to get ugly.

Her mother quit smoking years before—when Mia was around fifteen—but every once in a while, something would upset her and she'd go back to it. Whatever caused her to leave the party must have been the trigger.

"Nana will be all over you if she smells cigarettes."

Her mother tossed the butt into the flower pot outside the door. "Your grandmother will deal."

Mia stepped closer, trying not to let the familiar intimidation take over, but she had to admit to herself she wished Adam had stayed.

"It's too bad you left the party early, dessert was to die for."

Sitting at the table and refilling her wine glass, Mia noticed all the signs… one of Mom's outbursts was revving up. "You don't need dessert."

Mia shrugged. "Maybe not, but it was yummy."

"You have no discipline, you never have."

That hurt. But now, anger accompanied the hurt.

"You want to spit it out, Mom? Or are you going to give me the silent treatment for a few days and make me figure out on my own what's pissed you off? That's what you used to do, is it still your M.O.?"

"Don't take that tone with me."

"Oh, please. First, you call me 'undisciplined' and expect me to take you seriously. Second, you've smoked what looks like half a pack of cigarettes, and you're on your way to a hangover-worthy drunk. And finally, you left my thirtieth birthday celebration. You left. YOU owe me an explanation."

"I deserve your respect because I'm your mother, and I owe you nothing. Especially after the way you've treated me, and your sister's memory."

"Really? Aunt Regina doesn't feel I've been disrespectful. In fact, she told me she's proud of me. That *Dad* was proud of me."

Mom was silenced by that, and Mia hated throwing her aunt under the bus, but she needed all the help she could get. "So, Mom, you want to try this again and tell me why you feel it's necessary to make everything about you?"

"Why don't you tell me why that bastard, Greg Rhodes, was at your birthday party?"

The words were like a blast of ice water, freezing her from the top down. The burst of questions that filled Mia's head almost made her dizzy, but one stood out. *Why was she asking about Greg?* "Mom? You want to fill me in here?"

"You don't even realize the truth about the type of people you've been cavorting with. That pig is the one who left your sister, and obviously your boyfriend knows him. Birds of a feather, I guess."

The fluttering mess of emotions that had been swimming in Mia's head moved to her stomach as realization took over everything. "Greg is the one–"

"Who abandoned your sister."

Mia grabbed at the chair and sat down. "What?"

"Surprised? I'm not. Nothing good could come from you moving here. Now look what you've done."

"He's Ben's father. The adoption isn't final yet, and now I know who Ben's father is." Reality wasn't just smacking Mia in the face, it was beating her over the head.

"And we could lose him," her mother snapped. "You will say NOTHING."

Mia rubbed her hand across her chest, wondering how this happened. Had Adam known Sara, or known anything about her relationship with Greg?

She had to see him.

Ignoring her mother's tirade, Mia moved toward the door. Adam's house. She'd go there and he'd help her sort this out. Figure out how to keep Greg Rhodes out of Ben's life.

"Where are you going?" her mother screeched.

Still in a daze, Mia turned. "I'm going to Adam's. I need time to think. To talk this through."

Her mother bore down on her. "Are you crazy? You can't tell him anything. He'll take his friend's side and then Ben will end up with his no-good father."

"Stop it! He won't do that."

"God, Mia! Wake up! He's using you. Do you think he loves you? That he could actually love *you*?"

Mia froze as the words hit her full on. The old fears, the old doubts, the crushing insecurity came roaring back. Her mother sat there full of venom and condemnation, and Mia couldn't let herself believe it.

"He does love me. And I need to talk to him about this. I trust him, and that's all that you need to know."

"You really believe that, don't you?" Her mother blew out a stream of smoke from her most recent cigarette. "Dearie, think what you want, but men like him always leave. I guess if Adam leaves you, we'll have hit the trifecta. If he gets you pregnant, that would really take the prize."

Mia had no idea what her mother was talking about. All she could really keep her mind on was Ben and his biological father. "What are you talking about?"

"Ultra-masculine, competitive. A little dangerous. Those kinds of men."

"I'm not following, and I don't want to play games. I'm tired."

"One left me, one left Sara, and now one will leave you. You're probably knocked up already." She was babbling, but she had Mia's full attention. "Fuck 'em and leave 'em. That's what they do."

"Mom!" Mia walked toward her mother, cautious but

also angry. "What are you talking about?"

She shook her head, changing gears again. "Never mind. Go see your *boyfriend*. But his *buddy* is NOT getting my grandson. Ever."

Mia started to leave, but she stopped and looked back at her mother. She was a bitter, nasty woman Mia barely knew, and the distance between them suddenly made sense. Things started to click into place, and like a lightning bolt, the truth was right there. Mia was her father's daughter. Mia and Sara were different because of something else… something bigger. "Sara and I had different fathers, didn't we?"

Her mother stared at her hands, suddenly looking very old for her fifty-eight years. She didn't speak, and her silence gave Mia her answer.

"That's who you're talking about. The man who left you? You cheated on Daddy."

Mia drew a deep breath and the wash of pain, the flood of mistrust, almost overwhelmed her ability to think. "Is that what happened, Mom?"

"Your father and I dated for years. And he went into the Navy even when I begged him not to. I knew he'd be away all the time. So, I found someone else, but he left me the minute he thought I might want something more than a fling. I was pregnant when I married your dad. He knew right away Sara wasn't his. He was no one's fool."

"I can't believe he stayed with you. Knowing you cheated, he still stayed."

Her mother's head snapped up and anger simmered in her eyes. "You're lucky he stayed. If he hadn't, you wouldn't have been born. But your father was so damned...honorable."

He was that. And so was Adam. She had to have faith in her own instincts, and not let her mother destroy the best thing in her life. "Well, rest easy, Mom. Adam is not your lover or Sara's, he's mine. When I get back, you and I are going to have a long talk about my sister, and then you're going to leave. I'm done with you."

"So now you're issuing ultimatums?" Her mother was hard as ice, but she was terrified, too.

"I am. And if you're as smart as you keep telling everyone you are, you'll listen."

Mia shook her head and left the room, stopping only to put on her coat and grab her purse. Still too stunned to think or get upset, Mia's heart pounded with every step out of the house, and it positively ached when she thought about Greg Rhodes and Sara, and what this could all mean for Ben. Once she got into her car, Mia tried to take a deep breath to relax herself, then another. And another. It didn't work.

There, in the dark and cold, as she thought about the step-by-step turns she would need to take to get to Adam's house, the reality of the situation finally overwhelmed her. Tears burned her eyes at the same time dread filled her to the core.

She looked up at the beautiful old house and saw her

grandmother standing at the door. The look on her face told Mia she'd already talked to Mom. Leaning over the steering wheel, Mia turned the key and drew in a long breath. This would be okay. It would be okay.

It had to be okay.

Adam didn't like Greg much and he'd help her with this. There was no way she could say anything and risk losing Ben, but she had to understand more about what happened to her sister, and that's what this visit was all about. What did Adam know about her sister and Greg? Did he care about her? Did Adam know Sara at any point? Did he know she was pregnant?

Was this all a waste of time?

The ride to Gull's Point didn't take very long, but the roads were so dark, Mia almost missed Adam's driveway. When she pulled in, he was in his kitchen, sitting at the island. She could see him clearly in his plain white T-shirt, his dark hair mussed. He was reading something, and as she pulled her car forward, he noticed the headlights and stood.

Mia sat in her car, paralyzed by the knowledge that she could lose everything that mattered to her. Her family was a mess. She could lose Ben. After everything that she'd done to protect him, she could lose him.

THE HEADLIGHTS SHINED in his window just after one in

the morning, and Adam knew it had to be Mia. A glance outside confirmed it and he thought about the two reasons she would have come over—either something bad happened with her mother, or she wanted to spend the night with him.

He hoped it was the latter.

Stepping out the side door, Adam could see enough of a shadow to worry. Her hands still gripped the wheel, arms stiff. Not a good sign. He moved off the stoop and tapped on the driver's side window.

When Mia's head jerked toward him, he got his answer. She was crying. And from the red around her eyes, she'd been crying for a while.

Goddammit. He knew he shouldn't have left her. As soon as the lock clicked, Adam pulled open the door and pulled her close.

"What's wrong?" he asked. "What happened?"

Mia's fingers grazed her face and she looked at the wetness, then she looked at him and she broke. The tears came hard and fast. Her hands were freezing, her body shivering. Adam couldn't get her into the house fast enough.

"Oh, God, Mia. I shouldn't have left. I'm sorry."

Her head shook back and forth and he had no idea what she was trying to tell him. The grief he heard in each hiccupping breath, in each sob, was more than he could take. Pulling her into his lap, he let her cry. For the life of him, he couldn't imagine what could have happened to evoke this response. But whatever it was, he was sure Ellen DeAngelis was at the heart of it.

Mia sniffled and wiped the back of her hand across her eyes. Her voice, when she finally spoke, was low and hoarse. "I might lose him."

"Who?" Adam held her tighter than ever.

"Ben. I might lose him."

"No, you won't. Your mother won't take him from you."

Mia sniffed again and looked in his eyes. Tears tracked down her cheeks and her breath shuddered before she spoke. "Not my mother," she croaked. "His father."

Now it was Adam's turn to be stunned.

"What?" He drew another deep breath and had to force down his own panic. Mia would crumble if she lost Ben— natural mother or not, he was everything to her.

"Tell me what happened." He kept his voice deliberately calm so he didn't slip into his own kind of panic.

"When I walked in the house, my mother was waiting for me in the kitchen. She was downing wine like fruit juice and smoking. That's usually a clue she's not happy."

"Okay." Adam was trying to picture the very staid Mrs. DeAngelis as a drunk with a cigarette. It wasn't pretty.

"She blasted me about moving here, and about you, and how... how... you'd never love me."

Mia's head dropped, and Adam's heart broke. The cruelty of the statement made his blood surge. He held her close and spoke softly. "You have to know by now that I do love you, don't you?"

She nodded and held him tighter. "I know."

A sliver of relief settled in his heart. If she knew that he loved her, they could go forward from there.

"Finish the story."

"We argued about whether or not it was wise to bring Ben here, and after she told me what she thought of you, and that you were like the men who left her and Sara—"

"What? I'm not following."

"She was drunk, so all kinds of crap came pouring out of her. In a nutshell, she cheated on my dad, got pregnant, and was left. The child of that pregnancy was Sara. Then Sara got pregnant and the guy left."

"Wait, so Sara is…"

"…my half-sister, and my father was a damn saint."

"Holy shit," he whispered. There was so much to take in, Adam's head hurt. Poor Mia must have been on the verge of collapse. "So how did Ben's father come into this?"

"We know who he is, and I'm scared I'm going to lose him and—" her breath caught—"I can't lose him, Adam. I can't."

Somehow, as he listened, the truth was right there. He didn't need her to say anything; he just knew. "Greg."

What were the odds?

"Greg," she repeated. "He's Ben's father and now, and now…" She broke off mid-thought and started crying again. Anguished wails that tore at Adam's heart. "Oh, Adam. I c-can't let him go. I can't. Oh, God."

"Shhh. It'll be okay. Greg is not going to want custody. A kid would totally cramp his lifestyle. Don't worry," he soothed. "I'll be with you the whole way. He's not father material and he knows it."

There was quiet and then Adam felt the muscles of Mia's back tighten. This was not good. It only took a second for her to push away and look him in the eyes.

"What do you mean?"

Looking at Mia's face, he could see the anger, the fear... and that she never intended to tell Greg about Ben. "You have to tell him, Mia."

She pushed her way off his lap and reeled back from Adam. "Why would I tell him?"

Adam stood and took a step in her direction. Mia was pacing back and forth, frantic, running her hands through her hair.

"He's Ben's father. He has a right to know."

"HE HAS NO RIGHT TO ANYTHING!" she screamed. "Nothing. He wanted Sara to get an abortion. Based on everything I know, he threw money at her and walked out."

Unfortunately, that sounded like Greg. The guy he knew in college morphed into a giant asshole while he was playing pro. "Mia, I'm not excusing his behavior. But he still should be told. Odds are he's not going to want to be involved."

"How do you know?" She advanced on him. "How?"

"I don't, but—"

"All the hard work is done. The diapers and feedings and the sleepless nights. He could hire a nanny and never know Ben was around. I can't play those odds, no matter what you think."

"Mia—"

"NO! He was horrible to my sister. He tossed her off like nothing. He doesn't deserve to be Ben's father."

"But he *is* Ben's father."

"How can you side with him?" she choked out, distraught at the thought she might lose Ben.

"I'm *not*."

"Yes, you are." Mia dissolved into tears and sank to the floor. She crumbled in the middle of his living room. Sobbing. "He's going to take Ben if he knows. He's going to take him."

Adam lowered himself to the floor, knowing the extent of her anger when he reached for her and she curled away from him.

"Mia?" He could hear his own voice had gone low and rough. The possibility that he could lose her over this made his heart stop. He could not lose her. "Baby, please listen to me."

When she looked up, tears swam in her eyes and Adam reached out again, hoping that if he could touch her, she'd settle down a little.

"If he knows, I'll lose Ben, Adam. You can't tell him!"

"I won't tell him," he whispered. "But I think you

should."

She shook her head violently. "No. He'll take him."

"I don't think so." He scooted closer and reached out. "Come here. Please."

Mia stared at him, her eyes wild. But she did crawl toward him and settle into his lap. "Did you know Sara?"

Adam had been thinking about that since Mia dropped the bomb on him about Greg. Did he know Sara? He searched his memory and came up with nothing. "I don't think so. How did she know him?"

Sniffling, Mia wiped her arm under her nose. "She was a dancer."

"One of the cheerleaders?"

"Uh huh." Another sniffle.

"Teams forbid cheerleaders from having contact with players."

"She told me that."

"Honey, did she tell you anything about Greg?"

"That he cared about her and he wanted to be with her. She said he was wonderful."

Adam knew that was a lie, because Greg wasn't nice and he never cared about anyone but himself. He didn't even lie to girls about it. He was a prick; if they wanted to be with him, they dealt with it.

Adam didn't like where this was going. "Greg wasn't nice. To anyone. He took advantage of women all the time."

"Sounds like the kind of guy who'd take Ben away."

"Did she tell you it was Greg?"

"No. Just that he was a player, and that she couldn't wait for me to meet him. She fell apart when he wouldn't marry her. My mother knew, though."

That much made sense. It sounded like Sara was living in her own bubble.

"I never knew who he was," Mia continued, "but I heard stories. Heard my mother screaming that they would sue him."

"Why didn't they?"

"Sara wouldn't do it." He felt her draw in a deep breath. "Maybe she thought he'd come back to her."

How did he tell her the truth? That her sister wasn't in a real relationship, that Greg never had any interest in her beyond sex? He'd seen this too many times. Some guys were predators, dangling their money and status like a carrot in front of women who ate that shit up. Greg was one of them, he was a dick with women. But even with all that, they couldn't have the knowledge of Ben's parentage hanging over their heads.

Mia looked up. "What?"

"You need to tell him so the adoption is clear."

"I can't."

"You have to. It's the right thing to do."

"He should have married her like he promised. That would have been the right thing."

"I doubt he ever intended to marry her."

Mia sniffled and wiped her eyes. "How do you know that? They could have fallen in love."

"Greg doesn't love anyone but himself."

"She was beautiful."

"And he knew she couldn't say anything about sleeping with him or she'd lose her spot on the squad, so he took whatever he could get."

"He doesn't deserve to know."

"Maybe not, but you still have to tell him."

Mia pushed off his lap, furious. "I can't believe you're willing to take a risk like that. I could LOSE my son, Adam."

"Mia…"

"No! I have to protect Ben!"

"We will both protect Ben. But the truth has to come out."

She didn't want to hear it.

"I'm leaving. I can't talk to you about this." She was so angry her hands were shaking; he couldn't let her leave. Between the hysteria, the fact that she was exhausted, and that he didn't want her to walk out of the house hating him, he had to find a way to stop her.

"Mia, don't go. Listen to me."

"Listen? Are you kidding?"

"You have to tell Greg so there's no question about the adoption. He never had any interest in Sara. He used her, and he doesn't want Ben."

Watching her in pain was killing him. "How could you

say that?" she shot out. "How could you?"

"YOU NEED TO KNOW THE TRUTH!" he yelled. "Sara was living in a fantasy. Greg was never serious about your sister. He was never serious about anyone."

"But she told me..." Mia sniffled and wrapped her arms around her middle.

Cautiously, Adam took two steps toward her. He extended his hands, palms up, hoping she'd come to him. His own eyes were burning, because he was facing the possibility he could lose her and that couldn't happen. It couldn't.

"Mia, please. I love you. I love you with all my heart, and I would never want to hurt you. But the truth of this is that Greg had no interest in her, and he'll have no interest in being a father to Ben. Telling him, getting him to sign away his rights, will assure nothing will stop the adoption. You can be Ben's mother, legally, not just his guardian." He took another step. "We can both be parents to Ben. *Please.*"

She stood before him and her head dropped. Never had he seen anyone so defeated. Her mother spit venom at her, told her their life was a sham, she was faced with the knowledge of knowing the identity of Ben's father, and now she knew her sister had been living a lie. It was crushing her, of that he had no doubt.

"You believe I love you, don't you?" *Please answer me.*

"I don't know what to think. I'm so confused. My sister..."

"I don't care about your sister! I care about you," he

shouted. *God, he had to calm down.* Moving cautiously, he continued. "I love you. I love you, and what happened to your sister was tragic, but don't make another mistake because you think Greg Rhodes is a better man than he is."

Mia put her hands up and started to walk away. "Just promise me you won't say anything. That's all I ask."

"Don't leave like this. Please." His heart was skipping beats. Every time he thought about her walking out of his life, he had to force himself to breathe. "Mia, we'll work this out. We'll figure it out together."

"I can't, Adam. I can't talk to you about this. You don't understand."

With that, she walked out the front door.

He went after her, but when she turned and looked back, her eyes told him he should stop. He shouldn't try. All he wanted to do was grab her and make her see how much she meant to him. How much he needed her, that they would deal with this together. But right then, he could see she didn't want him in her life. At all.

And he didn't know if she ever would again.

Chapter Twenty-Four

MIA SAT IN the cab and watched the buildings on 8th Avenue pass by her window. It was cold outside, but the day was beautiful, and between the skyscrapers she could see blue sky and wispy clouds. As cities went, she loved New York—she'd made some wonderful memories here, first when she was a student and then with Adam.

Wiping at her eyes, she noticed the cab driver looking at her in the mirror.

"You okay, sweetheart?" His accent was pure New York, and Mia appreciated his concern, forcing a smile and nodding.

"I'm gonna tell you da same thing I'd tell my own *dawta*. If he makes you cry, he ain't worth it."

She nodded, but somehow Mia kept thinking that walking out on Adam was the biggest mistake of her life.

Everything he'd said about Sara was true. Once she thought about it, there was no denying her sister lived in her own world, and there wasn't anything that could justify her behavior. The more her mother went on about how the mess with Ben was all Mia's fault, the more she realized her mother felt guilty about what happened to her sister.

Mia hadn't talked to her mother since the blow-up in the kitchen where she'd pretty much turned Mia's world upside down. If she'd felt angry at Mom before, finding out about her infidelity was the breaking point. How could she look at her again? How had her dad managed all those years?

Talk about a mess. There were so many secrets, Mia didn't know what to believe. But she knew it was going to end with her. That's why she was going to talk to Greg. Adam had been right; nothing good could come from keeping Greg's connection to Ben a secret. But instead of having him with her, supporting her through this mess, she was alone, because she'd walked out on him.

She'd walked out on the love of her life over a sister who cared only about herself.

That was another wound that was going to take a while. Mia had been the "lesser" sister, the one who never measured up, and while Sara had always claimed she loved her "Little Sis", she fed into Mia's insecurity. She'd been the butt of her older sister's constant nerd jokes, criticizing everything from Mia's appearance to her grades to her music. Every accomplishment had been downplayed so Sara could feel confident.

Of course, her sister thought Greg would marry her. Having some time to think about it, it made perfect sense. She always got what she wanted, why wouldn't she get him? When it didn't happen—when she'd been rejected—and she was faced with a child to raise, Sara couldn't cope.

The cabbie kept looking at her, obviously a little worried. "You from around here?"

"Long Island," she responded.

"Really?" he asked. "You don't sound like you're from 'dere."

Again, she smiled. This man sounded more New York than anyone she'd ever heard, and he was talking about accents?

"Meeting your boyfriend at the hotel I'm dropping you at?"

"No. It's ah…" She hesitated. What was she doing? "It's a business meeting." That was all she was going to say.

From that point on, he didn't talk anymore, but Mia found she was still dabbing her eyes. It was all getting to her. Adam, Greg… everything.

A few blocks from the hotel, Mia rubbed a hand over her stomach, wondering if anything would calm down the bats that had taken up residence. Not knowing what she was going to say to Greg was only part of the problem. Keeping her wits, not breaking down into a slobbering mess, that was her bigger issue.

She figured she was pretty much screwed.

The cab pulled in right in front of the upscale hotel and a uniformed doorman was there, extending his hand to Mia. It was a genteel setting but Mia felt like she was walking into the lion's den. Just knowing how Greg treated Sara was enough to make Mia wonder how he would treat her.

The hotel was amazing—a true art deco palace. The front desk glowed with angled brass and the floors were polished marble. Fine leather-covered chairs and couches adorned the lobby and to her right was the lounge where she saw Greg, at a table near the bar. He was talking on his cell phone and jotting notes in a bound journal.

Her breath caught and she felt sick to her stomach. She knew she should get this over with, but felt frozen in place. She couldn't move. Finally, the clerk at the desk cleared his throat.

"Miss? Can I help you?"

"Oh, no. I'm meeting Mr. Rhodes." Mia raised her hand slightly, gesturing toward Greg, who by this point had seen her.

"Very good, miss." The clerk went back to his computer screen, and Mia nearly turned and ran back outside, but Greg was now moving in her direction. He was still on his phone, but he smiled, and extended a hand to her.

Without taking it, she walked past him and headed to the table where he'd set up a makeshift office. She could hear him now concluding his call, and with his sandpaper voice and imposing physical presence, Mia was scared. Out-of-her-mind scared.

"I'll call you back. My meeting's here." He followed Mia back to the small round table.

Mia went cold when he leaned in and kissed her cheek. Oh, yeah, he definitely had the wrong idea.

As she shrugged out of her coat, Greg's expression was tentative, like he didn't quite know what to say. It was interesting seeing the cockiness leech out of him, even if it was only for a minute. He took her coat, laying it over a chair, and before Mia could do anything herself, he pulled out her chair.

A waiter appeared and when Greg looked at her, a smile tilted the corner of his mouth. So much for humility.

"Would you like anything?" he asked.

"Ah, sparkling water is fine." she said, and he dismissed the waiter with a wave of his hand.

"So, are you going to tell me why you wanted to see me?"

Mia mustered a nod. The thick silence lingered and Greg blew out a breath.

"Sorry," she said. "I'm not feeling too well."

As she said it, the white-coated waiter reappeared with her drink. "A sparkling water for the lady."

"Thank you." Mia could barely hear herself. This wasn't the time to shrink into the woodwork.

"So? Why are we here?" Greg brought his coffee cup to his lips but didn't drink. Instead, he raised an eyebrow. "Get tired of Adam? Because if that's the case, I will consider this my lucky day."

"No, that's not it." His expression didn't change. "I want to talk about—" Mia took long drink of the mineral water. Her mouth was like a desert. "I want to talk about Ben."

Greg had taken a sip of his coffee, but when Mia laid the

topic on the table he put down his cup and stared into it. "What about Ben?"

Yeah, he wasn't flirting anymore. Now he looked as scared as she felt.

"You knew my sister when you played in Washington."

He chuckled. "Babe, I knew lots of women in D.C."

"My sister, Sara, was a cheerleader. Blonde, blue-eyed."

"Again, you're being kind of general here."

Mia was trying to keep her cool, but it was hard, because Greg knew what she was driving at and he was baiting her. "Don't be obtuse."

"Obtuse?" The arrogant grin that crossed his face really needed to be slapped off.

There was no use in dancing around this, so she blurted it out. "Ben? Is your son."

Bam. The air around them dropped ten degrees as he stared at her.

"Prove it." He sat back in the chair and started tapping something out on his phone.

The sputter that came from Mia was a result of the jumble of thoughts in her brain. Holy crap. *Prove it?*

Wow.

Now she was pissed. He thought she was there to make him take responsibility. His challenge forced her to see the man Adam had described—shallow, arrogant and cold.

"I'm not going to prove anything, because the last thing I want is for you to be in his life. I don't ever want to see you again."

Greg looked up from his phone and froze. "Wait, what?"

"I want you to sign away your parental rights. I want to adopt Ben and I can't, since we know the identity of his father."

He nodded slowly. "Oh. Fine. No problem there, but without sounding like a dick, are you sure he's mine? I mean…"

Mia leaned back in her chair, more disgusted than scared, and she folded her arms. "You aren't even going to put up a fight for him, are you?"

"Nah, I don't need a kid. You've done good with him. He's happy."

"Wow."

"Look, I've never wanted to be a father. I like my life."

"What could Sara have possibly seen in you? Good God."

"Money. Just like all the other women who claim they have my kid. You're the first who hasn't wanted me to write a check."

She shook her head, struck dumb. "I don't want anything but your signature on the papers that say I can adopt him. That's it.

"Fine. Have your attorney contact mine." Greg played with the spoon that lay next to his coffee cup. "Now, tell me again… who was your sister?"

The blinding heat that clouded her vision was so new,

Mia didn't know how to react. He didn't even know who she was talking about. He took Sara to bed, used her, treated her like crap, and he didn't even remember?

Mia understood she was naïve, and that Sara's life was full of stupid choices, but Greg's callousness raised Mia's anger to a whole new level.

He was still staring at her, confused, when his cell phone rang and he answered it, not thinking for another second about Sara, or Ben.

The asshole.

His voice dropped and a sly grin slid across his face. When she heard him say "Baby", Mia knew he was talking to a woman. His latest conquest, no doubt.

The rage which flashed a minute ago was now on a rolling boil as every word he uttered dripped with innuendo. Mia glanced at the table. There was a leather portfolio, a business card holder, a couple of pens and a laptop. The pens could do some damage, she thought, but hotel management might have a problem with bloodshed. Then, as she felt the bile rise in her throat, Mia's hand shot out and grabbed the phone.

"Sorry, sweetie. He's busy with me, he'll call you back."

Greg's hand was still posed as if he was holding his phone and his mouth was slightly open, stunned that little wallflower Mia had been aggressive.

He leaned into his chair, disgusted.

"I guess I'll call her back."

"You can dismiss me, if you want, but your disrespect for my sister and your son is disgusting."

"Is it possible you're overreacting?" he said. "I didn't disrespect your sister, I don't even remember her. And as for the kid, he's nice, but I don't think I'm exactly father material."

Mia's hands shook and without warning or knowing what she was going to do, she smashed his phone on the table. Then, without a moment's thought, she grabbed her drink and dumped it into Greg's lap.

He sucked in a breath at the shock caused by the icy cold liquid, muttered some colorful expletives, and glared at her. Fortunately, there were only a few people in the bar. Mia didn't give him a chance to speak. Instead, she leaned in and hissed.

"I hate you for the way you treated my sister. About the only good thing that's come out of this meeting is that you will be permanently out of Ben's life." She grabbed one of the business cards sticking out of the portfolio on the table. "My lawyer will be in touch."

"Fine," he said, growling. Mia grabbed her coat and started toward the door and as she did, Greg stood and started blotting himself with a napkin. Maybe the cold shock did some good because when she looked back, he looked a little sad. Very little, but he was still sad.

"Mia." She turned. His voice was low, serious. "How did your sister die?"

"She killed herself. Swallowed a bottle of pills, chased it

with alcohol."

He blew out a breath. "Because of me?"

Was it because of him? Was it?

No. Mia finally faced the reality of her sister's death.

It was as if someone smacked her upside the head. At last, Mia saw things with complete clarity, understanding her sister for the first time in her life. And as Sara's memory stepped down off the pedestal, Mia spoke, "As much as it would be easy to blame you, no. She died because she was weak, and because she gave up."

Something Mia would never do.

She stood there in her coat waiting for something from him, anything.

"I'm sorry." It was heartfelt, and she could see Greg wasn't comfortable speaking from the heart.

Mia nodded and left him standing there with a napkin in his hand and a big wet spot on his pants. It was a pathetic sight, but it wasn't nearly as pathetic as the shallow life he led.

It had been Sara's life as well, and Mia didn't want that for herself. She wanted her love story, and for the first time she believed she deserved one.

Adam's face flashed through her mind, and as she slid into the cab that pulled up in front of the hotel, she hoped it wasn't too late.

Chapter Twenty-Five

THE SNOW WAS early this year. Mia remembered her grandmother always said that if snow came to Long Island before December, it was going to be a rough winter. It was the last day of November, and it made sense to Mia that the coming season was going to be a tough one.

For lots of reasons.

The parking lot was getting slippery, and she was happy she'd worn flats, not the heels she was originally planning to wear. For some reason, she thought some height would make her more intimidating; then she'd thought about Greg, at six-three, and realized not much was going to intimidate him. Now she smiled inwardly as she reflected on the fact that she didn't have to worry about Ben. The adoption should go through without a hitch. When Fiona had taken a picture of her, Ben, and Adam three days ago at her birthday party, she'd joked that it was the perfect "family" portrait. When Adam leaned in and whispered that being a family was a dream come true for him, Mia believed that her life had really changed.

But now? Now everything was uncertain. Stopping at her

car, Mia reached out and touched the door handle. She thought about Adam and how she'd destroyed what they had. Blinking back the tears, she unlocked the door and wondered if there was a chance to save it.

First, she'd go home and let everyone know she'd come to an agreement with Greg. Then, she'd go find Adam. She'd find him and apologize, beg for his forgiveness if she had to.

She'd doubted his motives, his willingness to stand by her, and that had hurt him. Thinking back to the way he looked when she left, she hoped he had it in his heart to take her back. If not, she didn't know what she'd do.

The words about being a family, about being parents to Ben, echoed in her head and made her heart ache. God, what a mess.

ADAM MOVED THE couch in his grandmother's parlor three times. After an hour of watching her ponder the perfect placement, it ended up right back where it started.

"Yes, that works," she said.

"Grandma, you could have left everything where it was."

"I know, dear, but I wanted to explore some options."

"Options. Great." He flopped on the sofa and stared at the snow falling outside.

Grandma sat next to him and patted his knee. "Want to tell me what's wrong?"

"Nothing."

"Adam?"

Seeing the determined look on her face, Adam realized she wasn't going to let him go until he told her. So, he gave it up. "Mia and I had a fight."

"That happens with couples sometimes. You'll work it out."

He breathed out and shook his head. This wasn't going to be worked out easily.

"What? What happened, Adam?"

"Like I said, we had a fight. It was about Ben and his biological father. It went out of control. I don't think she'll be back."

"Oh, no. Is there anything I can do?"

"No, and you have to stay out of it."

"But…"

"No, Grandma. Stay out of it. Okay?"

She nodded, then reached out and took his hand.

"I don't know what I'm going to do without her."

"Oh, darling, it will work out."

He glanced down at her. "Are you saying I'll get over her?"

"Absolutely not. You'll never get over her, but I don't think this fight is the end. You two are meant to be together."

"I hope you're right."

"Have you tried to talk to her?"

"I called. Sent texts. No answer."

A chill settled around them. She didn't utter a word, but Adam could sense her mood had changed. He discovered he was right when suddenly, his grandmother stood.

"Adam, get out."

He looked up, blinked. "What?"

"Get out."

He rose. "You want me to leave?"

"You're sitting there telling me you called and sent texts... TEXTS? You want to put things right between you in a text message? Have you learned nothing?"

Adam looked away as his grandmother approached and laid a hand on his arm. Suddenly he felt like a coward. He'd done this before. He should have done something other than hide behind his cell phone.

"Go to her. Take in her in your arms. Get her to understand that you love her more than anyone or anything. That's what she needs. Not a blasted text message!"

He nodded and felt his eyes start to burn. Jesus. What the hell had happened to him? "She's everything to me, Gram."

When her fingers brushed across his cheek, Adam almost lost it. "Oh, my sweet boy, tell her that."

He drew a deep breath and understood what he had to do. "I'd better go."

Leaning in, he gave his grandmother a kiss and went to his truck. The snow was picking up and all he could think about was Mia. In his head he ran through the words he wanted to say, what he wanted to do. If he could get her to listen, he had a chance.

Sitting in the driver's seat, Adam slipped the key into the ignition and stopped. Three months ago, he didn't even know she existed. They meant nothing to each other. And now? Now she was everything. In his whole life, Adam never thought he'd feel this way about a woman, ever. Thinking about Mia, he knew he wouldn't have any kind of life without her.

It was her or nothing. He had to get her back.

The cell phone vibrating in his pocket made him stop and hope, but then he looked at the screen and swallowed. *Greg*.

Adam considered letting it go to voice mail, but at the last second, he answered. "Yeah?"

"Hey. Got a sec?"

"What's up?"

"I saw Mia today."

Adam's heart jumped into his throat. Damn. "Where?"

"She came to see me at my hotel. Had some news for me."

"Shit." Adam rubbed his fingers over his eyes. She went to see him. Alone.

"Did you know about the kid?"

"I found out a couple of days ago. What happened?" *Please, God,* he thought. *Let this have played out the way I said it would.*

"She told me, wanted to know about her sister and me. I couldn't tell her anything."

"Yeah?"

"She was pretty upset when she left. Dumped a drink in my lap."

"You didn't… wait… what about Ben?"

"Hell, I don't want a kid. She can keep him."

"Good," Adam said. His voice was hoarse as he thought of Mia dealing with Greg alone.

"I'm guessing he'll be yours too."

If I can get her back. "I'm on my way there now."

For a minute there was nothing, and Adam thought the call had dropped when Greg finally broke the silence. "I'll be flying back to Chi-town tomorrow. It was good seeing you."

"Have a good trip." *I hope I never see you again, asshole.*

Adam heard Greg take a deep breath. "If he ever needs anything…"

"I don't think he will, but I'll let you know if he does."

More silence.

"Thanks. Take care, man."

Before Adam could say anything, the connection was broken.

Thinking about Mia going to see Greg alone twisted Adam's insides. Even after the fight they had, she'd taken his advice anyway. He was glad the air was clear, but hated he wasn't beside her. The thought of her dumping a drink in

Greg's lap had him wondering, though. What the hell had gone on that Mia was that pissed?

Turning the key in the ignition, he was set to find out.

THE BUZZ FROM the dining room told Mia the family was home, and as usual they were all trying to talk over one another. Nana, her aunt, uncle, cousins, and Ben. The headache she was fighting all day threatened to make an appearance, but the relief she felt over Ben's adoption made the discomfort inconsequential. She'd check in with her family and then go find Adam.

If her luck kept running the way it had been, they'd be okay. They had to be okay.

A ball formed in the pit of her stomach. After hanging up her coat and bag on the hooks in the foyer, she stepped into the dining room.

Her entire family went quiet. Perfect.

Mia didn't wait for the question, she just blurted it out. "Everything is fine. There was nothing to worry about."

Ben bolted from his chair. He knew there was a question about the adoption, but nothing about Greg, and Mia planned on keeping it that way, at least for a little while. Since he knew Greg it would be strange, and at this point in Ben's young life, he didn't need any more questions about who didn't want him.

"You can adopt me?"

"Yes."

He didn't need to hear anything else. Ben's arms came around her waist, and if Mia ever questioned whether adopting Ben was the right thing, this settled it. He was her son and nothing would change that.

Looking at everyone there, Mia noticed the empty chair. "Where's Mom?"

Her uncle folded his hands and considered them before answering. "She went back to Charleston. She felt, we all felt, it was best for her not to be here. Reg agreed."

"She left?" Mia couldn't believe she left before she knew the outcome of her meeting.

"We decided, all things considered, that it was best."

Mia caught something in her uncle's voice, something firm and final. "She won't be back, will she?" she asked.

"No," Nana said. "Not for a while."

If that didn't beat all. Her mother had finally managed to get herself banished from her own family.

Uncle Rob made his way to her and rubbed his big hand across her back; her uncle was such a good man. He reminded her of her father. "Ellen is my sister, but this has to end somewhere. You deserve better, Mia. Hopefully, she'll get some help. Regina said she'd be in touch with us soon."

"Your mother was never happy," Nana said. "And I can't understand it. She had everything."

Mia shook her head. She didn't want to be that way. Regretting her life and her choices was a horrible way to live.

There was a light tapping on the door, but everyone stayed frozen in place. It had been quite a day.

Ben looked up. "Should I get the door?"

"Yes." Mia nodded, thankful someone was paying attention. "Check the side window to see who it is first."

"I will." He ran to the front of the big house, and that gave Mia the chance to adjust to the fact that she wasn't going to see her mother for a very long time. The surprising thing was, Mia didn't feel as badly about it as she thought she would. In a way, it was a relief.

"Mia." Her grandmother stood. "Sit, eat something."

"I'll eat later. I have to go out again."

Her grandmother's face dropped. "The weather..."

"Nana." Mia blinked hard as she spoke. "I have to see him."

Now that the drama with the adoption was settled, nothing was more important in her mind than fixing things with Adam. She'd gotten his texts, but the sooner she saw him, the sooner she could take his hands in hers, the sooner she would know if he'd forgive her.

But then, the space around her warmed and her skin tingled, and like magic, her worries vanished.

He was already there.

Turning slowly, Mia's eyes filled before she caught sight of Adam in the dining room archway.

He stood there looking at her with sadness his sea blue

eyes, letting her know he was as lost as she was. There was desperation in his stance, and fear, but he was there. He was still her guy. Tall, handsome, dusted with snow, and obviously in love with her.

Not caring about self-control, Mia burst into tears. Every fear, every worry, every emotion surfaced at the sight of Adam. If he thought twice about what he was going to do, she couldn't tell as he pulled her close.

"Shh, Mia, shhh. Don't cry. I love you. Don't cry."

"I'm so glad you're h—h—here."

She could feel his breath leave his chest in relief. "Thank God." He leaned back and his hands found her face. Pushing the hair back, he held her and kissed away her tears. "It's okay now."

Mia nodded and slipped her arms around his waist. "I'm sorry. You were right, about everything. I'm sorry I didn't believe you, that I blamed you…"

"We both made mistakes, but you have to know, I'm here for you and for Ben. You never have to worry about that."

"I know. I know."

He leaned into her, lowering his head to her ear. He spoke so softly, she was the only one who could hear him. "I love you," he said. "Marry me?"

Mia looked into Adam's eyes and found herself drowning in them. He was smiling, but in in his expression there was a seriousness, a sense of purpose, that told her how much she meant to him. Looking over at Ben, who was picking at his dessert, it was crystal clear they were the two most important people in Adam's life.

God, how did she get so lucky?

"You want your ring?" His whisper was now was a tease, and his smile was wide and playful.

"You have a ring!" Mia covered her mouth, but it was too late. Everyone heard her and she didn't care. Nana was up and over to them in a split second. Who knew she could move so fast.

"Ring?" Nana said. "What ring?"

Adam reached into his jacket pocket and pulled out a little blue box. "This ring."

Unable to speak, Nana pressed her fingers into her lips. Mia glanced over and saw the rest of her family respond. Ben was standing by the table, stunned. Her aunt, uncle, and cousins were beaming. It was perfect.

Uncle Rob cleared his throat. And both Mia and Adam looked over. "Adam, seems to me you need to have a conversation with someone before that becomes official."

Stumbling, Adam looked at her uncle. "Sir, uh…"

"Not me," he said. Then he pointed at Ben.

Mia felt her eyes well up. And Ben's face was… she saw he was trying hard to be the man, and fighting back his own tears.

Adam stepped away and approached him. "What do you think, bud? Think we can be a family?"

Ben at a loss for words was a rarity. Especially around Adam. The two would talk endlessly, and for her little guy to be speechless told her how much being a family meant to him.

Finally, Ben gathered his thoughts and looked up at Adam. "Would you adopt me, too?

Adam nodded. "I want to, if that's okay with you."

Ben nodded again. "This is so cool."

Watching Ben and Adam, Mia thought of everything it took for her to get to this point, and how for so long she thought she never would. But Ben had gained even more.

Mia took a few steps and slipped in next to Adam. Her hand found his and for once she didn't question it, didn't wonder if something was going to go wrong. This was right, and she knew it.

True North.

Her heart had found the way.

ADAM STEPPED ONTO the front porch holding two mugs of hot chocolate and enjoyed watching Mia admire her ring.

"I'm glad it fits." He handed her a mug and sat on the porch swing. They were both bundled against the falling snow, but Mia had wanted to come outside to watch it, alone, with him.

"It's so beautiful. I can't believe we're getting married."

He smiled. "Who'd have thought you'd end up with a jock?"

She smiled. "I know. Not me."

Not her mother.

"I need to tell you something." Her eyes locked on his. "Greg called me."

"He did?"

"He said if Ben ever needs anything to let him know."

"Let's hope he never does."

He took her hand, which was tiny and warm, in his. "Why did you go see him?"

Glancing down at her ring and then at him, Mia thought. "I couldn't keep looking over my shoulder. I had to know Ben was mine. I had to know about Sara." Pausing, Mia looked up and laid a hand on his cheek. "You were right."

"So, about Ben—"

"You were right."

"And your sister?" He took her hand in his, holding tight.

She sniffled, and then her head bobbed up and down. "You were right about her, too."

Looping an arm around her, Adam pulled her close. "I'm sorry about that."

"I hate that she was so alone."

Adam knew there was no easy way for Mia to deal with this new knowledge, but he didn't want her to feel guilty.

She'd martyred herself enough. It was time to look forward.

"I have something else for you."

When Mia lifted her eyes to his, he pulled a small box from Liam Jennings' shop out of his other pocket.

"What's that?"

"Open it."

Her fingers fumbled with the lid, and when she opened it, Mia drew a breath. In the box, lying on fine red satin, was a small brass Jennings compass. Mia held it in her hand and stared at the face. The needle shivered slightly, moved a little, and then pointed north, exactly as it was supposed to do.

"Look at the back."

Turning the instrument over, Mia saw the engraving.

"To Mia, With you my heart has found home. All my love, Adam"

Her eyes filled up and finally, truly happy tears glistened in her eyes. Holding her tight, Adam thought about the years he went in circles, the years he couldn't find anything worthwhile to cling to. Finally, Mia found him and gave him the life he'd been missing.

"Look at me," he said. When her gaze found his, Adam's heart skipped a beat. This was his beautiful girl and he'd never let her down. "We are going to have a great life. And we'll make a great life for Ben."

"I know we will, but..." She smiled, hesitated. "I was thinking. We've never talked about kids..."

"What about kids?"

"Well, uh…" She blushed. *She still blushed.* "If you want more."

Adam warmed to the core at the thought of seeing Mia pregnant with their child. He grew hot thinking about all the fun they'd have getting her that way. "We'll have as many babies as you want."

They settled into a comfortable quiet, and he wondered if they were both thinking about the same thing, about babies and their future. Then, without a word, Mia set down her mug, stood and extended her hand to him.

"Where are we going?" Adam asked.

"Home."

He loved hearing that. Loved that she was going to turn his house into a home. "Yeah?"

"Yeah. I think it's time to start that life I've had on hold."

Wrapping his arms around her, he gently kissed the tip of her nose. "Let's get to it, then."

The End

The Compass Cove series

Book 1: Then Came You

Book 2: You Send Me

Book 3: Waiting for You

Book 4: Coming soon

Available now at your favorite online retailer!

More by Jeannie Moon

Daring the Pilot
Men of Marietta series

Weekend with Her Bachelor
Bachelor Auction Returns series

Finding Christmas

His Forbidden Princess
Royal Holiday series

Until You

This Christmas
Christmas in New York series

Available now at your favorite online retailer!

About the Author

Jeannie Moon has always been a romantic. When she's not spinning tales of her own, Jeannie works as a school librarian, thankful she has a job that allows her to immerse herself in books and call it work. Married to her high school sweetheart, Jeannie has three kids, three lovable dogs and a mischievous cat and lives in her hometown on Long Island, NY. If she's more than ten miles away from salt water for any longer than a week, she gets twitchy. Visit Jeannie's website at www.jeanniemoon.com

Thank you for reading

Then Came You

If you enjoyed this book, you can find more from all our great authors at TulePublishing.com, or from your favorite online retailer.

TULE
PUBLISHING

Made in the
USA
Lexington, KY